REALMS SAGA

REALM OF STARS & SHADOWS

ALLISON SIPE

This book is a word of fiction. Names, characters, places and incidents are either the product of the author's imagination or are used fictitiously and any resemblance to actual persons, living or dead, events, or locales is entirely coincidental.

Text Copyright © 2024 Allison Sipe
All Right reserved

Book Cover Design by: Hannah Sternjakob

No part of this book may be reproduced, scanned, or distributed in any printed or electronic form without the explicit permission of the author.

For everyone who's taken the hard path,
and created their own destiny.
You are remarkable.

BOOK PLAYLIST

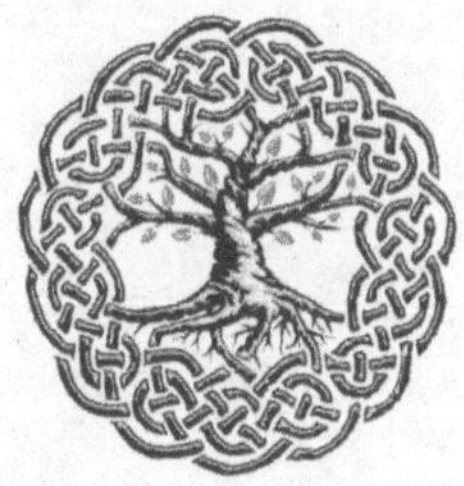

If you like to listen to music while you read, then you're in luck!
I've created a playlist just for Realm of Stars & Shadows. Enjoy
the music that inspired the story.

WE RECALL TWO SOULS,
BORN WORLDS APART.
THEIR HEARTS AND MINDS,
SET ON BECOMING LEGENDS.
THERE, UNDER THE BOUGHS
OF YGGDRASIL WE WOVE,
THEIR DESTINY INTO,
THE STARS AND SHADOWS.

CHAPTER ONE

KARA

My hand shook as I stepped away from Si. The raw, hungry Magik under my skin yearned for him like a moth to a flame. From the moment Freya earmarked him for Folkvang, his song was a melody in my bones I could sing in my sleep.

But I was no longer the same after what I did to Loki.

Sigurd's soul burned through me, slow and merciless as magma. My lungs tightened as I attempted to stifle the overwhelming urge to consume the untapped power of his soul.

Every muscle in my body ached with the effort to stay in control of myself. The rustle of fabric against my skin made me want to scream. And the constant current of lightning running through my blood left me teetering on the edge of fear and bone deep hunger.

I could do this. I could ignore the delicious melody of his soul.

I wouldn't be like the monsters Loki freed.

I pulled in a deep breath, filling my lungs with cool morning air. The smell of freshly turned earth, and leaves dripping with dew, was a balm to my frayed nerves. I let out a measured breath, clearing my soul of the dust, rubble, and Magik that suffocated me in the temple.

Si's soul was still acutely present and overshadowed the others, but the tremble in my hands eased.

He'd come for me. After what I did to Magnus, he'd still come for me. I'd forever be grateful that he put his grief aside and faced Loki on my behalf. But for the life of me, I didn't know how he could be so gentle and gracious with me.

A sharp sting of awareness buzzed under my skin, as if someone called my name from the other side of Yggdrasil. My legs wobbled and my vision blurred, but the power churning inside me kept me upright and alert.

Gods, I wanted nothing more than to lie down and find oblivion.

As I reached Talon, her gaze swept me from head to toe. "Everything okay?" She looped her arm through mine carefully to avoid the makeshift bandages Si wrapped around my arms when he freed me from my shackles.

"Mmhmm." I tried to ignore the unsettling ache of my soul morphing into something new.

She cocked an eyebrow, unconvinced, but she didn't press me further as we left the temple behind and ventured deeper into a forest I didn't recognize.

Beams of soft, golden light found their way through the canopy of trees, banishing the long shadows of night, and lighting the path ahead. It was serene, and so opposite of the dark, twisted knot inside me, it was almost laughable.

I took another intentional breath and counted my heartbeats.

A thousand questions swirled in my head. Why did they save me? Was I really a Disir? What did I do to Loki exactly? And why did it feel so empowering? Why couldn't I stop? Why do I want more? Uncertainty pulled at my soul, making me question who I was.

Thanks to the Disir and Loki's soul, I was alive when so many others joined the stars. Like Magnus. The thought of him was a punch to the gut. I killed him in cold blood. Flashes of the courtyard seared through me. My dagger at his neck. Blood on my hands. My stomach clenched as angry tears pricked my eyes.

He'd accepted me with open arms, despite being Sigurd's best friend. It didn't matter that Loki was in control of my every whim. All that mattered was that I wasn't strong enough to spare his life, nor the other people I killed under Loki's spell.

Their blood was on my hands.

Magik bloomed in my core like a rose unfurling its petals, slow and purposeful. It was different from Loki's sharp, urgent power. And the softness of it complimented Freya's Magik. I gave myself over to the purr of energy, letting it pull me deeper inside myself, until a foggy and frayed image tugged at the back of my mind.

"Let him be the first to fall in their line." A voice whispered from somewhere in the shadows of my mind.

Loki stumbled into my mind's eye, and I sucked in a breath. The red-haired Disir who saved me, grabbed Loki by his shirt and pressed her lips to his.

The vision—or was it a memory—fractured. Blue light flared like sunlight glistening off a lake, and my Magik snarled to the surface.

Loki grunted, as white light glittered from his mouth into hers.

Jealousy ripped through me. He was mine, the Magik roared in my blood.

His cheeks became hollow, his bones more visible as his eyes glowed the sapphire blue of the monsters he once commanded.

I stiffened and froze mid-step.

"No." My voice was deep and foreign, even to my own ears.

"Kara, what's wrong?" Her eyes bounced between mine as concern furrowed her brow.

"Loki." I shook my head and wiped a hand over my face.

"Where?" Talon spun, searching the trees for any sign of the trickster God.

"No, not here. I thought...I just..." Chills ran down every

inch of my body as Magik and fear collided inside me. "I think they turned him into a Draugr."

"What are you talking about?" I could feel her stare on me, but I refused to look her in the eyes.

I pinched the bridge of my nose. "The Disir," I said under my breath. "I think I can hear them…or see them." I let out a shaky breath. Images swirled in my mind from the temple.

Loki's terror. A flash of cobalt lightning. Hair like the sunset. Pain.

"What do you mean, you can see them?" Talon faced me, but it didn't go unnoticed how she was keeping a distance between us.

I was exhausted, physically, mentally, and emotionally. That's all this was. Right?

"I think I just need to lie down."

A branch snapped behind me and in the space between heartbeats, I pulled the dagger strapped to Talon's hip and whipped around.

Si and Daiman froze.

Both of them stared at me like I was a wild animal, and they were my prey. One small move and I might tear them to pieces.

"Kara?" Talon's voice was slow and even, as the sound of a blade being pulled from its sheath pierced the quiet morning.

My eyes fell from Sigurd's and Daiman's faces to the dagger in my trembling hand. I turned slowly to find her sword pointed at my chest.

"I'll ask again. Are you alright?"

Shame burned through me, and I dropped the dagger into the soft earth and leaves. She was afraid of me. Afraid of what I might do. Afraid of what I might be now.

"I…" I was half certain I was losing my mind, but with the way she was looking at me, I didn't think admitting it would gain me any favor. "I think it's just flashbacks."

"You said you could see them. Hear them." Talon glanced

away from me to the trees like she half believed there might be something or someone lurking in the shadows.

"It was like I was remembering a vivid dream." I shook my head. "Just snippets of voices, colors and…"

"And?" Talon said after a beat of silence.

"And Loki and the Disir who saved me."

Talon glanced over my shoulder, and motioned with a nod to Si and Daiman behind me. Their boots crunched through the dirt as they walked on either side of me. Si stopped by my side and picked up the dagger at my feet.

His eyes met mine for a fraction of a second and they seemed to say, *we'll figure this out.*

He gave me a slight nod, and though he hadn't spoken the words aloud, I heard them all the same.

"It's probably nothing," I exhaled. "I'm jumpy and need some rest," I said, as Sigurd joined Daiman safely behind Talon.

Talon sheathed her sword and closed the distance between us.

"Tell me exactly what you saw." She placed her hands on my shoulders.

I searched her dark brown eyes and found no judgment, only concern. The tension in my shoulders eased under her hands and I recounted what I thought I saw—or heard.

"It's not a memory." Talon dropped her hands from my shoulders. "I was in the temple from the moment the Disir returned and what you're describing didn't occur."

Panic tried to claw its way up my throat. I already had enough on my plate without hearing voices and having visions.

"Then I don't know," I snapped. "Maybe it's just wishful thinking." But I knew that wasn't true.

Because I wanted Loki's soul for myself. I balled my hands into fists as the taste of his essence filled my memory. I was too close to the edge of what I could handle at the moment. I needed to get out of here. I needed to breathe without three pairs of eyes on me.

"What happened in there with Loki—"

"I don't want to talk about that." I tried to sidestep her, but she stepped into my path.

A dangerous flare of anger roared through my blood.

"If you're a danger to the people of Folkvang, I need to know." This was Talon the Valkyrie speaking, not my friend.

I recoiled as if she'd slapped me. I could feel the sting in my eyes, and the heat in my chest, but I kept my face neutral as the ugly swell of hurt filled my heart.

"Finally, seeing the monster everyone else has the last hundred years?" I took a step away from her, and Loki's Magik flared in my blood, screaming to lash out.

Rationally, I knew I shouldn't turn on her. But I couldn't control the storm of emotions that were propelled by fear—fear of who I really was, fear of the Magik that was now a living part of me.

She wasn't wrong to question me, to want to protect Folkvang, but of all people, for her to look at me like a threat, hurt more than I cared to admit.

"You are not a monster." She jutted her chin in defiance. "But that doesn't mean you aren't dangerous." She cocked an eyebrow.

Anger, fear, and the helplessness I felt since learning Loki was controlling me, churned in my chest like the unforgiving sea.

"I was dangerous the moment I ended Sigurd's mortal life." My gaze flashed to him, standing a few feet behind her. "And yet you cleaned his blood from my hands. You welcomed me back to Folkvang with open arms." I held her stare as she assessed my every word, every flinch of muscle.

"But now you want to draw a line in the sand and make me the villain?" Sharp fury pricked my skin like freezing rain.

I wanted to tear Sol from the sky. I wanted to scream. I wanted to curl up in a ball and pretend none of this ever happened.

I was dangerous.

I'd been dangerous for a long time.

The sooner I accepted my role in this, the sooner I'd be free of the pain and guilt weighing me down.

"No one is calling you a villain." Her head fell to one side. "What happened in there—"

I opened my mouth, but she raised her hand to silence me. "The Disir, Loki, all of it… It's not your fault. You did what you had to, to survive. I'm on your side, Kara." Her eyebrows knit together. "Let me help you."

"Help me?" I scoffed. "You don't even trust me right now."

"It's not that I don't trust you," she sighed and took a step forward. "But for sorðinn sake, Kara. You almost killed a god," she said under her breath, as if Daiman and Si didn't witness the same horror.

The memory of Loki's breath against my skin, his soul running through my blood, and his Magik lighting the dying embers inside me flashed through my mind. Shame turned to acid in my stomach, followed by a hunger I was quickly becoming familiar with.

"He deserved it." My voice was cold and unflinching.

She blinked a few times, and she squared her shoulders as her fingers twisted for her blade once more. "Yeah, he did. But *you* shouldn't have that kind of power."

His Magik sparked under my skin, heating my temper. "I didn't ask for this."

Over Talon's shoulder, I saw Daiman and Sigurd take a step back.

"I know you didn't." Talon stepped froward and some of the softness returned to her voice. "I just want to make sure you're okay before we walk back into Folkvang and you have to face Freya and Bryn and everyone else who lost someone today."

I let her words sink in and counted to ten. And Loki's Magik curled up inside me like a house cat.

"If you're worried, I'll go on a killing spree, I think that's behind me now that the sacrifice ritual is complete." There was a bite to my words, but I was losing steam. I needed sleep and to be left alone to sort out who or what I was.

"Says the woman who pulled a blade on Daiman and Si a moment ago." She cocked an eyebrow at me. But there was a lightness to her voice that eased the guilt in my chest.

"Not on them," I said each word slowly. "I heard—,"

Her eyebrows rose to her forehead, and she pinned me with a look that said I was proving her point. And honestly, I was starting to doubt I'd heard or seen anything. The vision, or whatever it was, already felt slippery and hard to recall with any sort of clarity.

Maybe I was losing my mind.

"Look," Talon assumed a more relaxed stance. "You're crawling with Magik that doesn't belong to you. Magik, you can't begin to understand. Maybe what you saw was real. Maybe not. You, of all people, know how dangerous power is when the wielder doesn't understand it." She let out a tired sigh. "So I'll ask you one last time. Are you okay?"

She was right.

A ball of electric, hungry power curled in my abdomen, mingling with the Magik that sang in my blood. I didn't understand most of what I was feeling, nor did I know how to wield it or what it could do.

I nodded. "I'm sorry. I just…"

"I know. You're on edge, and that's to be expected." She shrugged. "I hate to add to this shit pile, but we still don't know how Loki could control you. And clearly, whatever you did to him is having a lingering effect."

What I did to him.

A wave of nausea rolled through me, and heat crawled up my chest and neck. I was grateful she wasn't calling me a Disir, but it was implied, and my heart squeezed to protect itself from shattering.

"You're right. So what do you suggest? Lock me up? Take my wings?"

"No one is suggesting that," Talon snapped. "Stop acting like a martyr."

My cheeks burned. She was right on every account. But fear was so much stronger than her logic. I hadn't felt like this since —since the day Sigurd died. The storm inside me passed, leaving behind waves of embarrassment.

I glanced at Daiman and Sigurd, who were pretending not to be listening to our conversation, then back at Talon.

I let out a breath, and my shoulders sagged with exhaustion.

"I understand your concern."

I did. She had every right to protect Folkvang, even if it meant going against a friend—against me. And if the roles were reversed, I'd do the same.

"I'm not okay," I admitted. "But I don't believe I'm a danger to anyone."

Her lips pressed together to form a tight smile.

"Innocent people died by my hands. Magnus died by my blade." Tears burned at the corner of my eyes, but I held them back.

Now was not the time to fall apart.

"And what happened with Loki and the Disir—I have no idea," I huffed. "I'm terrified about what it all means. And I think it's going to be a long time before I can say I'm truly okay." I closed my eyes and took a deep breath.

"That's all I wanted to hear." She placed a hand on my shoulder, and I opened my eyes.

"You shouldn't be okay. And as long as you can admit that, as long as you're not hiding from what happened in there," she pointed behind us to the ruined temple, "I'll be here to help you through it. But I can't help you. I can't fight for you if you keep me at arm's length."

I nodded, grateful to have her in my corner. There was little I'd thank the Norns for, but Talon was one of them.

"Talon," Sigurd's voice carried an edge that caught both of our attention. "I think you need to see this."

CHAPTER TWO

SIGURD

A SOFT BREEZE tossed the loose strands of my hair around my face as Talon and Kara continued their heated discussion.

"I wouldn't want to be Talon right now," Daiman said under his breath. "Kara looks like she wants to tear the color from the sky."

Unable to help myself, my gaze swept over Kara for the hundredth time, and my heart ached for her. Hurt and fear beamed out of her eyes as she argued with Talon.

I didn't know if she was really seeing things, or if the lack of sleep and trauma was taking its toll. I wanted to go to her and tell her we'd figure everything out together, but the unrivaled power rolling off of her warned me to keep my distance.

I ran a hand over my hair as the faint clash of steel caught my ear. Every muscle in my body tensed and I turned to scan the trees. Sunlight spilled through the branches, warming the dew laden forest. A fine mist rose all around us, glistening in the beams of light and creating a haze that made it difficult to see beyond.

I waited a beat and glanced at Daiman. He was searching the forest as well, one hand on the hilt of his sword.

The scrape of steel against steel cut through the heavy silence. Several Draugr and warriors from Folkvang fought in the distance. One of our own went down, disappearing in the brush as a deep voice bellowed orders.

"Talon," I called over my shoulder. "You need to see this!"

Kara and Talon were by our side in a heartbeat.

"The battle isn't over," Talon said, and she was right. It looked as if all of Folkvang was heading toward us.

"We need to make sure they don't escape. Gods only know what kind of damage they could do without someone to command them." The memory of Folkvang burning as the Draugr tried to destroy my home flashed through my mind. Never again.

"I'll cut them off on the right." I pulled my sword. "Daiman, you hit them straight on."

Daiman nodded and pulled his blade.

"Kara, are you well enough to take the left?" I searched her eyes for any doubt or hesitation.

"Don't go soft on me now." She glared at me. "I've fought beside you in worse condition."

I nodded and turned to Talon. "You take to the sky," I commanded without a second thought, even though both she and Kara outranked me.

"I'm going to need a weapon." Kara held out a hand.

I glanced at Talon, deferring to her judgment. If she trusted Kara to have a weapon, then that was good enough for me.

Talon nodded, and I closed the gap to Kara. Sparks tingled over my skin as I placed a dagger in her open hand. Her fingers trembled as they curled around the hilt, and she took a step back without looking at me.

Guilt punched through my stomach. I hated treating her like we couldn't trust her, but I wasn't willing to take any chances. We've already lost too much today.

A flash of Magnus bleeding out in my arms assaulted me and I sucked in a breath. I didn't have the luxury of giving into my grief. Not until we were safe—until Folkvang was safe. I pushed the memory of Magnus, and my heartbreak creeping like shadows across my soul to the back of my mind.

"See you on the other side." Talon smirked as her twilight and obsidian wings burst into existence. She shot into the air like an arrow and disappeared above the canopy.

Without another word, the three of us set off into the woods. I carved a path through the trees and waist high brush. My legs ached with each step, and the wound in my side throbbed, but I ignored all of it. In an ideal world, I would've had time to rest, and let Asheria's remedy take full effect before heading back into battle.

But this wasn't an ideal world. We were at war.

Running from tree to tree, I kept to the shadows as best I could. A roar split the din, and I froze. A spike of revulsion shot through me, sharpening my senses. I glanced around the trunk I was hiding behind and I could just make out the jagged edge of the rift.

The blood drained from my face.

There were still so many of them, spilling out of the rift like ants and scattering into the trees. The army Loki had assembled still looked mostly intact, which didn't bode well for Folkvang. My fingers tightened on my sword and I started forward with a renewed sense of justice.

I'd kill every last one of them if that's what it took to make my home safe again.

Three split off from the primary group and I started toward them, my sword raised and ready to strike. An axe cut through the air and one of them ducked out of the way. Taking advantage of the misdirection, I ran out of the cover of the forest and swung.

My blade cut across the front of his armor-free chest, sending a spray of black ooze to the leaves between us. The putrid stench of decay filled my nose, and I swallowed the urge to gag. His gaze fixed on me, and he snarled like a wild boar. Baring his teeth, he swung a dagger in each hand with wild abandon as he rushed forward.

I spun to the side, and one of the polished blades skated just shy of my cheek. *That was too close for comfort.* A flicker of irritation scrunched up his face as he squared his shoulders. The act was so human, it gave me pause.

It wasn't his fault he was like this. It wasn't his fault his life was stolen from him. It wasn't his fault he was a monster.

He lunged for me, and on instinct, my blade cut the space between us and sliced through the delicate skin of his throat. He stumbled backward, mouth gaping like a fish out of water.

It wasn't his fault, but it didn't change what he'd become. A monster.

He crumpled in on himself and sagged to the dirt. I closed the distance between us and yanked his head up by his grimy, stringy hair. Unnatural sapphire eyes stared up at me as I shoved my sword into his throat and pulled it through his neck. The glow around his iris flickered and went out as I released my grip, and he hit the ground.

How did so many of them go unnoticed for so long? The questions prickled the back of my mind as I edged closer to the fray.

Something wasn't right with all this. The break in the rift... Loki... the Draugr... Everything fit together too easily. No plan, no matter how carefully crafted, was ever executed with such effortless grace. If I've learned anything about war, it's that if something doesn't feel right, I should trust my instincts. And my gut was telling me there had to be someone on the inside helping Loki and the Draugr. But who? And to what end?

Daiman ran into my line of sight, sword raised and covered in black blood. I wondered if he could've been in on it from the start. He was with me the day we came upon the rift, and Freya had allowed him to guard it while keeping me away. Was there a bigger reason, or was I being paranoid?

Daiman shoved his blade through a Draugr's back. His sword penetrated all the way through the monster's chest with slick onyx blood. And an animalistic scream pierced the air so loud I flinched.

"Si, lookout!" someone yelled across the forest.

A wayward arrow pierced through a branch a few inches from my head. *For the love of Yggdrasil.* I looked in the direction the arrow came from, but I couldn't spot the archer anywhere.

Get your head in the game, Si.

"You alright?" Daiman asked, jogging up to me.

I opened my mouth, and the forest exploded. I crouched and raised my arm to protect myself as branches, rocks, and dirt pelted me from every direction.

Magik crackled around us, making the air sit heavy on my skin as the dull thud of rocks and leaves falling around us subsided. I dropped my arm as I rose to my full height, assessing the damage.

The smell of damp earth and ozone filled the air. Trees had been ripped from the ground, their roots reaching for the sky like twisted limbs. The blast had knocked several of the Draugr off their feet, but it wasn't enough to kill them. And in the center of the blast, Freya stood in full battle armor.

She looked like one of the vengeful gods legends warned us about. A smear of red and black blood coated the front of her armor, and her normally perfect hair was knotted with mud and black ooze. Bands of gold Magik licked down her arms and over the sword in her hand.

"Don't just stand there," she barked. "Kill them all."

Every shield-maiden, Valkyrie, and warrior jumped into action, unable to ignore her decree.

Freya's eyes met mine across the clearing. Her nostrils flared, and the prickly sensation of her Magik crawled over my skin like a snake.

Streð mik. I cursed.

I'd only seen that cold, hard look of fury on her face when she doled out a gruesome punishment. I sucked in a breath as she whipped around and cut down three Draugr with one swipe of her sword. Unease swarmed my stomach like angry bees.

My conversation with Bryn wouldn't be the only heated discussion I'd be having in the near future. I didn't know what was worse, the Draugr actively ripping apart my home or the thought of having to face a goddess who looked like she wanted to shove her sword through my gut.

"Sigurd!" The heavy *whoosh* of wings sounded overhead. And I looked up in time to see Talon reaching her hand out toward me.

I ran as fast as I could and launched myself off a stump. We caught each other's outstretched arms at the elbow. Using the momentum of her wings, she swung me around and let go of my arm, launching me toward a group of Draugr threatening to overpower one of our own.

I aimed my sword as I dropped to the ground. My blade found its mark and pierced through the skull of a Draugr. My arm jolted with the force of hitting bone, and I shoved the blade further into his skull.

Landing in front of him, I pulled a dagger from my hip and slit his throat. He toppled to the side, a shocked expression frozen on his skeletal face. I pulled my sword free, as a glint of silver shot past my vision, and pinned a Draugr to the tree in front of me. I searched the canopy of trees to discern where the arrow had come from and my back hit something solid.

I turned to attack, and Ezra's eyes met mine.

"Nice of you to drop in." He wore an amused expression that made me grit my teeth.

He'd never given me cause to dislike him, but something about his carefree arrogance had always rubbed me the wrong way.

I turned away to meet the next blow. "Looked like you needed help," I called over my shoulder.

"I think you like to hog all the glory." He grunted the last word as a body hit the ground to my right with a *thud*.

"I don't fight for glory. It just works out that way." I turned and threw my dagger, pinning a Draugr to a tree through their eye.

"Liar," he chuckled. "We all fight to have our names written alongside the gods."

He wasn't wrong, but I wouldn't give him the satisfaction of admitting that. Talon may be convinced of his innocence, but I was still wary of him. His presence in Kara's life was too convenient for my liking.

Pivoting to the right, I caught the edge of a blade across my shoulder. The pain shot through me like a snakebite, but it was the frustration burning under my skin that I felt the most. I was being sloppy and unfocused.

I shook off the thought of Ezra and Kara. The disappointment in Freya's gaze. The ache of losing Magnus. I let it all go as I focused my attention on the Draugr in front of me.

With both hands, his blade cut through the air. I raised my sword to block his attack, nearly losing my footing with the sheer strength he used to swing his weapon. He was stronger than some of the others, and the look in his eyes as he bore down on me had an awareness the others didn't.

I fought against the weight, freeing myself, and took a step back. He wouldn't be put down easily. I tightened my grip on the hilt, and we circled each other. He was waiting for me to attack. Intelligent indeed.

I waited for him to cross one foot over the other and shot forward. He met my blow with little effort. The bones and muscles of his face shifted into what I could only assume was a smirk, and he lunged forward, sword glimmering in the sunlight.

I twisted and raised both hands, holding my sword over my head, blocking his blow.

A flash of silver caught my eye, and I jumped back as he thrust a dagger toward my torso, narrowly avoiding another wound between the ribs.

"Need some help?" Ezra stepped into my peripheral. The group Talon had thrown me into had either perished or run off. It was just the three of us now.

I nodded.

I may not like the guy, but my ego wasn't so big that I couldn't accept help from him.

"Let's see what you can do." I gestured toward the Draugr.

Ezra stepped forward, and the half man, half monster, reacted immediately. I circled to the right, watching each swing, each step.

The Draugr favored his left, and always parried with the same flick of his wrist. He was brutal, but focused.

Ezra struck once more, getting the Draugr to leave his right side undefended. I jumped in, aiming for his ribs, but he turned on me and caught my sword with his bare hand.

Black ichor seeped from his closed hand, and a deep, menacing growl resonated through his chest. I ripped my blade free, cutting the gash in his hand deeper as Ezra gained his attention once more. I attacked again, my blade slicing through the air to meet his.

Ezra circled around the back of the Draugr. Wanting to keep the Draugr's attention on me, I channeled Ragnar. I swung again and again, not following any pattern and not letting him find an opening to put me on the defense. I was unpredictable and rough, lacking the usual grace I employed when fighting. And it felt good. With every strike, I channeled all my rage, heartache, and frustration.

Swing.

A blow for Magnus, the brother I would never see again.

My ears rang with the high pitch sound of steel scraping against steel.

Clash.

For all the pain and suffering Loki caused.

Hiss.

Anger propelled me forward, knowing that Freya kept my hands tied behind my back.

Ezra got hold of the Draugr by the neck and pulled his head back. I swung again and the two of them fell to the ground. I dropped to my knees and shoved my blade into his chest until it hit the dirt. I stared into his sapphire eyes. My hands shaking with rage. Ezra pulled a dagger across the Draugr's neck, and his head lolled to the side.

Pulling my sword free, I got to my feet. Ezra shoved the body and stood, clamping a hand on my shoulder.

"We make a good team."

"We're on the same side. But that doesn't make us a team." I rolled my shoulder out of his grasp and turned toward the rift.

Freya cut down a Draugr and sent his head flying into the bushes. She huffed out of breath as she returned to her full height and looked around the forest turned battlefield.

Kara and Talon landed a dozen paces in front of me. "More than a handful ran to the east." Kara looked like she was ready to collapse.

Talon placed a hand on her arm. "They can't get far without someone to command them. We'll find them."

Kara nodded as they came to a stop in front of me and Ezra. Her eyes met mine and the instinct to go to her pulled at me. I stepped toward her as Ezra pulled her into a hug.

"I heard Loki took you. Are you alright?"

"Fine." She wrapped an arm around him, but her eyes met mine, sending a pang of envy coursing through my core.

It should be me.

CHAPTER THREE

KARA

EZRA'S ARMS wrapped around me and the subtle melody of his soul brushed against my skin, making me stiffen. It was nothing compared to Si's soul, still running its fingers down my spine.

I glanced over Ezra's shoulder at Si, and disappointment was etched into every line of his face. I held his stare as some foreign ache unfurled in the pit of my stomach. Whatever path we'd started down together felt like it was crumbling before my eyes. It wasn't just longing or regret that stared back at me. It was heartbreak for the future that was shattered the moment I killed Magnus.

I dropped my gaze and pulled away from Ezra. His soul song was a whisper against my skin, but I didn't want to tempt the power simmering in me.

"Looks like you've had quite the day as well." I aimed for a cheerful, battle-worn tone, but my heart wasn't in it.

"Can't say it hasn't been eventful." His hands trailed down my arms, and I winced ever so slightly as his fingers grazed the fabric Sigurd had wrapped around my forearms.

My slowly healing wounds were another reminder of how close I'd come to a true death. Under normal circumstances, the pain would have already lessened, and I'd be well on my way back to myself. But the dull ache radiating up my arms was a constant reminder that nothing would be normal from here on out.

20

"You're hurt." His eyebrows knit together, forming a deep-v of concern.

"It's nothing." I stepped back. His concern for my well being after everything I did made my skin crawl. I didn't deserve his kindness.

His crisp blue eyes bounced between my arms and up to my face. He pursed his lips and took a step back as well. He'd been good about not pushing me for more than I was willing to give. And I'd never been more grateful for that personality trait than I was right now.

A flash of white caught the corner of my eye, and before I could react, a fist connected with my face. My nose cracked and thick metallic blood filled the back of my throat.

I raised my hands to defend myself as chestnut eyes filled with fiery rage stared back at me.

Bryn.

My heart sank, leaving me with nothing but an empty pit of despair in my chest. She must have heard about Magnus—about what I did to him.

I spit a mouthful of blood and steeled my nerves for the turmoil in her eyes.

"He never should've trusted you. I never should've trusted you." The crackle in her voice could only be from one thing— the gut wrenching scream of holding a loved one that's joined the stars.

"For sorðinn sake," Ezra exhaled somewhere to my right.

She stepped toward me, and her soul song was a featherlight touch against my skin that paled in comparison to Sigurd's. And I was starting to wonder why he had such an effect on me.

"Bryn don't do this," Si demanded, but she ignored him.

"You're a blight on the Nine Realms!" She shoved me, and I stumbled over the uneven rocks and leaves. She was strong on her best days, but it was nothing compared to the furious strength she exhibited now.

"How could you?" Emotion made her voice waver.

She kicked, and I twisted to the side, catching the blow against my ribs. A deep ache pulsed through my ribs, and I sucked in a breath. My body had already been pushed beyond its limits for one day, but I wouldn't turn my back on her heartbreak.

She punched again, and I raised my arms to block her. I took the full weight of her assault on my battered forearms. Sharp white-hot pain licked down the runes Loki carved into my skin and I sucked in a breath.

"Bryn, stop." Talon grabbed her by the shoulder, but Bryn grabbed Talon's hand, spun and shoved her backward.

"Let her be," I yelled at Talon and everyone else watching. No one else needed to suffer for my actions.

I planted my boots and stood my ground. Her fist pierced the air between us. I raised my arm to block the blow, but she shifted at the last moment. The glint of silver registered too late, and a dagger slashed through my trousers and across my thigh. I bit back the hiss on my tongue as the air hit my wound. It wasn't deep, but it stung.

"He took you in. Cared about you." She shoved me again, then swept my legs out from under me. My back hit the densely packed leaves, and the air ripped from my lungs. Every bruise, cut, and scrape on my body screamed in agony. The canopy of trees blurred and jumped back into focus, making my stomach clench.

I deserved this.

The hollowness in my chest swallowed me whole. I knew exactly how she felt. I knew precisely how much pain she wanted to inflict, because after Sigurd's mortal death I hated myself as much as she did now.

She dropped to her knees, and her murderous gaze nailed me to the damp earth. I was the only thing she cared about.

The woman who stole her love.

She straddled me, agony crisscrossing her brow like a map, detailing her pain. I understood all too well how every breath that filled her lungs felt like a betrayal to his memory.

I wanted to apologize. I wanted to tell her I understood. I wanted her to take her grief out on me, even if it only gave her a moment of peace. But there was nothing I could say that would ease her pain.

She fisted my dirty, tattered linen shirt and pulled me toward her. Her nostrils flared as she reached back and punched me square in the face. My head shot back and pain flared across my nose and cheeks. I choked on the trickle of blood making its way down my throat. She hit me again across the temple, and blue and white stars sparked in the dark as my vision went black.

I deserved the pain. She needed the release.

I'd let her break every bone in my body if it helped her grieve.

"That's enough!" The weight of her lifted off of me, but the weight of her emotional turmoil and my guilt kept me pinned to the dirt. My head sunk into the cold earth as a throb of pain radiated across my broken nose.

"She killed Magnus," Bryn screamed loud enough for everyone on both sides of the rift to hear.

"It's not what you think." Sigurd's voice was calm but firm. I rolled my head to the side as he took a tentative step toward her.

She pulled out of Talon's grip and stepped toward Sigurd. Her boots crunched through the leaves as she closed the distance between them and a spike of panic fluttered in my core.

"You were like a brother to him." Bryn's voice was calm, but it held a lethal edge. A warning flare went off in my head. I may deserve her wrath, but he didn't.

"He was, but—"

"But?" she practically growled. "How can you stand there and defend her after what she did to you, did to Magnus?"

"Because it wasn't her." His words tugged on the invisible thread between us, making my heart swell. He didn't blame me anymore. "It was Loki."

Hearing him say those words was like a balm to a wound that had been festering for a century.

Bryn snorted and shook her head.

I forced myself up on my elbow and tried to take a full breath. The sharp crack of pain down my side cut through me, and my arm shook with the effort to hold up my weight.

"You really believe her pathetic story?" She stalked toward him like a predator playing with its prey.

His eyes flashed to me. And I mouthed *don't*. Nothing he said would change how she felt, and it wasn't worth him getting hurt.

"I saw the truth with my own eyes." He looked away from me and squared his shoulders.

"You saw what you wanted because she warms your bed again." She was barely a foot from him, but he didn't flinch. "She's a vile monster, and she played us all." Her words were deathly calm, and a chill ran down my spine. One wrong word and the storm inside her would rain down on us all.

I forced myself to my feet. My legs shook and my nose throbbed, making my head spin. I ached in ways I knew I'd feel for days to come, regardless of Magik. I shoved my pain into the smallest corner of my mind and rose to my full height. I wouldn't let her hurt him or anyone else.

"I understand that's true for you right now, but she is not a monster." His brow softened as his eyes pleaded with her. The cracks in my heart quaked to see him so vulnerable with someone I knew didn't want his help.

Bryn grabbed the leather trim that connected Si's shoulder

guard to the chest piece and pulled him toward her. "Then why did you lie to us?" Every word dripped with poison, intending to strike at the heart of his betrayal. "Why didn't you tell us she killed Magnus before you asked us to run into battle to save her?" She shoved him, and he stumbled backward.

My hands balled into fists as I stalked toward her. Each step took more effort than I cared to think about.

"Leave him," I seethed, but no one acknowledged me.

"I was always going to tell you." Sigurd placed his hand over his chest. A pained expression crossed his eyes, and I knew his guilt was eating him alive.

"I thought I knew you. I thought I could trust you. Magnus trusted you." Her voice cracked on his name, and her pain seared through my chest as if it was my own. "But you aren't half the man he thought you were."

Sigurd squeezed his eyes shut, and my heart lurched for him.

"That's enough, Bryn." Talon stepped between her and Sigurd. "You were under Loki's influence, too. Have some grace."

I paused mid-step. When had Loki meddled in Bryn's mind?

"And yet no one died by my hand." Bryn rolled her shoulders back.

"You're right," I said, pulling her attention away from Si. "You were lucky enough not to have killed anyone. But I did." I put some bite into my words to keep her ire directed at me. "Your fight is with me."

"You'll both pay for your betrayal," she snarled, then launched herself at me. We tumbled to the ground.

Her elbow hit my ribs as I pulled her over me. She was hard to beat when I was at my best, and I wasn't anywhere near my best. A dagger kissed my throat, and the sharp bite of steel dug into my skin. Her hand shook as she stared down at me. I didn't want to join the stars, but I was so tired.

Tired of all the pain I've caused. Tired of trying to make amends. Tired of not being strong enough to save the people I cared about. I couldn't bring back Magnus or any of the others, but maybe killing me would soften the edges of her torment.

I didn't want to die. I just didn't want to feel anymore. I closed my eyes and let the Norns decide my fate.

"Enough!" Freya shouted. An icy breeze of Magik raised goosebumps on my skin, and everything slowed down. Magik roared in my blood as a melody that reminded me of the first kiss of rain sank into my bones.

Bryn's weight left my body, but I couldn't move. The ancient melody humming through my core made it hard to breathe.

I stared up at the trees as a pair of ravens took off from a branch. I tried to take a full breath, as my new Magik urged me to take the power calling to me.

"It's not your place to dole out justice. Now take a walk," Freya commanded and the monster inside me purred.

"Go," Freya said through gritted teeth, and the snap of Magik in the air smelled like sulfur.

Bryn's obsidian and gold tipped wings unfurled from her back as she stared down at me. "This isn't over," she said under her breath before launching into the sky.

"As for you," Freya looked down at me sprawled on the ground and the lyrical ballad of her soul wrapped around me.

"You're stronger than whatever pathetic display that was. You're a Valkyrie. Act like it." She looked me up and down like I was a half-dead animal dragged from the woods and then turned away.

I forced myself to my feet and propped myself against the nearest tree for support. Awareness pricked the back of my neck and I knew I'd been spared for a reason.

Not just with Bryn, but in the temple, too. Time and time again, my life has teetered on the edge of a blade, yet my heart still beats.

The Norns' haunting voices echoed in my memory.

You have a long journey ahead of you.

My life mattered to the Nine Realms. And as much as I wanted to slink away and lick my wounds, I wanted to know why more.

CHAPTER FOUR

FREYA TURNED AWAY FROM KARA. "The rest of you, back to Folkvang." She started toward the rift and the chill of Magik dissipated.

The others followed Freya, but I crossed the space between me and Kara. The crunch of leaves under my boots felt too loud in the now quiet forest. The stillness after a battle had always made my skin crawl, because it meant it was time to deal with the dead.

"You alright?"

A trail of blood dripped from her nose and smeared across her cheek. An angry red bruise spread across the bridge of her nose. Her hair was matted with bits of leaves. And the runes, Loki carved into her, were angry maroon blotches against her pale skin. She looked close to the worst I've ever seen her. And I could only imagine the pain she was in after being brutalized by Loki and Bryn.

"I wish people would stop asking that," she grumbled and took a stilted step toward Folkvang. The gash in her leg was much deeper than I first realized.

"Kara," I gently caught her by the crook of her arm. Her eyes met mine and a mix of exhaustion and pain flashed like lightning over a sea of green.

"I'm fine Sigurd." She sucked in a breath and looked away from me. I let go of her arm and she visibly relaxed. My chest squeezed. Already her walls were falling back into place, brick by brick.

I could let her push me away. It'd be easier after everything that's happened. But I didn't want to. I meant what I said last night. I was done pretending I didn't care about her.

"I'm sorry." I ran a hand through my messy, unkempt hair and tucked the loose strands behind my ear.

She halted and looked over her shoulder. "What do you have to apologize for?" Confusion furrowed her brow.

"Bryn." Her name felt like acid on my tongue as guilt curdled in my stomach. "If I'd been honest about you and—Magnus," I forced his name past the lump in my throat. "Then maybe she wouldn't have-"

"Tried to kill me?" She finished my sentence.

She closed the gap between us and placed a trembling hand on my shoulder. My heart leapt at her touch and the instinct to pull her close was almost impossible to ignore. Her features softened and the corner of her mouth lifted in a sad smile as she exhaled.

"Her pain is not yours to carry. She…" her gaze dropped to the ground, and she dropped her hand. "She lost the man she loves, and it was by my hand. I don't blame her for what she's feeling." Her eyes met mine again. "And neither should you."

"That's gracious of you."

She squared her shoulders, and her lips formed a hard line. "I understand what it's like to lose your heart and feel like there's no way back." She backed away from me. "Her pain is my burden and mine alone. Don't carry baggage that isn't yours."

I opened my mouth to argue as she held out the dagger I'd given her earlier.

"Thank you for what you said…to Bryn." She wouldn't meet my eye. "It doesn't change anything, but it was nice to hear." One corner of her mouth lifted ever so slightly in a sad smile.

I took the blade, unsure why she was giving it back to me. "I should've said it the day you arrived in Folkvang."

She took a measured step away from me and wobbled.

I reached for her, but she held out a hand to stop me. "I'm not your burden either, Si." She limped forward, and I let her walk away from me.

I glanced at the dagger in my hand and back at her retreating form. A beam of sunlight kissed her auburn hair, and a pit opened up in my stomach. Why did she return the blade to me? Did she really not trust herself?

My chest constricted as I watched her walk back to Folkvang. Kara may understand half of what Bryn is feeling, but I understood the other half. To feel betrayed by someone you trusted, to feel as if the Nine Realms were being ripped out from under you. I understood her rage. I'd felt it myself for more years than I cared to admit. But Bryn's anger was misplaced, and maybe I could help her see that.

I started toward the rift, my head and heart caught in a storm of guilt, anger, and frustration. Loki was to blame for all this, for controlling Kara, for killing Magnus and so many others. Should I ever lay eyes on the trickster God again, I'd make sure we all got our shot at him.

I took the last few steps in this foreign forest and stepped through the rift. Magik crackled over my skin and I sucked in a breath. The delicate mix of florals and rushing water filled my nose. Though I'd left one forest for another, there was a quality to the light dancing through the trees that felt like home.

My eyes searched out Kara of their own accord. She'd found another tree to lean against as everyone else gathered around Freya. She clearly wanted space right now, so I fought the compulsion to go to her and instead sidled up to Daiman and Talon.

A heaviness clung to the air and on the shoulders of every person around me. The only sounds that filled the morning were the shuffling of boots, the groan of someone in pain, and a cough that sounded a little too wet. It was the harmony of people taking stock after a fight they didn't necessarily win.

We were trained fighters, the best of Midgard. But that didn't mean we were ready to fight gods and monsters. My heart sank as I scanned the surrounding faces. How many of us would meet the stars before this was over?

"I thank you all for defending our home." Freya's hoarse voice showed how tired she might actually be. I may have been fighting to save Kara and stop Loki, but she'd been commanding her warriors since the alarms were raised.

"I know you're tired." Her shoulders slumped forward, but the spark in her eyes said she was ready for round two should it present itself. "And many of you have lost someone near to your heart." She placed a hand over the knotwork boar—the symbol of her Vanir bloodline—engraved on her metal chest plate. "Grief is an old friend to us all, one I know you wished to never encounter again."

The memory of Magnus on his knees in the courtyard clawed its way to the front of my mind. The storm clouds swirling inside me threatened to drown me in an ocean of sorrow.

"It's with a heavy heart I ask a little more of you today." She gripped the shoulder of the warrior closest to her. A mixture of blood and ooze stained their clothes, and their bone weary expression told a tale of exhaustion and loss.

"We need to clean up the bodies and prepare them for the burial rites. As well as make sure our borders are secure. Valt-trie, Hildr," she barked out their names. "Make sure no stone is left unturned. I want everyone accounted for, dead or alive. And no one goes anywhere alone."

"Understood," Valttrie and Hildr said in unison.

Talon glanced in my direction. It didn't go unnoticed that she charged someone outside our close knit group to make sure

Folkvang was safe. Unease prickled down my spine, and I shifted from one foot to the other.

"As for those of you who've been wounded, seek a healer," Freya continued. "I don't need any more losses today, not when it's clear someone means to break us." The compassion in her voice shifted to controlled rage. "They'll soon learn that Folkvang is not the weakest link in the Nine Realms. And before this is over, they will taste the strength of our will." A few people mumbled their agreement, but a cool wind dug into my exposed skin.

No one here knew the truth of what we were up against. None of them had ever experienced the raw power Loki unleashed in the temple when he freed the Disir. No one even knew who the Disir were or how powerful they might be. Hel, even I didn't understand the power we were up against and I was in the temple.

The thought of them roaming the Nine Realms, free of their stone prison, made my blood run cold. They'd bested every one of us, including Loki, seconds after their return. I could only imagine the damage they might cause once they were at full strength.

A gust of wind, followed by the heavy beating of wings, filled the clearing and threw loose strands of my hair in every direction. Freya's Hrafn landed just outside of the tree line. Its blue-black feathers shimmered where the morning light touched them.

"And the rift?" Daiman asked. "Should we stand guard?"

Freya turned slowly toward Daiman and every nerve in my body tensed.

"That won't be necessary." Freya looked at the protective border and I followed her gaze. "It's already healing."

The rift no longer disappeared into the sky. In fact, it was only a few feet wide now.

Relief washed through me, quickly followed by guilt. She

was doing something all along. I should have trusted her. I should have known she was trying to protect us. Instead, I was impatient and too focused on not getting what I wanted.

"You have your orders." Freya's eyes met mine and the sharp edge of her Magik prickled my skin. "Take care of one another. I'll see you all at the rites tonight."

She closed the distance to the Hrafn, and the bird lowered its head in greeting. Freya climbed on the back of the bird and they took off without so much as a backward glance.

CHAPTER FIVE

FREYA'S ORDERS spurred everyone into motion, but I stayed glued to the tree at my back. The acrid taste of battle sat heavy in the air, thick and foreboding. And while it was a relief to be alive and home, the last two days were just the beginning. The Disir were out there, and it was only a matter of time before they started killing.

"Guess Freya's not going to tell everyone about Loki and the temple?" Daiman commented to Sigurd.

A nagging sensation took root in my core as I watched Sigurd's makeshift family take stock and assess one another. I'd failed Magnus, and there was nothing I could do about it. But I could try to warn the rest of them of what was coming.

Be careful who you trust. The Norns' warning screamed in my head.

"You know she likes to keep things close to the chest." Sigurd shrugged and looked more defeated than I can ever remember seeing.

A thread tugged on my heart, begging me to go to him. But his song was still too strong. Stronger than any of the others—besides Freya's. So I pressed my back against the rough bark and didn't budge.

"Is it true?" Ragnar's question silenced the others as he stalked toward me. His expression didn't betray a single emotion. "Are you the reason Magnus will sail tonight?"

My heart throbbed at his words, and my stomach hollowed. A dozen pairs of eyes stared back at me.

"Yes." I kept my voice even and braced myself. Bryn wasn't the only one who lost Magnus. They all did.

"I knew you'd bring trouble down on us. He was the best of us." Hate simmered in his steely blue gray eyes. And an all too familiar feeling of dread wrapped its arm around me like a cloak.

I'd been here before. After Sigurd. When everyone turned on me, hated me.

"I'm sorry. I know—"

"You're sorry?" Ragnar snarled and stepped toward me. "You don't deserve the title of Valkyrie."

His words hit me like a physical blow, and I flinched. A desperate fear to keep my wings clung to my bones, and I squared my shoulders unconsciously. The foreign Magik in me snarled, and I pushed off the tree, not even feeling my wounds as I stepped forward.

"That's enough." Sigurd stepped between me and Ragnar.

Ragnar shook his head slowly and his lips formed a thin line as a beat of silence stretched between us. My heart thrummed in my chest so loud I was sure everyone could hear it.

"You're really going to defend *her*?" He shook his head, and his face contorted in disbelief. "You and Magnus were thick as thieves." He threw each word like a dagger.

Out of the corner of my eye, a pair of wings as dark as the ocean on a moonless night slowly unfurled. Talon.

I caught her eye and shook my head subtly. I couldn't let this turn into an all out brawl. If Ragnar and the others wanted to hate me, it was their right.

Sigurd stepped forward, and I grabbed his arm. The connection shot through me like lightning, and I sucked in a breath.

"He was like a brother to me, but Kara—" his voice softened and a lump formed in my throat.

"But nothing," Ragnar yelled, and a few nearby birds took flight. "She's a killer, Sigurd. When are you going to see her for what she really is?" Ragnar stared at Si with something akin to disappointment in his eyes and I dropped my hand.

"That's not entirely fair," Ezra stepped forward and Ragnar whirled on him. "We've all spilled our fair share of blood."

Heat flushed through my body, and I dug my nails into my palms. Why couldn't it have been Ragnar instead of Magnus? I balked at the thought, and shame burned through me like I'd swallowed hot coals.

"Not innocent blood," Ragnar snarled at Ezra. "The both of you make me sick. Is your loyalty so fickle that a woman spreading her thighs will have you turning your back on your friends, your family?" He looked between Si and Ezra with disgust.

"This had nothing to do with loyalty," Ezra rolled his eyes. "We all lost people today. Magnus isn't the only boat we'll burn tonight."

"He's right." Talon stepped forward, her wings nowhere in sight. "This is war. Unlike anything you've seen before. Magnus won't be the last of us to meet our end."

"I'm well aware of the consequences of battle, for sorðinn sake. We all are. But killing to save your life, the lives of others, differs from killing innocents in cold blood," Ragnar argued.

"You're right," I stepped next to Si. "Magnus was innocent, along with the other souls I destroyed." My heart faltered, like the emotional cracks were becoming physical and permanent, but I kept the pain out of my voice. There'd be plenty of time later to hold the tiny shards of my heart together.

"That Loki destroyed," Si said through gritted teeth, like his will alone would change everyone's minds.

I met Sigurd's gaze. "It isn't Loki's hands stained with their blood."

His jaw ticked and his eyes crinkled like he wanted to argue with me, but he held his tongue.

"Good to know the monster can take accountability for her actions," Ragnar sneered.

"You want to talk about monsters?" Sigurd closed the gap to Ragnar and shoved him. "What about everything you said and did under Loki's influence?"

Daiman stepped forward, a hand on the hilt of his sword. Talon's wings snapped from her back and Ezra put himself between Ragnar and Si, placing a hand on each of their chests.

Ragnar bared his teeth. "I didn't kill—"

"You would've killed Daiman if I hadn't stopped you," Sigurd practically growled.

"If you're so skilled at defusing Loki's Magik, then why didn't you stop her?" Ragnar yelled. "Where were you when she sent our friend to the stars?" Ragnar shoved Ezra aside, and Daiman stepped up and steadied Ezra.

Sigurd fisted Ragnar's shirt, their faces inches apart. "I was on my knees, bound by Magik, helpless to do anything." He tossed Ragnar like he was nothing. "Did you know she tried to kill herself first?" Rage burned in Si's words, just as hot as the Magik running through my veins. "She turned Loki's dagger on herself, so she wouldn't have to kill anyone and Loki undid her sacrifice with a snap of his fingers."

"You what?" Talon whirled on me, and my cheeks flushed.

"It was all I could think to save them," I snapped. "I have no problem being everyone's punching bag. But Si's right. I tried to save everyone in that courtyard. I tried to stop Loki, and it wasn't enough."

I wasn't enough.

Ragnar's eyes met mine as I seethed.

"And what did Loki want, exactly?" Ragnar's tone softened like maybe, just maybe, I wasn't the monster he made me out to be.

"They deserve to know," Daiman's calm demeanor eased the fire burning in my core.

"Know what exactly?" Ezra stepped closer to Daiman.

The memory of him telling me not to make decisions for him flashed through my mind. It had only been a few days since we had that conversation and already I was wondering if not telling him everything was the right decision.

Daiman was right. They had a right to know.

"Is anyone going to tell me what you lot are hiding?" Ragnar looked at Talon, Daiman, and Sigurd, waiting for an explanation, and I let out a heavy breath.

The Norns told me to be careful with who I trusted. But considering half of Folkvang saw what Loki and I did in that courtyard, it was safe to assume the horse had left the stables.

My gut told me we could trust Ezra, but Ragnar was a tossup. We'd spent the least amount of time with each other since my return, and I didn't know if I could trust him or if it would bite me in the ass.

I stared at Ragnar, and he held my gaze without flinching.

"Loki released the first Valkyrie. They go by the name, Disir." Either we could trust him or we couldn't. But we wouldn't win this fight by keeping people at arm's length.

"He used me to kill eight people, including Magnus and Si, to complete his ritual." Each word was like acid in my mouth, but I forced my emotions behind a mask of cold indifference.

Ezra's expression remained open and curious. While Ragnar remained stoic. Whatever he was thinking, he was keeping it well hidden.

"And I take it the Disir are different from the two of you?" Ezra motioned between me and Talon. "Considering Loki went to great lengths to free them."

"Correct," Talon said before I could form a response, and I thanked the stars.

I wasn't ready to explore my connection to the Disir, and I sure as Hel didn't want to label myself as one of those monsters.

"All this drama and death for some Valkyrie?" Ragnar raised an eyebrow at me. "What aren't you saying?"

"The Disir are the ones who created the army of monsters we've been fighting." I motioned to the bodies lying at our feet. "They consume the souls of warriors chosen by the gods. Warriors like you."

Ezra snorted a laugh, and Ragnar's eyes widened ever so slightly.

"Wait, you're serious?" Ezra's smile faltered.

I nodded.

He looked at the dead Draugr closest to him. "Why turn men into monsters?" He grimaced, and his head cocked to the side as he inspected the Draugr.

"Does the reason matter?" Sigurd's words were sharp, and I shot a glance in his direction.

He didn't like Ezra and had voiced his concerns after I went on a killing spree. Was it jealousy that Ezra was the one to welcome me back to the Nine Realms, or was there something more to his mistrust?

Ezra shrugged. "Maybe not. But, unlike some, I like to understand the full picture before I pass judgment." He cocked an eyebrow and Sigurd's jaw popped.

I didn't have time to hold their hands or coax their egos. They were big boys, and if any of us were going to survive Ragnarok, they'd need to set their egos aside.

Sigurd scoffed. "Some men wait around and wax poetic over battles and strategies, others are on the front lines, taking action."

Si was quick to make judgments based on the information in front of him. His instincts and intuition have saved him more times than I can count. But he often found himself cleaning up messes that could've been avoided by learning all the information upfront.

As for Ezra, I knew little about his history. But he was right about one thing. He didn't let the gossip mill taint his perception of me when I arrived.

"Seems to me like I was the one taking action." Ezra's eyes flicked in my direction, and a wicked grin pulled at the corner of his mouth.

Great. A pissing match.

"You're both big powerful men." Talon rolled her eyes. "Can we act like there's at least half a brain between you?"

"They want power," I answered before either of them could take another dig at the other. "With every soul they take for themselves, they grow stronger. Strong enough to kill the gods."

Ragnar scoffed.

"Is that even possible?" Ezra's brow furrowed.

"They did it once." I nodded. "Freya stopped them before they could take over, but it appears her solution was temporary."

"But to kill the gods is to invite Ragnarok, is it not?" Ezra glanced at the others as if needing confirmation that he was right.

"Which is why we need to keep this quiet..." Talon's words landed between us all as an order.

"Easier said than done." Ezra ran a hand through his hair. "We lost good people today. The survivors are going to want answers."

"Freya will give them answers," Talon said.

"Just not the truth?" Ragnar raised an eyebrow.

"Freya doesn't know the truth," I said. "The Norns were very clear about keeping the gods in the dark about the Disir's return."

"I think that ship has sailed," Ragnar grumbled.

"He's right," Daiman jumped in. "She must have known they

were in the temple. She tasked us with finding out who'd brought the Draugr here. And she was explicit in telling us not to go near the temple."

"When I spoke with Freya about the Disir—" Sigurd started.

Talon visibly balked at his words. Daiman's brows almost disappeared into his hairline, and Ragnar's rage simmered to the surface.

"You know, maybe if you kept fewer secrets, Magnus would still be alive." Ragnar shook his head.

"I was commanded to keep quiet by our goddess."

"When did you become such a weak man?" Ragnar looked Sigurd up and down with disgust. "The man I met years ago had fire in his veins. He didn't take orders like a dog."

"You would've done the same." Si raised his chin.

"No, I wouldn't have. I turned her down. I chose myself."

"When did that happen?" Daiman asked.

"Before your time," Ragnar answered.

"Now, who's keeping secrets?" Sigurd said.

"We all keep truths hidden in the dark. All of you need to stop acting so surprised." Talon rolled her eyes.

"What I don't understand," Ezra paced in front of me, "is why the Norns told you to keep the gods in the dark? It doesn't make sense."

"Doesn't it? It would mean war across the Nine Realms if the gods found out the one thing that can kill them, and kick off Ragnarok are alive once more."

"Maybe a world without the gods wouldn't be so bad," Ragnar mused.

"Watch your tongue," Talon snapped in his direction.

"If they're strong enough to kill the gods, then what makes you think we stand a chance?" Ezra turned back to me like I was the answer to all our problems.

"We have to try, don't we?" Daiman shrugged.

"Maybe you do, but I don't want any part of this," Ragnar

said. "And if any of you," he motioned to Daiman, Sigurd, and Ezra, "have an ounce of sense left in you, you'll walk away from her too." He turned on his heel and stormed off.

My eyes met Sigurd's, and my heart plummeted into my bowels. Ragnar was right, he should walk away, they all should.

time today I noticed her bracing herself or stepping away when someone drew near. I wondered if it was it involuntary, or was she afraid of being close to anyone now?

"I guess it could've been worse," she sighed without looking at me.

Folkvang was bathed in the golden morning light, but it was the remnants of battle that took my breath away. Black smoke billowed from various buildings still on fire. And to the left, nestled at the base of the blue mountains, an entire block of longhouses had been reduced to timbers and ash.

A passionate fury ran through my veins like a thousand horses at seeing what those vile creatures did to my home.

"They can burn all the buildings they want." Anger dripped off my words. "It's the people that carry the soul of Folkvang. And so long as one of us is left standing, Folkvang will never fall."

Out of the corner of my eye, I felt her studying me. "I hope you're right." She stepped out of the cover of the trees and started down the path toward Asheria's.

I took another moment to memorize the scene in front of me. The fires still burning, the anger and frustration boiling under my skin. The homes and lives lost. I let it all flow through me, sewing this moment into the fabric of my soul so I'd never lose sight of what I was fighting for.

Taking a deep breath, I swore to the Norns. To Yggdrasil. And anyone else who was listening, that I'd fight until my last breath to free the Nine Realms from the terror Loki unleashed.

I exhaled, feeling the weight of what was to come settle into my bones, and started after Kara.

Before either of us knew what we were getting ourselves into, we agreed to work together. But after everything she went through in the temple, I didn't know if that promise still carried any weight.

"Kara," I called after her. "Can we talk?"

Green eyes snapped over her shoulder at me. Now that we were away from curious glances, I could see just how exhausted and angry she was.

"Whatever it is, can it wait?" She said as she exhaled.

"I'd rather it didn't." I understood that she'd been through a lot. We all had. And while I'd love nothing more than to lick my wounds and sleep for a week. Now was not the time.

"I'm really not in the mood to deal with anything else."

"And you think I am?" My words came out harsher than I intended. A clear indication of how fried my nerves were.

"You're the one who wants to talk." She continued along the path toward the city center.

"This is important," I argued.

"In case you haven't noticed, Folkvang is falling. So whatever it is, it can wait." I could feel her slipping through my fingers, and my resolve hardened.

"No, it can't." I caught her arm and pulled her into an alley. I didn't need or want an audience for this conversation.

"Sigurd, please. I'm exhausted." She didn't pull free from my grasp when we both knew she could.

"So am I." She may have gone to Hel and back, but we all had.

"Then let's not." She snapped and tried to walk away. I pressed my hand to the wall, creating a barrier. I needed to know if we were on the same page, whether she liked it or not. We were at war and I didn't have time to wait for answers.

"Move." Anger and something ancient rippled off of her in waves.

"Or what?" I cocked an eyebrow. We both knew I wasn't really holding her here. She could fly off whenever she wanted. Which meant she wanted to be here.

"You really want to test me? After everything you've seen?" She looked up at me, her green-grey eyes piercing through me like a fiery brand.

I cupped her cheek, careful to avoid the bruises. Her pupils blew wide open and lips parted.

"I'm not afraid of you." A ripple of Magik pulsed between us, and I sucked in a breath to steady myself.

"You should be," she breathed. "My hands have more blood on them than you could ever know." Her words were soft and menacing and she shoved me—hard. I stumbled back a step, but still she remained instead of flying off.

"That's been true since the day I met you." I punctuated each word. She needed to understand that whatever happened in that temple didn't change who she was in her heart.

"It's not the same now and you know it." She stepped toward me. "Magnus is gone forever because of me." Her eyes were glassy with pain.

The cracks in my heart split open, and a swell of agony rippled through me. "I'm well aware."

"And yet here you stand acting as if I'm not capable of ending you too." Her voice cracked and the cut on her lip bled again.

"Would you prefer it if I hated you?" I raised my voice. My own emotions getting the better of me. "If I was just as angry and hurt as Bryn? Because I am."

Her face crumpled, and she took a step back like my words were a physical blow.

"I'm furious that Magnus met his end," I practically growled. "The memory of him in my arms as he bled out is a weight on my soul that I'll never shed. I want to hunt down the Norns and force them to give him back. I want to scream until the Nine Realms crumble and I feel nothing."

I closed the distance between us, unable to ignore the need to be close to her. The smell of rain, lavender, and the metallic tang of blood filled my nose as she looked up at me and I wiped the blood from her lip. She sucked in a breath and her shoulders stiffened as she pressed against the wall.

"But I'm not angry at you." My heart thrummed wildly in my chest as I stared down at her. "It's Loki who holds my ire, and if he's still alive, I'll use every breath I have left to end him myself." I lowered my voice. "But I don't have the luxury of letting myself fall a part right now. And neither do you."

I took a step back, my hands shaking and eyes burning with tears that desperately wanted to spill over. I wiped my fingers across the sleeve of my ruined shirt. Swallowing the lump in my throat, I tried to force the ache in my chest into the darkest shadow of my soul.

"It's all I can do, not to lose myself to the hands of guilt and anguish clawing at me," she exhaled. "Every breath aches like a festering wound. I should have met the stars today." Her voice grew louder with each breath. "I accepted that my time had come to an end. And yet here I stand," she threw her arms out. "Alive when others more deserving are not." Tears threatened to spill down her cheeks.

"You deserve to be here." I held her gaze, willing her to believe she was worthy of living.

"Don't look at me like that." A tear coasted down her face.

"Like what?"

"Like I didn't kill your best friend. Like what happened in the temple didn't change everything. Like you still know me." She looked up at me, eyes filled with so much agony it ripped a hole in my heart.

I closed the gap between us and placed a hand on her hip. She flinched at my touch, but didn't pull away. She must be hurt far worse than I realized.

"What if the temple didn't change anything?" Her eyes danced between mine and she sucked in a breath. "What if losing Magnus only made it more apparent that we need to work together?" I gently pulled her toward me, and she acquiesced.

"What if, no matter what happens, I'll always know who you

are in your heart?" I placed my hand on her chest. Even through her armor, I could feel the thrum of her pulse.

"You can't know who I am." She wrapped her fingers around my wrist and squeezed like she wanted to hold on for dear life, but instead she removed my hand from her chest. "When I don't even know myself anymore."

"Kara," her name dripped off my tongue like a caress.

She closed her eyes, and she leaned into me. "Please don't try to make me feel better. Not right now."

"Alright, I'll let it go for now." I stepped back, reluctantly letting my hand fall from her hip. "But we still need to talk—"

"Gods," she rolled her eyes. "Whatever it is, it can wait." She started toward the main street.

"I thought we agreed to be cautious," I called after her, not ready to be done with this conversation.

She looked over her shoulder. "Cautious about what?"

"About who we trust with what the Norns said." I did my best to keep the emotion from my voice.

She turned back around. "You don't think the others have the right to know everything?" She cocked an eyebrow, and her eyes met mine. Fire simmered beneath the surface of the look she pinned me with.

"Or is it just Ezra you have a problem with?" She folded her arms over her chest, and I swear I could feel her frustration prickle over my skin.

Fine, right to the point then. "He wasted no time in getting close to you the moment you arrived."

"And what's so wrong with that?" Her eyes met mine with a challenge. "Just because you avoided me like the plague doesn't make it a crime for someone else to get close."

"You're not worried about why he inserted himself into your life?"

"I'm pretty clear on why he came into my life." She sauntered toward me, closing the space between us. "Is my friendship with

Ezra really such a problem for you that we need to have this conversation right now?"

"It's not a coincidence that he was there the day you lost control." I ignored her jab. I had a gut feeling about Ezra and I was done ignoring my instincts.

"You were also there, just outside my door when I lost myself." She jabbed a finger into my chest. "And I was with you the first time I lost control. Should I suspect you?"

"Why tell him now, when you were against it before?"

"I changed my mind." She shrugged, like it was no big deal.

I bristled with irritation. "Based on what, exactly?"

"Correct me if I'm wrong, but weren't you the one who argued that I should tell him?"

"That was when he was sharing your bed," I said through gritted teeth. I was losing patience with her careless attitude. Maybe this wasn't the right time for this conversation, but it was too late to drop it. "He deserved to know that you might try to kill him while he lay defenseless next to you."

The corner of her eyes crinkled ever so slightly. "He deserves to know whether I'm sleeping with him or not."

"This isn't about who you're—" I took a deep breath to regain control of my thoughts and emotions. I hadn't felt this out of control since my days in Midgard. I'd always attributed my hot head and passion to living in a mortal world, but no. It was this infuriating woman who made me lose all sense of control.

"I just want to be on the same page." I was coming off like a jealous ass when really this had nothing to do with who she wanted to sleep with. Even if she ignited something, I thought I lost the day my mortal life ended. I wouldn't burden her with my feelings if she didn't return them.

"You want to stop the Disir, right?" She leveled her gaze at me and I nodded. "Then I don't see how telling Ezra changes that."

"I don't trust him." My eyes flicked over her. "Not to mention Ragnar." My hands balled into fists. "He had no right to say the things he did."

She held up her hand. "Ragnar has every right to be angry. And for what it's worth, I told him the truth because it's what Magnus would have done. But whatever's between you and Ezra isn't my problem."

"You may be right, but we agreed we were in this together. Neither of us can make decisions blindly, or we'll lose this fight."

"We agreed to walk this path together, but we are not in this together." Her voice hitched, the only clue that she was brimming with emotion. "You weren't forced to kill anyone. Nor were you strapped to that slab of stone and bled within an inch of your life." She placed her hand on my chest and fire burned in her eyes. "We may be on this path together, but we don't have the same dog in this fight."

I folded my hand over hers, keeping the warmth of her touch pressed to me like a lifeline. "I'm well aware we are not the same."

She flinched.

Immediately I realized the error of my words. "I know Loki's twisted plan has taken a great toll on you." I cupped her cheek and Magik sparked across my palm, heating my skin.

Seeing her so close to a true death ignited a deep and ancient fear inside me. I'd always seen her as indestructible. And even when I wanted to hate her, I could never picture a world without her in it.

"And I know the Disir saving you has implications we don't fully understand." My thumb brushed her cheek, and she leaned into the touch. Maybe she wasn't as closed off as I believed.

"But all of this started with my mortal death. You aren't the only one with skin in this fight. You can shut me out of your bed and heart, but I won't stand by and let you shut me out of this fight."

"It's been a long time since I've seen you push for something you want." She pulled my hand from her face and let out a frustrated sigh. "It's something I've always loved about you, your passion and determination." Her eyes traced my face and her brow furrowed in pain.

I could feel her throwing up her walls again. And I had to fight the instinct to hold on to her and never let her go.

"My plan to end this with you by my side hasn't changed." She took a step away from me and added another brick to the wall between us.

"The real question you have to ask yourself is if you're willing to do this with me. With everything you know now, and with inviting others in."

Another step back, another brick.

A desperate panic I didn't understand crawled up my throat.

"Because we can't do this by ourselves. Not if we're going to stop Ragnarok. So think about what you really want." She turned and walked out of the alley.

The moment she was out of sight, the panic subsided as if a spell had been broken.

As much as everything in me wanted to scream yes, I hesitated. The ache in my heart for Magnus, the hunger in her eyes when she consumed Loki, made me pause. I owed it to both of us to let her words sink in and truly understand what she was asking of me.

I followed her out of the alley, my mind swirling with each step. She was right in more ways than one. I needed to be sure I was ready to walk this path with her. No matter where it led.

CHAPTER SEVEN

SIGURD

WE REACHED Asheria's after a very silent walk through the city. Not only was I lost in my own thoughts, but the normal hustle and bustle of Folkvang was somber. Most of the residences were off making sure there weren't anymore Draugr lurking about, and the few that stayed behind were cleaning up the dead.

So much loss, and for what?

Kara pushed open the door to Asheria's and stepped inside. I followed her over the threshold, and the cloying smell of fire and herbs hit me like a wall. It didn't matter that the windows were thrown open, the stench of the dead and dying lingered and soured my stomach.

Asheria barely glanced up as we walked in. "Give me just a —" She did a double take. "Kara?" Her eyes widened and her hands froze over the bloody rags she was in the middle of cleaning up. "You look like you've had a row with the World Serpent?"

"It's been a long few days." She ran a hand over her hair. "Talon insisted I see you." She shrugged and motioned to her injuries.

Asheria grabbed Kara's arm and twisted it from side to side. Her gaze zigzagged over Kara's face, and she pursed her lips as she inspected the damage that Loki and Bryn had inflicted upon her.

"Is it just superficial?" Asheria assessed Kara like she was trying to see any damage beneath her armor.

"My ribs have seen better days." Kara touched her side and closed her eyes. My gut churned and fear trickled down the back of my neck. I'd never seen Kara hurt like this. In fact, I'd never seen any Valkyrie in the state Kara was in.

"You're not healing as quickly as you should."

"I'm fine, really. Just need some rest." Kara stepped back from Asheria, and the Valkyrie nodded.

"There's some food in the back and warm water to clean up." She motioned with her head toward a forest green curtain that separated the surgery from Asheria's living quarters. "Why don't both of you head back while I finish up here?"

Kara nodded and stepped around Asheria. I followed quietly behind her as she brushed aside the dark fabric curtain.

A small bed with dark brown furs sat in one corner. A small fire burned in the middle of the room, filling the space with the aromatic scent of smoky pine. And a table sat off to the left of the room, with a platter of fresh fruit, bread, cheese, and meat.

The floor boards creaked as I crossed the space to the platter. I tore off a piece of warm bread and tossed it into my mouth without really tasting it.

Kara exhaled a grunt of discomfort catching my attention. She was trying to undo the straps that wrapped around her torso, but as she reached for the buckle, she winced and abandoned her efforts.

"Can I offer you a hand?" In days gone by, I wouldn't have hesitated to get her out of her bloody clothes. But there was a century's worth of walls between us I was still navigating.

"I can do it myself," she huffed and tried again, but failed to unfasten the strap.

"I know you can," I stepped toward her. "But you don't have to." Her gazed flicked up to mine and her answer sparked in her eyes.

She sighed and her shoulders sagged as she nodded her consent.

I crossed the room in two strides, and she raised her arm to expose the straps of her armor. I stepped into her space, and warmth radiated off of her. She turned her head to the side. Blood was caked and dried into her hair, next to the bruise on her temple.

My eyes skated down the length of her neck, and my heart thrummed in my chest at her closeness. It never ceased to amaze me how much of an effect this woman had on me.

Kara closed her eyes and swallowed as I gently pulled the first strap back to free it. She sucked in a breath and grabbed my bicep, digging her fingers into my muscle.

The fire popped as the unmistakable caress of Magik warmed my skin.

The strap flipped free, and I moved to the next one. Her hand slid to my shoulder and the memory of her hands sliding up my chest as she rose to kiss me burned to the surface of my mind. My pulse quickened as I pulled on the next strap.

Her fingers gripped my shoulder, and she let out a shaky breath.

Guilt splashed through me. She was hurt, and I was letting my desire for her cloud my mind.

I moved to the final strap on her right side and freed it from the buckle easily. Kara exhaled a heavy breath and slumped forward, pressing her forehead to my chest.

"How bad is it?" I kept my voice low and rested my hand on her waist. She'd been down playing how hurt she was, but I didn't want whoever might walk into Asheria's overhearing us. There'd be plenty of people looking to take advantage of her weakened state after Magnus's death.

"I'll be okay." She lifted her head but wouldn't look at me.

"That's not what I asked you." I bent slightly to catch her eye.

Her gaze searched mine. A flicker of emotion kissed her lips.

"You don't have to worry about me." She took a half step back, but my hand squeezed her hip to keep her in place.

"Since the moment we met, I've worried about you." The corner of my mouth twitched. I moved to the fasteners on her left side, and her hand found its way to my other shoulder like a perfectly choreographed dance.

"And look where it's gotten you." Emerald green eyes met mine and my heart ached with all the emotion in her gaze threatening to spill over. She was hurting. And not just physically. All her bravado and posturing was gone.

This was the Kara I knew. The woman without all the masks, without the armor.

Just her.

"I'm right where I need to be." My concern for her had always been unfounded. She was stronger, faster, damn near god-like. But my mortal heart couldn't help wanting to protect her. Caring for her wellbeing was like breathing. I couldn't stop even if I wanted to. I tried for a century without success.

The first strap slipped from the buckle easily as I held her gaze.

"Si," she breathed, and it sent a shiver down my spine. Her eyes searched mine, like she was begging me to go, but her grip on my shoulder pleaded for me to stay. "You can't mean that, not after everything."

The second strap came loose, and I moved to the last one without breaking our gaze.

"Are you calling me a liar?" I cocked an eyebrow and a spark of life lit up her eyes.

"Everyone's a liar about something." The final strap came loose, and she rolled her shoulders.

She stepped back and made to pull her armor over her head, but I gently gripped her upper arms.

"That may be true. But when I say I wouldn't want to be

anywhere other than here, I mean it." I tucked her hair behind her ear.

"If you're not lying about that, then what *do* you lie about, Sigurd?" She drew out my name like she was tasting every letter and tilted her head back. She looked so deeply into my eyes, every thought emptied out of my head.

It would take no effort at all to press my lips to hers. To lose myself in the sultry promise in her eyes. Magik crackled between us and the air warmed with her breath. It would be too easy to forget that we were at war. That I'd lost friends, and would likely lose more before this was over.

My hand slipped under the hem of her top to the small of her back. My fingers brushed her bare skin and I swear her Magik flared at my touch.

Giving in would be as easy as my next breath. And for a moment, I wouldn't have to grieve, or think, or feel anything outside of us. My heart banged against my chest like a caged animal. It'd be so easy to remind myself of what it feels like to be alive.

I brushed the back of my hand against her cheek and her eyes closed. But using her to shut out the swirling shadows of guilt and heartache wasn't fair to me or her.

I swallowed hard and forced myself to gain some control of my emotions.

"The only lies I tell, are the ones I tell myself." My voice was ragged with unclaimed desire.

With a concentrated effort, I lifted the heavy lamellar armor over her head and placed it at our feet.

"Thank you." She wrapped an arm across her middle with a shutter.

My heart seized at the state of her. Blood stained the cream top in more places than I could count.

"Kara, this is..." My hands balled into fists to keep from

touching her again. And my heart let out a pulse of anger tinged with a cold spike of fear.

How close had she been to meeting the stars?

"I've had worse." She took a step back, and the air cooled between us.

"Now that *is* a lie."

"Sigurd, I'll look at your first." Asheria burst through the curtains.

"Go take care of yourself." She nodded toward Asheria, but wouldn't meet my eye. It was as if the distance between us allowed her to think clearly again and her walls were back up.

I hesitated. Rationally, I knew she'd be okay if I left her here, but my gut screamed at me to keep her close. Like whatever part of me could see a battle play out before the fight, knew that leaving her now would be a choice I couldn't undo.

"Go," she mouthed. "You're worse than a mother hen."

Reluctantly, I turned away from her, and my gut churned. The constellations in my soul rearranged themselves for the course ahead, leaving me with a sick feeling in the pit of my stomach.

I made my way past the green curtain and into Asheria's surgery. Just as quickly as the tug on my core came, it vanished. The feeling of dread swirling in my stomach settled as if the course was set, and the stars realigned.

"Let me guess." Asheria whirled on me. "You didn't follow my orders and ran right into battle when you should have been resting?" She cocked an eyebrow, and the child in me shriveled from her disapproving gaze.

"You know me," I shrugged, aiming for casual nonchalance as I tried to see behind the curtain. "Can't resist the call to arms."

"Mmhmm. Was it the call to arms that had you putting your injury at risk, or a certain someone?" She glanced toward the curtain, then her eyes swept over me like every one of my thoughts was being broadcast in aching clarity.

"The call to battle lives in all our blood." I kept my eyes on the glass containers over her shoulder. They were filled with different herbs, dried leaves and tinctures, only Asheria understood how to use properly.

"I've seen half of Folkvang today." Asheria grabbed a few clean rags. "I know Kara was staying with you. And I know Loki took her."

She wiped off the dark wood table between us with a wet rag.

"I know you and a handful of others went after her. And I know that the Draugr were up to something on the other side of the rift, that reeks of dark deeds. Let's not pretend you have any secrets?" She pinned me with a look that seared right through me.

The gods work hard, but the rumor mill works harder.

"What would you have me do? Sit around like a child, nursing my wounds while others fight to save our home? To save her?" I met her hazel eyes, and they softened at the edges.

"Can I assume your concern for her well-being means you've forgiven her?" She lowered her voice and raised an eyebrow.

"I thought you already knew everything," I fired back.

A soft laugh escaped her lips. "I know more than you'll admit to yourself."

"You have the gift of healing, not mind reading."

Water dripped and sloshed from behind the curtain where I left Kara. It took all my careful control not to glance in that direction.

"I don't need to read your mind to see what's plain on your face." She met my stare, then looked over her shoulder in the direction of Kara. "You're worried about her and not just about her injuries."

"You didn't see what Loki did to her." I said through gritted teeth. The image of her bleeding and screaming as she rose from the stone played in a loop behind my eyes.

"No, I didn't. But I know her heart. She'll be okay, she always is." She rounded the table and came to a stop in front of me.

"I'm well aware of how capable she is."

"Then you should have stayed put, and let the Magik do its job." She shoved my shoulder. "Now sit." She pinned me with a stare I used to see on my mother's face when there was no arguing with her.

I sat.

She made a lifting motion with her hand. "Take that off. Let's see the damage you've done."

I unfasten my armor with deft fingers and placed it on the floor next to me. Crossing my arms, I grabbed the hem of my top and lifted it over my head with a wince. The adrenaline was wearing off, and the pain of my injuries was beginning to make themselves known.

Asheria groaned as she took in my injured arm. But it was the reopened wound on my side that made her purse her lips. Dark purple bruising spilled across my ribs and lower abdomen. It looked worse than it felt, thank the gods.

"Why do you lot never listen?" She shook her head. "You act as if Magik grows on trees." Her warm fingers gingerly pressed along each rib, and I squirmed at her probing touch.

"I didn't really have a choice. We're at war in case you haven't noticed."

"I'm well aware." She raised my arm over my head and knelt to get a closer look at the gash in my torso. "But there's something to be said for restraint." She pressed on the skin around the wound and I winced.

"Where's the fun in that?" I said through gritted teeth.

She rolled her eyes and let my arm fall back to my side. "Sometimes I wonder if Freya deliberately chooses warriors with only half a brain." She made her way to the other side of the table and began pulling jars off the shelves.

"You think any of us got here by having wool for brains? We're warriors, we fight. It's in our blood." I rubbed at my sore ribs, careful to avoid the throbbing she provoked.

"You have a warrior's spirit, but that doesn't require you to have a death wish." She placed the jars on the table and grabbed the mortar and pestle.

"Death comes with the job. The fallen know that better than most."

She glanced up at me as she crushed a dried flower in her palm and dumped the contents into the mortar.

"Are you so eager to join the stars?" Her voice was soft and curious as she added small dark seeds to the mixture.

I sighed. More than once over the last few days, I'd accepted I wouldn't see another sunrise, but that didn't mean I wanted all this to end. Especially not when things were getting interesting again.

"I was in no danger of meeting my end." My gaze flicked toward Kara hidden behind the curtain, and the memory of exploding stone pelting me from every direction flashed through my mind.

"Your bravery is second to none. I'll give you that." She poured a handful of dried cloud berries into the mortar. "But you're no use to anyone on your deathbed."

"I thought I was here for some healing, not a lecture."

"You don't want my help, the door's behind you." She ground the ingredients in the mortar with a saccharine smile.

I held her stare as she pulverized the herbs and berries, but I didn't make a move to leave. The wound on my side pulsed with my heartbeat and a headache was starting to take up residence behind my eyes. I needed her to heal me, and we both knew it.

The sound of heavy objects hitting the solid wood floor

came from the backroom, and I was on my feet in half a heartbeat.

"Sit." Asheria commanded, and there was no room for arguing in her tone as she made her way to Kara.

One heartbeat, my hands balled into fists. It was too quiet. Another heartbeat and I grabbed my sword.

She's fine. I chanted to myself.

A flash of Loki throwing Daiman across the room splintered into my mind.

Two more heartbeats and sweat beaded on my forehead. The memory of Kara screaming echoed through my bones.

I jumped to my feet.

I've spent way too long letting others take charge, when I should be the one jumping into action.

I was across the room in three strides and about to rip the curtain from its fitting when Asheria brushed the fabric aside and froze on the threshold.

She placed a hand on my chest to stop me from pushing right through her.

I looked over her shoulder for anything out of place. But all was quiet.

"Kara?" I stepped around Asheria. Kara's armor and bloody tattered clothes sat in a pile on the floor, and a stack of books was strewn across the space.

My stomach jumped into my throat as anger pulsed through me. I gripped the hilt of my blade and ground my teeth so hard, I was sure they would crack under the pressure.

"For sorðinn sake."

She was gone.

"I wouldn't worry." Asheria clapped a hand on my shoulder. "She'll come back round. She always does."

I wanted to believe her, but after everything that's happened in the last two days, I wasn't sure she'd be back anytime soon.

The front door of Asheria's creaked open, and I rushed back into the main room, sword drawn and ready for anything.

Daiman stood on the threshold with a worried expression on his face.

"What is it?" I lowered my blade.

"Freya wishes to speak with the both of us. Now."

"Will this cursed day never end?" I turned back to Asheria. "Any chance we can make this quick?"

CHAPTER EIGHT

KARA

COOL AIR WEAVED between the feathers at my back as I glided into another realm. I could still feel the heat of Sigurd's fingers against my skin, and the siren call of his soul haunted my every breath. Each note carefully crafted to torment me.

Guilt tugged on my gut like a fish on a hook, and Magik overwhelmed my senses. I sucked in a breath, but I couldn't breathe as the Nine Realms shimmered all around me. My heart raced and the compulsion to pull on Folkvang's tether seared through me.

No. I clamped down on the swirling power inside me and swallowed hard.

I left for a reason.

I needed to breathe, to think about my next steps, and grieve without the constant hum of temptation clawing at me. Even as a novice, I'd never felt this out of control. But this, this was all-consuming, and almost impossible to ignore.

Folkvang was safer with me gone. Si was safer.

And if he wanted to walk away from me now, I wouldn't stop him. I lived without him in Midgard for a century. I could live without him again, even if a part of my soul would never come back from losing him.

Banking to the left, my wings rustled against the resistance, and my ribs ached from the beating I'd taken from Bryn.

I had such high hopes for my return to the Nine Realms

after a century. But I should've known I couldn't escape the past. From the moment Loki forced me to kill Sigurd, my hopes and dreams for the future ended.

My chest throbbed, and the cracks in my heart threatened to break beyond repair as I flew over the misty, snow covered mountains of Niflheim. The frigid air bit into my skin and froze the tip of my nose and cheeks. It was enough to numb my physical ailments, but I feared it'd take more than a blast of frigid air to numb my emotional wounds.

I crested over the highest mountains, and pushed Si, Bryn, Magnus, and Folkvang from my mind. I'd left to put some distance between me and the people I hurt, not wrap myself in thoughts of them.

Dipping into my Magik, the threads of the Nine Realms reached out to me like leaves on a branch. I wrapped my heart and mind around a new destination and tugged. Obsidian flecked with bursts of cobalt swirled around me and the freezing alps of Niflheim fell away as a sea breeze kissed my cheeks.

CHAPTER NINE

Svava—Freya's lap dog and pain in everyone's asses—escorted us toward the long house Freya conducted the day-to-day ruling of Folkvang in.

My upper arm burned under the dressing Asheria hastily wrapped, and the bandages around my chest gave off an earthy medicinal aroma. I could only hope Asheria wouldn't need to mend me further after this summons.

The double doors opened upon our arrival and Svava motioned us inside with a saccharine grin that grated against the last shred of my patience. If I knew Svava—and I did—news of our presence here would be twisted into an ugly lie and spread across Folkvang within the hour.

Wood pillars, carved to look like the trees surrounding Folkvang, lined the path to Freya's throne. Lanterns hung off the branches of the pillars, their soft, warm light casting a glow throughout the space.

There were no windows to let in the natural light and fresh air on purpose. Sweat beaded on my forehead, and my heart beat so loud I was sure everyone could hear it. I'd never been called before Freya in this manner before. Being close to her had afforded me enough leeway that meant I was never reprimanded the way the others were.

Freya stepped out from behind a gold shimmering curtain and took a seat upon her throne. Her armor was gone, replaced by a blue linen dress and a decorative gold corset. The design easily could have been mistaken for Thor's hammer upside down if you didn't know better.

Her eyes met mine, and a flash of rage simmered beneath the surface, and my mouth went dry. As we reached the bottom step, Daiman and I dropped to one knee.

"Do either of you care to explain what possessed you to cross the rift?" Her eyes flicked between me and Daiman, and settled on me with the last word.

Crossing the rift had been my idea. I wouldn't let Daiman take the fall for following my lead.

I cleared my throat. "I was trying to save Kara and stop Loki."

"Stop, Loki?" She looked away from me in disgust. "You're no match for an Aesir. No matter how skilled you think you are."

Her dismissal of my skills festered in my chest, making my heart beat like a war drum. It didn't matter that she was right—I was no match for the gods—but her declaration of my usefulness hurt more than I could put into words.

"What was I supposed to do, let Loki continue to wreak havoc on Folkvang? Let Kara die?" Bitterness laced my every word.

"A few months ago you would have." She pinned me with an icy stare, and shame burned up my chest and neck.

"I told you I was done sitting around and hiding from the real threat." My hands curled into fists as I tried to temper the insubordination in my voice.

She was trying to provoke me, and it was working. She knew how conflicted I'd been about Kara upon her return, but two could play that game.

"It's better to die trying than to sleep comfortably, while others pay for your inability to close the rift and protect them."

Her nostrils flared and a wave of glacial Magik raised the hairs on my arms.

Daiman flinched next to me. "Are you trying to force her hand?" He said under his breath.

I knew I should be afraid of her wrath, but I refused to cower from her. If this was how I met my end—protecting my home and the people I cared about—then so be it.

"We were only doing what we've trained for," Daiman offered. "A friend was in danger. Folkvang was in danger." I didn't miss the plea in his voice.

Freya reigned in her power, but a heaviness still permeated the air, and left a charge on my skin.

"You should have informed me of Loki's whereabouts the moment he showed his face." Her eyes darted to the side—one of her tells.

And it all fell together. She was furious that Loki had snuck into her realm undetected.

"I would've handled him and put a stop to his meddling in our affairs." The corner of her lips quirked, and she inspected her nails, like it would have been all in a day's work to dispatch a son of Odin.

"There was little time for conversation when he was aimlessly slaughtering people." I did my best to keep my voice even, but the helplessness I'd felt in the courtyard was a living entity under my skin.

"You had plenty of time to regroup, and have Asheria tend to your wounds, and yet no time to inform me? Spare me your pretty words, Sigurd." She punctuated my name with a flick of Magik, stealing my next breath.

She was right. We had time. But my trust in her had wavered, and if I was being completely honest, all I cared about was saving Kara and stopping Loki. Following protocol wasn't high on my list after Magnus died in my arms.

"I was under the impression you'd been informed of Loki's

arrival," Daiman tried to salvage any credit we had left with Freya. "No one gets into Folkvang without your awareness. Isn't that why you had us patrolling?"

Smart, but dangerous. I eyed him, waiting for Freya to respond.

"You were on patrol." She aimed her wrath at Daiman. "Because our border had been breached. Which means you should have informed me of Loki's movements the moment you were aware of them. There's a chain of command for a reason."

The temperature plummeted as Magik stabbed down my spine like icy rain.

"We should have told you instead of acting on instinct." The urgency in Daiman's voice told me he was feeling the grip of Freya's power as well.

I kept my gaze on the stretch of floor just in front of her throne. Let her think me subservient.

"While I understand your motives, it doesn't explain how you were able to leave Folkvang. You should have died the moment you crossed the rift."

My gaze snapped to Freya and my chest tightened. She had to be lying. If crossing the rift was a death sentence, then why hadn't she raised the alarm for all of Folkvang?

"So the fact that you're kneeling before me means you're not telling me the whole story." She leaned forward and her gaze bounced between the two of us.

"What do you mean, we should have died?" I did my best to keep my tone civil, but I was teetering on the edge.

"You are no longer mortal." She leaned back like she was bored. "You can't walk the lands of the living. The moment you crossed the rift, you should've succumbed to the wounds that ended your mortal life."

"Forgive me if I'm mistaken," Daiman kept his gaze on the floor. "But you sent me and the others to patrol across the rift and monitor the temple. We survived."

"So long as you were serving my interests, you were under my protection. But crossing the rift to stop Loki was of your own accord. Therefore negating my Magik. So, I ask again, how did you survive?"

I glanced at Daiman and realized my reckless plan should have landed both of us in boats tonight.

"Your silence is disturbing."

"Loki used his influence to lure all of us to the courtyard," I said, grasping at straws. "Is it possible that his Magik allowed us to cross unscathed?"

"You think he compelled you to find the temple?" Freya considered the explanation. "The only problem is, Loki doesn't command souls in their second life."

"Then what do you call the Draugr? He seemed to command them?" I said without thinking.

Freya's head snapped toward me and my blood went cold. "Speak out of turn again and I will revoke any favor you have left with me."

I shut my mouth, knowing I'd reached the limit of her patience.

She waved a hand, and Svava appeared out of the shadows. "Look into their claims. I want to be sure it was Loki who commanded them, and not someone or something else."

Svava nodded once and vanished back into the shadows.

"As for the two of you." She glanced between me and Daiman. "You're banned from patrols and training. If I get wind of you touching a weapon, I will have you put down without a second thought. You are to help the Valkyrie with anything they ask of you, and you will not step a toe out of line until I'm satisfied."

Every fiber of my being wanted to argue, but I followed Daiman's lead and inclined my head.

We both got to our feet and Daiman turned to leave.

I cleared my throat. "May I ask, just one thing?"

"Pressing our luck, are we?" The corner of her mouth curled as she looked at me.

"I only wish to know what you plan to do with Kara."

Her eyes hardened. "That's none of your concern."

Daiman pulled on my arm. "Si, come on."

"She wasn't in control of her actions," I explained. I knew Kara wouldn't want me to say anything on her behalf, but she'd already been through enough.

"What I do with my Valkyrie," she rose from her seat and closed the distance between us. "What I do with my realm." Her fingers wrapped around my throat and thick bands of Magik crawled over my shoulders and down my chest. "Will not be decided on the whims of your emotions."

A bone deep shiver rocked my body, and my knees threatened to buckle.

"I will do with her what I see fit." Her grip tightened, her nails digging into my throat. "And you will remember your place." Sparks burned my skin as her Magik engulfed me. "I am a god and you will speak to me as such." She closed the gap between us so our faces were an inch apart. "Are we clear?"

"Yes," I croaked.

She released me, and I sucked in a ragged breath.

"Get out of my sight."

CHAPTER TEN

I STOOD on the shore of Folkvang lake once more. The air was crisp and a cool chill wafted off the water. A handful of the brightest stars blinked into existence overhead as Mani chased Sol out of the sky. Every muscle in my body throbbed, and though Asheria's Magik left me feeling a score better than this morning—her administration only went so far—and my sore muscles screamed for a bed.

Kara was still nowhere to be found, and I was fairly certain we wouldn't see her in Folkvang for some time. My heart ached at the thought of her being out of reach again. I knew she was more than capable of taking care of herself, and I knew many wouldn't welcome her at the rites. But it didn't stop me from wondering where she was, and if she was well.

Talon, Daiman and Ragnar stood by my side as Freya reached the boats closest to us, and I swallowed the lump in my throat.

There were too many boats. Too many lives lost forever.

A vengeful rage settled into my bones and my chest. I couldn't help but feel responsible for each soul that now belonged to the stars.

I should have done more. I was born to do more.

I grit my teeth, my jaw aching with the pressure as flashes of the previous two days assaulted me. My axe slicing through flesh. The snarl of a Draugr. The chaos of bodies crushed together, fighting to the death.

A flash of auburn as Kara walked past me, hand in hand with Loki.

The beat of wings overhead. Magnus on his knees, blood dripping from his throat. An explosion of stone as the Disir awoke. Bryn's strangled cry of pain. Kara, ashen and bloody as Magik tore her a part.

I should have done more. I should have fought harder.

My gaze found Freya at the last of a long line of boats. She looked ready for war, with her dragon scale cloak, dark leather trousers, and a silver chest plate that accentuated her strength and power as our ruler.

Something twisted and soured in my gut as she bowed her head over the dead and walked to the center of the beach. There was a part of me that blamed her for what happened today. This was her domain to protect, as she so lovingly put it. And yet here we stand, boats filled with our brothers and sisters.

Flames sparked out of the corner of my eye, and I stepped up to Magnus's boat to say a final farewell. I placed my hand over his and my eyes burned with unshed tears.

"You were the best of us." My voice was thick with emotion that threatened to bring me to my knees. "It's been the greatest honor of my life, knowing you."

I pulled a dagger from my belt and pulled it across my palm. Blood sprang to the surface, and I squeezed my hand into a fist, letting my lifeblood drip into his boat.

"Death is not the end, brother. I'll carry your memory with me, just as you'll carry my blood with you." A chill shivered up my forearm, raising the hairs on my arm.

"Rest easy, my friend." My chest ached as I took a step back.

I'd avoided reality all day, keeping my heartache at bay. But there was no running from it now. Magnus, my friend, my brother, was gone. My breath stalled, and I balled my hands into a fist, digging my nails into the cut on my palm. The sharp bite of pain was just enough of a reprieve and I sucked in a shaky breath.

Bryn stepped forward, her expression blank. Whether she was numb, or feeling entirely too much to show any of it, I wasn't sure. I'd never seen her so subdued. It was like someone reached into her soul, tore out all her vibrant colors, leaving her with nothing but shades of gray. A wave of shame washed through me as I watched her step up to Magnus's boat.

I should have done more.

Bryn pulled something from her pocket and placed it on his chest. It was the trinket I'd seen them pass back and forth a thousand times.

She opened her mouth to say something, but if any words passed her lips, they were too soft for me to hear. A single tear skated down her cheek and I looked away. Watching her grief felt like an invasion of a private moment I had no right to.

Not after I lied to her about whose hand took her love's life.

Turning away from Magnus, she started toward our group. Her dark eyes met mine, and her lips formed a hard line. The hollowness in her stare sent a chill down my spine. Her flat expression was so much worse than her display of brutality this morning. She stalked past us and I stood with some of the other Valkyrie a few feet away. A clear line being drawn in the sand.

"Many lives were lost." Freya's voice carried over the silent mourning crowd. "Their absence weighs heavy on us all." There was a melancholy spirit to her words that tugged on the unease simmering in my heart.

"We were unprepared today. Loki took advantage of our weak defenses. It cannot happen again." The sorrow in her voice turned menacing. "I chose you for your bravery, your honor, and, above all, your strength." Each word was punctuated with a passion I've yet to see from her and it was terrifying.

"The time to prove your worth has come. This fight is just

beginning, and many more of you will meet the stars before this is over. It's time to rise to the challenge and cement your name in the history of the Nine Realms. It's time to fight for their memory." She motioned toward the dead and an invisible force pushed the boats into the water.

Ripples fanned out from each boat as they made their final voyage.

"It's time to remind everyone just who resides in Folkvang." Freya raised her arms, and the sharp static of her Magik brushed along my bare skin.

Embers from the bonfires filled the twilight sky on her command, flickering on the wind and falling over the several dozen boats like shooting stars. As the first embers caught, a bitter fury erupted inside me.

The weight of each loss sat heavy on my heart, making it difficult to stand still. My soul craved retribution. My hands craved blood as payment for every soul touched by death.

Freya was still speaking, honoring the dead, but her words didn't reach me as I watched the last boat catch. Flames crawled up the wood and cast a reflection in the water, making it look as if the fires of Muspelheim were rising from the depths of the lake.

The hair on the back of my neck prickled, and dread seeped into me like fog. A rustling of voices and boots shuffling reached my ears, and I turned to see what all the commotion was about.

Everything slowed. The crackle of the flames, the breeze, Freya's words. The Nine Realms paused and held its breath. My heart raced, and my intuition flared, the same as it did before a battle.

A figure stalked forward with broad warrior shoulders. The hood of his cloak was drawn up, hiding his face. A crow sat on his shoulder, its eyes tracking each person as it passed.

With each step, the stranger grew closer and my instincts

told me to run. A wave of bitter Magik rolled off of him, making my stomach turn.

One more step and we were shoulder to shoulder. Subtly, I placed a hand on the hilt of my sword and his head snapped in my direction.

His beard was tied into a braid, and a shimmer of gold kissed the left side of his face where his eye should have been. I swallowed, and my hand trembled on the hilt of my sword. One blue eye stared back at me from the shadow of his hood.

"Alfather," I exhaled and inclined my head.

He looked me up and down, his bird mimicking the motion and cocking its head to the side like it'd be happy to pick my bones clean. Fear spiked in my core, and I took a slow half step backward.

I'd always had a healthy fear of Odin, purely because of who he was. But after learning what he did to Kara—taking her wings as payment for my death—I hoped to steer clear of the Alfather all together.

"You dare disrupt our rites?" Freya barked and Odin's attention snapped in her direction, releasing me from his all-seeing gaze. I loosed a breath, and the tension in my body eased a fraction.

"Where are they?" he demanded, the deep timber of his voice rippling across the shore as he took a step toward Freya.

"Now is not the time." Freya threw her shoulders back and raised her chin in defiance.

Adrenaline raced through my veins, making me hyper-aware of Freya's movement. She was putting on a good show of not backing down, but the flex of her jaw and the slight widening of her eyes told me her bravado wasn't entirely real.

I knew there was bad blood between them. She had spoken of him poorly enough that there was no debate about where her loyalties lay. But seeing her bravado falter made me angry on her behalf.

I glanced at Talon beside me, but she was staring holes into the back of Odin's head like a scorned lover. Was she angry on behalf of Kara, or did Talon have her own fraught history with Odin? Barely contained rage seeped out of her and I placed a hand on her arm.

She glanced at my touch and up at me. My forehead crinkled in question and she silently shook her head as if to say, not now.

I'd heard stories—rumors that Odin wasn't beloved among the Valkyrie, but it never occurred to me to ask any of them why. Just another thing I let slide over the last century. Shame blistered my heart. My mortal self would hardly recognize the complacent man I've become.

"I'm only going to ask one more time." Odin's commanding voice was deathly calm, making my blood run cold. He may be in Freya's domain, but he was the one in control here.

Nothing good could come from this. In the hundred years I've been here, Odin hasn't once graced us with his presence. To interrupt our rites and demand answers could only mean one thing.

He knew about the Disir.

"Where are they and that vile creature you call Valkyrie?" He spat the last word.

Freya glanced in my direction for a split second and fear poured into me like I'd been plunged into a frozen lake.

For the love of Yggdrasil. He was talking about Kara.

Ancient, primal fear unfurled inside me, dragging its claws over my soul. My pulse shattered, and I clenched my fists so tight, I bled again. The stars above me quaked and my vision narrowed on the Alfather.

Thank the Norns Kara wasn't in Folkvang. Her disappearance from Asheria's left me with a bitter taste in my mouth, and too many unanswered questions. But she was safely away from Odin right now. And that was all that mattered.

"You do not command me." Sparks of Magik slithered along

Freya's fingers. Odin clearly unnerved her. But the woman I've come to know over the last century never let her emotions get the better of her.

"Maybe not." Odin peeled the hood of his cloak back and murmurs went through the crowd as everyone else recognized who was in our midst.

His rich cedar hair was pulled back in braids and twisted down the center of his head, forming a thick ponytail tied with a leather strap. A tattoo covered the shaved side of his head. The prominent black ink created an intricate design of swirls and runes.

"But will you let them suffer to save a woman who has proven repeatedly that she's a menace to the Nine Realms?" Bands of pale light wrapped around his forearms like snakes. "Not to mention the vile creatures your lack of foresight has unleashed on the Nine Realms once more."

"Do what you want with the Disir. But the Valkyrie in question is mine to deal with."

"You've had your chance!" His voice echoed through my bones, and I flinched at the venom in his words. "And you failed. I will not allow your incompetence to undo everything I've worked for." Wind whipped across the shore, sending dirt and pebbles flying into the air.

A wave of raw, furious power hit me square in the chest, knocking me to my knees, along with everyone else at the rite.

Everyone but Talon.

Out of the corner of my eye, I watched as she lowered herself to the ground of her own accord. *What in the name of Yggdrasil?*

Another ripple of his power rushed over me, and fire ripped through my veins, burning through my blood and searing me alive. I writhed in the dirt, trying to fight against the wall of Magik bearing down on me.

I broke out in a sweat and tried to roll onto my back. But a fresh wave of blistering pain ripped through me. Someone cried out, and my vision blurred.

Another wave of Odin's Magik hit me so hard it was like falling from a horse. I coughed, and the air was ripped from my lungs. My chest ached, my blood burned, and the corner of my vision went dark.

I tried to suck in a breath, tried to fight against the cloying blanket of Odin's will, but my limbs gave out and I collapsed.

My eyes fluttered closed as my heart rebelled against the shadows creeping into my soul to claim me. We were all going to die.

"You kill them, and I'll consider it an act of war." Freya's words sounded muffled, like I was hearing them from underwater.

"Tell me where she is." Thunder rumbled overhead, and the sky darkened.

"Release my people, or those words will be your last." A flash of lightning cut through the darkness, threatening to consume me.

A gentle caress that felt like rain on a blistering day brushed over me, and the fire that had burned so hot a moment ago was extinguished.

I sucked in a desperate breath and then coughed until it felt like my lungs were trying to escape into the fresh air.

The sound of dozens of people gasping for air and groaning filled the charged shore.

"Last chance, tell me or I won't hesitate to kill them all where they lay." Odin snarled as a taste of his power bristled against my raw nerves.

"Your guess is as good as mine," Freya cooed. "She left shortly after daybreak."

"We both know you can track her. Do it."

"It's not that simple." The sharp bite to Freya's words made me flinch.

Logically, I knew giving up one to save many was the only option. But I couldn't live with myself if I let Freya turn Kara over to Odin.

"Freya." Odin grabbed her by the throat with one hand and squeezed. "You, of all people, should know what happens when someone lies to me."

A smile spread across her face that turned my stomach. "Don't make promises you can't keep," she croaked.

He shoved her away, and she stared at him with a challenge in her eyes that sent a shiver down my spine.

"I'll give you a fortnight to deliver her, and then I'll tear Folkvang from the fabric of the Nine Realms and make you watch as I destroy everything you hold dear."

"She won't come willingly."

"Oh, I think she might," Odin swiveled and his eye met mine. "With the right pressure point." Magik curled around my wrists and up my arms like chains.

"She's still fond of this one, is she not?" He cocked an eyebrow as the chains forced me to take a step forward.

My muscles strained, and I shook with the effort to stay put, but it was useless. The Magik tugged me forward.

"He's one of mine." Freya's words reverberated through me. I'd thought I'd lost all favor with her, but clearly her hatred for Odin was far greater than her ire toward me.

Odin clicked his tongue. "He was never yours. You stole what was mine for some misguided retaliation."

Never Freya's?

Odin's Magik deposited me in front of them, and Odin clapped a hand on my shoulder. Worry gnawed at my insides like a rabid dog.

"Do find the girl quickly. I'd hate for him to meet his end when he still has so much potential."

Lightning hit the shore and everything went dark.

CHAPTER ELEVEN

KARA

IT HAD BEEN an age since I was last in Jotunheim. I closed my eyes and took a deep breath, filling my lungs with the briny sea air as I strolled down the main promenade. An ancient memory flashed through my mind like brush strokes on a canvas.

Sticky hands, birds squawking, my father's laugh, water lapping at our toes, and the bright and decadent aroma of citrus and fish cooking over an open fire.

I breathed out a tendril of heartache, letting the memories push back the shadows threatening to consume me. This is why I'd finally settled on visiting Jotunheim. To remind myself of happier times, to warm the ice in my soul, and figure out how to face the others no matter the consequences.

Hungry gulls squawked in the distance, looking for scraps to fill their bellies. Families sat on the low wall overlooking the sea, their feet dangling over the water as they enjoyed the spiced fish and fresh fruit.

Laughter pierced the din as the rhythmic plucking of a string instrument carried on the wind. The juxtaposition to Folkvang sent a pang through my gut.

There was so much pain, heartache and loss in Folkvang that it was hard to imagine there was still love, laughter and joy in the Nine Realms. It felt like a crime that these people were unaware of the devastation I'd unleashed.

I wasn't new to the notion that war often lived in its own

isolated bubble while the rest of the realms continued to live normal lives. But none of us would escape Ragnarok, unless I found a way to stop the Disir first.

I rubbed the back of my neck. My body ached more than it should. I was so exhausted from the swirling Magik inside me, it felt like my nerves had been held to a fire day and night. Whatever I awakened in the temple and consumed from Loki was crawling through me and making itself at home.

With an unseemly groan, I settled down on the low wall, and let my feet dangle over the water. Ships of every size sat in the harbor, their masts reaching for the sky like a naked forest as aquamarine water that rivaled the sparkle of gemstones lapped at their hulls.

My feet throbbed, free of the weight of my body. And the tell-tale nausea, along with the sharp sting in my right eye, signaled a headache that would take more than a good night's rest to shake. I should have taken advantage of the food Asheria offered, but with the smell of blood still fresh in my nose, I had little appetite.

"And here I thought you'd come visit me first chance you got," a familiar voice said behind me and my heart leapt into my throat.

"Davlin?" I balked, surprised to see a friendly face.

He took a seat next to me, a wide grin spreading across his tanned face.

"What are you doing here?"

"I could ask you the same thing? Aren't you supposed to be in Folkvang wooing lover boy?" He cocked an eyebrow at me.

Sigurd standing in front of me, pain etched into every line of his face flashed through my mind.

"Even if he forgives me, I don't think I deserve it," I said under my breath.

I looked away, watching the last rays of sunshine turn the sky into a mix of burnt sandstone and dusty rose.

"What happened?" I could feel his eyes burning a hole in the side of my head.

"Too much." I swallowed the lump in my throat and stared at the glittering horizon.

Guilt simmered in my core like a predator waiting to strike. I should be in Folkvang. I should be paying my respects. But I couldn't face them after what I'd done—not the living or the dead.

I glanced at Davlin, who was watching me with kind and patient eyes, while I tried to find my voice.

"Have you ever done something you couldn't forgive yourself for?" I watched a pair of gulls soar over the harbor.

"Haven't we all?" There was no judgement in his voice. Something I always loved about him.

"How did you move past it?" I finally looked at him.

"Who says I did?" He raised an eyebrow. "Does this have anything to do with your curse?" He was testing the waters, trying to see if he could goad me into telling him what happened.

"You could say that." I picked at a loose thread on the dress I borrowed from Asheria.

"How bad is it?" He asked when I looked up at him.

Tears pricked my eyes, blurring the sea and sky in a cacophony of colors. "World ending." I didn't have the strength to mince my words. I was physically and emotionally stretched beyond my limit.

His eyes traced my face and dipped to my broken and healing body. He brushed his fingers over the purple bruises covering my arms and his brow furrowed.

"I would say you're being dramatic, but this," he turned my wrists over.

The mostly healed slash across my forearm said more than my words. They looked better than they did this morning, and my nose no longer felt broken, but it was clear to anyone who knew me—something was wrong.

"This is just—did Odin do this?" His eyes flicked to mine, cold as steel.

I shook my head. "It was Loki. And one pissed off Valkyrie."

His bottom lip fell open, and he sat back, keeping one hand on mine. "You've only been gone a few months and already pissed off another god?" The corner of his mouth lifted. He was trying to lighten the mood, but I was beyond his usual tactics.

"If only that was the reason." I leaned back and stared at the horizon as Sol started his final descent.

"Out with it then. I can't help if I don't know what's going on." He abandoned all pleasantries.

A humorless laugh escaped my throat. "You can't help me."

"Ahh, this again." I could hear the sarcasm in his voice and it made me bristle.

"This isn't like last time," I snapped and sat back up.

He cocked his head to the side. "Looks like last time."

"You don't know what I've been through the last few months." Anger bubbled beneath my guilt.

"Then enlighten me." He turned his body toward me, folding one leg under him.

I looked at him and wanted to scream, cry, tear the realms apart. Anything but have a calm and civil conversation about the destruction I caused.

"I know that look." He leveled his gaze at me. "And it will not make you feel better to spiral and explode."

I let out a huff. Just once, I wished I could give into the storm of emotions instead of taking the high road.

Where do I even start? Magnus, Loki, Sigurd, the Disir? It all felt like too much.

"Kara," Davlin's voice was gentle. "Whatever it is, whatever's happened, you'll get through it."

"One minute at a time," I repeated his mantra, and he nodded his head.

"I found out why I killed Si." I started with the beginning.

"Oh? And how is prince charming?"

I grimaced at the memory of Sigurd on his knees, watching me kill Magnus in cold blood.

"That bad?" he eyed me.

"It's complicated. We're..." I didn't know how to finish my sentence. Two days ago, we were on the path to being friends—well, maybe more than friends, but that was besides the point. But now. I shook my head.

"I killed his best friend." I settled on the truth of the matter. Because no matter what Si and I felt for each other, there would always be too much blood between us.

"The plot thickens." He cocked an eyebrow.

"It was all part of Loki's plan to bring back the Disir. He used me to kill eight people. Sigurd was the first and Magnus—" I let out a shaky breath. "He was the last." Nausea rolled through me as each death played through my mind one bloody attack at a time.

"And was Loki successful in freeing the Disir?" The calmness of his demeanor didn't match his tone.

"He was." My stomach roiled.

"Their affinity for turning the realms upside down is legendary." He ran a hand over his short cropped blond hair. "At least things will be interesting again."

"You speak as if you know them?" I studied him as he watched a small crew ready a ship in the distance.

He nodded. "Doesn't everyone?" He brushed a piece of lint off his trousers, which was his tell. He was keeping something from me, but what? And why?

"Are they as terrible as I've been warned?" I was curious to hear more about the Disir from someone other than the Norns.

"We're all monsters in someone's story." He shrugged.

I flinched and wondered how many people thought of me as the villain.

His eyes skated over my face, my shoulders, and my fingers as I picked at my cuticles. "You're leaving something out."

"It wasn't just killing eight people that brought them back. It was me. My blood."

His eyes narrowed as he looked at me.

"What exactly are you saying? Because if it's what I think, you just got mildly more interesting." He cocked his head and the ghost of a smile touched the corner of his lips.

"Their blood runs through my veins." My heart jumped into my throat.

I knew what I was. I felt it in my soul as I consumed Loki's life force. But I still wasn't ready to say the words out loud.

"You're absolutely sure?" Davlin didn't bat an eye at my admission, and warmth spread through my chest as if he hugged me. I don't know how I got so lucky to have him as a friend.

"I'd like to say no, but the ritual worked. The Disir are free and…"

"And?" His eyes widened.

If I was going to even attempt to accept this part of myself, then I needed to be honest about what I did to Loki. "Do you know what the Disir do to gain power?"

He nodded, waiting for me to say the words.

"Well, the only reason I'm sitting here now is because they gave me Loki. I took his soul for myself." The hunger deep in my stomach curled around Loki's Magik like a dragon around its egg. There was something more in me now, something that didn't belong to Freya or the Disir. And as much as I hated to admit it, I liked the feel of power within me.

Davlin threw his head back, and a laugh bellowed out of him.

"So the prick finally got what he deserved." His smile reached his eyes, and it eased some of the tension in my chest.

"You understand what I'm saying, right?"

He wiped a tear from his eye. "Let me guess, you've turned this into a negative somehow?"

"It's hard to put a positive spin on literally sucking the life out of someone." I laid it out in black and white because his reaction was not proportional to the threat that lived in my blood.

"Well, it saved your life, right?"

"Yes."

"And he'll no longer create chaos and leave a trail of bodies behind him." His eyebrows nearly met his hairline as he stared at me.

"Sure, but—"

"No buts." He waved me off. "Loki has played with fire since the moment he learned what it is. If he's no longer a problem, then I say good riddance."

The vision I had earlier of the Disir turning him to a Draugr flashed through my mind.

"There's a chance he's still alive. He vanished before I could..." How was I supposed to even end that sentence? *Before I could kill him? Finish him?*

"At the very least, he's less than he was. From what I understand, there's no going back. He'll never get back what you took from him."

How much did he know about the Disir? I wondered.

"Aren't you at all concerned that I can consume souls?" I pointed out the obvious because I didn't think he was getting how serious this was.

He let out a sigh, and a soft smile touched his lips. "Not one bit."

"Of course not." I let out an exasperated sigh. Somehow, when I felt like the sky was falling, he always remained calm. It's both what I loved and hated about him.

"You're still you, Kara. You've always had the ability. Knowing it doesn't change you."

I thought about how good it felt to feel Loki's soul pouring into me. It was as if I was drinking the mead of the gods, and tasting the Nine Realms for the first time.

"It changed something in me." I bit my bottom lip. "There's a part of me that wants more, to feel powerful like that again. It was…intoxicating."

My conversation with Freya when I first returned to Folkvang played in my mind.

Had she known then what I was?

"Okay." He leaned forward and studied me like he might see the power hungry Magik under my skin. "But are you willing to kill innocents to feel that power again?" There was no judgment in his expression and I knew if I said yes, he wouldn't balk. He would help me because that's what he's always done.

"No." I shook my head. "Of course not."

"Exactly." He sat back, satisfied with himself. "You aren't the same as them."

I understood what he was getting at, but a little voice in my head snarled at his words and unease settled in my gut. One doesn't go from being good to evil with one action. It's a slow descent into darkness, one decision at a time. And if I wasn't careful, I'd end up just like them.

"I think that's enough doom and gloom for one night." He got to his feet and held out a hand to me. "How about some dinner and a good night's rest?"

I gripped his hand and let him pull me up. I winced at my stiff legs and muscles, and his brow furrowed.

"And a hot bath," I groaned.

I looked at the horizon once more. The burial rites would be happening right now. Sigurd and the others will be standing on the shore to say goodbye to the fallen—to their friends.

To Magnus.

I squeezed my eyes shut at the memory of his death. The warmth of his blood on my hand, the way his body slumped to the ground at my feet. More than anything, I wished Loki hadn't returned that memory to me. I could've lived the rest of my life not knowing how numb and heartless I was when I slid that dagger across his throat and took his future from him.

I placed a hand over my heart and swore I would avenge him.

"Rest easy Magnus."

CHAPTER TWELVE

THE FLICKERING of firelight on the other side of my eyelids brought me out of the darkness of unconsciousness. My mind felt heavy, like a blanket of fog had settled over my faculties, making it hard to discern if I was awake or still dreaming.

Muffled voices reached my ears. I could just barely make out a few words through the fog, though none of it made sense.

I took stock of my body. The gash in my side burned, and my arms were shackled above my head and tingled painfully. If the pain in my arms was any indication, I'd been here for a while.

My eyelids fluttered open and fell closed almost instantly. The urge to fall back under the haze was almost too much to ignore. My eyes burned as I opened them again. My head swam and my vision blurred as exhaustion tried to drag me back under.

Fighting the urge to close my eyes, I looked around, trying to get a sense of my surroundings. Torchlight flickered in a sconce on the wall across from me.

I'd been stripped of everything but my trousers, shirt, and boots. My armor was gone, my weapons were nowhere in sight, and Magnus's flask was missing as well. It made freeing myself and getting out of here in one piece that much harder.

I scanned the area again, looking for anything that might

help me escape. The walls were dirt and stone. Carved out of the mountain, much like Ragnar's caves.

The floors were stained with dark patches of what I could only assume was blood. There were no openings to let in fresh air or light. The torches along the walls were the only glimmer of warmth and illumination. In the corner to my right, there was a single wood door. The only way in or out.

A pang of uncertainty pulsed through my empty stomach. Freya had a fortnight to spare my life. And I had no idea how many of those days had already passed or if it had only been hours since the burial rites.

Would she give up one of her own to save her realm? To save me? Or would she sacrifice me and risk a war with Odin?

The door swung open, and I stiffened. The Alfather stepped into my prison with a knife and a ruby-red apple. He'd shed his cloak and armor, making him look younger and less menacing. With his casual dark blue tunic and leather trousers, he almost looked like Ragnar or Magnus. Almost.

"Good, you're awake." His sapphire eye skated over me, and my heart threatened to beat out of my chest.

Indignation heated my blood, knowing he was using me to get to Kara. But I kept my mouth shut. I didn't care why he was here or what he had to say. I was well aware my chance of survival was slim, and I'd rather meet the stars with my dignity intact.

He came to a stop in front of me, the tips of our boots almost touching. A heavy note of ale, mixed with something sharp and cloying, filled my nose.

"There is much to bring you up to speed on." Some long forgotten survival instinct screamed through my blood to put distance between myself and the self proclaimed ruler of the Nine Realms.

He turned his back on me and walked away, a move that indicated just how little of a threat I was.

"Did you know you were meant for Valhalla?" The deep timbre of his voice resonated through the cave like prison and he started to pace.

I met his stare but said nothing. What did it matter if I was meant for Valhalla? I'd been chosen for Folkvang and I made my peace with that long ago. I wouldn't let him get under my skin now.

"I suppose you wouldn't, would you?" He pulled his knife over the apple, separating the skin from the fruit beneath. "Freya is many wondrous, devious things." He shot me a knowing look, the corner of his mouth pulling into a grin that made my skin crawl as he flicked the apple skin to the ground. "But not very forthcoming."

I watched him carefully, studying the way he moved, the way he held the knife. Of how he subtly didn't put all his weight on his left foot.

"She gets first pick of the fallen. A deal I've sorely come to loath." He said the last part under his breath. "But you were always earmarked for my realm." He carved off another piece of crimson skin and flicked it to the stone floor. "Your bloodlust and cunning strategy caught my eye. But it was your ability to discern the changing tide of a battle that made you stand above all else."

I had to fight the urge not to roll my eyes. The gods really did like to wax poetic when given a captive audience. I just couldn't see the point of this if he was going to kill me when Freya inevitably didn't supply him with Kara.

"Tell me Sigurd." He stopped his pacing and turned fully to face me. "Do you feel the tide changing once more?" His unnaturally blue eye bore into me as a wave of Magik swarmed me like a thousand bees.

I'd always had a knack for picking up the tiny details others ignored. It allowed me to sniff out the path to victory with ease. It wasn't just the Norns' words to Kara that set the tone of what was to come, but the rift in Folkvang, Loki, the Draugr and the Disir. Even the Magik I'd grown accustom to felt different—weaker over the last few years.

The Nine Realms was changing, the ground beneath our feet no longer stable.

But what did it matter if I could sense the change in the air, the same way I could smell rain before a storm? I was stuck here, nothing more than a bargaining chip that would either make or break the path the Norns set us on.

So I remained silent.

"Freya may tolerate your lack of respect," he closed the gap between us. "But I will not," he growled and backhanded me so hard I tasted blood. "Answer the question."

I waited for the sting to subside and spit a mouthful of blood. Turning slowly, I met his stare. "Yes," I growled.

"Yes, what?" The sickly sweet scent of the apple wafted between us.

"Yes, I can feel the winds of change."

"Good." He continued to wear a path in the layer of dirt and grime covering the stone floor. "I'm glad to see you have some self preservation left. It'll make this next part easier. I have a proposition for you." He carved a slice out of the apple.

"Not interested."

"Speak out of turn again and I'll make sure that Valkyrie you're so fond of is torn apart feather by sorðinn feather." He raised the blade to his mouth and ate the slice of fruit off the edge of the knife.

Fear punctured my chest like a dull blade. I had no doubt he'd take pleasure in making Kara suffer. If he ever got his hands on her.

"I suspect Freya won't turn over her little pet project," he grimaced. "She's always been oddly protective of that foul abomination. Something you, unfortunately, have in common with her." He started in on the apple again, cutting away the flesh and tossing it at his feet.

A bitter tang filled my mouth as I swallowed my words. How could one Valkyrie garner so much ire from the Alfather?

"And while you may have been a favorite of Freya's." He gave me a knowing look. "I can almost guarantee she won't hand the Valkyrie over to save you."

"Then why…" confusion furrowed my brow as I scanned his face.

A devious smile crept over Odin's lips and a sick, oily feeling slithered down my spine. "You want war." This wasn't about Kara or the Disir, they were just a convenient excuse.

He turned toward me and popped another slice of apple into his mouth. "I want balance."

Balance? What the Hel was he talking about?

"The Disir have returned." He paused and studied my reaction as if he was testing me. To see if I'd play dumb or be honest about what I knew.

So I said nothing once more. Let him make of that what he will.

"And Freya is to blame. She allowed their blood to survive. She thought she could tame the shadows that lurk at the edge of the universe." Malice dripped off each word.

"She thought she was stronger than the Disir because she bested them. But I knew. I always knew this day would come." His careful mask of indifference slipped.

This was personal for him. A vendetta who knows how long in the making.

I let him ramble. The likelihood of me surviving to tell someone any of this was unlikely. But in the event I made it out of here in one piece, I wanted to learn as much as I could.

"And so I waited. I let her take you. I let her keep that half-breed. And I turned a blind eye when Loki freed the Draugr."

"You knew?" Shock and disgust twisted inside me and soured my stomach.

Boats burned because of those men turned into monsters. Friends were lost to the stars and my home was ripped to pieces. And he knew.

My grief turned molten, and I lunged forward, unbridled rage burning so hot in my blood I barely felt the manacles dig into my wrist. A smile slowly crept over his face, like he knew he finally had me.

"People died because of the Draugr. Good people."

"You think anything happens in the Nine Realms that I'm not aware of?" His gold eyepatch shimmered in the firelight and my mouth went dry.

"All those lives lost." I shook my head.

"They were chosen—by Freya," he sneered. "If they met the stars, then they didn't belong in Folkvang, and the Draugr rectified their placement in the universe." He skinned another sliver of apple in one quick motion.

"Not a single one of them deserved to meet their end." I ground my teeth and swore to the stars that I'd make him pay for the role he played in their deaths—in Magnus's death.

"Do you carry the same rage for the innocent lives your Valkyrie took to wake the Disir?" His words hit me like a punch to the gut.

"We both know she was under Loki's influence," I said through gritted teeth as I tried to rein in my anger.

"Was she? Or did he just wake what was already in her?" He sliced through the flesh of the apple and cut off another piece.

"You, of all people, should know how dangerous she is. How utterly ruthless and bloodthirsty for power she is." He stepped toward me slowly, and slid the apple slice off the knife and into his mouth.

"Your fight is with the Disir, not Kara." My empty stomach turned, and unease crept over my chest.

"They're one and the same." He narrowed his eye at me and my blood stilled. "The sooner you learn that, the sooner you'll be free."

"Kara isn't who you think she is," I argued. "She just wants to live."

He closed the gap between us and looked down at me. "You're blinded by the potential of who she could have been for you, not who she is at her core." He tossed the half-eaten apple over his shoulder and it rolled to the corner of the room.

"Freya's the same. She saw Kara as an asset of what could be. But she is nothing more than a murderous liability."

I huffed a laugh. "I think you fear her. Not because she's a Disir, but because of her potential to topple the Nine Realms *you* built."

The butt end of his knife cracked across my face with a sweeping punch. An explosion of pain radiated through my jaw and eye socket.

I'd hit a nerve in his indifferent facade. Good.

Satisfaction rose in me like a bonfire. It didn't matter that my jaw was most likely fractured. I blinked through the searing pain and pushed it to the back of my mind. I'd endured far worse. And the stakes were too high to waste energy on something as trivial as pain.

"Look what she's done in just a few months of being free of your curse?" My words came out in a grunt, but the rage in his snarled expression was worth the splintering pain of speaking.

I spit a mouthful of blood and saliva and it hit the floor with an audible *thwack* between us.

"You kept her in Midgard like a caged animal, but now she's free and it just won't do." I closed my left eye as pain throbbed across my face in tempo with my racing heart. "Why else would you go to such lengths to get her in your grasp?"

He fisted the knife in his other hand. "She killed my son. That's more than enough of a reason to call for her head." He swung again, and my vision exploded and then went dark. Pain shattered across my face. My eyes, nose and teeth throbbed as a trickle of hot, thick blood slid down my throat.

I breathed through the pain and forced myself to open my eyes. Odin moved in and out of focus, and my head spun. The edges of my vision started to narrow, but I pushed against it. I would look him in the eye so long as I was alive to do so.

"Loki had it coming. He's the one who woke—" His knife kissed my throat. The cool, sticky edge of the blade dug into my windpipe as the sweet smell of apple crawled up my nose and turned my stomach. Embers of molten Magik crackled over me as the blade broke my skin and blood dripped down my throat.

Doubt tinged with panic soured in my core. I'd pushed him too far.

He grabbed my face. I winced at the pain that shot across my jaw. Definitely broken. "Speak another word against my son, and I'll let Fenrir feast on your flesh."

He released my face, and I sucked in a shallow breath. The threat of coming face to face with Fenrir, the wolf destined to swallow the sun and end the Nine Realms, as we know it, sent a shiver down my spine.

"Back to the matter at hand." He removed the blade from my throat, and I breathed a sign of relief. For a split second, I worried I'd miscalculated Odin's desire to keep me alive for the time being. "What do you know of the blade named Gramr?"

"The sword that was used to slay the dragon who once guarded Yggdrasil?" I pressed my back into the stone wall and rose onto my toes to give my arms some slack. My shoulders slumped a few inches and relief washed through me. "My mother used to tell me the legend as a bedtime story."

"It's no legend. The sword was created for one thing, and one thing only," he paused, and a secret smile pulled at the corner of his mouth. "To kill what cannot be killed."

"Feeling inadequate, now that the Disir have returned?" I

cocked an eyebrow and relished in the idea that Odin may not be all powerful like I thought.

He threw his knife, and it embedded itself in my thigh. Heat followed by the sharp sting of pain shot down my leg and I grit my teeth.

"Next time," he crossed the space and pulled the knife from my flesh. "You lose something valuable."

Blood dripped down my leg as he turned on his heel and took his position across from me once more.

"I took a trip to Mimir's island and paid dearly to learn a truth long forgotten." He pointed the tip of the bloody blade at his gold eye patch.

"To learn of Gramr's true destiny. Of *your* true destiny. It's why I earmarked you for Valhalla. It's why I've brought you here now." His eye met mine, and an awareness brushed over my soul that made my heart race.

"The sword was meant for you." The path forward shifted as my ears rang and every instinct in my body screamed.

"You are destined to end the threat of Ragnarok forever."

CHAPTER THIRTEEN

HE KNEW.

Odin knew Ragnarok was on the horizon.

The blood drained from my face, and my heart sunk through my body and hit the floor. I stared at him and firelight glistened across his gold eyepatch as he watched me absorb the gravity of his claim.

You are destined to end the threat of Ragnarok forever.

His declaration rang true in my soul. And the warrior in me jumped at the notion of getting into the middle of this fight. But the voice in the back of my mind said it was too good to be true. If he had a weapon that could kill the Disir, why not use it? Why play this game with me, Kara and Freya?

I reeled my emotions back in. He didn't know the Norns had warned Kara—and in turn me—about Ragnarok. Though their insistence about the gods staying in the dark seemed moot at this point. He also didn't know how much Freya shared with me about the Disir. It gave me the upper hand, and I needed to play it just right if I was going to get out of here.

"I don't believe you. This is a part of whatever game you're playing with Freya."

"Do you think I would've gone to such great lengths to secure you in *my* realm if the end wasn't looming?" Odin narrowed his lapis eye at me.

"If you're telling the truth, why not share with Freya what you learned? I'm sure she would've allowed—"

"How little you know her." A short, humorless laugh escaped his throat. "Did you ever think to ask why she kept you out of the line of fire?"

"How did you know that?" His words struck a cord and my frustration at not being utilized to my full potential bubbled to the surface.

"I have eyes everywhere, Sigurd." His lips twitched, and I recalled the raven perched on his shoulder at the rites. It was rumored that the Alfather's pets roamed the realms and reported back to him, but I didn't expect him to admit it.

"Freya stifled your growth. Made you soft," he stepped toward me. "She made you weak." He came to a stop in front of me and my heart beat against my chest, making the wounds on my face throb.

"You lost your friend and so many others because she allowed it. You and I both know it." There was an edge to his voice that stirred a long forgotten warriors passion in me.

I didn't want to agree with him. Every morsel of my soul wanted to scream that he was wrong. But hadn't I accused Freya of exactly that? Allowing us to die instead of sealing the rift?

She had sealed it, I argued internally.

Guilt squeezed my heart. Freya went toe to toe with Odin to save us all. She fought alongside us to defeat the Draugr. Odin was using my grief to twist my mind and loyalty.

"Freya rules with grace and compassion," I seethed.

"She's weak and idealistic," he snarled, and a sizzle of Magik burned up my arms. "And so are you. But we can fix that." I hated the glimmer in his eye as he looked me up and down. Like I was some animal that he couldn't wait to whip into shape.

"Freya may have caused this mess by protecting that Valkyrie, but the Norns are gracious to those who serve their interests." He crossed the space between us.

"What do the Norns have to do with all this?" Confusion rippled through me.

The Norns were helping Odin? But why? And why would they grant Kara's request when they've been silent for so long?

My intuition prickled along the base of my neck. I needed time to think, to piece everything together. Because I was certain everything that's happened since Kara ended my mortal life was connected in more ways than we realized.

"The Norns made sure a warrior would come to be." He stepped in front of me and lifted my chin with the tip of the knife. "A warrior who could wield Gramr, and end the Disir once and for all."

What nonsense had the Norns whispered in his ear? And why didn't they tell Kara?

"You want me to kill the Disir," I exhaled. "Kill Kara." I flinched just saying the words. "I won't harm her." Heat swelled in my blood, and my heart cracked open. I'd rather join Magnus in the stars than lay a hand against her.

He took a step back, and bright golden Magik sparked down his arm. He threw the knife, and it pierced the stone floor like it was nothing more than sand.

"It's not about what I want, it's about what's written." The gold patch over Odin's eye flickered in the firelight and a door within me cracked open and perked up at his words.

He turned his back on me and headed toward the door. "Prove you're worthy of the task, Sigurd. Free yourself from those chains and I'll show you just how powerful you can be under the right tutelage."

I glanced at the knife, its bone white handle taunting me. When I looked back up, Odin was gone. I swallowed the lump in my throat. I had more questions than answers, but at least I had a way out of here.

I stared at the knife, just out of reach, and hope blossomed in my chest. The tide of the Nine Realms was changing, and if I had anything to say about it, it wouldn't favor the gods.

My EYES FLICKERED OPEN, *and blue starlight danced in the darkness, casting shadows on the cave like walls. My eyes fluttered closed as energy radiated around me like a warm blanket. The low hum filled my ears and settled in my bones, and I shivered. Goosebumps washed over me from head to toe, and I breathed a sigh of relief.*

"Ge—tttt— uuu—" words drifted over me like falling leaves and I was too slow to catch them.

I opened my eyes again and stared at the light shimmering above me like I was at the bottom of a clear lake looking up. The patterns moved with the rhythm of the energy singing around me and I exhaled.

"Ka—ra."

I plucked my name from the sky and bright green eyes came into focus above me.

"Get up." Her face flashed in and out of focus, but I caught the urgency in her expression. Her energy was familiar, but so at odds with the calm, soothing warmth of this place.

Where am I?

"There's no ti—" Her words fluttered past me, some landing and other passing me altogether.

"You m—t embra—." Her words were like rocks tumbling in a stream, almost silent to the dreamer wandering in the forest.

She flashed in and out of focus again and the starlight flashed, blinding me. I closed my eyes and raised my arm to shield the light, but it was everywhere, pulling on me and banishing the gentle hum with loud banging voices.

"Sigurd." *I turned my head, trying to catch another word, hear another rock tumble past me, another leaf gliding on the wind, but there was nothing but the bright, all-consuming light as a heaviness settled over me.*

My body ached, and the sound of metal scraping sent a shiver down my spine.

"UUUUUPPPPP." *The sound came screaming from my bones, resonating through my body, and my heart stuttered.*

I shot upright, gasping for air, sweat clinging to my skin. My heart felt like it was going to run out of my chest and my tongue was dry and stuck to the roof of my mouth.

"Just a dream." I huffed.

But it didn't feel like a dream. It felt like a warning.

CHAPTER FIFTEEN

MY ARMS WENT numb hours ago. Or at least I think it's been a few hours since Odin's departure. Despite several attempts, I wasn't any closer to pulling the knife from the stone floor and freeing myself.

I was both glad and anxious that I couldn't feel my arms anymore. Glad because the excruciating pain shooting down my arms and into my shoulders was gone. But anxious, because I knew if I didn't get my arms down soon, I might lose functionality forever.

My head throbbed like someone had taken up residence behind my eyes and was beating on a drum. And my leg had stopped bleeding, but was stiff and tender if I put my full weight on it.

Odin's words rang through me once more, nagging at the back of my mind.

It's not about what I want, it's what's written.

If he was telling the truth, if I'm the one who's meant to kill the Disir—all the Disir—then the Norns are going to have to change the truth of the universe. Because I wouldn't kill Kara. Not in this life, or the next. And certainly not for Odin.

The slow creak of a door squeaked open, then swiftly banged closed, echoing through the prison. I closed my eyes and strained to listen.

Another screech and clank. Door number two.

Silence stretched between each breath. My heart throbbed against my ribs, making every bone in my face ache. And the too sweet aroma of the apple Odin tossed in the corner clung to the air.

A deep groan. A heavy thud and clank. Door number three.

The soft tinkle of metal—keys possibly—sounded close, and my eyes shot open as the thick wood door to my prison glided open with a groan of its own.

A woman entered, carrying a small wood tray with two small rolls, a handful of cloudberries, and a carafe. Surprise flickered through me. I thought I'd go hungry until I agreed to Odin's terms. Although I was still chained, so eating would be impossible if I didn't free myself.

And I realized that was the point. A small, yet fulfilling reward.

I studied the woman as she took three steps into the dimly lit space. Her corn silk hair was down to her waist, and she wore a simple maroon dress with a brooch fastener on each shoulder. She had a strong build, and her hands were scarred—no, burned.

I'd seen burns like hers plenty in Midgard. Men and women alike, burned and disfigured when they refused to join the conquering army's ranks.

My heart ached for her as she placed the tray on the floor across from me.

"Excuse me," I kept my voice soft so as not to frighten her. "Do you know how long I've been in here?"

Her gaze flicked to me, and she started toward the door.

"Please," I begged. I had no way of counting the passage of time and it left me feeling lost and disorientated.

"You arrived last night." Her voice was soft, too delicate for a place like this.

"Thank you," I exhaled, and she made a quick escape.

It had only been one night. I leaned my head back and stared at my arms. Dried blood streaked down my ghostly white arms from pulling and twisting against my shackles.

I took a deep breath. Looked at the tray of food, my gaze settling on the carafe as a muscle in my calf spasmed. I needed water, desperately. It was now or never.

I walked forward as far as my chains would allow and angled my body sideways. I filled my lungs with stale air and exhaled.

I placed all of my weight on my back foot and then swung my right leg out with a kick. The toe of my boot hit the knife, and hope flickered through me. My chains yanked me backward and my shoulder collided with the wall, sending up a spray of dirt. Lightning shot down my ribs, my leg throbbed, and I grit my teeth.

The spark of hope twisted into frustration. I'd lost count of how many times I'd thrown myself at that damn knife.

Taking a beat to ignore the pain throbbing all over my body, I tried again. Letting my irritation propel me forward with every ounce of strength I had.

I missed. By a foot.

Again. The cuts on my wrists screamed in agony as my body swung forward. My foot caught the knife, and it wobbled before I was pulled back.

"Streð mik!" my voice echoed off the stone floors.

Frustration, anger, and disappointment churned through me like choppy waters. Maybe Odin was right—I'd gone soft. I didn't see the attack on Folkvang coming. I couldn't stop Kara from killing. I couldn't save Magnus. Bitter tears pricked the back of my eyes as I stared at the knife.

I may have lost my edge. But I wouldn't die in here. I took another deep breath, and repositioned myself.

One.

Deep breath.

Two.

I leaned back on my left foot.

Three.

I exhaled and swung my body forward. I heard, rather than felt, my wrist pop and heat poured down my arm as my boot connected with the handle and the knife clattered free.

I might have collapsed from relief if not for the chains keeping me upright. Reaching for the knife with my right foot, I stepped on the blade and dragged it toward me. The metal scraped against the stone floor, making the hairs rise on the back of my neck.

Leaning against the wall, I positioned the knife between my boots, with the hilt facing me. With the toe of my boot, I gently turned the blade so the sharp edge was facing the ground, and pressed the knife between my boots.

I took a deep breath, and readied myself. Pressing my back as hard as I could into the wall, I tightened my core, and raised my legs. My back slid off the wall, putting my full body weight on my already battered arms.

As quickly and controlled as possible, I raised my legs and curled my head forward, pressing my chin to my chest. I spread my knees, pressing my boots tighter together. The hilt of the blade stuck out between my boots, and with every quaking muscle, I brought the knife toward my face.

My whole body trembled, and sweat dripped down my forehead. Bringing my legs closer, I leaned forward and grabbed the hilt of the knife with my mouth. It tasted of dirt and apple, but I wouldn't have cared if it tasted like dung.

I was one step closer to getting out of here.

I dropped my legs and leaned against the rocky wall in relief. I sucked in a breath around the hilt and leaned my head back.

Taking a moment to gather my strength, I pushed up on my toes and my arms dropped a few inches. The tension in my shoulders eased a fraction, and I breathed a little easier.

That took more effort than I cared to admit. And shame

colored my cheeks. I had gone soft in the last century. But when I got out of here, that would change.

Alright, Sigurd. Time to prove what you're made of.

I looked up at my pale and unsightly hands and wiggled my fingers. I couldn't feel them, but I could still make them move. Good. I wrapped them around the center chain and sucked in a breath as a wave of nausea rolled through me.

Reaching up with my left hand, I pulled myself up the chain and my boots left the ground. The movement rocked me gently back and forth as I reached up with my right hand and pulled. Pain shot down my wrist and I clamped my mouth tight as I groaned.

My gaze traveled the length of the chain and I had to force myself to focus on the next few inches instead. It didn't matter how far I had to go. All the mattered was the next step. And then the next.

Left hand. Right hand. The chain draped against my body, creating a loop. Left hand. Right hand. My arms were bent at a comfortable angle, and I tucked my elbows into my chest. A warm, tight sensation of blood rushing back to my limbs sent a bolt of panic through me. I needed to move fast, before the numbness gave way to the agony I knew was waiting for me.

My fingers tighten around the chains, but as I tried to pull myself up, my right hand gave out and slipped.

My body jolted as I fell a few inches, and my stomach bottomed out. My pulse skyrocketed, a high-pitched ringing pierced my ears, and my mouth filled with saliva as my left hand held on for dear life.

Though I wasn't that high off the ground, if I fell, both of my shoulders would dislocate and the bones in my wrists would surely snap. And I'd be left to dangle until someone put me out of my misery.

"Move," I yelled at myself as pins and needles moved down my shoulders and into my upper arms.

I reached up with my right hand again, grabbed the chain, and pulled myself up. Just a few more and I'd be able to place my foot in the loop of the chain.

Left hand. I bit down on the knife handle. Right hand. I pulled myself up with a grunt.

The chain knocked against my boot and I searched for the foothold blindly. My foot found the opening, and I tested my weight on the chain. It held.

I wrapped my left arm around the chain, securing a better hold as my heart pumped furiously. Pain shot down my arms, up my arms, through my arms. It was worse than I expected. My wrists burned from the manacles tearing through the skin. Sharp burst of hot white pain shot down my shoulders and through my back. And the pop I'd heard earlier in my wrist throbbed with its own heartbeat.

I ignored all of it as I removed the knife from my mouth with my right hand. I stretched my jaw and took a full, deep breath.

Step two done.

Now to free myself.

I inspected the manacle on my left wrist, but the craftsmanship was second to none. They weren't coming off until Odin wanted them off. I changed tactics and studied the chain. The links were crude, old, and covered in rust.

And then I saw it. Another foot up, there was a broken link. Just one. Just barely. My chest swelled with hope.

I placed the knife back in my mouth, grabbed hold with my right hand and untwisted my left arm. My body swung from the momentum and my shoulders stiffened, sending a jolt of pain down my spine. I sucked in a breath and flexed every muscle in my body.

Almost there.

I pulled myself up one more time, coming face to face with

the broken link. I wrapped my left hand around the chain and grabbed the knife.

Adjusting my grip on the handle, I inhaled deeply. Sweat coated my forehead, and I was so light-headed I wasn't sure how much longer I'd be conscious. My hand shook as I forced the tip of the blade into the small crack in the link. If I dropped the knife now, it was over. I didn't have enough strength to do this again.

I applied some pressure, forcing the crack to widen just barely. My left arm started to shake like a leaf in a storm, and I knew I couldn't hold myself much longer. I shoved the knife deeper into the crack and forced the link to split.

Just a little more and it should break entirely.

I repositioned the knife once more, getting a better angle to press the two halves of the link apart.

My heart slammed against my ribs. Here goes nothing. I exhaled and applied pressure. Pain shot through my wrist as I quaked with the effort.

The link split wider, and I unwound my left arm from the chain, getting ready to drop. With everything I had left, I pried the link open.

And then my hand slipped.

The dagger hit the floor with a clatter I felt in my soul. My heart swelled and filled with desperate anger. I was so close.

I stared at the partially open link as I gently swung back and forth. The flames in the torches flickering at my failure.

It was almost wide enough to slip the link below off the chain. Almost. I looked up at the ceiling and screamed. Letting all the pain, frustration, and shame burn through me.

I was so close.

Resolve settled in my gut like a stone. I only had one option left. Let go, and hope my weight and momentum, rips the chain open wide enough to separate itself.

I looked down at the ground. The fall wouldn't kill me, but if the chain didn't snap, I was a dead man.

I sent up a silent prayer to anyone who might take pity on me and let go of the chain. I pulled my arms in tight to my chest and braced myself.

I kept my eyes on the weak link as the warm, stale air whipped past me. The chain caught and yanked my arms upward, and I let out a yelp of pain as I came to a sudden halt and then I was falling again.

The chain snapped, and I hit the ground so hard my teeth clattered. Cold, sharp pain ricocheted through my body as I rolled to my side and laughed.

I was free.

Thank the g—no. I'd never thank the gods for anything ever again.

CHAPTER SIXTEEN

SIGURD

LAYING ON THE FLOOR, I rested my hands on my chest and let the cool stone soothe my aching muscles. I stared up at the broken chain dangling from the ceiling, still swaying ever so slightly.

Everything hurt.

There wasn't a single part of me that didn't ache or throb. I knew eating and drinking would help with the constant pounding in my head, but I couldn't be bothered to move just yet. I was exhausted, not just physically, but emotionally. My soul needed rest after pushing through the pain, not to mention everything Odin spewed at me.

For just a brief moment, I wanted oblivion.

The clang of a door closing nearby sent a pang of disappointment through me. I let out a heavy breath and sat up with a groan. Of course, there wouldn't be a reprieve. I pushed to my feet, my arms hanging heavy at my side. Though the pins and needles were fading, a bone deep ache was setting in.

I grabbed the knife off the floor. Palming the bone white handle, I pressed my back against the wall. I took a moment to feel my exhaustion, feel every bruise and ache pulsing through me, and then I pushed it all to the back of my mind.

The door to my cage creaked open and every muscle in my body went taut.

"Bryn?" My heart thundered in my chest as I scanned her

from head to toe. She wore standard leather trousers and a dusky blue top—the color of mourning. Her white alabaster hair was down, but the braids and jewelry that once adorned her hair were gone. She wore no weapons, but that didn't surprise me when she was a weapon herself.

"You look the way I feel." She wrinkled her nose in disgust as she closed the door and leaned against it with a casual attitude.

Realization flooded through me, and my heart sank into the pit of my stomach.

"You aren't here to help me escape, are you?" I wanted to be wrong. But the way she sauntered in here, like she owned the place, painted a pretty clear picture.

My stomach turned as she moved through my prison like a cat on the hunt. Bryn was lethal on her best days, and she'd handed my ass to me frequently. But that was training. This was real, and I knew she wouldn't hold back.

"Afraid not." She no longer wore her heart on her sleeve, and her grief, whatever was left of it, was carefully masked under hardened features. "Odin told me he was keeping you down here and thought I'd pay you a visit."

"He told you?" My chest tightened, and heat flushed through me at her admission.

Her lips twitched, but a genuine smile never touched her features. Realization flittered through me, hot and urgent, making me grip the knife tighter.

"It was you. You went to Odin about Kara and the Disir." Images of her attacking me and Kara flooded my mind, making my heart race.

She was out for blood, and what better way to achieve her revenge than to turn us over to the Alfather. My heart squeezed as it broke a little more for her and Magnus.

"Freya wouldn't make things right." She bent down and grabbed one of the rolls off the platter. "So I found someone who would." She took a bite of the bread and rose to her full height.

Irritation prickled my skin.

"But how did you know about the Disir? You weren't in the temple." I searched my memories for her face in the shadows and dust as stone exploded around us. But all I could recall was Daiman's pale face, Kara's screams and Talon challenging Loki as the Disir broke free of their stone cage.

She tossed the roll to the dirt covered floor and shook her head.

"Loki's Magik isn't as strong as Kara would have you believe." She leaned against the wall across from me and folded her arms over her chest, mirroring me.

"Once I was free of his influence, I tracked you to the temple. I wanted to help." A short, humorless laugh escaped her throat.

Adrenalin coursed through me, making me light-headed as I scanned every corner of my prison on instinct. I already knew there wasn't anywhere to run. I was trapped, and at the mercy of the woman whose heart I betrayed.

She stalked toward me. Her boots echoed off the stone. "I saw everything," she said through gritted teeth. "The Disir. Loki. Kara." She came to a stop in front of me and I stood a little straighter.

"I left to warn Freya of what I'd seen when I ran into Valtteri." She cocked her head to the side like one of Odin's crows and chills ran down my arms.

I realized I've only ever know Bryn as a friend. I've never met Bryn the Valkyrie before, and she was terrifying.

"Valtteri told me he was sorry for Magnus."

His name hit me like a physical blow spoken from her lips, and my stomach bottomed out.

She closed the gap between us, her face inches from mine. "He went on and on about how he couldn't believe Kara killed him."

Her eyes closed and her brow furrowed, her mask of indifference slipping for a fraction of a second.

"And you did nothing." She turned away from me. "You lied to all of us," her voice echoed off the stone. "To save her," she growled, no longer in control of her emotions. I gripped the knife tighter. I didn't want to fight her, but I wouldn't let her kill me either.

I stepped toward her. "It was Loki who—"

She whirled on me, and her hand connected with my face. Sharp, hot pain flashed across my cheek and my vision blurred.

"Loki died by her hands. Just like Magnus." I could hear the pain in her voice as she shoved me. My head cracked against the stone, adding to the throbbing ache.

I took a breath and shook off the pain. I deserved that hit for lying to her. For lying to all of them about what happened when Magnus died. But I wouldn't blame Kara for it. Not again. Not when I saw up close and personal that she wasn't in control.

"Loki deserved it." I met her angry stare and squared my shoulders. If she needed someone to take her heartache and rage out on, I was happy to oblige. Magnus wouldn't abandon any of us in our grief, and I won't abandon her.

"And what about Magnus?"

She might as well have hit me again. Grief hollowed out my stomach, and my chest ached with the memory of him dying in my arms. "He was innocent."

Her face soften and her bottom lip quivered. Tears sparkled in her eyes, and the urge to embrace her tugged at my soul. I wanted to give her a shoulder to lean on, to feel everything and fall to pieces.

Maybe I wanted that for myself, too.

"He didn't deserve to meet the stars." I reached for her hand and she stepped back.

My shoulders deflated, and I leaned against the rocky wall.

"No, he didn't." She straightened her shoulders and seemed to compose herself. "So, what are you going to do about it?"

"There's nothing to be done. He's gone."

She shook her head. "Nothing to be done? Come now, we both know that's not true."

"Loki paid for Magnus's life." I felt like I was teetering on the edge of a cliff. And at any moment, she'd stop giving me the time of day and shove me off the edge to my death.

"And what about Kara?" She yelled at me. "What about the Disir?"

My brow furrowed as I stared at her. I should have known she wasn't here just to talk about Magnus. She wanted revenge. She wanted blood. And she wasn't going to stop until Kara paid for his death. But I never thought she'd join forces with Odin.

"The Alfather sent you here to convince me to take up arms against the Disir. Didn't he?" I shook my head in disappointment and let my arms fall to my side. "I won't kill Kara."

"You will." Her lips pulled into a grin that would haunt my dreams. "For Magnus."

Heat bloomed in my chest, and anger boiled in my blood. "He wouldn't want me to kill anyone in his name."

"Magnus doesn't want anything anymore," she snapped.

"I know you're angry, so am I."

"You aren't half as angry as you should be." She whirled on me with wild eyes and the torchlight flickered on the wall behind her.

"Don't pretend to know what I feel," I fired back.

Now that I knew she was here doing Odin's bidding, I didn't fear her retaliation.

"He was my friend long before your eyes wandered in his direction. I'd give my life if it meant he could be here instead of me. But I can't. He's gone." The last word got stuck in my throat. As much as I was trying to reason with her, my pain was still too fresh to remain unaffected.

She stepped forward, a kernel of hope in her eyes at seeing my heartache.

"That's right, he was your friend, your brother. What you and I feel is only a fraction of the pain she's caused. And you can make it right. You can bring justice to the people she hurt. You can end the Disir and cement your name in the history books alongside the gods."

She was good, I'd give her that. Playing up the glory of what she wanted me to do. A lesser man may've fallen for the honeyed trap.

"I don't need your revenge plot or Odin's delusions to find glory."

"There are ways to make you concede." She huffed a laugh and turned away.

"I'm glad Magnus can't see you now. It would break his heart."

She whirled on me, closing the distance lightning fast, and her fist connected with my stomach. Before I could double over, she grabbed me by the throat. Her nails digging into my windpipe and cutting off my air supply.

"Go ahead, kill me," I croaked as I held her gaze.

The pressure in my head was almost too much to bear as the drumming turned into a murderous tempo. My lungs burned and the corner of my eyes blurred.

"Killing you would be too easy," she spit in my face and released me.

I sucked in a breath, and coughed so hard I was afraid my lungs might actually crawl up my throat and splatter on the floor.

"I think..." I heaved, wiping the spit off my face as I sucked in another breath. "You can't kill me...otherwise you would have already."

"I don't want you dead, Sigurd," her jaw flexed. "I want your help. I want you to do what's right." Tears sprung to her eyes. "I want you to use your heart and end all the bloodshed." A tear fell down her cheek.

"I am thinking with my heart, Bryn, my broken heart. And ending bloodshed with bloodshed isn't the way."

"And what about the other Disir? Are you going to let them run free to wreak havoc on the Nine Realms?" She gave me a pointed look.

I opened my mouth to say no, but that would only prove her point further.

She smirked and wiped the tear from her face. "I didn't think so." The cold steel was back in her voice, dropping the emotional act. "If you won't let them live, then you already know what the right thing to do is."

She headed for the door and, as she reached for the handle, she looked over her shoulder. Her face was soft, her eyes kind and sad.

"Think about, Si," she said and then pulled the door open and slammed it closed behind her.

"There's nothing to think about." The words echoed against the stone walls, and my heart felt a little lighter.

I sunk to the floor and leaned my head against the wall. Her logic was sound, but she was overlooking one crucial fact. Kara has never killed an innocent person of her own volition. And she wasn't going around consuming souls.

Except for Loki's.

I couldn't find an ounce of compassion for what happened to Loki. Nor did it make me fear Kara. If anything, I was glad she did it. And I was glad she was still alive because of it.

The memory of removing her armor at Asheria's, the way she held my gaze and gripped my arm, flooded my mind, heart, and body. A calm washed over me, and a clarity I hadn't felt in over a hundred years settled in my bones.

A smile pulled at the corner of my lips. Kara wanted me to think about what I wanted. If I could take the next step knowing everything we know now. If I could trust her despite everything. I knew my answer in the alley, just as much as I knew it now.

I've never had a choice when it came to her. My decision was made the day I met her and the day she stole my heart forever. And even if the path before us sent me to the stars. I'd still follow her to the end of the Nine Realms.

CHAPTER SEVENTEEN

KARA

MY DREAM from the other night haunted my every breath. I couldn't shake the feeling that I was missing something. Like it was on the tip of my tongue, but no matter how hard I tried, I just couldn't figure it out.

Davlin waved his hand in front of my face. "You still in there?"

"Yeah, sorry." I shook my head, trying to dispel the nervous energy growing inside me. "What were we talking about?" I glanced over his shoulder at the ships sitting in the harbor, water glistening like a sea of jewels, and groaned. Why did I agree to this excursion when I should be searching for more information about the Disir?

"Does it matter?" Davlin's brow furrowed as he studied me. "What were you thinking about?" He asked as the boat rocked hard to my right.

"Do you think people can communicate through dreams?"

He adjusted the steerboard, and the wind tossed my hair over my shoulder.

"Is this a philosophical question, or are you trying to tell me someone's hijacked your dreams?" He gave me a pointed look.

"Must you always answer a question with a question? It's insufferable," I snapped at him. He didn't deserve my short fuse, but my patience was thinner than paper after several nights of being woken up by the same dream.

He stood and released the anchor. "There are many who believe our souls walk the realms while we sleep and interact with others to awaken some hidden truth."

"What do you think?" I asked as he moved past me toward the mast.

"The better question." He pulled the rope and lowered the sail. "What do *you* believe?" He looked over his shoulder with a grin that made me want to throw him in the water. I hated this game of forcing me to give up my every thought while he stayed neutral.

"I don't know about my soul wandering the realms, but I think the Disir might be trying to communicate with me." I looked out over the water.

It was a beautiful day for sailing. The sea was calm, the sun was warm, and the breeze was cool. But it did nothing to quell the storm building inside me.

I could press him for an answer, but he was just as stubborn as me, and it would only end in a stalemate of silence. Which I didn't have time for.

"There was a rumor that the Disir had grown powerful enough that they could communicate with each other across great distances. Some believe it's how they almost bested the gods," he said matter-of-factly as he pulled out a satchel out from under his seat, and sat back down.

I swear Davlin's lived a thousand lives. He never ceased to surprise me with a new tidbit of information or history. And I cursed myself for not digging into his brain sooner.

"You know more about the Disir than you're letting on." I leveled my gaze at him. "Don't you?" A small wave crashed against our hull and splashed some cool sea water across my lap.

"There's that cunning intellect." He glanced up at me and winked. "As a matter of fact, I know a great deal." He pulled out a bottle of mead and two cups. "I was there when Freya encased them in stone—all except one."

"Why didn't you say anything the other day? When I first told you about them returning?" Irritation prickled my skin.

"Because you didn't need more on your plate at that moment. You needed a friend, some sleep, and time to grieve what you just went through." He gave me a pointed look that reminded me of my father.

"That wasn't your call to make." I stood and my legs wobbled as the boat gently rocked to the cadence of the sea.

"I planned to tell you everything. That's why we're out here," he waved his arms at the wide open sea, "away from prying eyes and ears."

"You're toying with me, and I don't appreciate it." I sat back down on the wood bench.

"I've watched you fall apart before." He poured a cup of mead and handed it to me. "And I won't be the reason you fall apart again. Telling you a few days after you've rested and healed is hardly the end of the world."

Guilt colored my cheeks, and I took a sip of the mead. I didn't like that he was treating me like glass. But I couldn't blame him. He'd seen me on my darkest days—my most destructive days. And as much as I wanted to be angry at him, I knew he was only trying to protect me from myself.

"Fine. What else are you keeping from me? Did you know I was like them?" I grabbed the satchel and pulled it toward me.

He rolled his eyes. "Yes, I kept the truth of your bloodline from you, just so I could see the look on your face when you learned you're related to those harbingers of death," he said deadpan.

"I'm serious." I glanced up at him.

He let out a heavy sigh and stopped me from rifling through the bag. "On my honor—"

"Which you have very little of." I raised an eyebrow at him.

"On the last shred of my honor," he amended. "I swear I didn't know you shared their bloodline. Only that Freya spared one of the Disir." He took the satchel from me, pulled out a leaf wrapped meal, and held it between us. Notes of citrus and smoke hit my nose, and my mouth watered.

I put down my cup and took the offering, unwrapping the leaf on my lap. A warm puff of steam wafted out of the leaves, filling the air with the decadent aroma of fresh grilled fish, herbs and citrus. He was lucky he brought my favorite dish.

"Alright, then tell me everything." I pinched off a piece of fish and popped it into my mouth. Flavor burst on my tongue and I closed my eyes. It had been an age since I tasted the buttery fish seasoned with the perfect blend of aromatics.

"The Disir were not so dissimilar to yourself and the other Valkyrie when I first came across them." He unwrapped his own meal. "Their Magik was different, more unpredictable, having been born from Bor's ignorance. But they were kind, smart, and devastatingly beautiful." A sheepish look crossed his features.

"Please tell me you didn't sleep with any of them?" I leveled my eyes at him.

A devilish smirk he reserved for courting pulled at the corner of his mouth.

"You're drooling."

"You would be too, if you could see my memories," he tapped his temple.

"If I wanted to be subjected to torture, I'd call upon the Alfather."

"As if listening to you agonize over lover boy for fifty years was a walk in the park." He pinched off a piece of fish and tossed it into his mouth.

"On second thought, I might actually pity the Disir you took to bed. I'm sure being turned to stone was a welcome respite after your ministrations."

"You have about as much charm as a dragon," he rolled his eyes and smirked.

"Enough about your sex life." My Magik flared with my irritation. "Can we get back to the Disir?"

"No need to sink the ship." He held his hands up in surrender. "The gods have done well to erase their true nature from the consciousness of the Nine Realms." His eyes met mine and I could feel the foreign Disir Magik slither against my bones, like it knew we were talking about it.

"Much like you and your sisters, they were supposed to ferry worthy souls to the gods, but their hunger for power outgrew any loyalty they had to Bor. It wasn't long before the Disir realized that by consuming a soul, they could grow more powerful than anyone living, including the gods. And they couldn't have that, now could they?"

"That's why the punishment for killing your charge is so severe," I said under my breath. "I just thought they were being cruel, keeping me from the Nine Realms for a hundred years. But it's because of them, isn't it?" I took another bite of my fish and licked my fingers. Not even the topic at hand could ruin how delicious this meal was.

"Precisely. They couldn't risk any Valkyrie becoming too powerful again."

"Why not kill me? After Sigurd and save everyone the trouble?" The tattoo on my back prickled, and Odin's words echoed through my bones.

You're lucky Freya's Magik binds me from making a true example of you.

"If I had to guess," he shrugged. "It might be because you've never taken a soul for your own."

Until Loki. I thought.

The vision of him with blue eyes made me shiver, and I prayed to Yggdrasil he was dead and not a Draugr.

"None of this explains why Freya spared one of the Disir? Wouldn't she want them all locked up?"

"Freya claimed," he leaned forward as if he was worried the water was listening. "She wanted to know her enemy better."

"You don't believe her?" My eyes narrowed.

"There were rumors she found a way to take their Magik from them." He picked the meat off the bones and ate a healthy portion of fish. "Make them like any other Asgardian citizen."

"And?" I turned my focus back to my lunch.

"Your guess is as good as mine," he shrugged. "When I confronted her about it, she swore the woman would never see the light of day again. So whether she figured out how to tame the Magik, or if she just wanted to understand them better, only Freya knows."

"And just how were you privy to any of this, or even granted access to Freya?" I took another bite of the fish and washed it down with the mead.

"You think you're the only one who has a history with the gods?" He raised his brow suggestively.

"You never said anything?" I shook my head.

I knew Davlin. I trusted him with my life. But I was beginning to realize that he knew me better. Guilt colored my cheeks, and I looked down at my favorite fish. I've spent so much time wrapped up in my own mess that I hadn't gotten to know him as well as I should have.

"My relationship with the gods wasn't relevant to our friendship, and my path changed long before I met you."

"Sure. Why share your history with the one person you've spent the last fifty years with?" I may've been wrapped in my own turmoil when I met him, but he'd also been careful to always steer the conversation back to me. My guilt wasn't unfounded, but a relationship went both ways. I should have asked more questions about him, and he should have shared.

"When you've been alive as long as I have, it isn't easy to encapsulate one's life into something digestible."

"That's crap and you know it." I shook my head. "I can understand not telling me every detail of your life, but you knew I was a Valkyrie, you knew I killed Sigurd, and you never shared any of this. Why?" Magik flared under my skin and I had to fight to rein it back in.

"I've interfered where I shouldn't have in the past, and I paid dearly for it. I wasn't going to make the same mistake twice. Not when the path you walk is so precarious."

"What the Hel are you talking about?" I stared at him like he was one of the Norns, spouting off prophecy as a cryptic message.

He held my stare, both of our meals forgotten. The sail wafted behind me, the breeze tousled my hair, and the water went still.

"You're at the beginning of a very long journey, one I can't help you with this time. What you do, how you move forward, every step you take, all of it has to be your choice."

He broke eye contact and picked at his fish once more, breaking the spell.

"Having information wouldn't change that." I turned my attention back to my half eaten fish.

"Wouldn't it?" If you knew all this before you went back to Folkvang, would everything have happened as it has? He popped another bite of fish into his mouth and licked his fingers.

"Then why tell me now?" A gull squawked overhead, surely eyeing our food, and I leaned forward to protect my meal.

"Because you asked. You confided in me when it would have been easier to not say anything. And asked me what I knew."

I mulled his words over. Part of me felt betrayed that I'd spent so much time with him and he'd kept this from me. But another part of my mind argued I wouldn't have listened back then. Not when my entire world had been ripped from me. None of this would have made sense without the context I have now.

"Any other secrets you're harboring?"

"You have no idea," he chuckled and folded up his leaf once more.

"Do tell."

"Like I said, I'm not interfering this time. The Norns would have my balls, and not in the fun way."

"You're insufferable," I laughed and for the first time in days, I felt a little lighter. This may be just the beginning, but at least I wasn't completely in the dark anymore.

"Fine. Keep your secrets. Just tell me one thing?"

"Depends if I have an answer." He reached over the side of the boat and dipped his hands in the water.

"When you went against the Norns and interfered." He stiffened ever so slightly. "Was it worth it?"

His gaze fell to the planks between us and I got the impression he was lost in the memory of what he did.

"Only time will tell." A sad smile kissed his lips as his eyes met mine. "Enough about me, though." He got to his feet and clapped his hands. "Let's get to why I really brought you out here." He raised his brow suggestively.

"Is this where you toss me overboard and tell me to swim back to shore?

"Nope." He rubbed his hands together like a scheming child. "I want you to test out your new Magik."

I froze with a piece of fish halfway to my mouth. "I'm sorry, what?"

CHAPTER EIGHTEEN

THE LACK of celestial light gliding across the sky made it impossible to know if it was day or night. The only indication of time passing was the delivery of food each morning by the same young woman.

Five trays sat discarded in the corner, every crumb and drop of water gone. It wasn't much, but it allowed me to keep my strength up. Even so, I hadn't managed to remove the manacles. And my knife was a little worse for wear from trying to pick the lock on my door.

It had been days since Bryn visited, and still our conversation clung to me like old, dirty clothes. I understood her pain and her quest for revenge. I'd felt that fire burn within me for more years than I cared to think about. But revenge wasn't the answer with Kara. And maybe that meant revenge wasn't the answer for the Disir, either.

The thought soured in my stomach as I leaned back against the wall. The cool, rough surface was a relief from the stagnant warmth of the prison. While I appreciated the light from the torches, it kept the prison too warm, and made it hard to get a good night's rest.

A door groaned open somewhere beyond my prison. It didn't sound the same as when Odin and Bryn graced me with their company, and I wondered how many paths there were in and out of this place. Would I even be able to find a way out if I escaped this room? Or would I end up lost in the dungeons, with no hope of escape?

A grinding sound echoed through the stone walls. As if someone was rolling something heavy down a corridor. My heart picked up in tempo and I got to my feet. The grating grew louder, closer, and I picked up the battered knife. It was better than nothing, I told myself.

As I moved into a defensive position, everything went quiet. The only sound that pierced the air was the steady flicker of the torch. I half wondered if I was going mad, and then the heavy clank of my prison door being unlocked resounded through the room.

The door creaked open slowly, and a dark wood table was rolled toward me. My heart beat at a steady pace as I quickly assessed this new threat. The surface of the table was empty save for a leather bundle, tightly wrapped with a thin strap. A kit of some sort. Most likely instruments of torture.

So it'd come to this.

Adrenaline burned through my veins at the notion, and I stood up a little straighter. My gaze turned to my would be torturer.

Tall. Close to my height. Lean. Built.

The hood of his cloak hid his features. Only the edge of his nose and the cut of his bearded jaw were visible. He wore dark leather trousers and a dark green top that looked a shade too big on him. And he wore a belt wrapped around his middle with an empty dagger sheath.

Smart. If given the opportunity, I'd have made that weapon mine.

He wore no armor, which was mildly unsettling. Did they really not see me as a threat? Or was I really so powerless here that even a modest man could break me to his will?

"If you're here to convince me to take Odin's offer? Don't waste your breath," I said as he turned his back on me and closed to the door.

"You're very confident for someone who may never see the light of day again." His voice was deep and smooth as honey. I could imagine him weaving stories over a fire, captivating anyone who listened.

He stepped to the right side of the table and unrolled the leather pouch. Silver gleamed in the firelight like dancing embers. I steeled my nerves for what would come next. It wouldn't be my first time going under the blade. But it'd been an age since someone tried to sway me to their cause through torture.

He moved to the other side of the table with a quiet grace.

"If Odin wanted me dead, he'd have killed me already."

"You think just because he requires your assistance, he won't still kill you?" He pulled a platter out from a hidden compartment under the table.

A roasted bird sat in the center of the plate next to a loaf of bread, cheese, and berries. My mouth watered and my stomach let out a groan of need. They were providing me with one meal a day, but it was just enough to sustain me.

He looked up at me, his hood falling back just barely. A scar cut across his cheek and disappeared behind his ear.

"Let me make something perfectly clear." His dark eyes met mine. "If you don't agree to his terms, he will kill you and find another way. The Alfather's will is ironclad and near impossible to escape." He rolled the table closer to me and upon further inspection, the torture instruments were utensils.

He stood on the other side of the table and procured two plates from the hidden compartment. The decadent aroma of herbs and spices hit me like a punch to the chest.

"That may be true of lesser men, but I think he'll find me harder to break." I didn't move from the wall, even though my mouth was watering and my stomach groaned loud enough for both of us to hear.

A small smile touched his lips, and I noticed the flecks of gray in his beard as he served a piece of meat to each dish.

"Harder yes, but all who come here only leave one of two ways. Dead or broken." He set one of the plates on my side of the table. "Either way, you'll need your strength."

Pushing off the wall, I stepped up to the table and placed my knife on the polished wood surface. Let him see I wasn't a pushover. If it came to it, I'd fight until my last breath with only a chipped knife to my name.

I glanced at the food and back at him. I was tempted to dig in, but for all I knew, the food was poisoned or tainted with Magik that would enslave my mind and soul.

He tore off a piece of bread and took a bite, as if sensing my hesitation. Then held out the loaf between us. I took the offering and pulled off a piece for myself. Against my better judgement, I took a bite and prayed to the Norns it wasn't a mistake. It was warm and soft, with a hint of herbs. My mouth watered as I tore off another piece.

"You're a fierce warrior." He grabbed a handful of berries and popped a few into his mouth. Following his lead, I added some berries to my plate as well. "And one of Freya's most treasured fallen." He stated with an authority that made me wonder just how much he knew about me. "But you let the flame in your heart rule you, and it will be your undoing."

"I didn't realize gossip from Folkvang would reach your ears here in—I actually don't know where we are, to be honest." Based on my conversation with Odin, I assumed we were in Valhalla, but assumptions wouldn't do me any good if I managed to escape.

"You're in Asgard." He stabbed a piece of meat and took a healthy bite.

Surprise flickered through me and I froze with a piece of bread halfway to my mouth. Freya said we couldn't survive outside the lands of the dead and yet here I was, in another realm, and my heart was still beating. Either she was mistaken or something was seriously wrong in the Nine Realms.

Never in a million years did I think I'd find myself in Asgard. Even if it was the dungeons. My mother used to tell me fantastical stories that described the city and surrounding islands like an oasis of beauty and culture. My heart yearned to see if her stories were true, but deep down I knew it was unlikely I'd ever see Asgard's beauty with my own eyes.

"Gossip is such a harsh word for someone who craves to be known. To be remembered." He smiled and the scar across his face wrinkled. "Even if they only speak your name because of the company you keep." His gaze settled over my chest. Where the scar Kara gave me hid beneath my clothes.

Instinctively, I rubbed my hand over the spot. "Since you seem to know so much about me," frustration laced my words. "Then you must know I won't kill Kara."

"Believe me, I know the truth in your heart. You're loyal to her. Even if you shouldn't be."

A flash of anger burned through me. What did he know of my loyalty to anyone, let alone Kara? A short, humorless laugh escaped my throat as I cut off a piece of meat and took a bite. It tasted even better than it smelled. It was juicy, smokey with a hint of spice. I fought the urge to tear into the bird and gorge myself.

"I get the impression the only loyalty that's rewarded here is the kind where I subjugate myself to the Alfather's will."

The corner of his lips twitched. "Loyalty is a tricky bedfellow. Some would say it's impossible to be loyal to one who holds power over you. The mouse will always fear the cat's wrath and therefore cannot be truly loyal in their heart."

"Is this the part where you tell me Odin is a just ruler and worthy of my loyalty? Because I hate to break it to you, but being locked in his dungeons doesn't breed any sort of warm regards toward the man."

"No." He laid down his utensils. "This is the part where I ask if you can truly trust the Valkyrie. You know the power she carries within her, do you not?"

I refused to answer and instead tore off a piece of cheese.

"You're smarter than Odin gives you credit for, but it's a fool's errand to play dumb with me. We both know what happened in that temple."

My heart raced and my stomach went hollow with each word he spoke.

"What Kara did to Loki." He tilted his head to the side and my mouth went dry, turning the bread in my mouth to ash. "What she truly is."

I forced myself to meet his gaze.

He wanted to get a rise out of me. Rile me up, so I'll admit what I knew. But I wouldn't tell them a single thing about Kara or what happened in that temple. He could question my loyalty all he wanted, but he was right about one thing.

I did let the fire in my heart guide me, and it's never been wrong before.

"Whether you want to admit it or not. When push comes to shove, you're the mouse and Kara is the hungry cat, trying to ignore her instincts." He cut off another piece of meat and took a bite with an air of indifference that made my blood boil.

"Odin is also the cat in this scenario of yours. And didn't you say yourself that Odin would happily send me to the stars, even if it thwarts his plans?"

"The point is not to align yourself with Odin or the Valkyrie, or even Freya, for that matter. The point," he tore off another piece of bread. "Is deciding what kind of man you want to be. You have the power to save lives. Your destiny can free the Nine Realms of chaos, pain, and destruction. You are not the type to let innocents die for the love of a woman. A woman, I'll remind you, who ended your mortal life."

Blood rose to my cheeks, and I gripped the fork in my hand so hard it dug into my bones.

I forced myself to swallow the food in my mouth. "You have no idea the type of man I am."

"I know exactly the type of man you are. I know you want to drive that fork into my neck. I know you want to prove that you know better than the Alfather. I know you gave your heart to Kara the day you met her. But I also know there is a kernel of doubt brewing inside you that you're ignoring. And I know you'll fail, not only yourself, but the people you love if you continue to fight this. They will all die. Ragnar. Daiman. Talon. Bryn. They will all die if you stay on the path you're so determined to."

I shook my head and dropped the fork onto the plate. I hated every word out of his mouth. "You can threaten me and mine all you want. But you can't know the future. Only the Norns know the path we're on and from what I hear, even their vision has shadows they can't see beyond."

"I don't need the Norns to know what I've seen with my own eyes."

I took a step back. The tide of the conversation was shifting. My eyes burned and my hands shivered as his gaze met mine.

"You will choose Kara, but she won't choose you. She can't ignore the darkness in her. And before long, she will succumb to it."

"I don't believe in prophecies and fate. I don't care what you've seen or what you believe to be true. This will not end with her blood on my hands."

"It does. One way or another. It's up to you to decide how many people you'll let die before you finally stop her."

"And why should I believe you?"

He lifted his hands and removed his hood, letting the firelight illuminate his face fully.

"Because I am you. And we stop her, but far too late."

I sucked in a breath and my body took the blow of his words like a punch to the gut. My vision tunneled, and emotion crawled up my throat, stealing the words from my mouth as the firelight flickered against a breeze that didn't exist.

I studied him. His brown eyes, the scar on his cheek. The dark hair flecked with strands of silver. There was a likeness to him that was familiar, but the man before me bore scars, and history that did not belong to me. This had to be a trick, another one of Odin's games.

"Impossible." It was the only word I could manage.

"The future is but another realm. And now that the Magik of the universe is failing, a great many things are possible. I know you can feel it. The unease in your stomach, the prickle along your skin like you've been out in the sun too long." There was an urgency in his voice that set my nerves on edge.

I did feel it. I just didn't know what I'd been feeling over the past few months.

Is that why Freya took so long to fix the rift? Because she couldn't fix it? Is that why Odin was so Hel bent on getting his hands on Kara? Was she the reason Magik was failing?

"Magik may be failing, but I'm no fool. Not even the gods have access to the future." I grabbed my knife off the table and put some distance between us.

"The gods," he scoffed. "They're blinded by their own arrogance. Too caught up in their egos to see what's right in front of them. Much like you at the moment." He scanned me from head to toe with pity. "We both know there's nothing I can say that'll make you believe me. You have to come to that conclusion on your own."

"On that, we can agree. I've seen enough Magik and illusions to know when something foul is afoot. If Odin wants me to do his bidding, he's going to have to do better than you."

"You're right. Odin is the reason I'm here. But not for the reason you think. I didn't take him up on his offer. And I'm here now, to ask you to be stronger than me. Because I failed. I waited too long to do the right thing. And now the veil between realms grows thinner by the day."

"You expect me to believe that Magik is failing in the Nine Realms, because I won't kill Kara?" This was absolutely asinine. I expected more subtlety from Odin, not out right desperation.

"Magik is failing because the Disir stir once more. And Kara is a Disir, whether you want to accept it or not. There will come a time not too far from now, when their power will be unstoppable, and the balance in the Nine Realms will shatter."

Balance?

There's that word again. Odin said he wanted balance. Maybe there was something to what this man was saying, even if he was lying about who he was.

"That's what has allowed me this brief encounter with you now. The rift in Folkvang isn't the only tear in the realms." His mention of the rift gave me pause. Was it already common knowledge, or had Odin's spies penetrated deeper into Folkvang than we realized?

"The rift in Folkvang appeared before the Disir. Your logic doesn't add up."

"It appeared after Kara's return to the Nine Realms. She's the catalyst."

I shook my head and opened my mouth to tell him he was wrong, but the words remained stuck in my throat. All I could think of was Ragnar, and how he thought Kara's return was distracting us from the bigger picture.

Could he have been right all along?

"I don't expect you to believe me. I wouldn't believe me either. Not yet, at least." He grabbed my plate and dumped the rest of my food on the platter.

"But there will be signs. When you see lightning on a clear day, you'll recall my words, and that ember of doubt in you will grow." He dumped his plate as well and deposited both of them in the hidden compartment.

"And when you lie under the stars of another world, you'll feel the call of her Magik and know you're losing her to the darkness." He picked up the half eaten platter of food, and it too disappeared under the table.

"And when you are asked to make a sacrifice to a queen with a crown of bones, you'll know I've spoken the truth. And you will do what I could not. You will spill her blood." He lifted his hood and his face fell back into the shadows.

"If this is so important, why be cryptic? Why not give me hard proof that what you say is real?"

He wheeled the table backward toward the door. "They're only cryptic to you now. But they'll be key moments on your path that'll be impossible to ignore. And only you will know them for what they are. Omens of what's to come."

He unlocked the door and pushed the table into the dark hall. Footsteps echoed close by and he glanced over his shoulder as he stood on the threshold.

"Wait," I stepped toward him. "I can't do anything if I'm trapped in here. Let me go. I'll find a way to stop the Disir and save Kara. But I can't do that in here." I hated the note of pleading in my voice.

He shook his head. "Your place is here for now. But Sigurd, you've always known the right path. Don't do as I did and fight the current." He closed the door, and the lock fell into place with a clang.

His words settled into my chest, and I threw my knife at the closed door. It stuck into the wood with a thud and I started to pace to shed the anxious energy buzzing inside me.

He knew enough of the right things to say. He knew parts of my history that were easy to regurgitate. But there wasn't a chance in Hel that man was my future. At least not any future I wanted a part of.

CHAPTER NINETEEN

THE INSISTENT THUD of someone banging on wood jolted me awake with the acrid taste of a scream still on my tongue. My heart beat with a fever I felt in my ears and eyes, and a cold sweat made me shiver. I couldn't recall my dream, but the lingering desperation clung to my bones.

"Just a dream." I exhaled and took a deep breath. Hushed angry voices sounded from the main room, and a blanket of fear settled over my shoulders.

Sliding out of the disheveled bedsheet, I slipped the dress I borrowed from Asheria's over my head. Grabbing a dagger, I headed out the door and down the hall to the main living quarters.

The fire in the hearth had burned to embers, casting the room in dark shadows that called to the Magik inside me. I quickly acknowledged the power, then coaxed it back into the recesses of my soul, like we'd worked on all day. It was hard to manage from a dead sleep, but I was able to cut down the sharp edge of lethal hunger swirling inside me.

"Who the Hel's banging down your door at this hour?" I kept my dagger hidden in the folds of my dress.

"You tell me?" Davlin swung the door open wider.

Deep midnight blue wings filled the doorframe and a soft melody that sounded like a quiet night under the stars tangled with my Magik.

"Talon?" I loosened my fingers on the dagger and tightened my grip on my Magik. "What are you doing here?" Confusion swept through me once I reined in my Magik.

"Gods, I've been looking for you everywhere." She gave Davlin a pointed look, and he stepped out of her way. Her wings clipped the door as she stormed into the house.

"Why? What's happened?" Worry pierced my heart as I took in the dark circles under her eyes.

"Odin's taken Sigurd."

Her words hit me like a physical blow, stunning my whole body. A fissure cracked open in my heart, and panic bled into my chest. I didn't know it had any room left to break.

I tunneled into my Valkyrie Magik for the familiar call of Sigurd's soul.

Please be okay. I silently begged.

He was further than I expected as I sifted through the realms for him. I pulled on the tether to Asgard and surprise flickered through me when the cadence of Sigurd's soul lapped at the shore of my heart.

My Disir Magik perked up its head at the call of a worthy soul, and I clamped down on the connection.

"Is he…?" Davlin asked.

I let out a sigh of relief and my shoulders slumped forward. "He's okay," I confirmed, and angry tears pricked the back of my eyes.

"Odin's using him as a bargaining chip." Talon rolled her shoulders and her wings vanished in a puff of smoke and Magik.

"Bargain for what?" Davlin asked as he crossed the room to the hearth.

A sinking realization pierced through me. "He wants me." The Disir Magik rattled against the cage I'd shoved it into, and I had to fight the urge to let it free.

Talon nodded. "He gave Freya a fortnight to turn you over. Or he'd kill Sigurd and destroy Folkvang."

"For the love of Yggdrasil, Kara. I've never met another soul so intertwined with disaster." Davlin added kindling to the embers.

"Your commentary isn't helpful," Talon shot him a look that promised pain if he didn't keep his thoughts to himself.

"Never said I was trying to be helpful, love." He winked at her and I swear Talon bristled.

"Is he always like this?" Talon asked under her breath.

"Charming and devilishly handsome?" Davlin cocked his head to the side and looked her up and down.

"Can you not be you, just this once?" I stared daggers at Davlin. Normally, I was all for his easygoing attitude toward the world, but right now, I'd strangle him if he spoke one more word.

"That's like asking the sun not to rise." The kindling ignited and cast a soft, flickering glow across the living space.

I turned my back on him and folded my arms over my chest. "If he wants me, so be it." Hot, bright tendrils of revenge curled around my heart, my lungs, my every breath. "I'm done with his threats."

"It isn't a threat. He's out for blood." The fear in Talon's voice fanned the flames growing inside me.

"Then he'll have it." I snapped at her. "I won't let Sigurd or Folkvang pay for what I am."

"Honorable of you. But you're thinking like a mortal." The fire burned brighter and I could clearly see the desperation in her eyes now. "Use your head, not your heart." Talon's words were unyielding as she stared me down. "It's not just you he wants. Otherwise, he would have demanded your head the moment you set foot back in Folkvang."

"The Disir," I said through gritted teeth.

Talon's gaze flicked over my shoulder to Davlin.

"He already knows everything." I waved off her concern.

Surprise flickered across her face and she appraised Davlin once more.

"You may not know me yet, but you can trust I'm loyal to Kara." I could hear the smile in his voice.

"Loyalty for loyalty's sake isn't a virtue." Talon's lips pressed together.

"He was there when I had no one." I glanced at Davlin. "He's family."

"Very well." She sighed. "I believe Odin wants Folkvang for himself. Taking Sigurd is clearly to draw you out. But threatening Freya and Folkvang," she shook her head. "It seems illogical to start a war over you. He was waiting for a reason to light the battle torches."

"And when Loki…freed the Disir…"

"It was the perfect opportunity," Talon finished my thought.

I was so tired. Tired of running, tired of losing people I cared about. But mostly I was tired of the gods and their games.

"How could he possibly know what happened in the temple already?" My gaze flicked between Talon and Davlin. Only a handful of days, and already I'm being hunted for the blood in my veins.

"The Alfather has eyes everywhere," Talon said. "I'm honestly surprised he waited until the rites to confront Freya."

"From what I remember, he has a flare for the dramatic." Davlin folded his arms over his chest and sighed.

Talon looked at him with renewed interest.

"You have experience with the Alfather?" She cocked an eyebrow at him.

"You could say that." He looked her up and down.

Talon glanced at me, and her brow furrowed as if to say, *who is this guy?*

Impatience prickled my skin. "While I'm sure it's a very interesting story, can we please get back to the matter at hand?"

There was no room for warmth in my voice. "How do we get Si back? And stop a war."

My wings shot from my back of their own accord, responding to the anxiety and panic swirling inside me like a turbulent sea.

"Hold on," she grabbed my arm. "We need a plan. We can't just storm Asgard. That's exactly what Odin wants."

"You can't gain access to the dungeons. It's near impossible," Davlin informed us.

"Nothing's impossible," Talon said through gritted teeth.

"This is. Trust me. If you ever want to see Sigurd again, you'll need Odin to bring him to you." It was rare for Davlin to sound so serious, and it gave me pause.

"How do you know so much about the Asgard dungeons?" Talon raised a brow, but she wore a curious smirk.

"I've lived many lives."

"Haven't we all," she sighed. "And for your information, no one is storming Asgard without a plan. The others already have a half cocked rescue mission brewing."

"The others?" My gaze shot back to Talon.

"Ragnar, and Daiman." She waved a hand.

"How are they going to help? They can't leave Folkvang."

"They can. They have, in fact. To save you."

Her words settled into me and I opened my mouth to tell her she was wrong, but she wasn't.

"Crossing the rift is one thing." I shook my head, determine to leave them behind and go after Si myself. "But leaving Folkvang altogether isn't possible."

"It might be. The Magik of the Nine Realms is failing," Davlin supplied.

"And just how do you know that?" I shot him a pointed look.

"I can feel it. Can't you?" He flashed a grin that didn't meet his eyes.

"Failing or not, they're human. They're not meant to travel the realms."

"Don't tell them that," Talon scoffed. "You won't convince them not to go. Sigurd is their brother in arms." She folded her arms over her chest.

"I don't like putting their lives at risk."

"You aren't their keeper. If they want to risk their second life to save Sigurd, that's their choice," Talon said in a huff like she's already had this conversation with them and lost.

"Alright." I let out a breath. "Alright, fine. What about Freya? Where does she stand?"

"She's made it very clear. She won't bend to Odin's threats," Talon grumbled like she disagreed with the decision, but I'm not sure where that left me in her eyes.

Did she want Freya to hand me over? Or was she just disappointed that Freya wanted war over peace?

"She'll let him die, and risk Folkvang to spare my life? I don't buy it. She's up to something." My intuition flared, mixing with my Magik, and every bone in my body told me something wasn't right.

"She isn't afraid of war with Odin. She's had the first pick of the fallen for over a thousand years. Her army is stronger than his, and she knows it," Talon said. But it did nothing to quell my determination to spare Folkvang another fight.

"Maybe, but they're also grieving and still regathering after the assault from the Draugr."

"I know it's been a long time since you've led the fallen, but we both know they are more than capable, even in their current state. So what's this really about?" Talon demanded.

"She doesn't think she's worth the fight," Davlin said point blank, and I stared daggers at him.

"If it makes you feel any better, I think Freya's been itching for this fight with Odin since way before your name was tossed into the ring." Talon ignored the tension rolling off of me. "We all know how much she despises him, but she'd be a fool to declare war on him. You're just the catalysts to a fight that's been brewing since before you were born."

"Is that supposed to make me feel better? People are going to die because of some spat between the gods?"

"People have died for a lot less," Talon reminded me, and my heart sank.

"You think I don't know that?" My temper flared and Magik swirled through my core. Talon's shoulder stiffened, and she took a step back.

She was afraid of me. My heart shuddered and my anger floated away on a breeze. Talon had stood by me through more than I cared to remember, and she never looked at me differently. Until now.

"Deep breaths, Kara," Davlin reminded me.

I curled my hands into fists and forced the Magik churning through me into submission. I let out a shaky breath and my shoulders eased.

"I know you're taking this personal." Talon's voice was calm and kind, though she kept her distance. "You have every right to. But if the gods want a war, there isn't anything we can do to stop them. We have to focus on what we can do. And we can save Sigurd."

I nodded. "You're right." I didn't entirely agree. There was a way we could save Folkvang and Sigurd. Or at least there was a way *I could*. "I'm just sick of stumbling into everything blindly."

"Whatever it is you're keeping to yourself," Davlin said under his breath and gave me a pointed look, as if he could read my thoughts. "Don't let your guilt and fear dictate your actions. Those are old habits you'd do well to keep dead and buried. Especially with your new found Magik."

His words struck a cord, a desperately broken cord in me. I knew he was speaking to the woman he found all those years ago. The woman who would do just about anything to take away the pain of killing Sigurd. And while I was no longer that woman, she still lived with me. Bandaged and bruised. And that part of me would always feel like it was my responsibility to do something. To fix all of this no matter the cost to myself.

"What's he talking about?" Talon looked between the two of us.

"He's afraid I'll do something stupid." I held Davlin's gaze. "But I'm not that person anymore. I know there's innocent blood on my hands that I'll never be able to wash away. I can live with that. I have to live with that. But I'm done standing by and allowing others to play this game better than us."

"Your bravado is all well and good, but what happens if Odin gets his hands on you?" Davlin demanded. "If he…" His gaze drifted over my wings and they fluttered at his meaning.

"He won't," Talon said it with such confidence I couldn't help the smile that pulled at the corner of my mouth.

Gods, I was grateful to have her on my side.

Davlin looked between the two of us and rolled his eyes. "Sorðinn Valkyrie. I swear you all have a death wish."

"No, we're just not afraid of walking hand in hand with odds that are stacked against us," she fired back with a smirk, and Davlin rolled his eyes.

"We're wasting time." I ruffled my wings, ready to take flight. "Time Si doesn't have."

Talon's wings materialized, deep blue swirls of Magik wafted around her like the night sky. "Then let's get the others and rescue Si."

Magik pulsed under my skin like lightning, and the threads of every realm made themselves known to me. I reached for the familiar thread of Folkvang.

"Wait." Davlin looked between the two of us.

I nodded and let go of the Magik that would take me home.

"One minute." She glance between us, her gaze lingering on Davlin before she stepped away.

A small, sad smile touched his mouth. "Promise me something?"

I nodded.

"If it comes down to saving yourself," he placed a hand on my shoulder and squeezed. "Or him. Choose you."

"You of all people know I've never had a choice when it comes to him."

He dropped his hand and for the first time since I met him, I felt like our paths were diverging.

"You always have a choice, Kara." He leaned forward and kissed my forehead. "Never forget that," he said as he pulled back and smiled down at me.

I took a step back and let my Magik flood my veins.

"Talon?" Davlin gave her a pointed look. "Take care of her and yourself."

She nodded once and glanced at me. "Ready?"

I nodded and grabbed onto the thread of Folkvang as an explosion rumbled the earth beneath my feet. My brow furrowed, and I glanced at Talon as a scream pierced the night, freezing me to the spot.

CHAPTER TWENTY

KARA

Dust fell from the ceiling as another explosion made the building groan. Talon pulled her sword from its sheath, and Davlin started for the front door. I grabbed one of the swords lying on the table, and the hairs on my arm rose. I glanced at the front door as a wave of apprehension hit me square in the chest.

Not again. I chanted to myself.

This felt too similar to the morning I sent Magnus to the stars. I crossed the room and shoved my bare feet into the boots I'd discarded earlier.

Davlin swung the door open, letting in a burst of fresh damp air. Talon took one step and froze. I pushed past both of them, my Magik aching for release as I gripped my sword.

Flames licked up the side of the homes across from us and two bodies lay in the street. My breath caught in my throat as I ran toward them.

A fine mist of marine layer prickled my skin. And the hairs on the back of my neck rose as I slowed to a walk and approached the bodies. Their eyes—my mouth went dry.

"No," I breathed.

I knelt next to the younger of the two. His hollow cheeks and bright blue, unnatural eyes were a dead giveaway to what happened to him.

"Draugr," Talon growled under her breath behind me.

"The Disir are in Jotunheim."

Just saying their title made my Magik prickle with terror and excitement. As if it could taste their Magik in the air. I glanced up and down the street, searching the shadows, but there was nothing but flames, crumbling buildings, and cries for help.

The body twitched, sending my heart into my throat. I wasn't sure how long it would take for him to animate into the monsters I've come to know, and I didn't want to find out.

I stared down at the innocent man, turned Draugr, and pulled back his head, exposing his neck. I raised my sword with my other hand and came down on his throat with all my strength.

"Kara," Davlin yelled behind me as I dislodged the Draugr's head from his shoulders. "What in the name of the gods are you doing?" He grabbed my arm and hauled me to my feet.

Horror lined every inch of his face like I'd never seen before, and I ripped my arm out of his grasp.

"He's a Draugr," I snapped at him. "It had to be done."

He glanced at the dismembered body and back at me. His shoulders dropped, and guilt pinched his face as Talon removed the head from the other victim.

"I'll take care of the bodies. You two search for any others."

"I'll take the east, you take west," Talon blurted as she shot into mist covered sky.

"Be discreet." Davlin called after me. "The people of Jotunheim have no notion of the Draugr and Disir. They'll only see you killing their loved ones."

I nodded and headed west. A damp chill crept into my bones and I wasn't entirely sure it was because of the weather. My Valkyrie instincts were in full force with all the death around me. Thankfully, none were mine to ferry beyond this realm, but the melody of so many on the brink of death was breathtaking. The Disir Magik in me rattled against its cage, and I shook with the effort to keep it at bay.

As I rounded the corner onto the main street, dark gray smoke billowed into the sky, making the air heavy with the scent of wood, ash, and despair.

The citizens of Jotunheim ran from their homes, while others ran into buildings, hoping to rescue something or someone dear to their heart. Others huddled away from the burning buildings in their nightclothes, shivering and scared.

A guttural roar pierced the chaos, and a man fell to his knees as a body was dragged out of a burning house.

I ran toward the group huddled around the body, and my breath caught as my eyes landed on the prone form lying in the damp street.

She was so young, barely out of childhood. Her white nightclothes were stained with ash and charred along the hem. Her raven black hair was singed around the edges, and soot stained her pale skin, making it look like she was covered in bruises.

The burly man who screamed scooped her up in his arms, tears streaming down his cheeks, mouth wide open in a silent cry.

"Let me see her," I commanded with as much compassion as I could lace into my voice. I needed him to let me look at her, and I was sensitive to the position he was in. But if she was a Draugr—

I held my breath as the man who I assumed was her father laid her body back down.

There was nothing I could do to save her. Even without the Magik in my blood, I knew that her soul had already moved on from this realm.

Feigning like I might be able to save her, I felt for a pulse first—nothing. With a hope and a prayer to Ymir, I lifted the girl's eyelid. Hazel, unseeing eyes, stared up at the stars.

She was unchanged.

I closed her eye and sat back on my heels. My relief that she wasn't a monster was quickly replaced with sorrow for the ones she left behind.

"I'm sorry."

"She's all I have left," the man croaked and ran a hand over her hair. "Please." His hazel eyes, so much like the girls, met mine, glassy with tears. He grabbed my hand, engulfing mine with his larger than human grip. "Please."

"She's already at peace." It was the only thing I could offer him as I pulled my hand free. He slumped over the girl like a mountain, trying to protect the one he loved.

I'd seen more than my fair share of death and grieving. I'd mastered my emotions long ago when it came to the pleading of the living. It was easy not to take on their pain when I knew their loved ones were in their second life.

But the agony etched into the lines of his face. The way he looked at me like I was his last kernel of hope. It broke something in me.

Maybe it was because my grief was still fresh. Or maybe it was simply because I was tired of all the death.

"Hail to the beloved dead." I placed a hand on her cold arm as I recited the death prayer.

"Stand with us if you would," a chorus of solemn voices joined me. A crowd had formed around us and hands touched the father's shoulders.

"Smile on us, if you will. And may your light shine upon the realms, for all time."

I took my leave, letting the people who knew the family best bring the father comfort as I surveyed for anymore dead.

Lightning blazed across the sky, and unintelligible whispers whisked passed my ear, sending a shiver through my soul. I adjusted the grip on my sword and turned in a circle, searching for a glimmer of where the voices were coming from.

But there was no one. It was as if the shadows themselves had crept from their hiding place and lurked just out of sight.

I started down the street again and a shiver snaked up my spine as mist dotted my face. My gaze panned left to right, over my shoulder and straight ahead. There was nothing. No one who didn't look like they'd run from their bed, fire nipping at their heels.

It made little sense. Why attack a city just to watch it burn? I'd seen my fair share of attacks on sleepy villages, but it was for pillaging gold, raiding supplies, or, on several occasions, revenge. But that always ended in blood filling in the street.

This felt impersonal and nonsensical.

Another streak of lightning and the hairs on my arm rose as the tang of Magik filled my nose and called to my blood.

Kara. More than one voice slithered through the misty rain.

I turned around, scanning the faces of the men and women shivering in the cold, staring at their demolished homes.

Kaaarra. The voices purred in unison as warmth splayed across my stomach and tugged me to the right.

I moved toward a building whose fire had all but burned out. Embers glowed along the earth, but there was nothing but charred remains left. Stepping through the burnt remains. My boots crunched through the debris as I looked around for the source of the Magik calling to me.

Nothing.

I turned back the way I'd come and halted mid-step. The world before me was silently frozen.

Across the way, a woman with dark untamed hair wearing a gray sleeping gown was frozen mid-wail over a body in the street. Her mouth open wide, eyes scrunch closed, shiny tears staining her cheeks.

A few buildings over, flames engulfed the window so slowly I watched each lick of fire sway and dance as it destroyed someone's home.

Another structure to the right was mostly ash, except for the charred timbers. Tendrils of smoke stood frozen like sentries over the rubble.

And ahead of me, a smattering of sparks filled the sky. Embers hung in the air like bright stars methodically placed by the universe.

Time was warping around me. Slowing every person, every drop of water, every natural thing in Jotunheim.

Except me.

Kaaarra. The voices called from behind me and I turned in their direction.

"What do you want from me?" I yelled at no one and nothing.

Lightning streaked across the night. Each jagged strand traceable like a river on a map. It lit up the sky like Sol himself had risen from his slumber and carted the sun up just for me.

I followed the path of the lightning moving across the sky like an artificial horizon to a giant oak tree up on a hill.

Its branches stretched and twisted from the house sized trunk like the hungry tentacles of a monstrous sea beast reaching to the sky. The massive roots tunneled into the earth, fat and heavy, with enough strength to crush a horse. The canopy reached clear across the hilltop, looming like dragon wings over the city.

There was something about the lifelike branches that pulled at the back of my mind and I stepped toward the oak.

The Gods. Gooddssss. A harmony of voices hissed in my ear.

Must pay...they must pay for what...pay for what they've done.

The vitriol in their words pierced my heart and rage oozed through my blood, slow and merciless.

It was Odin's fault I was stuck in Midgard without my wings, my family, my friends. It was Loki's fault I killed all those innocent people, and ended Sigurd's mortal life.

The gods were to blame for everything! Power surged

through me and I balled my hands into fists as my heart threatened to beat out of my chest.

Kaaarrra. Their voices fanned the lava in my veins as my body moved of its own accord. There was no escaping their blind rage as it spread through me, echoing my own.

"They deserve to pay for what they've done," I said through gritted teeth as I reached the gnarled roots of the tree.

Lightning flashed again, and I was released from the trance. The rage receded like a wave leaving the shore for deeper waters, and the anger in my heart gave way.

I wiped the mist from my face and looked up at the canopy of leaves. They swayed to the ocean breeze and the lightning almost made them look like they were glowing blue.

I scanned the vastness of the tree. Looking for the Disir, when I noticed delicate burn marks across the middle of the trunk. I stepped closer and fear rooted me to the spot. They weren't some random markings, they were words...words meant for me.

There must be balance.

When you're ready, you'll know how to find us, Kara.

I ran my fingers over the rough bark, tracing each letter.

They brought me here. They wanted me to see this.

Lightning flashed so brightly, I lifted my arm to shield my eyes. A roar of thunder shuddered overhead, followed by the unmistakable snap of wood. A woman's broken sob pierced the air, and the crackle of fire returned.

"Kara!" Davlin's voice pierced through the fog, but the call of the Magik still held me in place. I read the words carved into the trunk again.

"Kara!" the Magik snapped, releasing its hold on me, and I let out a heavy breath as I turned toward the sound of his voice.

He wore a worried expression as he walked toward me. "You alright?"

I was still standing in the middle of the burned out building.

And the world around me resumed at normal speed. But the giant oak was nowhere in sight.

They'd done all this. Burned the city to the ground. And killed innocent people to send me a message.

Rage like I'd never felt before burned through me and something slithered through my core, hungry for revenge.

Talon dropped out of the sky, landing a few feet behind Davlin.

"I'm fine." I glanced over his shoulder at Talon. "Just pissed."

Talon flourished her sword and sheathed the blade. "Then let's put that anger to good use."

CHAPTER TWENTY-ONE

KARA

THE SOFT AROMATIC scent of earth and florals filled my nose as Folkvang bloomed under me. The streets were quiet, but the scars from the battle with the Draugr could still be seen everywhere I looked. A long row of homes below me had lost their roofs to flaming arrows, and some long houses had all but caved in. Patches of dark blood stained the cobbled street, marring the beauty of Folkvang. But it was the quiet that made my skin crawl.

It was the hush after a battle of too many heavy souls. It was the quiet of people taking stock of who and what were left. Folkvang was no longer the bright and merry home of the fallen, but a tomb that told the story of those who joined the stars most recently.

"Do you think the others are still up at this hour?" I asked as our boots touched down.

"After what happened at the rites, no one's been sleeping much." The flames in the lanterns above us glistened over Talon's dark skin and wings as she walked ahead.

"What exactly happened at the rites? I stepped in line with her.

As we walked through the quiet streets, she painted a picture of the horrors Odin unleashed on the mourners of Folkvang, and the threats he made if I wasn't delivered to him.

No one deserved to be tortured and threatened because of

some sick obsession the Alfather has with ending my life. Magik roiled inside me, slow and merciless in its quest to take over my senses. I had half a mind to give into the foreign Magik, and give Odin a reason to truly fear me.

I balled my hands into fists and breathed through my nose to keep my composure. I'd already put Talon on edge once tonight. I didn't need her thinking I was at risk of rupturing at any moment. Even if it might be the truth.

"Suffice to say, Odin made enemies of everyone at the rites. No matter how the others feel about you, they won't abide threats to their own." Talon stopped in front of a longhouse I'd never been to before.

"He has that effect on people." Warm light flickered in the windows, and the strained tone of muffled voices made it clear there was a heated discussion taking place.

Talon rasped her knuckles against the door, and the voices fell silent. The solid thud of boots against wood echoed through my chest like they were walking on my heart. I was nervous, and rightfully so. Ragnar wanted nothing to do with me, and Daiman regarded me with a haunted expression after everything he witnessed in the temple.

The door screamed on rusty hinges and a pair of curious eyes swept over the two of us before opening the door fully.

The tang of ale, mixed with the cloying smell of a fire, hit me as Asheria waved us inside with a tight lipped smile. Talon made her way across the threshold without hesitation.

"You're looking more like yourself," Asheria said under her breath. At least she didn't seem to hate me.

"Looks can be deceiving." There was no trace of warmth in my voice, and Asheria's brow furrowed in concern. "It's been a long night, for us all, by the looks of it," I amended. It wasn't her fault all my walls and armor were up for this meeting.

"Indeed," she sighed.

"What the Hel is she doing here?" Ragnar shot up from his seat at the large oak table that took up half the room.

"Be civil," Talon snapped as she pulled out a chair and took a seat. "We all want the same thing."

Chills ran up the length of my body as a heavy wave of soul songs crashed over me and I stilled.

"Do we?" Ragnar stared daggers at me, and it didn't go unnoticed that Daiman was quietly studying me as he threw another log on the fire.

And then there was Ezra, leaning against the far wall, looking as aloof as I've ever seen him. Surprised tinged with suspicion flickered through me at his presence. Based on how Si felt about him, I didn't think Ezra would have an interest in seeing Sigurd rescued. Though, I had to admit, it was nice having another person in the room who didn't look at me with some level of discomfort.

I allowed the Magik to rip through me slowly, like Davlin and I practiced. Then, little by little, I coaxed the hunger into submission piece by piece until I could fill my lungs with a breath that didn't make me want to devour them all.

I turned my attention to Ragnar. "I know you don't trust me, and that's fair. But let me make something perfectly clear." I closed the door and leaned against it now that I was fully in control of myself. "I will see Sigurd safely returned to Folkvang."

Ragnar's sea blue eyes scanned me from head to toe as the fire crackled quietly in the center of the room. No one spoke and I'm pretty sure no one breathed as we all waited for Ragnar to pass judgement.

Ezra pushed off the wall. "Then let's get to it." I appreciated his attempt to break the tension.

Ragnar's head snapped in his direction like a snake striking at prey.

Ezra shrugged. "You want to get him back? We're going to need all the help we can get."

"She's more likely to kill us than help us." Ragnar slammed a hand on the table, rattling the cups of mead and knocking an empty one over.

"Or am I the only one still mourning Magnus?" Ragnar stared at each one of them.

"You're being dramatic." Talon rolled her eyes and took a seat at the table. She grabbed the nearest cup, and tipped it toward her, inspecting the contents.

"Look around you." Ragnar threw his arms out, indicating the rest of the living space. My gaze travelled around the room with a quick sweep. Off to my left, behind a half draw curtain, a bed sat in the shadows. It was the only sign that this wasn't a small mead hall of some kind. This was someone's home.

"Look how few of us are left because of her." He pointed at me and I felt the stab of his finger from across the room.

"You're right." Talon folded her arm across her chest. "Magnus is gone. Si's been taken. Our friends are few and far between. We *can* storm Asgard just the five of us," she shrugged as if she didn't have a care in the world. "And maybe, if every-thing goes perfectly to plan, we can save him on our own. But she," Talon gestured in my direction. "Gives the three of you a better chance of seeing another sunrise."

"You know what gives us a better chance of not meeting the stars?" Ragnar raised his chin and narrowed his eyes at me in challenge. "Handing her over."

My stomach dropped, and the Magik in my blood snarled at the threat. But he was right. It would save them from me, but not Asgard.

"It would be safer," Daiman finally spoke up and my heart sank. He may have come to my aid, but it was clear he'd taken a side now that he knew the truth about Magnus.

"You could turn me over," I said, even though the Magik in me burned at the admission.

"Kara—"

"But," I cut Talon off. "It won't guarantee you'll ever see Si again." I let my words settle in the room like hot coals. "Odin could keep Si in Asgard, or kill him." The words tasted like ash in my mouth. "Even if Freya hands me over, it doesn't mean Odin will hold up his end of the bargain."

"She's right. If we want Sigurd home, we have to work outside of the gods." Asheria stepped forward, and all eyes swiveled toward her. "Besides, if Freya wanted to hand Kara over, she would've hauled her ass in here the moment Odin disappeared."

"She has a point," Talon agreed, and in doing so another chip fell in my corner. "If Freya was going to do something about Sigurd, she would have already."

Ragnar let out a huff of frustration, like a dog who knew he was beat. "You really think Freya would let war come to Folkvang just to protect her?" Ragnar addressed Talon.

"Freya would do a great many things, I fear to prove a point to Odin." Talon gave Ragnar a sympathetic look.

He was young, and idealistic about the gods and the justice they dolled out. But the Aesir and Vanir lived by their own rules, and their brand of justice rarely fit with a mortal's sense of right and wrong.

Ragnar stewed in silence as I waited to see what his next move would be. Was Sigurd worth it to him to work with me? Or would his hatred win out?

He turned toward me, slowly, as if it took all his strength. His jaw flexed like he was fighting the words as they formed in my mouth.

"A whiff of foul play from you and I'll gut you like a fish."

My Magik hissed at his threat as if to say, let him try.

"I'd expect nothing less." I nodded once in his direction and was ready to move on.

He shook his head, as if agreeing to work with me was the worst thing he's ever done. Which I highly doubted. He grabbed a stein off the table and stomped across the room to the small kitchen off to the left.

It wasn't a welcoming invitation, but it was as good as I was going to get. I didn't need them to like me. I just needed them to work with me to save Sigurd. Gods only know what manner of torture he's being subjected to.

"Alright then," Talon clapped her hands together. "Now that we're all on the same page. Let's get down to the details."

"The first thing I want to know is how you're able to leave Folkvang?" I asked. "Your second life is bound to this realm and Freya's Magik?"

"We haven't been bound to this realm for quite some time," Ragnar answered as he poured himself a mug of ale from one of the large casks set against the wall. "The rift that opened up a few months ago wasn't the first. It was just the first above ground." Ragnar walked back toward the group with the smug saunter of a man who knew more than the rest of us.

Ass. Both my mind and Magik were in agreement.

"I've been leaving Folkvang for the better part of a decade."

His words knocked the breath from my lungs. It was impossible for those in their second life to leave a realm of the dead. Once their soul was tied to Folkvang, Valhalla or Hel, the only way they could leave was by finding their way to the stars, or by the command of the god they were bound to.

"Ten years the wards have been failing, and no one knew?" I glanced around the room, waiting for someone to refute his claim.

"You think you're shocked?" Daiman scoffed. "Try being friends with the guy and finding out he's been keeping the Nine Realms to himself."

Ragnar looked like he wanted to shove a dagger into Daiman's eye. They were on the same side, but clearly there was tension there.

"These other rifts?" I asked. "They weren't healed when Freya repaired the one the Draugr came through?"

"Nope." Ragnar pulled out a chair at the head of the table and made it his throne.

"How has this gone unnoticed for so long?" I glanced at Talon again.

"My guess," Talon shrugged. "Freya knows the wards are failing, but there isn't anything she can do about it. Which is why it took her so long to *repair* the rift above ground."

"Are you telling me the rift is still an issue?" I asked.

"Yes and no, her Magik is keeping it together, but it's a temporary solution. It won't hold. It's already weakening." Talon reported the stability of Folkvang's defenses like a weather update.

"It would explain why patrols were doubled over the last few years," Daiman offered. "It's possible she wanted to make sure nothing got in."

"Or no one got out," I said under my breath.

"I hate to admit it, but red is right." Ragnar took a sip of his drink and refused to even look in my direction.

"Red?" I gave him a pointed look as he swirled the liquid in his stein, spilling a few drops on his shirt.

"Seems fitting, considering your hands are covered in blood."

My hands in question balled into fists as the Magik snapped in his direction.

"The same can be said for everyone in this room," Talon argued.

Ragnar's eyes met mine, cold as ice. "That may be true, but we are not the same."

Asheria cleared her throat and pushed off the wall. "We're all willing to spill blood to save lives, and in this case, Sigurd's. Let's focus on what's important."

"You won't get an argument from me," I glanced away from Ragnar to Daiman, only for him to give me a bored and slightly frustrated sigh.

"Talon was right about one thing," Ragnar started, ignoring the tension in the room. "I believe you're are an asset we can use."

"I don't know how I feel about the word *use*." I folded my arms over my chest.

Ragnar gave me a pointed look. "Odin knew you'd want to save Si. He said as much at the rites. We need to use that to our advantage."

"What like bait?" Asheria cocked her head to the side. "We can't trade one life for another."

"We won't be," Talon said with all the confidence in the world. "We just need Odin to think we're handing Kara over."

"He's going to want assurances we aren't playing him. He'll already be wary that Freya isn't the one making the trade." Daiman mused.

"We need to play our hand carefully," Talon splayed her hands on the table in front of her.

"Maybe he doesn't need to know that Freya isn't willing to trade," Ezra offered with a smirk.

"We're already going to have one god pissed at us," Daiman shook his head. "You really think faking a raven from Freya will do us any favors?"

Asheria pushed off the wall and stepped forward. "He's right, if she finds out—"

"Then we'll make sure she doesn't." Ragnar got to his feet and paced.

"As one of her personal guards, I can send the raven without drawing any suspicion." Talon offered without an ounce of hesitation.

"Once that's done, we make our way to Asgard and wait for the trade. Once Sigurd is produced, we grab him and get the Hel out of there." Ragnar continued with all the air of a king, mapping out his plan for world domination.

I can only imagine what a nightmare he must have been in his mortal life, if he was this self assured in his second life.

"You make it sound easy," Asheria snapped. "But we'll be lucky if we all get out of this alive."

"Even if that plan wasn't complete and utter garbage. It doesn't account for my freedom."

"You're the blood-thirsty Valkyrie. It should be easy for you to escape." The corner of Ragnar's mouth twitched, and I fought the urge to punch him through the wall and prove him right.

"Are you trying to start a fight?" Talon leveled her gaze at Ragnar.

"Not only does your plan not give Kara an exit," Asheria paced the small space. "It also doesn't guarantee Sigurd's rescue. Odin didn't say he'd return Si to whoever turned Kara over. He want's Freya to bend to his will."

"It depends on what game Odin's playing. Does he want to force a war with Freya or does he want Kara more?" Ezra mused.

"I'm guessing he wants both, but I can assure you, he wants to get his hands on me," I begrudgingly admitted.

"Don't you think highly of yourself?" Ragnar's words dripped with venom.

I curled my hands into fists and ignored him. "He took Sigurd, knowing it would draw me out. He's been torturing and punishing me for the better part of a century, and he wants the satisfaction of finally breaking me to his will."

"Why? What's so special about you?" Ragnar looked at me over the rim of his stein.

My heart battered against my ribs, and Daiman stiffened across the room. Ragnar didn't know what happened in the temple. He didn't know I carried the Disir's Magik inside me. I glanced at Daiman, and a kernel of gratitude bloomed in my core. He saw what I did, and yet he said nothing to Ragnar.

"Does it matter?" Talon snapped.

"If we're risking our lives, I think we should know why Odin has such an obsession with her."

"Is Sigurd not enough of a reason to risk your life?" I said through gritted teeth. He was wearing on my very thin nerves. "Is saving your home not enough of a reason?"

"None of this would be happening if not for you," Ragnar rose to his full height with a challenge in his eyes. "Your secrets have already gotten one of my brothers killed. I won't go into this fight blindly. So tell us. Why does he want you so badly?" Anger rolled off of him in waves, matching the fury burning in my blood.

"She killed Loki," Daiman blurted and my whole body froze like I'd been plunged into icy waters.

Panic crawled into my veins and turned me to a statue. I couldn't breathe. I wasn't ready to share my connection to the Disir. Especially not after all the trouble they went to, to leave me a message in Jotunheim.

A flash of Loki's soul song echoed through my bones, and his Magik curled through my core as Ragnar looked me over.

"You killed a god?" His eyes bore into me like he was searching for the lie buried in my soul.

"I did." My voice was husky with the taste of Loki's Magik.

"Good riddance." Ezra leaned back in his chair. "The man was a menace."

Ragnar sat back down, and I took a full breath.

My eyes met Daiman's, and he inclined his head ever so slightly. I wasn't sure what game he was playing or if he was playing a game at all. But I was grateful for his intervention.

"Can we move on?" Talon huffed. "It's not as if time is of the essence or anything."

"If someone has a better plan, I'm all ears." Ragnar placed his stein on the table.

"We need to find our way into the dungeons." Daiman stepped forward and took a seat at the table.

"I can help with that," Asheria perked up.

"What do you know of the dungeons in Asgard?" Ragnar's brow furrowed as he studied her.

"I'm one of very few who've found their way out without Odin's blessing." A secret smile touched her lips.

All eyes fell on Asheria as shock rippled through me. I had no idea she had been in the dungeons before.

"It's a story for another time." Asheria stepped forward and placed a map of Asgard in the middle of the table. "There." She pointed to one of the larger islands surrounding the mainland.

"You're sure?" I glanced at her. I'd flown over those islands a thousand times and there was nothing but beautiful beaches and untamed forests.

She nodded. "The prison is underground, far beneath the sea. It makes escape near impossible. Unless you know the paths in and out."

"Well then, isn't it lucky we have you?" Ezra clapped a hand on Asheria's shoulder.

"I wouldn't count any who lays a foot on that island lucky. Even if it's by choice." She tapped the island absently and the ghost of her past haunted her eyes.

"Asheria, if this is too much," Talon started. "We can find another way."

Asheria rolled her eyes. "I know you make it your job to worry about everyone, but I'm more than capable of deciding what I can and can't handle."

"I'm not saying you can't do this. I'm asking if you should? We can find a way that doesn't jeopardize your wellbeing."

Talon's words gave me pause, and I studied Asheria. I was

willing to sacrifice myself to save Si, but that didn't mean I'd force others to face their demons.

"Do you think so little of me, sister?" Asheria's brow furrowed, and she folded her arms. "Do you think me incapable?"

"I think we should weigh our options before we rush into anything."

Asheria scoffed. "You're unbelievable," she looked away from Talon. "Tell me this isn't because of what happened with Sif?" She cocked an eyebrow.

"Had we been more cautious, Sif wouldn't have ordered our heads piked," Talon grumbled.

"I distinctly remember you deviating from the plan and causing the fire that nearly destroyed her beloved ship."

"That was—"

"I'm sure this is a story for the ages, but is now really the time?" I interrupted them.

The two of them stared at each other, some silent conversation happening between them. The air in the room became thick and a spark of Magik sizzled over my skin.

Ragnar stood, shoving back his chair. "Either take it outside or get over yourselves. We don't have time for a pissing match."

Her gaze met mine and her lips formed a thin line. "If you ever want to see Sigurd alive again. This is the only way."

My heart rioted in my chest and I grit my teeth. Screw the Disir, screw Ragnarok, and screw the gods. I'd turn the Nine Realms inside out and let it all fall to ruins if it meant Si could live out the rest of his second life in peace. And if she was willing to go back into that prison, to save him. Who was I to stop her?

"Tell us everything you know," Ragnar spoke the words on the tip of my tongue.

It appeared we *could* agree on something.

CHAPTER TWENTY-TWO

WITH A POUNDING HEADACHE, I stepped out into the night and left Ragnar's longhouse, and made my way to Sigurd's place around the corner. We agreed to stay close by and get a few hours of rest before heading out at first light.

I heaved a sigh of relief as the cool night air hit my skin. It was a welcome reprieve after the heated discussion over the last few hours. I'm not sure what we did more of, argue over who was right or disagree on how to move forward. I knew working together wouldn't be a walk in the park, but gods, I wanted to rip my eyes out by the time we all agreed on a plan.

Ragnar was damn near insufferable. Anyone who managed to get along with him for any length of time was a glutton for punishment.

Daiman had been mostly pleasant by the end, but more than once I caught him watching me, like he was waiting for me to pounce and consume the souls of everyone in the room.

I couldn't blame him. Not after what he witnessed in the temple. If I could kill a god when I barely had the strength to hold myself upright, then how could he stand a chance against me?

As I reached Sigurd's place, my heart leapt into my throat and I hesitated at the door. The last time I was here, I'd spent the night lying next to Si with the promise that we'd figure things out together. My soul ached with the heaviness of how things had gone so wrong so quickly.

I'd give anything to go back to that night. Before Magnus, before Loki, and the Disir. I would have enjoyed the fragile peace we created. And I wouldn't have been so quick to keep him at arm's length.

I forced myself to turn the handle and pushed the door open. It wasn't a surprise that he left his door unlocked, most did in Folkvang. Until a few months ago, there wasn't anything they needed to protect themselves from in their second life.

I stepped inside and it felt smaller, emptier without him here. My heart contracted at the thought of where he was right now and I suppress the compulsion to abscond to Asgard without the others.

I closed the door behind me and the scent of wood, leather, and ash filled my nose. A flood of memories shot through me.

The desperate heat in his eyes when he said he was done pretending he didn't care about me. The brush of his lips that curled my toes. The feel of his skin under my fingers. And the way he held me close to him throughout the night.

My chest squeezed at the sweetness of that night, and tears pricked my eyes. I would get him back. I told myself for the millionth time since Talon showed up on Davlin's doorstep.

I moved further into his home, letting my fingers trail over the back of a chair. Moonlight pooled on the couch I spent half a night on, and spilled onto the floor in front of me. The blankets and furs on the bed were still mussed from when we left for breakfast with Magnus and Bryn.

I let the emotions I'd hidden away since I was last in Folkvang rise to the surface. Dark, oppressive clouds of grief and bolts of anguish consumed me.

I reached into the center of the storm swirling inside me and pulled on the constant thrum of my Valkyrie Magik. My skin pebbled with gooseflesh, and I sucked in a breath as I cleared my mind and opened myself up to the call of Sigurd's soul.

He was easy to find now that I knew where to look for him, and I sucked in a breath as the first note sang in my blood. My shoulders slumped, and I closed my eyes, basking in the melody that my heart knew all too well. Magik soared in my chest, but the relief of knowing he was firmly in the Nine Realms outweighed the hunger for power.

"I thought I might find you here." A voice said from the shadows and I turned on my heel, dagger half drawn and heart racing. My Magik turned its attention away from Sigurd and snapped toward Freya. The call of her soul, the power coursing through her, made my head spin and my hands shake.

"Your fondness for him is heartwarming, truly." She stepped fully out of the shadows and I took a step back. The Magik swirling off of her suffocated me, making it nearly impossible to see straight.

"If you're here to—" I exhaled as I tried to rein in the Magik. But this was all-consuming, like stepping into a fire and burning alive.

She raised a hand in dismissal. "I'm not here to hinder your plans to rescue Sigurd."

I took another step back and settled my dagger into its sheath. The last thing I needed was a weapon in my hand when the weapon inside me was struggling for control.

"Then to what do I owe the pleasure of your company?" My patience was razor thin and my body screamed for another taste of a god.

"I only wish for you to reconsider your involvement in his rescue." She stepped into the patch of moonlight. Her cream linen dress almost looked like it was glowing.

I took a deep breath and the sharper edges of my Magik ebbed. Allowing me a measure of control over my emotions.

"I thought he meant something to you? Do you not care

what happens to him?" The words felt like acid on my tongue. I didn't want to acknowledge their relationship.

"I don't envy the position *your* Sigurd is in." I didn't miss the emphasis on the word 'your', as if she was trying to quell the storm of jealousy inside me. "But he's stronger than you give him credit for." She huffed a humorless laugh. "Than I gave him credit for."

I took another deep breath, and I sat on the edge of the couch. Tendrils of Magik wove through my lungs, around my heart and into the depth of my Magik, trying to gain control. It wanted her power. I understood why the Disir didn't resist the call of the gods. I only had one taste, and now I couldn't take a single breath without wanting more.

I won't give in! I yelled inside my head and balled my hands into fists on my lap.

"He's no match for an angry god," I said through gritted teeth.

"No, he's not. But it's you Odin truly wants." Her gaze traveled up the length of me and her Magik hummed between us. "If you go to Asgard, he will find you, Disir."

My Magik snarled as icy cold shock flashed over my skin.

"You know?" The words were barely a whisper on my lips as I fought the surge of desperation flooding my senses and making my heart race.

Her eyes hardened. "Of course I know." She raised her chin with an heir of superiority. "I can feel it in your blood."

A tendril of her Magik slithered up my arm, and the Magik that belonged to the more unsavory parts of my ancestry slithered to the surface in a quiet, deadly rage.

Freya's soul pulsed around me and I dug my nails into my palms to hold on to a tiny window of clarity.

"You can feel—" Does that mean she's known since my first wing ceremony, when I was barely out of adolescence? "How long have you known?" The words came out like a growl.

She raised her chin and looked down at me through thick lashes. "I've always known."

Rage pumped from my heart like ink. Spreading through my body, poisoning every inch of me until there was nothing left but blind hatred.

The gods must pay for what they've done, echoed in my soul once more.

She knew I was like them, knew I might kill for power, and she said nothing. She knew when I asked her about Sigurd. She knew when she sent me to the Norns. She always knew, and she lied to me.

Liar! The Magik hissed, and I shot to my feet. I needed to move. I needed to scream. I needed to make her pay for—

No. I would not give into the rage inside me. I needed to get a grip. I took a deep breath and bit the inside of my cheek, drawing blood.

"Why didn't you say anything?" I barely recognized my voice as all-consuming fury shed its cocoon inside me and grew into a beast of its own.

"It was inconsequential." She waved a hand like my question was nothing more than an annoying horse fly.

"To you, maybe." Anger propelled me across the small space. "Everything that's happened over the last hundred years is because of the blood that pumps through my veins."

"Your story was already written," Freya continued like she didn't notice the Magik in me was changing the very air that she swallowed.

"Telling you what you are wouldn't have changed anything."

A short, humorless laugh escaped my throat. "You're wrong."

Her head snapped in my direction, but her face remained expressionless.

"The path I'm on wasn't written. It was created by some perversion of Magik."

Her lips twitched, but otherwise her features remained neutral.

"Created, written." She waved a hand. "Call it what you like. Your days have been numbered since the day you were born. But you have a choice to make now. Save yourself or save Sigurd."

The ballad of her soul pierced my bones, and my whole body shook with the effort to ignore it. I didn't want to be like them. I didn't want to crave the Magik inside her. But my bones ached with the effort to stay in control of my mind.

Don't fight it. A soft voice whispered into my ear.

I closed my eyes and took a deep breath. "I won't leave him to Odin's wrath."

"Let the others go in your stead. Your life is too precious to waste." There was an edge to her voice that raised the hairs on the back of my neck.

"Waste? Sigurd is not a waste." I snapped. I'd never spoken to Freya with such malice before, and I was more than a little surprised she wasn't putting me in my place. Unless she knew it was worthless to try.

"I know he's not. But Odin will kill you. He's feared the Magik in your blood for longer than you've been alive." She didn't look at me as she recalled the memory.

"Why didn't he kill me then when I was born?" The words were almost a plea. My death would end so much suffering.

"I stopped him." Her eyes were soft as her gaze met mine. "I believe the Norns bring everyone into the Nine Realms for a reason. And you were just a babe. Harmless. Innocent." She stared at the ceiling, her gaze on the past.

"I convinced him we should let you become a Valkyrie. I believed my Magik could tame your ancestry. And it did for a time." Her gaze met mine again, and a chill ran down my spine.

"Until Loki," I said, and she nodded.

She knew what happened in the temple. She knew I took

Loki's power for myself, and yet she didn't want me to die. My curiosity was peaked making it mildly easier to ignore the torrent of Magik swirling inside me.

"Now that the Disir have risen, not even I can erase the blood on your hands. I've delayed his hand for as long as I can. There is no staying his wrath this time. He will find you."

"Let him find me," I said through gritted teeth. "I'm not afraid of him anymore." The truth of my words burned bright in my heart and a swell of pride crashed over me. I'd spent too long fearing the Alfather. And if nothing else, this all-consuming Magik freed me from those chains.

"She's feisty, I like her." Both of our heads jerked toward the door. The air grew thick with the sultry melody of another god, and my skin flushed with the rush of Magik.

"Brother," Freya sneered. "What are you doing here?" She pushed her shoulders back and a mask of haughty indifference slid over her features. It was both amazing and terrifying to see her so easily flip between personalities.

Freyr walked into Sigurd's house like it was his own. A forest green cloak trailed behind him, and the hilt of a massive sword was visible at his side. He pushed the hood of his cloak back, and his bright green eyes locked on mine. Magik snapped through me like a whip and I took an involuntary stepped toward him.

"Whispers have reached my ears of your tiff with Odin, sister." He didn't take his eyes off me as he spoke.

His reputation didn't do him justice. He was devastatingly handsome, and it was no wonder he was rumored to warm every bed in Asgard. His chestnut hair was parted to one side, the other shaved, showing the swirls of a dark tattoo across his skull.

He wore a white shirt that shimmered in the torchlight from what could only be threads of silver woven into the fabric. And leather trousers that hugged his thighs. He was a beautiful man, and he knew it.

"Gossip from one of the many wives whose company you keep, nothing more." Freya played the role of annoyed indifference well.

"Then who is this spirited beauty?" He stepped closer, and I held my breath. His gaze travelled up my body, heating my skin. My Magik turned molten as the soft tune of his soul echoed through my chest.

"She's no one of consequence," Freya snapped at her brother, which only seemed to intrigue him more.

He clicked his teeth, and turned toward Freya. "If you must lie to me, then I won't bother sharing what else a little bird cooed in my ear."

Freya met his stare, the two of them having a silent battle of wills, giving me a moment to try to rein in the Disir Magik, begging for a taste.

"If you have something to say, Freyr, then go right ahead. Otherwise, I have a realm to command."

"Tell me who she is. Who she really is." He folded his arms across his chest, making the muscles in his arms bulge.

Freya turned toward him, stepping out of the beam of moonlight and casting her face in the shadows. "It appears you already know."

"Whatever you have to say, I doubt it's pertinent?" I sneered. "If memory serves me, you're the god of harvest and weather. Neither of which are helpful at the moment."

He sauntered toward me. "Don't forget fertility," he smirked.

I took a step back and folded my arms across my chest. "Another useless skill where I'm concerned." I sucked in a breath as I strained against the insistent Magik looking for the chink in my armor.

He cocked an eyebrow at me and I swear the corner of his lips twitched.

"Say what you've come to share or get out," Freya ordered.

"Fine," he grumbled. "If it means you'll pull the stick out of your ass, and stop acting—"

"Choose your next words wisely, brother," Freya's Magik turned the room glacial. "Or I'll freeze your prick right off of you." Her words were punctuated with tiny puffs of breath.

"Point made." He pulled his cloak tighter, as if he knew she wasn't bluffing. "Odin plans for war, even if he gets his fat fingers on her." He nodded in my direction.

"You think I don't already know that?" She scoffed.

I stepped forward, shoving the Magik aside as the desperate need to protect my home out weighed the hunger inside me. "You can't go to war with Odin, he'll—"

Freya snapped in my direction. "You forget, I've spent centuries curating my army, knowing this day would come."

"And she has me," Freyr winked.

"Once again, you show up at the end to collect a piece of the glory. Pathetic." The chill in the room renewed. I let my wings unfurl gently and wrapped them around me for warmth.

Ignoring the frost in the air, he stepped closer to his sister and pinched her chin between his thumb and forefinger. "You've always been an entitled brat," he breathed, a puff of warm air escaping his lips. "Too good for the rest of us, too proud. Mark my words, it'll cost you."

She shoved his hand away and her eyes darkened. "As if it hasn't already cost me everything."

"You still have a realm. You still have your life, your Magik. Some would say you haven't lost a thing. Not yet."

Shivering, I realized they were talking about something bigger.

"Are you threatening me?" Her voice was lethal, and Magik filled every crevice of Si's home. My head swam with the heady ballad of their souls as exhaustion settled deep in my bones.

"I'm warning you. This is bigger than one, Disir." He

motioned over his shoulder at me. "He'll stop at nothing to take Folkvang for himself."

Freya smiled, and the ice in the air dissipated. "You underestimate me, brother."

"I wouldn't dare." He held his hands up. "But you should know, he's made a trip to Lyngvi island."

Freya went visibly stiff and her eyes widen ever so slightly.

"I see." She turned to me, and the haunted look on her face made my skin crawl. "Then it's time we prepare for Ragnarok."

Every nerve in my body zapped to attention. Fear and confusion poured into my chest as my Magik prickled along my skin. I'd failed the Norns. I'd failed us all if Ragnarok was so close Freya could taste it.

She crossed the room and placed a hand on my shoulder. "You alone must choose your path." Her eyes met mine and my skin flushed with nerves. "You survived the temple for a reason. Don't throw it away on the whims of your heart."

She stepped around me, and the door creaked open. I could feel that they were gone before the door softly closed.

Fury and a desperate need to expel the energy inside me propelled me across the room until I reached the bed. I grabbed one of the pillows and screamed out all the rage and heartache into the down feathers. My lungs ached and my throat burned as rage far beyond my own soul poured out of me.

Show the world who you really are. The voices whispered, and this time I didn't try to ignore them.

SIGURD

IT HAD BEEN another two days since my visitor when the lock on my door sounded, pulling me out of my slumber. As I sat up, the door swung open and Bryn appeared on the threshold. She still wore her mourning colors and leather trousers, but this time, she wore a sword at her waist and a chest full of armor. Her alabaster hair was tied up in dozens of twists and braids, making her look more like a Valkyrie than I'd ever seen her.

I waited for her to say why she was here, but she just walked toward me without closing the door. I glanced over her shoulder, but there appeared to be no one with her. Had she come to her senses? Was she here to set me free? A blossom of hope unfurled in my chest as she grabbed the chain connecting my manacles. Her dark brown eyes met mine, and it was as if all the life had gone out in her gaze.

This couldn't be good.

The woman I laughed with. Who teased Magnus and exuded warmth was gone. She was cold, hard and empty as she pulled on my chain, forcing me to step forward as she started toward the door.

Curiosity mixed with trepidation destroyed the bud of hope before it had a chance to take root. Either Freya made the deal, and I was being handed over, or it was time to meet the stars.

I thought about asking her where she was taking me, but if

she was going to tell me anything, she would have. So I stayed quiet as she closed the door to my prison behind us.

The hall was much darker than I expected. Cool, damp air brushed over me, and it was a welcome reprieve from the stale air of my prison. The smell of freshly turned earth filled my nose, removing the last remnant of Odin's rotting apple.

A faint glimmer of torchlight flickered up ahead as Bryn turned toward the left. I marked the first change in our route as she guided us down a crudely dug out tunnel lined with heavy wood doors that looked just like mine. As I passed one of the doors, gooseflesh pebbled my skin. How many prisoners did Odin keep down here?

Bryn turned again—another left—dragging me with her, and my heart beat a little faster. There was a helplessness in this place that settled into my bones and sucked the light and hope from my soul.

For a brief moment, I considered making a run for it, but my instincts tugged on my core. As much as I hated being patient, it was better to hold position and learn what I could before making a move.

All was silent except for the small telltales signs of the other prisoners behind their doors. The jangle of chains, a wet cough, boots pacing back and forth, soft weeping, and the familiar whoosh of wings. My stomach hollowed and my heart spasmed at the symphony of suffering.

A quick right turn took me off guard and then another left. I was sure she was leading me in circles. Which meant she didn't want me memorizing the route we were taking. Which also meant she probably wasn't leading me to my death. There was no point in trying to confuse me if I was about to meet the stars.

We walked, and walked, and walked. Another left, then right. Through a door, then to the left. I thought we were moving further underground when the temperature dropped, but the steep incline said otherwise.

"While I enjoy a good mystery, are you ever going to tell me where you're taking me?" My voice boomed off the stone floors and echoed around us as she led us up a stone staircase.

She glanced over her shoulder at me. "Odin wished for you to see something."

"Can't imagine the horrors he has in store," I grumbled. I had no doubt this was another ploy to get me to do his bidding. But whatever it was, I wasn't interested. I'd made up my mind about Kara.

We made it to the top of the stairs and walked down another long corridor. She slowed to a stop and instead of turning one way or the other, Bryn unlocked the door in front of us and pulled it open.

Bright golden light poured over me, and I shut my eyes, unable to bear the harsh light after days spent in the dark. A cool breeze wafted over me, and I inhaled deeply. The salty-sweet smell of the sea banished the shadows I'd been living in and made me feel alive once more.

As my eyes adjusted to the morning light, I looked out across the horizon. Islands, some small, some large, peppered the sea as far as the eye could see. And at the bottom of the hill, a ship sat in the breaking water, carrying a dozen warriors all armed to the teeth.

My stomach tightened as a wave of adrenaline swirled through me. There was more than enough brute strength in that boat to take on a small village. Which begged the question. What did Odin want me to see exactly?

"Go on," Bryn pulled me forward. "We don't have all day." She scoffed and yanked on my chain, guiding me down a slope of sand and wild flowers.

As much as I didn't like the idea of getting in a boat with a handful of warriors loyal to Odin, I didn't resist or try to run. There was something about the crisp morning air and the hiss of the sea as it covered the sandy beach that felt familiar. Like I'd been here before.

My boot sunk into the sand as I reached the shore and my heart sped up as Bryn tugged me forward. The wind rustled my hair as I stepped up to the boat, and I knew without a doubt I would not return to this island as a prisoner.

Bryn handed my chain to one of the men, and I hauled myself on board. A wave crashed on the shore, and the boat gently rocked under us.

I turned toward the beach as we pushed off into the sea. Wild flowers of every color, and tall grass covered the hills leading to the sandy beach. Beams of sunlight broke through the clouds, shining down on pockets of charcoal rocks atop the highest hill. A handful of birds flew overhead as a wave crashed on the shore. It looked so serene that for a moment it was hard to believe what lay beneath.

Guilt pierced my core. How many innocent lives were still hidden under the flowers? How many would never see the sun again or taste a breath of fresh air? If I survive this, I promised I'd come back one day and free everyone from the depths and bring them back into the light.

"It's starting," one of the men yelled, pulling my attention away from the island and toward the prow of the ship. A small boat came into view from behind one of the smaller islands ahead, and I stepped forward to get a better look.

A torch stood at the prow of the boat, the flame whipping in the breeze. Bright blue florals mixed with an array of greenery lined either side of the ship, trailing into the water. And in the center of the boat, I could just make out a figure lying amongst the flowers.

My heart sank as the sun moved behind the clouds and the warmth of the morning light dulled as another boat came into view. It bore a torch and flowers as well, but instead of a prone form, there were three people sitting in the center of the boat, all dressed in a midnight blue.

"Who's burial rite is this?" I glanced at Bryn out of the corner of my eye as another boat carrying the dead rounded the corner.

"This is the last rites for all those killed by Kara."

An icy chill crept out of my heart and through my body, freezing me to the spot. Another boat carrying a family of four followed the deceased and my heart all but stopped.

"Odin offered their families the honor of an Asgardian burial."

I had no words as I watched boat after boat, filled with the dead, and their mourners gently glided past us on the calm water.

One more boat followed the procession, larger than the rest. And where the others had flowers, this ship was lined with torches and soldiers. Toward the back of the ship, Odin stood proudly. He wore the morning colors as well under heavy gold armor and his gaze held firm on the boats ahead. He looked like the god I'd heard about in stories, proud and powerful.

I couldn't help but look on with reverence as he gave these families what little peace he could offer their grieving hearts. And though I'd already said goodbye to Magnus, I took a moment to hold his memory in my heart.

"I know you believe Kara can be saved," Bryn kept her voice low. "I understand that now." I glanced at her, but her entire focus was on the boats in front of us. "But too many have already suffered at her hands. How many more boats have to burn?" She turned to me and her eyes met mine. "Before you accept that the woman you care for died when your mortal life ended?"

An ancient ache formed in the pit of my stomach as I took in each grieving family. Even though I knew their loved ones were in their second life, safe and on a new path, I couldn't help the anger that rose in me.

None of them should have died.

But if I wanted to get out of here alive, I needed to start playing along.

"Maybe she isn't who she used to be," I finally said. "But it's hard to let go of the past when it still feels within reach."

A raven landed on the dragon head stationed at the prow of the ship. The bird's head cocked to the side, studying us as it bounced on the smooth wood surface. It looked like the same bird that was perched on Odin's shoulder at the rites in Folkvang, and the hairs on my arms stood on end. Its onyx eyes blinked, and it let out a caw before it took off toward the west.

"I don't envy the position you're in," Bryn sighed. "But you have to make a choice. It's her or the rest of us." Her words echoed my visitors, and an overwhelming sense of dread filled my chest.

CHAPTER TWENTY-FOUR

KARA

RAGNAR GUIDED us by torchlight through a series of tunnels that led to the rift he'd used to leave Folkvang over the last decade. Thankfully, the tunnel was both tall and wide, giving me breathing space to control the Magik inside me. I was getting used to the call of their souls, but it still took a substantial amount of effort to ignore it.

I adjusted my shoulders, getting used to the weight of the armor typically reserved for Freya's personal guards. Talon had arrived at Sigurd's just before dawn and insisted I wear the impenetrable breastplate. And heavy shoulder guards that reminded me of horse blinders. I felt a little ridiculous, considering my wings, and Magik had always been my best defense.

Not to mention the newly acquired power coursing through my veins.

I glanced up at the ceiling made of dirt, rocks, and dangling roots, and I wondered how Ragnar even found this place. The smell of damp earth filled the cave, and my lungs ached for a breath of fresh air.

Mist clung to the floor and swirled around our boots with each step. A twig snapped like a bone and every nerve in my body went taut. The scuff of boots and rustle of rocks dislodging themselves around us made my skin crawl. Gods, I hated enclosed spaces.

Time was running out for the Nine Realms. And yet, we

were taking the slow route to Asgard when we should be flying. I had half a mind to leave them all and let my wings take me to Asgard.

"Breathe," Talon leaned in the moment I reached for my Magik.

"I am," I said through gritted teeth.

She glanced at me from the corner of her eye, and I took a deep breath to prove the point.

"Is it the mission or something else?" She asked under her breath. The lie was on the tip of my tongue. It would be easy to tell her I was worried about Si and Odin. Which was true, but it was only half the reason every nerve in my body was strung tighter than the strings of a tagelharpa.

"Freya paid me a visit last night." I kept my voice low and slowed my pace as Ragnar veered toward the right.

"Things are far worse than we realize." I met her eye.

Talon glanced at the others ahead of us and looked back at me, eyebrows raised in question.

"Not here." My eyes found Ragnar in the firelight.

"You don't trust him." She glanced at Ragnar and back at me.

"Do you?" My brow furrowed. She knew him better than I did, but I couldn't imagine he was any more likable or trustworthy after a few decades.

She shrugged. "He's difficult, keeps his cards close to the chest. But he's never given me a reason to doubt him."

"And what about him leaving Folkvang for the better part of a decade with no one knowing? Gods only know where he's been, what he's been up to, or what alliances he's formed outside of Folkvang." My fears tumbled out of me. I didn't trust a man who kept as many secrets as he did.

"You've been gone a long time. You forget how mundane their lives are now. Can you blame him for seeking adventure?" She shrugged, like his leaving Folkvang was the most natural thing in the world.

"It's his ability to keep a secret, even from those closest to him, that makes me wary."

"We all have secrets." She stared ahead, and I got the impression she wasn't just talking about Ragnar. "Will you punish him for his when you guard yours with every weapon in your arsenal?" She gave me a pointed look and frustration heated my chest and face.

"We're here," Ragnar called over his shoulder and placed the torch in a sconce on the very solid wall in front of him.

It was a dead end.

The hairs on the back of my neck stood straight up and Magik ignited like tinder to a flame under my skin. I reached for the dagger at my thigh discreetly. I knew I was being rash, but I slept very little after Freya's departure, and my wariness of Ragnar had ramped up my paranoia.

A cool breeze caressed my skin, and the torchlight flickered. We were deep in the mountains. There shouldn't be a breeze here.

"So, how does it work?" Ezra stepped forward and reached a hand out toward the wall.

Ragnar grabbed his arm. "Patience. You wouldn't want to get lost in the void."

"The void?" Asheria asked, as Ezra pulled his arm out of Ragnar's grip.

"The place beyond this wall is the absence of life and existence." Ragnar turned toward the group. "It's both beautiful and terrifying. And from what I can tell, it doesn't seem to be a part of any realm. It's the space between them, leading everywhere and nowhere if you're not careful."

"He can't be talking about what I think he's talking about, can he?" I glanced at Talon, but she was watching Ragnar with renewed interest.

"I've never heard of anyone other than Valkyrie being able to access the Nowhere." Talon glanced at me and back at Ragnar.

"And we pass right through it," Asheria added as she sidled up next to me. "It never occurred to me it might be a physical place as well."

My conversation with Talon in the library—what felt like eons ago—came to the forefront of my mind. If someone like Loki could access the Nowhere, then maybe that's how he evaded the Norns' vision.

Neither of us thought it was possible at the time, but many things have changed since then. It explained how Loki and the Draugr gained access to Folkvang unnoticed and how he carried out his plan to wake the Disir with little effort.

"I have two rules." Ragnar eyed everyone in the group, his gaze lingering on me for a beat longer than the rest. "Don't let go of the person in front of you. And never stop moving, no matter what you might see or hear."

"That's not ominous at all," Daiman joked, but by the set of his shoulders, he was anything but relaxed.

"Right." Ragnar turned around and pat his shoulder. "Everyone, grab hold of someone. We've got a man to bring home."

Talon shuffled to the front of the group and placed a hand on Ragnar's shoulder. Daiman was next, then me. Ezra stepped behind me, and Asheria picked up the rear.

Ezra gave my shoulder a reassuring squeeze. "I knew getting to know you would be an adventure."

Not for the first time, I wondered why Ezra was joining us on this mission. From what I could tell, he and Si were barely acquaintances.

"Don't sound too excited. You may meet the stars before this is over."

"If I do, then at least I'll be doing something worthwhile for a change."

Guilt pierced my heart, and I wondered if my Magik was making me paranoid. Talon was right. They craved adventure and while Folkvang was wondrous, it lacked the genuine risk that made life worth living.

"Everyone ready?" Ragnar called.

One by one, we sounded off.

Ragnar took a step, then another until he stepped right through the wall and disappeared. My eyes widened and surprise flickered through me. He really was telling the truth.

Daiman took another step, and he was through the wall, half of my arm disappearing with him, and then it was my turn. I stepped into what should have been a solid, damp and rocky wall, only to pass right through it. Magik prickled along my skin like ice and a light breeze pulled loose strands of my hair in every direction.

With each step, the path ahead of me grew darker and darker, until there was nothing. Not the outline of anyone in front of me. Not the faint shape of the cave walls on either side of me. Complete and utter darkness like I've never experienced before.

I took another step and when my boot touched down, I could no longer feel the solid dirt beneath my feet. It was almost like I was flying, but there was no pull on my body toward the ground. I felt untethered, set free from the ties of the material world.

For the first time, I understood why Si hated flying so much. It was the lack of control, the utter feeling of hopelessness as the world at your feet disappeared.

I looked up, down, left, right, and over my shoulder, but everything was the same nothingness. As if we'd stumbled upon some unwritten part of the universe. Unease slinked through me like rotten food and turned my stomach. I didn't know how to move forward, or if my next step would be one too many and I'd lose myself to the darkness between realms.

The smell of rain against stone and fragrant peppermint leaves filled my nose. A smile kissed my lips at the familiar scent of Nidavellir, as the thread of the dwarf realm called to the Magik inside me like a friend.

This really was the Nowhere. The darkness between realms that I've passed through like a shooting star a million times. There was a beauty to the darkness I've never been able to enjoy before. Like being swaddled in a velvet blanket of Magik and it soothed my frayed nerves.

As we continued our march through the void, an earthy, smokey scent I'd known anywhere wafted over me.

The poppies of Asgard.

It was a delicate aroma. Almost too soft to notice, but I played in fields of poppies as a child and their elusive perfume was burned into my memory.

After a dozen paces, tiny pinpricks of light winked into existence and dotted the darkness in every direction. Their light was faint and felt both distant, and right in front of my eyes.

Looking around, the shadows lessened. Giant tangled arches and gnarled structures loomed over us and all around us. Their twisted form took on a familiar shape as more specks of light filled the emptiness.

They were roots.

Roots so massive they looked like distant mountains that blended with the sky. The sheer size of them was so overwhelming they didn't look real against the black canvas all around us.

"Is that...are we?" Ezra's voice was a reverent whisper behind me.

"Yggdrasil." I stared up at the gargantuan tree of life.

More bright blue stars—no, not stars, leaves—glowed all around us like the night sky.

"So, you're telling me, Yggdrasil, the tree of life was just through one of Ragnar's tunnels all this time?" Daiman scoffed, and I shared the sentiment.

"Yggdrasil is everywhere all the time," Talon's words almost sounded muffled. Like the nowhere was feeding on the sound of our intrusion.

"It's no more here than it is in Folkvang, in Midgard, in Jotunheim. It exists in every realm, all at once," Talon explained, like she was telling a bedtime story. "You only see it now, because there's nothing to turn your gaze. No sky or sun or life for it to hide behind."

"You've seen it before?" Ezra's deep voice was close behind me and it sent a chill down my spine.

"Not like this. We pass through here faster than lightning."

My gaze travelled the length of one of the massive roots to my left, all the way to the trunk. My eyes rose, up, up and up. The trunk looked more like a cliff side, until branches speared off of it in every direction.

"It's beautiful," I exhaled. A quiet calm settled over my chest as I stared up at the tree that brought life to the Nine Realms.

"I'd never seen it's equal." Ezra echoed what I felt.

"We have to keep moving. The longer we dither, the harder it'll be to find our way." Ragnar called from the front of our line, and I forced my eyes back to the path ahead.

A faint light flickered directly in front of us like a flame dancing upon a wick. And I knew in my bones where it would lead. Asgard.

A screech pierced the darkness, shattering the peace. We all froze as one and my heart leapt into my throat.

"What the sorðinn Hel was that?" Ezra snapped behind me.

Shadows took shape on either side of us, and the Magik inside me opened a curious eye.

"Run," Ragnar yelled as the closest shadows lunged toward us.

CHAPTER TWENTY-FIVE

KARA

LONG OBSIDIAN CLAWS reached for me and I dropped to my knees, losing my grip on Daiman. I pulled the dagger from the sheath around my thigh and another screech vibrated through the Nowhere.

The wraith passed over me. Their cloak of shadows, and midnight torrent of untamed hair, billowed like a capsized sail in water. Its bone white complexion was almost translucent, dark veins crisscrossing its face. Its sharp angular cheekbones and nose bore the hint of femininity. And its large pearlescent eyes stared right into my soul. A shiver crawled over my skin, and my mouth went dry as the first prickle of fear bloomed in my chest.

"What the Hel are those things?" Ezra panted right behind me.

"Mara, wraiths of the night. They're lost souls that bring your nightmares to life." I scanned the area, but they were impossible to see in the dim lighting. "Don't let them touch you. One touch and they'll get inside your head and kill you."

He nodded, blade already drawn as another ear splitting screech crashed around us, like waves on the shore. Gooseflesh rose all over my body and I sucked in a breath. I tried not to focus on the prickling sensation bubbling inside me. They could smell fear and once they got their claws into your mind, it was almost impossible to escape.

"Weapons won't do you any good." Asheria huddled next to us. "So long as there is a soul alive that fears the dark, they'll thrive."

"We need to get out of here." I stood and grabbed Ezra's hand. "Don't let go," I ordered.

I pulled on my Magik and searched for the threads of Asgard. Every realm twisted together like gnarled roots, making it impossible to tell where one realm started and another ended. I couldn't grasp onto any of them as a surge of helplessness blurred my vision.

On foot it is.

I started in the direction we'd been going and hesitated. There was no one in front of me. Not to my left, nor right. Ragnar, Daiman, and Talon were gone. Either they'd already escaped, or—fear spiked in my heart and my lungs sucked in one too many shallow breaths. The bitter taste of the Mara's Magik coated my tongue as the temperature plummeted. I started forward, remembering one of Ragnar's rules—Don't stop moving.

Out of the corner of my eye, the darkness rippled. I turned, dagger raised as razor sharp teeth snapped toward me and bit my dagger in half. The Mara cocked its head to the side like a bird and its lips curled into a toothy grin. Several rows of teeth gleamed in the dim blue light as it leaned in and sniffed me.

I threw the broken dagger to the ground and kicked with all my strength. The Mara bolted into the air and I ran, dragging Ezra along with me.

I had no idea if I was going the right way or if I was driving us further into the darkness. The beacon of light guiding us to Asgard had vanished. I looked in every direction, but the only light came from the blue leaves of Yggdrasil.

My legs burned, and my heart raced as I pushed forward, searching for a way out of the dark, when Ezra's hand was ripped from mine and a deep guttural scream pierced me like an arrow.

"Ezra!" I came to a screeching halt and turned in a circle, looking for him.

He screamed again, the sound coming from above me.

Two Mara tossed him back and forth like a child's toy high above me. I could barely make him out, as they moved further into the darkness.

It couldn't end like this. I couldn't lose someone else.

Fear and anger bubbled up my throat, and my Magik crackled to life. My wings erupted from my back, and I shot toward Ezra. He screamed again, and I was close enough to see the deep gashes in his arm as he thrashed against the Mara.

"Kara, behind you," Asheria yelled from somewhere below me. I banked to the right as dark shadows swirled toward me. A flash of white caught my eye, and I tucked my wings in tight and flipped backwards. My wings snapped open, catching me in midair.

Three Mara floated between me and the monsters toying with Ezra.

My hands balled into fists as I stared at each of them. Fury burned through my veins as the Disir Magik in me begged for release.

The Mara in the center licked its teeth.

"We haven't seen one of your kind in an age." The one on the left spoke in a raspy, serpent voice.

I didn't have time to wonder if I should let my Magik free, when Ezra whimpered and his head bobbed back and forth lifelessly. I let every ounce of Magik burn to the surface. My skin felt tighter, my senses sharper. The darkness was no longer menacing as light bloomed around me.

I wouldn't let him die when I could do something about it, even if it meant channeling the darkness of the Disir.

Sparks burst behind my eyes. Every muscle in my body flexed and burned as a well of Magik spilled over and flooded my senses. My heart slowed to a steady beat and a deep sense of calm and clarity settled over me.

"Allow me to remind you what my kind are capable of."

Magik rippled off of me like a dozen honed arrows and I shot forward, grabbing the robes of the Mara to my right as the other two scattered.

Sharp finger like talons bit into my skin as it wrapped its hands around my forearms. The Mara's Magik needled along my arm like a thousand bee stings. I met its stare and let a wave of Magik from deep within me fall over the Mara like a tidal wave. I poured every ounce of hatred and grief into my Magik. I let it feed on all my sorrow and heartache, drowning the Mara in my misery.

It felt good to let go, to let the Magik take hold and let it scream through me. It was death by fire, burning me from the inside out, releasing me from the guilt, pain, and anguish.

The Mara's eyes widened, its mouth opened in a soundless cry. The light in its eyes flashed once, twice, and then went dark.

I released my grip, and the Mara fell like a stone through water, disappearing into the depths of the Nowhere.

The two monsters fighting over Ezra snarled, their screams ripping through the air, making the blue leaves shutter and wink. As if their anger alone could blot out the tree of life.

The Mara dropped Ezra and stared at me for a heartbeat. "Monster," they snarled, then scurried back to the shadows where they came from.

"Kara," Ezra bellowed, and I dove after him with my heart in my throat.

I killed that Mara to save Ezra, I told myself.

Yes, but didn't it feel good? Powerful? A voice purred in the back of my mind.

Wings of night shot out of the shadows and headed right for Ezra. "I've got him," Talon yelled over her shoulder as she caught Ezra. "Find Daiman." She flew off without another word.

My wings slowed my descent, and I hovered for a beat, letting my nerves unclench. I searched the endless sea of nothing below me, the shadows and leaves above me. I dashed to the right, eyes peeled for any sign of Daiman, then doubled back to the left. But there was nothing, and no one.

My heart thrummed against my ribcage with a renewed ferocity. And a drop of fear poisoned my blood. The Mara's teeth chattered like a thousand birds pecking the bark of Yggdrasil, echoing all around me, but they didn't show their faces.

I doubled back, hoping I'd find Daiman if I flew lower, when my Magik tugged on my core and I halted. It was as if I'd reached the end of a long rope tied around me and I couldn't move any further. Chills ran the length of my arms and legs, and my mouth went dry. The undeniable sensation of being called to someone's death was one I was familiar with. My heart sunk into my stomach as the first note of Daiman's soul song burned my bones like a brand.

A waterfall of blind terror bombarded me. "No." The word escaped on an exhale. Daiman couldn't die. He couldn't meet the stars.

I wouldn't let anyone be taken in this soulless void.

Magik surged in me, making it easier to see, easier to fly. Easier to feel the music of a soul leaving the universe.

I doubled back and frantically scanned the darkness. "Come on Daiman, where are you?"

The roots of Yggdrasil stood proud and ominous on my left. The glow of the blue leaves dangled closer as another low, soft note sang through the darkness, and I veered to the right on instinct.

"Daiman," I called for him, but my voice was swallowed up

by the endless expanse of nothing. My wings beat faster, propelling me through the Nowhere like a ship with the wind at its back.

A flash of silver darted across my vision so quick I almost didn't notice it. I dove, scanning the area as another peel of music soared inside me.

There.

My eyes zeroed in on Daiman, dragging himself with one arm, sword drawn in the other. His long dark hair was caked to his face with blood and his skin was ghostly pale.

A dozen Mara hunted him. Shadows swirling like a whirlpool around him. Claws tore at his legs as he swung his sword at the empty air.

Fury burned in my blood as I tucked my wings. I shot toward the wraiths of the night like an arrow shot from the bow of the hunter god, Ullr.

My hair whipped past my face as Magik zipped along my skin. My skin flushed and my heart raced as a scream tore through me.

A long sharp note whined off Daiman, making me suck in a breath. He didn't have long. Fear punched through me as my eyes met his through the snarl of cloaks and claws.

A dozen sickly pale white faces all turned toward me as I landed a few feet away. Daiman dropped his sword, and his body slumped to the ground behind them.

Teeth and tongues lashed out at me as the Mara swarmed like hungry fish.

"Hold on Daiman," I ordered, but the only acknowledgement I got from him was a quiet plea for death to come quickly.

Magik surged in my chest, begging me to take his soul for myself. And a wave of hot disgust rolled through me. There'd be plenty of time to hate myself later. All that mattered right now was saving Daiman.

The first Mara flew toward me, then the next. A sharp strike of Magik jumped off me like a snake on instinct. The power of it took me by surprise as it incapacitated one of the wraiths.

The heat of this Magik differed from the Disir Magik I channeled earlier. This was full of calculated rage and mischief.

This was Loki's Magik.

I smiled, welcoming the crash of power inside me and stepped toward the Mara. A kernel of energy grew in my core, its roots tunneling into my soul.

Movement caught my eye to my right, and I threw out a hand. My fingers wrapped around the Mara's throat and its eyes widened. My skin glowed, like the sun was rising from inside me. The Mara screamed, an awful dying animal sound that echoed through the dark. It squirmed and kicked. It tried to claw at my arm, but the light burned its talons the moment they touched me.

The others shot off in every direction, scattering like rats.

"Let...it...go," Daiman struggled to breathe.

I looked away from the Mara to Daiman, lying on the ground unable to lift himself up. His dark eyes met mine and all I could see was Sigurd. Magnus. And all the other souls I was forced to kill.

But I didn't care. Not when my Magik rippled under my skin, making me feel powerful. Unstoppable.

The Mara screamed again, fighting against my light with everything it had.

"Kara," Daiman croaked. Another deep strum of music hit me and the Disir Magik made my head swirl. "Don't give...in" he sucked in a breath like it might be his last.

My hand shook as I looked back at the Mara. I wanted to kill it. I wanted the wraith to feel the pain and fear they caused Ezra and Daiman. I wanted it to pay for laying a hand on them.

Take your revenge. Whispers swirled around me. *Embrace your power.*

A deep, sorrowful note caressed my soul, and my eyes darted to Daiman.

I let go of the Mara, and it vanished into the Nowhere in half a heartbeat.

Daiman sagged to the floor, relief clear on his face.

I took a step toward him. *Thump.* The beat of a drum echoed in my chest. Another step and my vision blurred as the melodic plucking of his soul thrummed through me.

Thump. Thump.

The drums picked up their tempo, joining the low, sultry notes of Daiman's soul.

I knelt next to him, my Magik making me feel drunk and heady. I could take his soul for myself. I could end his suffering. I let out a shaky breath as another note soared through the darkness and into my bones.

His hand reached for mine and our eyes caught. A memory of him laughing while we played Ragnar's stupid drinking game flashed in my mind.

I sucked in a breath as my ears started to ring.

Snippets of Daiman and Si fighting in the temple washed over me and a moment of clarity hit me like rain on a hot summer day.

Daiman was a friend.

I pulled back and his brow furrowed as he stared at me.

"Give me a second," I exhaled as I forced the Magik back into the dark recesses of my soul. My hands shook with the effort and the Magik snapped and snarled like the Mara as I retook control of myself.

Grief poured back into me tenfold and my chest ached like I'd been stabbed. I swallowed the lump in my throat and let all my emotions tear through me anew.

It was like plunging into freezing water. Needles prickled all over my skin, and I sucked in a breath as the last thrash of Magik snarled into submission.

Daiman's soul song softened to a manageable melody that I no longer felt in my blood. I reached out my hand to him, but he hesitated.

"I'm alright," I tried to reassure him. "But you're not. We need to get you out of here." My voice was husky and raw, as if the Magik had taken a piece of me with it into the shadows.

He searched my eyes and slowly, as if he realized he didn't have any other choice, he took my hand.

Another screech from a Mara echoed in the distance. I wasn't sure how long we had until they regrouped and came after us. I might be able to scare off a few with my new found Magik, but I didn't want to find out the limits to my power. Not when Daiman was in desperate need of help.

I pulled him against me. He was heavy and his legs started to buckle as I wrapped my arm around his waist.

"Just hold on a little longer." I shifted his weight to get a better grip on him and my wings lifted us off the ground with little effort.

I started in the direction Talon had flown off with Ezra. It was all I had. Between trying to save Ezra, fighting the Mara and rescuing Daiman, I'd lost the path out of here.

Daiman's head went limp against my shoulder, and an icy sting of panic flooded my chest.

"Kara," Talon's voice sounded from below us.

My wings fanned out, grinding us to a halt. I searched the darkness under us and a twinkle of light caught my eye. There, through the shadows, hiding in what I thought was the ground, was the glow of Asgard.

"Daiman," Talon yelled his name. This time I saw her, standing in the frame of the light like a beacon of life.

Thank the Gods.

I tucked my wings, and we dropped from the sky like a stone. My hair whipped past me and I held onto Daiman with a death grip.

As we drew closer, the air swirled around us, and the glowing blue leaves shifted, mimicking the stars in the night sky. The gentle glow of Asgard was no longer below us, but in front of us.

I hated this place. There was no sense of stability, nothing to ground you.

My wings fanned out, catching the current, beckoning me into the light. Fresh damp air hit my face and the delicate scent of poppies filled my nose once more.

Talon reached a hand toward us and I landed a few paces from the entrance. The sunlight pouring into the Nowhere was blinding and I shielded my eyes.

"He needs Asheria." I tried to place him on his feet and his knees buckled. I caught him before he could hit the ground, wrapping his arm around my shoulders.

"She's waiting for him." Talon rushed forward.

"And Ezra?" I glanced over her shoulder.

"Safe on the other side."

"Let's get the Hel out of here."

Talon wrapped an arm around Daiman's waist, hoisting him up and taking some of his weight off of me.

You've done well. A voice slithered down my spine.

I looked over my shoulder, and the icy grip of fear strangled me.

There, at the base of the roots, stood eight shadowy figures. One of them stepped forward, her dress billowing around her like she was underwater. And even from a distance, I recognized her.

She was the Disir who saved me.

You're so much stronger than you realize. Her approval wrapped around me, and I felt myself being drawn to her.

"Kara." Talon's sharp voice broke the spell holding me hostage.

I turned away from them, more than a little terrified by my

willingness to go to them. Using the Disir Magik was a mistake. It was too easy to tap into, and it almost cost Daiman his soul.

I shook my head as we stepped into the light. I didn't look back as the three of us left the Nowhere behind.

And I swore I wouldn't use the Disir Magik again.

CHAPTER TWENTY-SIX

KARA

The ground sloped downward, becoming rocky and solid as we left behind the dark shapeless void of the Nowhere. With each step, my body anchored to the earth under my boots. The untethered feeling like I might float away on the breeze dissipated, and I exhaled in relief.

The roar of the ocean meeting the shore echoed through the rocky tunnel, and my Magik hummed at the familiar warmth of Asgard. A mix of nostalgia and dread filled my chest.

I grew up in Asgard, but my return didn't feel like a homecoming, as our group limped into this realm.

"Hold on, Daiman," Talon said under her breath like a silent prayer as she took the brunt of his weight off of me.

He wasn't that heavy, but I was feeling a little hollow and weak around the knees after using so much Magik. My body wasn't used to that kind of raw power, and I was more than ready to sit down for a moment and catch my breath.

Puddles and small rocks littered the ground as the waves crashing on the shore grew louder. A fine salty mist carried on the breeze, and a chill ran over my exposed skin. Light danced along the rocky ceiling, reflecting off of the water ahead, creating a rippling effect that echoed the waves of Magik inside me.

As the tunnel grew narrower, the ground turned to sand and my boots sank deeper with each step. Sunlight peaked into the tunnel, lighting up the warm sand colored walls, and pearlescent shells stuck out of the rocks like gemstones.

Just ahead was a natural arch, big enough for one person to squeeze through, that led to a rocky beach. Sunlight fractured across the midnight blue water, making me squint against the brilliant shimmer.

"You go first," Talon said, adjusting his weight. "I got him."

"Hold on a little longer, Daiman," I released my grip on him.

I stepped into the calf deep water, and my whole body tensed. Even through my trousers, the cold seeped into my bones almost immediately. I ducked as I made my way through the opening and stepped up on a large boulder once I was on the other side. A deep boom thundered as a wave crashed on the beach, followed by the hiss of the water receding.

Talon shuffled one step at a time as Daiman tried to stay upright. Once they were through the narrowest part of the opening, I looped my arms under Daiman's arms and pulled him the rest of the way through. Talon quickly followed, and the three of us waded through the shallow water and rocks toward the others.

"What the Hel happened?" Ragnar barked as he and Ezra hurried toward us.

"Gods," Ezra gasped. "I thought I had it bad." His sky blue eyes met mine and my heart swelled with relief. His arm was bandaged, but the color had returned to his cheeks and he looked entirely like himself once more.

Ezra and Ragnar grabbed Daiman from us, looping his arms over their shoulders.

"The Mara nearly killed him." Venom laced my words. "Monsters you should have warned us about." I directed my indignation at Ragnar. I knew we shouldn't have trusted him.

My worry over Daiman was quickly transforming into a dangerous rage. I should have come alone. None of this would've happened if I'd left Jotunheim and come straight here.

But I'd let Talon convince me otherwise, because I didn't trust my instincts right now.

But I should've listened to my gut. I should have come alone.

"They've never shown themselves before." Ragnar grumbled.

I scoffed. "I find that hard to believe." My Magik stirred like it could taste the lie on his tongue. "Daiman might meet the stars, because you kept pertinent information from us." Malice punctuated every word as Magik cascaded down my spine, forcing my shoulders back.

"There are many monsters that prowl in the dark. You expect me to know every horror that lurks in the shadows?" Ragnar snapped over his shoulder like that was enough of an explanation.

I didn't buy a single word out of his mouth. He was lying about something. I could feel it in my bones. His eyes shifted around the beach, and his brow furrowed when he glanced at me again.

"I told you to keep moving," he said under his breath as we reached Asheria on a sandy part of the shore.

Boulders rose out of the sand, tall as buildings, creating enough privacy to keep our group hidden until we could regroup. They lowered Daiman to the ground, and he went still. He looked even paler in the sunlight, and a pang of fear shot from my heart, through my core. I opened myself up just enough to listen to his soul song, and it hit me with the force of a battle-axe.

"He doesn't have long," I exhaled and shut the Magik down with some effort.

"For the love of Yggdrasil," Asheria balked as her eyes skated over Daiman's ghostly and bloody figure. "Get his armor off," she ordered, and Ezra went to work.

"I warned all of you she'd be the death of us." Ragnar got to his feet, his hands curling at his sides. "I've been traveling safely through the void for a decade. One time with you," he pointed a finger at me, "and monsters come crawling out of the shadows." He cocked his head to the side. "Why do you think that is?" He stepped toward me, murderous rage written in every line of his face.

Magik prickled my fingertips, and I itched to force the truth from him. I itched to make him pay for Daiman. I clamped down on the urge and grit my teeth.

"Maybe," Ragnar sauntered closer, "they were attracted to you. Like calls to like, does it not?" He raised a cocky eyebrow, and the desire to drop him from the highest cliff made the Magik across my back twitch.

"Careful," I warned him and balled my hands into fists. I didn't want to prove him right, but it was oh so tempting to put him in his place. I took a deep breath. The ocean air filling my lungs and keeping me from doing something I might regret.

"Or what?" His eyes sparked with challenge. "You'll show your true colors?" The corner of his lips twitched.

He wanted to get a rise out of me. He wanted to push me to the edge and see if I'd snap. Magik set my soul ablaze with resentment.

"We need to regroup." I tried to ignore the pounding in my veins and focus on what was important. Getting Si back.

"We need to cut our losses. Another day with you and we'll all meet the stars." Ragnar turned his back on me and the warrior in me wanted to strike.

I dug my boots into the sand. "You want to go after Si on your own? Be my guest." I threw my arms out and shook my head. "You don't stand a chance against Odin."

If Ragnar wanted to die, I wouldn't stand in his way. I understood why he didn't trust me, why he didn't like me. But this... trying to provoke me. It's where I drew the line. I was here for Sigurd, and I wouldn't let anyone get in my way. Especially not Ragnar.

"It's you we don't stand a chance against." Ragnar pulled a dagger and stepped toward me.

Surprise flickered through me. I wasn't sure if I should be impressed that he thought he could go toe to toe with me, or horrified at how brazenly stupid he was.

"Magnus would be alive if not for you." He yelled at me as another wave assaulted the shore. "Sigurd wouldn't need rescuing, if not for you." He gestured toward me with his dagger. "And Daiman wouldn't be fighting for his life, if not for you." Anger scrunched up his face, and his cheeks flushed with passionate hate.

"You're the one who led us into the Nowhere." I took a calculated step to the right. Out of respect for the others, I wouldn't fight Ragnar. But I wouldn't let him catch me off guard, either.

"Ragnar, don't be a fool," Talon ordered, but he ignored her.

He crossed one foot in front of the other, moving a step closer to the shore. "She'll get us all killed." The hiss of the water receding charged the air between us.

"I just saved two out of three of you." I pointed to Daiman and Ezra up the beach. "If I wanted you all dead, I'd have left you to the Mara."

"We wouldn't need saving if it weren't for you." He stepped toward me, dagger gripped in his hand like he meant to carve me to pieces.

"I get that you're pissed, but now is not the time." I pivoted my body as he took another step.

He stiffened and his jaw flexed as he ground his teeth.

"It's past time someone did something about you. I should have put you down the moment you arrived in Folkvang."

My temper flared, and I had to fight the Magik rising to meet it. "You want someone to be angry with? Look to the gods. Loki's the one who let the Draugr into Folkvang." My voice shook with rage and Magik danced along my arms.

"Odin's the one who took Sigurd." My heart hammered in my chest.

They deserve to pay. Whispers skated over my skin as Magik heated my blood.

"And yet, it all revolves around you." He shot toward me and swung.

I jumped, and my wings carried me over his head in an effortless flip. I landed perfectly behind him. Grabbing his dagger hand, I pulled it behind him and twisted. The blade fell from his grip into my waiting palm, and I kicked the back of his knees. He dropped like a bird falling out of the sky and I pressed his dagger to his neck.

His soul beat with a fervor and I leaned closer to him, taking it in and letting it wash over me.

"You're a skilled fighter, but you're no match for me," I said against his cheek. The sentient power within me purred at his racing pulse. Sparks flashed through me, and I shook with the effort to stay in control.

He tried to jerk away, but I twisted his arm to the edge of breaking.

"Enough. We have Si to think about."

His shoulder jerked and his body tensed. One more movement like that and he'd snap his arm in half.

"I am thinking about him. He's our brother," Ragnar spat with renewed passion. "You're just the whore who killed him."

A hundred years of heartache, anger and guilt exploded inside me and danced with my Magik.

Do it. Gooseflesh pebbled my skin as the whispers filled my mind.

I threw him into the sand face first and flipped him over. Straddling him, I pressed the tip of the dagger to the hollow of his throat. Wild sparks of Magik crawled toward him in the sand as I stared down at him. His eyes met mine and his lips pulled into a crooked grin.

"Let him go." A woman's voice bellowed across the beach, and my body went stiff as it registered who it belong to.

I looked up to my left, as if in slow motion and my heart skipped a beat.

"Bryn," her name fell off my lips in a shocked gasp.

She wore standard leather trousers and a midnight blue tunic under her armor. Her snow white hair was twisted up into a smattering of braids.

Pain swelled in my chest as her betrayal registered. She was the one who told Odin about the Disir. About me. As I met her eyes she quickly glanced away. Any shred of the friendship we had was long gone, twisted by sorrow and bitterness.

I wish I could say I hated her for running to Odin. But I understood better than most the rot that fed on grief and loss. And how it could drive someone to make choices they might not otherwise.

I got off of Ragnar and threw the dagger into the sand next to his head. He got to his feet with a satisfied grin and my heart sank.

We were surrounded. All of us except Ragnar. Talon and Ezra were on their knees, swords held against their throats. Another stood behind Asheria, sword pointed at the back of her head, while she continued to work on Daiman.

Archers sat perched on top of the tower size rocks, arrows drawn and pointing at every single one of my companions, except Ragnar.

I whirled on Ragnar. "How could you?" Anger flashed like lightning through me. "Did you ever plan to rescue Sigurd?" I stepped toward him, rage bringing my Magik to the surface.

"One more step and they all die," Bryn informed me.

I raised my hands. Ragnar may think I'm a monster, but I'd go willingly if it meant everyone on this beach, including him, went free.

"I told you," Bryn called my attention back to her. The ends of her hair twisted around her face in the ocean breeze, and her eyes sparked with revenge. "There's only darkness in her." She motioned someone forward, and my heart swelled and cracked as the cadence of a song written on my soul pierced the ocean air.

"Sigurd," I exhaled.

Relief flooded my chest, my bones, my every nerve. I knew he was alive, but seeing him in flesh and blood made all the tension in my body unclench despite my current situation.

He was mostly unharmed. I heaved a sigh. Though his lip was cut and a few bruises colored his face. It was far better than I expected to find him. He looked down at me, strands of his dark hair falling across his eyes as his gaze met mine. A flicker of doubt crossed his features and my heart crumpled like stale bread.

"Maybe now he'll see you for what you really are," Ragnar whispered against my cheek as muscular hands grabbed me and forced me to my knees.

I didn't fight them. I didn't have the will to do anything but look up at Si and try to decipher what he was thinking. His expression was guarded, haunted even as I stared up at him. But there was a tenderness in his gaze that gave me pause. Was it kindness or pity?

My arms were pulled behind my back and a slice of pain bit into my shoulder. I ignored it. Let them think they had the upper hand. Shackles clamped tightly around my wrists, the steel cold against my heated skin. But I paid them no notice.

Bryn leaned into Si, and he stiffened at whatever she whispered to him. Heat crawled up my throat as I watched her lips curl into a smile and she pat his chest. My body went rigid as his gaze locked on mine and warmth spread through me.

I know who you are in your heart.

His words from the alley seared through my mind, like he

was shouting them from the top of the rock as he held my gaze. He swallowed and his lips parted, then clamped shut.

The tenderness in his gaze turned cold. He rolled his shoulders back, as if making a decision, and he looked away from me. Unease tugged deep in my core. Had he'd been poisoned against me? I waited for him to look at me again, to give me any sign that he was still the man who gently removed my armor and held me less than a fortnight ago.

Firm hands grabbed my head and forced it to one side. A flicker of worry spurred my Magik as someone brushed the hair off my neck and Bryn smiled down at me. My eyes flicked back to Sigurd, trying to understand their dynamic. His jaw flexed as he watched what was happening behind me, and his hands balled into fists. He took a step forward and Bryn yanked on the chains tied to his wrist.

The embers of my Magik turned to a slow rolling fire deep in my core. Her fight was with me. Not Sigurd.

His head snapped at her, and his features softened as he said something that was muted by a wave crashing on the shore. Hot, angry tears stung my eyes as I fought against the inferno building inside me.

His eyes met mine again, and worry creased his forehead.

"Bryn, don't do this," Ezra shouted across the beach and a stab of fear punctured through the flames under my skin.

Out of the corner of my eye, Ezra was punched so hard he fell sideways, just as searing steel kissed my neck.

Ice cold shock burned through me and I sucked in a breath. My stomach soured as my flesh sizzled like meat over a fire. My vision blurred as blinding agony shot down my neck, shoulder, arm. My Magik rose to meet the pain, but was batted down by an invisible force.

Fight it. A voice snarled inside me.

Magik flared in my core, ripping through my veins. My head swam as unyielding power unfurled inside me. But every flare of Magik was met with ice so cold it scorched my bones like dragon fire, and shut off a piece of my soul. The burning hunger of my Magik faded to a whimper as door after door shut inside me.

But I refused to scream, or whimper, or show any signs of the inferno ripping through me. I was a Valkyrie, and we were born through pain.

Still, I watched Si's blurry figure atop the tower of stones and waited for him to say something. Do something. But he just stared down at me, devoid of emotion as my Magik was stripped from me, drop by drop. My eyes welled with vengeful tears. And the smell of flesh burning filled my nose as the final embers of my Magik flickered and died.

The brand left my skin, and I was shoved forward. Someone screamed my name from the other side of Yggdrasil as I hit the warm sand.

"Get up," a gruff voice ordered.

The Nine Realms halted, and I didn't move. Sigurd's soul song was carried away on the wind, along with Daiman's and every other melody on the beach. I couldn't feel a single one of them and, for a moment, I was relieved. Until the hollowness of being left without Magik engulfed me. Fear ate away at my bravado as the endless expanse of nothingness consumed me.

You are not alone. Whispers carried on the wind.

"I said, up." Someone kicked me in the ribs and my stomach heaved.

Using my shoulder, I pushed myself upright. My gaze sought Sigurd of its own accord, but he and Bryn were gone.

I got to my feet an empty shell of who I was a moment ago. Odin was about to get everything he wanted. Me and a war with Folkvang.

CHAPTER TWENTY-SEVEN

SIGURD

MY HEART FELT like it was going to riot in my chest as I turned away from the scene below. I pulled in a thick breath of salty sea air that burned my throat, forcing me to swallow the howl of outrage.

It took every ounce of training I had to keep a neutral expression when my very blood craved vengeance. Watching her take that brand without a word hardened my resolve to follow Kara to the end. Even if that end was today.

"Do you see who she really is now?" Bryn said, pulling me closer by my chain and I grit my teeth so hard my jaw popped. Her obsidian and gold tip wings stretched out from her back. A warm sea breeze brushed over my skin and rustled her feathers as she wrapped a stiff arm around my waist.

"She would've killed Ragnar today if I hadn't stopped her." Bryn jumped off the rock without preamble, and my stomach flipped end over end. I really hated flying, no matter how short the distance was.

Her gaze searched my face as my boots sunk in the soft sand. And I knew what I had to do. If Kara and I were going to get out of this in one piece, I needed to make Bryn, make everyone think they'd been successful in turning my heart against her.

I stepped back and glanced at Kara as she was hauled to her feet. She wore a stony mask of defeat as a breeze tousled her hair. Odin's men dragged her toward the boat hidden on the other side of the rocks, and I locked my heart behind a steel cage.

"The woman I cared for." I shook my head and met Bryn's eyes. It was easy to manipulate the anger burning inside me and pretend it was toward Kara. "She never would've hurt Ragnar."

The words fell from my lips with ease, because they were true. She wouldn't have hurt Ragnar anymore than the rest of us while sparring. The Kara I knew—the one who tried to kill herself to save everyone in the courtyard, the woman who took a beating from Bryn as payment for the blood she spilled— would never hurt an innocent soul to save herself.

Bryn scrutinized every flicker of emotion on my face. "And Magnus?" A wave crashed on the beach and hissed up the shore as the tide came in.

Her mask slipped, and I saw the broken woman underneath for just a moment. She didn't care about Ragnar. Or anyone else on this beach. All she cared about was hurting the person who stole Magnus from her.

"I'm sorry." My voice broke as I placed a hand on her armor clad shoulder. I was sorry she lost the person she loved. I was sorry Magnus was no longer with us. I was sorry I didn't tell her the truth from the beginning.

And I was sorry that I would never avenge her heartbreak, so long as she blamed Kara. The water receded and I exhaled with it.

"I wanted to believe she wouldn't kill him in cold blood," I continued. "That it was all Loki's doing." I straighten my shoulders and lifted my chin to sell my next lie. "But I can admit that I was wrong." I arranged my features into a hard mask of vengeance and dropped my hand. "She'll be the death of us all."

I let the grief in my heart bleed into my chest and drown me. I stared out at the glimmering sea, so at odds with the torment raging inside me, and forced the next words from my mouth.

"Tell Odin I'm ready to take up arms against the Disir."

Another truth neatly packaged to fit their narrative. I did want to rid the Nine Realms of the Disir. But no one could convince me that Kara was one of them, even if she carried their blood. There's more to a person than the family they're born in to.

Bryn closed the gap between us, her face inches from mine. "Just know this." Her gaze bounced between my eyes. "If you're lying, if you think you'll still find a way out of this. I'll spend the rest of my everlasting life making you wish for death."

"Let's get this over with." I started toward the others as Odin's soldiers loaded Kara, Talon, and Ezra into the boat.

Ragnar was allowed the freedom to board himself, and a bolt of betrayal seared my heart as I watched him sneer at Kara. I knew he wasn't overly fond of her, and after Magnus, he had every right to be angry. But this? Siding with Bryn and Odin. Betraying our friends. It wasn't the man I knew.

The boat gently rocked in the surf as Daiman was laid in the back with Asheria's aid. Water crashed over my boots as I sent a silent prayer to Yggdrasil that she'd be able to heal Daiman before long.

I hoisted myself into the boat and had to catch my balance as it rocked in the surf. As I looked up, my gaze fell on Kara like she was the sun and I was the moon, desperately chasing a glimpse of her.

The late afternoon light lit up her auburn hair and soft, pale skin. She looked calm. Too calm. Like a vibrant sunset before a storm. A wild strand of hair caught on a breeze and she looked up at the sky. Standing there, in the middle of the boat, she looked just as she did the day she stole my heart forever.

Wood creaked under my boots as I was inexorably drawn toward her.

"Interesting company you're keeping these days." Talon's warm voice tugged me back to myself. I glanced down at her, arms bound in rope, and legs kicked up as she leaned against the ship wall without a care in the world. "I hope you haven't gotten any moronic ideas into your head."

"No more than usual." I cocked an eyebrow and glanced at Ezra next to her.

He was less casual and wore a hard, determined expression as he watched Odin's men ready the ship. His arm was freshly bandaged, and I wondered what they'd encountered that left both Daiman and Ezra in need of healing. I may not like the man, but he'd risked himself to come here on my behalf.

I kicked at Ezra's boot. "You alright?" I nodded toward his arm.

Ezra looked up at me, and the corner of his lips twitched. "I'll live." He turned in his seat and looked back at Kara. "Can't say the same for her, though." His eyes met mine, and narrowed like he was searching for the truth hidden behind my mask of indifference.

My attention turned toward Kara once more and lingered. She leaned her shoulder against the mast, her arms still tied behind her back, and only one of Odin's fallen standing nearby. That was a mistake. Even without her Magik, she was a force of nature. Which begged the question. Why was she allowing them to take her so easily?

"She can't run from the blood on her hands forever." I pressed my lips together as my gaze traveled over her.

Ezra scoffed. "I don't know what she sees—" His words were cut off with a groan. I spared him a glance as he rubbed his bandaged arm.

"The feeling's mutual." I stepped away from them and wished he could trade places with Daiman.

I stepped over one of the chests that doubled as a row seat as I made my way down the ship. I don't know why I bothered trying to mend bridges with Ezra. We've orbited around each other for decades and never attempted a friendship. There was no point in starting now.

The boat rocked again, and a cold mist of sea spray kissed the side of my face and cleared my mind. Another breeze kicked up and Bryn shouted orders from somewhere behind me. The heavy slap of the mainsail pierced the air, and the boat lurched forward. My eyes found Kara once more as the undercurrent pulled at the keel and we settled into the water.

She turned her head to the side, looking out at the deep blue sea as a breeze tossed her hair over her shoulder. The red, angry brand on her neck was far worse up close and I grit my teeth. My heart thrummed with fury and I swore the men who put that mark on her would pay with their lives.

I needed her to look at me. I needed her to know I didn't condone what those men did to her. I needed her to know that my alliance was still with her.

Look at me. I begged as the boat tipped side to side and settled into the sea.

Her emerald eyes flicked up and caught mine like she heard my silent plea. My heart stopped, and everything melted away like butter on a hot day. The boat under my feet, my friends, our enemies. They all blurred into the background as my entire focus zeroed in on Kara.

I could still feel the heat of her breath on my neck when I removed her armor. I could still feel her smooth skin against my fingertips, and I balled my hands into a fist. It was going to take more effort than I thought I possessed to keep up my charade of indifference.

I took another step and Kara's eyes skated over me in an intimate perusal that heated my skin and tugged on the invisible thread that was a living thing between us.

Whatever she felt, she kept closely guarded as she watched me. She was a master at schooling her features. She kept every thought, every feeling from showing up in the curve of her lips, the line of her brow, the set of her shoulders.

We could have been strangers for how indifferent she

seemed. But I knew her. And I knew she was anything but unaffected. I could see it in her eyes. The slight glint of hope. I could see it in the steady rise of her chest, too quick to be unbothered. And I knew in my bones the tension in her neck and shoulders wasn't just from the pain of the brand. She was fighting to keep her boots rooted to the planks under her feet.

I took another careful step as the oars were dropped in the water. Her breath caught, making every muscle in my body go tight. I could do this. I could play the game to save her life, even if it killed me.

Our shoulders brushed as the boat rocked. I leaned in, our faces an inch apart. The scent of lavender and rain punched me in the gut, and I steeled my nerves for what needed to be done.

"You asked me once if I thought there was anything stronger than love." My voice came out rough and full of emotion. To everyone else, it would sound like I was holding back my rage and disgust. Only I knew the distaste in my voice wasn't aimed at Kara.

Her lips parted, and she sucked in a shallow breath. "Let me guess, your answer's changed?" Her face hardened, but her shoulders slumped ever so slightly, like her last shred of hope relied on whatever I said next.

"It has." I needed her to know I wouldn't let Odin have her without a fight. I shifted my body so no one could see my hands. "Revenge is stronger than anything I ever felt for you." I brushed my index finger across her palm. Her eyes widened for a fraction of a second before her mask slammed back into place.

"Death follows you like a loyal dog," I continued and ran my thumb along her fingertips.

She raised her chin, and her fingers curled around mine. Pride swelled in my chest as understanding flickered in her eyes, and I let out a shaky breath. She knew my words were false, which gave me the courage to put the final nail in the coffin.

I squeezed her hand back, then pulled away. "It's time someone put you down for all the blood you've shed." If I lingered any longer, I wouldn't be able to walk away, and I'd give myself away as the liar Bryn accused me of being.

Ezra scoffed behind me, but I ignored him. His ire was the least of my concern.

A deep laugh rumbled in Kara's chest, and she leaned toward me with a menacing grin. "I'd like to see you try." Her words cut through the air like a knife and if she hadn't grabbed on to me like a life line a moment ago, I might have believed the hatred in her gaze.

"He's going to do more than try," Bryn said from behind me and shoved me forward. "He's going to make sure you never destroy another life again."

Kara turned away from Bryn without a word, and I continued down the boat, finding a seat on the other side of Daiman.

"You should tread lightly. It's a dangerous game you're playing," Asheria said under her breath as she placed a bandage across Daiman's cheek.

The sight of him so pale and bloody hardened my resolve. He shouldn't be here and in this condition. None of us should.

"I don't play games I don't intend to win."

A warm breeze made the hair on the back of my neck prickle, and the boat rocked hard to one side. The current shifted once again, down a path not written in the stars, but in the choices we'd make from this moment forward.

CHAPTER TWENTY-EIGHT

KARA

STARS SWIRLED *around me in the darkness like moths circling the flame of a candle.*

Tiny explosions of light shot over my head like a thousand flaming arrows. I was barefoot, and wearing a flowing night dress that reached my calves. I felt younger, less burdened. Which is how I knew I was dreaming.

I could still hear the others in Asgard. Whispered words between Talon and Asheria. Ezra's boots—tap, tap, taping—against the stone. Daiman's heavy breathing, in…and…out.

I searched the darkness that reminded me of the Nowhere and heard a wave breaking on the shore. My feet moved of their own accord, and chilly water splashed between my toes. But the cold didn't bother me, instead it felt like a dip in the coolest lake on a hot day.

Sand fell from above like a million tiny pricks of gentle rain. A warm breeze whispered against my skin that felt like Sigurd, and my hair was brushed over my shoulder.

Still, the stars fluttered around me like the landvaettir sprites found in Folkvang. I closed my eyes and inhaled the fragrant scent of wildflowers and salt. It felt both familiar and foreign, like I was lost in a memory that didn't belong to me.

Another thunderous boom shook the ground beneath my feet and a fine salty mist coated my face. I opened my eyes and a sense of wonder filled my heart like a warm cup of tea. Stars sparkled overhead, reflecting on the black ocean in front of me, and sand stretched as far as I could see on either side of me.

The moth-like stars brushed against my skin one at a time, then shot across the ocean. They took their place in the cosmos and formed the Seven Hens just above the horizon.

The back of my neck prickled with awareness and as I glanced to my right, a woman with long auburn hair down to her waist strode toward me. She wore a simple cream dress like my own. And her crimson, saffron, & amber wings were on full display, the tips trailing in the sand behind her like wildfire. They shimmered in the moonlight and glowed unlike anything I'd ever seen before.

I blinked, and she was in front of me, as if she crossed the distance between us with one step. Her hand reached for me and she caressed my cheek. "You've done well, Kara." Her voice was like honey, soothing and sweet.

"Who are you?" I stared into her hazel eyes that reminded me of a forest in spring.

A cool breeze pulled at the corner of her lips and leaves brushed across my bare feet. I glanced down, and the sand was gone, replaced with bright verdant grass and damp soil.

Trees rose around us as tall as mountains. Sunlight filtered through the leaves, making everything glow with a warmth I felt in my soul.

"I'm here to help." A crown of wildflowers bloomed on her head like as she motioned for me to follow her.

I took a step toward her.

And the tap...tap...tap of Ezra pacing faded on a breeze like daffodil seedlings.

"That doesn't answer my question." I asked as I felt myself fall deeper into the dream. The colors of the forest brightened, birds chirped in the distance, and the smell of rain filled my nose.

"You've been cut off from your Magik." Her night dress transformed into a gown that trailed behind her. Vines and delicate flowers crawled up the cream fabric, like she was becoming part of the forest. "But I can give you an ember of my own."

She turned toward me, and a single fleck of fire danced on her palm.

"It's yours," she held out her hand with a melancholy smile. "If you want it."

The ember in question burned a little brighter at being acknowledged, and I reached for it without a second thought.

It floated toward me, gliding over my fingers and up my arm. The tiny flame warmed my cool skin as it made its way over my chest. It hovered for a moment, as if waiting for me to open my heart to its power.

Bands of green and purple light filled the sky, plunging the forest into a magical glow. I didn't know if any of this was real or if it truly was just a dream. There was only one way to find out if what Davlin said about dream walking was true. So I pressed the ember to my chest and chills ran down my body as the ember settled deep in my core.

"You must embrace it. Feed it." She placed a hand on my shoulder and sparks danced across my skin. "Or the light you've been gifted will burn out before it's had time to flourish."

"I can't." I dropped my gaze, and the forest darkened like the sun had been chased behind a cloud. "I won't use it to hurt anyone."

"You already have." A sad smile touched her rose-colored lips. "When you took Loki's soul for yourself, there was no going back."

"You know about Loki?" The clouds grew darker overhead, transforming the forest. Branches twisted overhead, flowers died and the caw of a raven pierced the din.

The woman's eyes darted to the clouds as the flowers on her dress wilted and died.

"Loki was just the beginning."

"What happened to him?" I blurted. Rationally, I knew I should ask her a million other questions, but I needed to know if what I saw after the temple was real, or if I was truly losing my mind.

Lightning flashed overhead, and I heard someone call my name.

"The woman who saved you took care of him after the temple."

"So he's dead?" My heart raced as a bitter wind whipped through the forest.

"In a manner of speaking." Her eyes grew darker and the vibrance of her wings dulled as the raven cawed overhead once more. *"But he's not important. You are."* The reverence in her voice spoke to the Magik in me.

"The Nine Realms cannot survive if you don't embrace—"

Thunder rumbled overhead and Talon's voice bellowed like a god through the forest as she called my name.

The woman grabbed my shoulders, and the desperation in her gaze made me go stiff. "You mus—embra—Magik." Lightning flashed so brightly it was as if night turned to day.

I blinked to shield my eyes from the light and when I opened them, the forest was gone.

My eyes fluttered open to a dark, cold prison, and Talon's warm chestnut eyes stared down at me.

Don't be afraid of who you are. The woman's voice echoed through me as the last remnants of my dream released their hold on me.

"Time to get up." Talon helped me to my feet. "Someone's coming."

I rolled the ache out of my shoulders from sleeping on the stone floor and rubbed the sleep from my eyes. My dream was already fading. The fresh scent of leaves and wet earth, snuffed out by the moldy smell of cold stone. The flames of a fire flickered in the corner of my mind as stars winked out behind my eyes.

And yet, the ember of Magik remained, and flickered in my blood. It wasn't just a dream. She was real.

The door swung open, and a hoard of guards stood on the other side. Time to see if the ounce of Magik I'd been given would do me any good.

CHAPTER TWENTY-NINE

KARA

THE SOUND of boots shuffling and steel clanking echoed off the winding stone staircase as we were escorted to our fate. Thin beams of light cut into the stone walls pierced the otherwise dark tower, lending enough light for me to see the two bulky men ahead of me.

Their armor bore the three interlocked triangles that made up the Valknut sigil—Odin's symbol for the fallen. While several others marched behind me. And even though I was short on Magik, it still boosted my pride knowing they saw me as a threat.

The others, Talon, Ezra, Asheria and a much better looking Daiman, each had their own escort up ahead of me. It was obvious that Odin didn't care about the others. Talon and Asheria could fly out of here at a moment's notice, with Ezra and Daiman in tow. A point I made several times over during the hours since our capture. But of course, all of them were too stubborn to listen to reason.

I wish they understood that this wasn't their fight. This was about me and the Disir. And now that Odin had me, I'd make sure he held up his end of the bargain and let Sigurd go. There was no need for them to risk the stars, but I should've known better than to argue with hardheaded warriors.

A door clanged open ahead, and a warm golden light spilled into the stone spire. As I drew closer, I squinted, and was reminded of the lightning in my dream. The hazy image of a red-headed woman wearing a crown of flowers flashed before my eyes. The ember of Magik deep in my core flickered, and the sensation of trying to remember a place I've never been before made my heart sink.

One of the fallen behind me shoved me forward. With a glare over my shoulder, I stepped into the light and onto a bridge. Fresh air filled my lungs and the setting sun warmed my face.

Across the bridge, flanked by two guards, was Sigurd, standing in a beam of afternoon sun, and my breath caught at the sight of him. He looked liked he belonged in Asgard among the gods.

I took another step onto the bridge and his eyes shot to me like I'd called his name. My heart swelled and a palpable force sizzled between us. The ghost of his covert touch made my fingers itch for another caress, and I balled my hands into fists. His eyes tracked the movement and the ember inside me burned a little brighter.

He looked better than I'd last seen him. His hair was slicked back and bound at the nape of his neck, and his clothes were no longer stained with grime and blood. Instead, he wore a midnight blue long sleeve top with the sleeve rolled up and a pair of dark leather trousers. He still wore manacles, but was clearly receiving better treatment than before.

I wasn't sure I'd see him again after they unloaded us from the boat and we went our separate ways. His gaze flicked over me briefly and I watched his features shift into a mask of mild disinterest, before he turned away. I knew it was to keep up appearances, but his indifference stung more than I cared for.

Not for the first time, I replayed his gentle display of solidarity on the boat, and reminded myself of the words he spoke so fervently in Folkvang.

What if, no matter what happens, I'll always know who you are in your heart?

Whether our connection was written in the stars or created by forces beyond our understanding, I'd always been able to count on him. And I wasn't going to stop now.

Bryn and Ragnar stepped out onto the bridge near Si, from a similar stone turret. The smug look of satisfaction on Ragnar's face made the ember inside me flare with indignation. It wanted revenge. I wanted revenge for Ragnar's betrayal.

I had to remind myself that he was doing all this for Si. And as much as I didn't want to align myself with a single shred of the man, I understood why he did it. Even if I wouldn't have done the same.

Bryn motioned for Si to join her, and he stepped toward her without hesitation. Unease swirled in my stomach as he stepped into line with her, and I did my best to ignore it. My own guards shuffled around me, forming a circle and ushering me into position behind Bryn, Ragnar, and Sigurd.

It was hard to believe I was being served to Odin on a platter, and I couldn't find an ounce of fear in me. I spent too long looking over my shoulder. Too long wondering if he'd come back and take more than my wings.

I was done running.

Two ravens cawed overhead, and Bryn whistled in return. The fallen around me seemed to understand the signal and started forward in unison. We marched down the bridge, prisoners of a war that had only just begun toward the Hall of the Gods.

Gold statues lined the path on either side of me. One for every god Odin found worthy of immortalizing for all to worship. No surprise, most of the statues amounted to nothing more than an elaborate family tree.

Enormous stained glass doors opened of their own accord as we approached The Hall of the Gods. Sunlight filtered through the meticulously cut glass, depicting a battle won many moons ago, sending a spray of color across the polished stone path.

The artist captured Odin's eight legged horse, Sleipnir, in a powerful pose as it reared up on his hind legs. The dark glass cast a shadow through the explosion of color around him. Odin sat atop the beast, clad in a gold so vibrant it made the sun look dull. An array of marigold, amber, and honey colored glass formed vibrant flames that licked up the panels, and kissed the stars dotting the cosmos.

Pearlescent Magik shimmered along the panels, creating movement in the design as the sun passed through the glass. At just the right angle, you might think the glass was alive with the past. It was breathtaking. Even if the subject left something to be desired.

"Wow," Ezra exhaled behind me.

We passed over the threshold and the doors groaned closed behind us. A cool breeze brushed my cheek and sent a chill down my arms. Magik cloaked the air. Each breath was thick with the acrid taste of Odin's wards. They were stronger than I remembered them being. But there was something off about them. Like walking through a forest of cobwebs.

Surprise snapped through me at the state of The Hall of the Gods. Long shadows crawled across the marble floors, and the mural that stretched along the ceiling looked as if the color was actively bleeding out of the painting.

Even the bronze rays of sunset skittered away from the shadows that crawled these walls. The decorative gold paint that used to shine had lost its luster. The marble floor no longer reflected light, but seemed to suck every flicker of torchlight into the floor for warmth. The trees that once welcomed dreamers were now twisted and barren. And their sweet floral aroma was replaced by the heavy scent of mud.

Decay filled the hall, and my Magik cowered inside me like it was afraid of the tomb this place had become. I couldn't help but wonder if this was another effect of Magik failing throughout the realms. Odin wouldn't have let this place fall into such ruin if he could help it.

A tremor of anxiety fluttered through my chest. The Disir's return was still fresh. Could they have done this much damage to the fabric of the Nine Realms already?

The ember of my power shuttered, and I curled the fingers of my will around the tiny flame thrumming inside me like a second heartbeat. I refused to let the last drop of my Magik flicker and die. Even if it was the Magik of the Disir. Deep down, I knew if it was snuffed out, it'd only be a matter of time before the flame of my soul was extinguished as well.

Bryn and Si reached the stairs at the bottom of the Dais and halted. Bryn turned and faced the way we'd come, and Si followed suit like he'd been doing this his whole life.

His eye caught mine for a fraction of a second, and his mask broke. His brow furrowed and his jaw clenched in what I could only guess was worry mixed with wonder. His gaze flicked away and his mask fell back into place as he focused on the double doors at the end of the hall.

The fallen to my right stopped short and placed a hand on my shoulder. His meaty grip was unyielding as he forced me to turn and face the way we'd come.

The doors creaked open again, and I held my head high. The last time I saw Odin, I was a broken, hopeless thing. I let him tear out pieces of my soul without a fight.

But not this time. I stood a little taller, as adrenaline made my heart beat faster.

This time, I would go down fighting.

Odin was the first through the doors. He wore a gold chest plate over his leathers that was engraved with elegant twists and knots. Raven feathers so dark they seem to suck in the surrounding light, adorned his shoulders and flowed down the trim of his cloak. A gold chain was wrapped around his fist and—

"Gods," I exhaled, my eyes going wide.

A chorus of curses and gasps rustled through the hall.

It took all my practiced strength not to take a step back as Fenrir, the Sun Eater, padded through the doors a few paces behind Odin.

I'd heard stories about the wolf, legends, really. None did the beast justice. He towered over Odin like a mountain, casting a long shadow over the men at his feet. His dark black fur was the deepest shade of midnight with a dusting of gray like stars sprinkled throughout his coat.

Gold chains, glowing with Magik wrapped around his body. Another chain wrapped around his neck, with Odin holding the lead in his fist. It was hard to believe this was his smaller, tamed form. The mere thought of him in his true form, free of the chains, sent a chill down my spine.

Fear thundered in my chest and quaked down my legs. Odin wouldn't have to lift a finger this time to dole out his punishment. Fenrir would do his bidding and tear me in half with a single look from his master. My mouth went dry, and I tried to swallow, but the truth of my fate was lodged in my throat like a stale piece of bread.

None of us were going to walk out of here today.

I looked over my shoulder at Si, who stared at the beast in horror. His face paled and my heart broke. Whatever he was secretly planning just died before his eyes. Not a single person in this room was a match for Fenrir.

Maybe in another life. I thought as I stared at Si.

His eyes found mine and his head cocked to the side as if to say, *let's go down fighting one last time.*

The corner of my lips twitched into a defiant smile, and I nodded once before turning back to face Odin and his beast.

Fire burned in my veins as I stared up at the wolf. A purely murderous rage curled his lips back, showing the sharp points of his canines. I'd tear this entire hall a part, I'd throw myself to the literal wolf, I burn my last ember of Magik to ash, if it meant my friends—if it meant Si—would see another day.

I looked at Odin, full of rage, and he was already staring at me. A small smile crept over his lips. The tendril of Magik in me flared, as if it recognized the cadence of Odin's essence and found it repulsive.

"Bryn," Odin bellowed as he drew closer. "I must say, I'm pleasantly surprised you've managed to make good on your promise and deliver Kara so quickly." Fenrir's footfalls were all but silent except for the tremor that rumbled through the floor, and into my bones.

One of the Fallen whimpered, and I didn't blame them. No manner of training could prepare them for the reality that they were among gods and monsters.

"Your loyalty will be rewarded." Odin's every word was measured and calculating. The way one might string a bow and carefully aim at their target.

"And you." His gaze fell on Sigurd behind me, and my heart leapt into my throat. My muscles burned with the compulsion to put myself between Odin and Si. The corner of his mouth twitched like a predator toying with its prey. "I hear you've finally come to your senses."

"I have." Sigurd's voice was devoid of emotion.

Odin's gaze swept up and down the length of me, disgust evident on his face. The feeling was mutual.

"Is that so?" The Alfather stalked past me. His boot steps echoed through the hall with the same cadence of an axe hitting wood. Slow, merciless and precise.

Against my every instinct, I turned my back on Fenrir. Odin moved toward Si, slow and methodical. He was testing his will, looking for cracks, but Si remained still, emotionless. He could've been carved from stone with all the humanity he displayed.

I'd never seen him so rigid and stoic as he held Odin's gaze. For a mortal soul, he acted braver than any god I'd ever encountered. Pride swelled in my chest. I'd always known Si was a man above measure, but watching him stare done the Alfather like he was the one in control, made the ember in my core light the kindling in my soul and simmer to a slow burn.

The fresh taste of Magik was like coming up for air after being submerged for a breath too long.

"She's proven time and time again, she can't be trusted." The venom in his voice was so convincing, my heart squeezed at his words.

I trust you. I chanted at him like he might hear my silent solidarity.

"The question is, can you be trusted?" He raised Fenrir's gold leash, and the wolf let out a low, menacing growl that reverberated in my chest and sent a bolt of blazing fear down my neck.

I looked over my shoulder, unable to ignore the shadow of death as Fenrir crept closer.

"I've found the human spirit to be wild, too encumbered by emotions." Odin yanked on Fenrir's chains and the beast lowered his head slowly and with considerable effort. It was as if he was trying to fight against Odin's command. But there was no use.

Ancient wrath boiled under my skin. Odin had no right to tame Fenrir and make him his slave. My hands shook as the memory of the Disir's rage flooded my veins.

He had no right to temper our power. I wasn't sure who spoke the words in my mind. The voices that haunted my soul or my own.

"Fenrir cannot ignore the Magik that binds him. My will is his command." Hatred settled into the pit of my stomach and spread like ink through water. "You'd do well to remember that." Odin's attention zeroed in on Sigurd, and I shook with the effort to stay rooted to the spot.

The large double doors behind me groaned open once more, and every nerve in my body went taut as the single flame in my core flared to life.

What fresh Hel could be joining us now?

Every pair of eyes turned to look down the hall as a streak of bronze afternoon light spilled across the floor and banished the shadows.

CHAPTER THIRTY

FREYA MARCHED INTO THE HALL.

Sunlight trailed her like a river, as if all the light in this desolate place was drawn to her warmth. Her dress looked dipped in liquid gold to match the perfectly sculpted chest plate. And brilliant gold dragon scale armor adorned her collar and arms. She held her chin high, and her lips pressed firmly together in a murderous expression as she glided into the hall.

A spasm of uncertainty squeezed my chest. This wasn't going to end well. I'd never seen her look so terrifyingly godlike in the hundred years I'd known her. A prickle of awareness sent a shiver down my spine as the balance of power shifted. Whether it was swinging in our direction remained to be seen.

"Come to save your little pet?" Odin's deep voice resonated through the hall.

"I'm merely here to witness the justice that must be served." Freya's words were passive enough, but her tone cut across the hall like knives.

Fenrir let out a low grumble as Freya moved closer, and every person in the room inched away from the beast.

"I'm afraid your honeyed words are hollow. I know what you truly whisper in the dark." Odin sounded bored by the intrusion. Almost like he was expecting her.

"I see you have a new bird squawking in your ear." Freya

shot daggers at Bryn and a prickle of wintry Magik filled the hall as she moved past Fenrir without breaking her stride.

Odin glanced at Bryn, and the corner of his lips twitched.

"Loyalty is a fickle companion. You'd do well to keep your own on a tighter leash, lest they find a master worth serving." Odin glanced between Bryn and Freya and unease twisted my gut.

Freya's eyes met mine as she stepped between me and Bryn, and the telltale shimmer of her Magik wrapped around me like a warm embrace.

Relief flooded my senses, and the tension in my shoulders eased. Whatever ill will she held toward me on Folkvang didn't seem to extend to the present circumstances.

"Unlike you," Freya stepped past me and started up the stairs. "I have no desire to keep those who would rather serve another." Freya raised a hand, the veins in her arm glowing as a swell of Magik shook the ground.

The snap of Bryn's black and gold wings bursting from her echoed through the hall, and the force of it sent a gust of air over me. She let out a strangled cry as she was forced to her knees.

Color leeched from her black and gold feathers, turning them ashy gray. Bryn sucked in a strangled breath as Freya turned to face us. Ancient, world ending fury sparked in Freya's eyes as she stared down at Bryn. Another spark of Magik made gooseflesh rise on my skin as embers ignited on the tips of her feathers.

Bryn screamed.

Her strangled cry echoed off the marble floors, and I felt the blood drain from my face as her fingers clawed at the impenetrable stone. She may have betrayed Kara and Freya, but she didn't deserve this.

"For the love of Yggdrasil," Ragnar stared down at Bryn, a look of concern and trepidation marring his features. It was obvious he didn't think his alliance with Bryn through. To betray Freya was to court a true death.

I looked over my shoulder and finally allowed myself to look at Kara. The pain in her eyes was almost unbearable as she stared at Bryn. She rolled her shoulders and her body went stiff as Bryn let out a whimper.

Realization hit me with the force of a battle-axe.

This is what Odin did to her. This was how she paid for ending my mortal life.

"Stop," Kara shouted, and the tremor in her voice made my heart riot.

A savage fury burned through my veins, making my head spin. I looked past Freya to Odin. A satisfied, smug expression twisted his face into the vengeful god he pretended not to be.

My hands balled into fists. I wanted to kill him.

Freya released her hold on Bryn, and her body slumped forward. The spark of Magik vanished, but her wings were half charred and brittle. And she shook with every breath as she sat up.

"You would fight for her when she's betrayed your life?" Freya's brow furrowed as she glanced between the two Valkyrie.

Bryn's wings hung from her back, like they were too heavy for her to support. And her shoulders caved toward her chest, like a crumpled sheet of parchment. Gone was the anger and bravado.

All that was left was a broken woman who lost her love.

My gaze found Kara once more, and understanding flickered through my chest like knives. She was fighting for Bryn because she understood her. Another brick of guilt settled heavy on my chest for being so ignorant to her pain over the last century.

"She's grieving. She doesn't—"

"Don't speak for me," Bryn yelled from her place on the

ground. Her words echoing through the hall like the screech of a bird through a canyon.

It would destroy Magnus to see her like this. Another fissure formed in my heart, and my chest ached. She was the physical manifestation of the heartbreak I was actively trying to keep at bay.

I knelt and reached my hand out to her. There wasn't anything I could do to bring him back, or take her pain away. But she didn't have to grieve him alone.

She looked at my outstretched hand and slapped it away. But I swore I'd keep trying to reach her for Magnus.

"There's been enough heartache, enough devastation." Kara pleaded. "Spare her the agony I once suffered. Let it all die with me."

Die? The word hit me square in the chest like a physical blow. I stared at Kara, and I knew she meant it. She would trade her life for ours. Just like she tried in the courtyard with Loki.

I took a step toward her instinctively.

And she shook her head ever so slightly, as if to say, *don't come another step closer.*

I froze. I couldn't protect her from the gods, but I couldn't just stand here and let her die on behalf of us.

"While this little display of theatrics is entertaining," Odin grumbled. "Bryn is under my protection. Singe another feather and I'll consider it an act of war."

The tension between Freya and Kara fizzled as Freya reared on Odin.

"You have no authority over *my* people." The flames flickered in their torches as a blast of Magik erupted off of Freya.

"I do when they come to me for sanctuary and claim you're unfit to lead." His sapphire eye glimmered.

Magik crackled through the hall and Bryn had the good sense to look terrified as she pushed to her feet. Her eyes bounced between Freya, Odin, and Kara. There was no easy way out of the mess she'd made. She'd sold her soul to Odin and, without his protection, she'd be at Freya's mercy.

At this point, I wasn't sure which was worse.

"You'd like that, wouldn't you? Claim my throne. My people." Magik prickled over me, raising the hairs on my arms and heating my skin. "My realm," Freya seethed. "Over my rotting corpse."

"Over hers actually," Odin nodded toward Kara, and my blood went still.

"She isn't the problem." Freya said through gritted teeth. "It's the Disir you want."

"She is a Disir." Odin's voice was deafening as he closed the gap between them. Fenrir snarled at Freya, as if Odin's rage overflowed into the beast.

But Freya held her ground as her head tilted toward the wolf.

"Control that mongrel, or I will," she snapped.

Odin's laugh was deep and menacing. "Your traitor was right," Odin looked between Freya and Bryn. "Your judgement is severely lacking."

He stalked across the dais like a lion on the prowl. "You have one Valkyrie who's betrayed you for her own vengeance. Another who's murder spree might very well bring Ragnarok upon our heads. And a band of traitors who circumvented the Magik that binds them and stormed my realm while your head was turned."

"You have no right to question my rule, when it's your bastard son that's brought all of this upon our heads." Freya shouted at Odin, and I held my breath.

Odin backhanded Freya and thunder rumbled through the hall. The torches blew out, their smoke curling into the shadows to escape the wrath of the Alfather.

Freya touched her cheek and slowly turned her head back to Odin. "Your touch has grown soft in your old age."

The hall rumbled once more, and the ground shook with the force of a stampede.

"Say one more word about my son and your Valkyrie won't be the only one to lose their head today."

Magik crackled over Freya's arms, lightning to Odin's thunder.

"Threaten my realm again, and I promise Ragnarok will be the least of your worries."

Odin stared at Freya, his one eye more menacing that it had any right to be as he assessed the goddess in front of him. No one dared speak or even breathe, as a battle of wills played out silently between them.

The rumbling subsided, and the heaviness in the air dissipated.

"You can keep your realm for now." Odin's gaze flipped to me as he held out his hand to Freya. "I already have what I want."

Freya placed her hand in his and he pulled her against him.

"But I keep the ones who trespassed into Asgard." He nodded toward Talon, Ezra, Asheria, Daiman and Ragnar.

Panic clawed its way up my torso as I looked at my friends.

"Like I said, I have no interest in keeping anyone who defies my command and betrays the home I've given them." Freya looked over her shoulder and her eyes met mine. "You can have them all."

My mouth went dry and my heart fell out of my chest.

A familiar caress of Magik ran up my arms and warmed my chest. Freya.

She glanced toward an alcove to the right of the dais, and her lips curled into a smirk. A firm tug on my core heightened my senses, and I felt the ground shift under me. Only it wasn't the marble stone that was moving. It was another path forward, taking shape in the shadows.

Something was hiding in that alcove. Something Freya

wanted to make me aware of. Maybe she wasn't leaving us to Odin's mercy after all.

"I do enjoy your vengeful side." Odin's eye danced over Freya, and just like that, their spat appeared to be over.

"Alfather," Bryn's voice broke the tension. "Ragnar was instrumental in delivering Kara."

My eyes shot to Ragnar. And he stared daggers at Bryn for bringing everyone's attention back to them.

Odin's head whipped in Bryn's direction and a wave of heat blasted through the hall. "Speak out of turn again, and I'll let Freya pluck the Magik from your bones until you go mad."

Bryn lowered her head in submission, and Ragnar took a step back. He looked like he wanted to make a run for it, but Fenrir let out a hot, heavy breath.

"I hope Fenrir enjoys the taste of traitors," Ezra said under his breath.

I swore I wouldn't sit on the sidelines anymore. And even if Ragnar deserved to be a dog's dinner, I couldn't in good conscious let that happen. I cleared my throat, and my heart threatened to beat out of my chest as I took a step forward.

Freya and Odin's attention turned to me, and my inside shriveled under their stare.

"If you want me to do your bidding, let them go. All of them." My voice was firm and clear even though fear coursed through me so hot I thought I might be sick. "Or I swear. I will never touch Gramr."

"You're not in a position to be making demands," Odin eyed me, but there was curiosity in his gaze.

"Aren't I?" I cocked an eyebrow with a confidence I didn't feel as I stared down the ruler of the Nine Realms. "I was under the impression it was my destiny to end the Disir."

I heard someone lose a breath behind me, and I could feel Kara's gaze digging into my back.

Not now, I thought as I did my best to ignore every soul I now bargained for.

Odin's lips formed a hard line.

"Well, isn't that an interesting development," Freya cooed.

"Destinies can be rewritten." Odin's Magik hit me like a poisoned arrow. And I fought to stand my ground as a searing pain expanded across my chest.

It was just as the visitor said. He'd kill me even if it meant he had to rearrange the stars himself to get what he wanted.

I shoved the pain to the back of my mind and squared my shoulders. Folding my hands in front of me, I shrugged as my knees tried and failed to buckle.

"If that were true, you wouldn't have gone to such trouble to convince me to take up arms against the Disir."

"This is your doing," Odin snapped at Freya.

"As much as I would love to take credit for this," she waved a hand at me. "His penchant for overstepping is legendary." Freya's eyes sparkled with approval. "Keeping him in line has been a full time job." Her Magik sparked against my skin again and the oppressive weight of Odin's lessened.

There was still a battle of wills going on between them, even as they calmly stared out at all of us.

"Very well," Odin grumbled, and the blanket of his Magik vanished. "Thor," Odin glanced at the alcove, and the Nine Realms narrowed around one single point. Everyone and everything disappeared as the path in front of me started to take shape.

"Bring forth Gramr."

I glanced at Freya, and she nodded just once.

CHAPTER THIRTY-ONE

THOR STEPPED out of the shadows with a purposeful and assured stride, carrying what I could only assume was Gramr wrapped in blood red fabric. He was tall as a mountain and his gold and blue tunic clung to his arms and shoulders, showing off his imposing stature. He wore his infamous long blond hair, in traditional plaits that were surprisingly elegant for a god known for his brutality.

His lack of armor was evidence enough of his power, especially with Mjölnir—the massive dwarf made hammer—strapped to his side. It glimmered even in the shadows. The knotted design coming to life and slithering along the metal. Just its presence filled the air with a thick petrichor charge.

Doubt crept under my skin like a ship taking on water. I was an exceptional fighter, one of the best in Folkvang, and I've always been able to hold my own against the Valkyrie.

But Thor was a god.

Each of Thor's steps took an eternity as shadows stretched and reshaped themselves in the corner of my vision. The taste of metal filled the air and an ancient fear prickled the back of my neck.

Thor held out the red cloth, like he was handing over a babe. My entire focus zeroed in on the hum that seemed to emanate from the package in Thor's arms. Odin peeled back one corner of the fabric, and time seemed to slow. Piece by piece, he removed the covering until the last shred of cloth slid away from the blade.

My breath caught and my vision doubled as the sword was exposed to the hall. An urgent, heady Magik, unlike anything I've ever felt before, settled into my bones, making me restless.

Surprised murmurs sounded behind me, but their words could have been the rustling of woodland creatures for all I cared.

Every piece of me strained toward the sword. My fingers itched to hold it, my heart ached to feel its strength in my hands. A gentle pulse of Magik flashed across the surface. Lighting up runes that glowed like the setting sun. It was magnificent.

Odin picked up the sword, and its shine dulled, like it didn't like being held by the Alfather. A jealous spark burned through me as he held up the blade and inspected the weapon like a prized horse.

His eye met mine, and he motioned me forward. I hesitated for a moment as my gaze skated up the blade. The urge to take it from Odin and feel its power in my hands sent a thrill through me. But I also knew there was no going back once I picked up that sword.

This was the diverging path, I realized. We'd either die as Sol's chariot plunged beyond the horizon tonight, or we'd be hunted for the rest of our days. Either way, Gramr would be the one to tip the scales.

I glanced at Kara, surrounded by guards, and her wide, trusting eyes held mine. Despite all the odds, her fate was in my hands, and yet she looked at me with a warmth that made me want to fly. The Norns may have woven our lives together for their own purposes, but I chose to tie my life to hers the moment she walked into my village.

I choose you always.

Her lips twitched into a secret smile, and I turned my back on her to make another choice today.

Step.

My boot echoed through the hall like the beat of a drum. The shadows in the corner of my eye seemed to lean closer, like they were watching history unfold.

Step.

A beam of sunlight glinted off of Gramr, and a hum resonated through my bones.

Step.

Odin turned the blade side to side and I could swear starlight flashed along the steel.

Step.

The scent of wet earth and sunlight filled my nose, and a calm washed over me.

Step.

The Magik in the air turned cold, and my gaze flicked to Freya. The corner of her lips twitched, and she raised her chin with a haughty expression.

Step.

Destiny swirled around me like a wild storm.

My visitor's words about the future were a bitter wind biting at my skin. The Norn's warning to Kara roared in my ears. Magnus's death, pelting my soul with sharp rain. Bryn's anger clung to the air, making it hard to breathe without drowning. And Kara was the bolt of lightning illuminating the choppy waters, threatening to drown us all.

A tidal wave of clarity hit me, and I knew exactly what I had to do.

Step.

With sweaty palms, I came to a stop in front of Odin, Freya, and Thor. A man among gods.

"Bring the Disir."

I turned to watch as two of her guards pulled her forward. She didn't fight them, and a swell of pride filled my chest. As they reached the top of the stairs, Thor stepped forward and yanked her forward.

Kara stumbled as his fat fingers dug into her skin. My jaw popped as I grit my teeth. Thor threw Kara at Odin, and she skidded across the marble floor. It was a testament to his strength, how easy it was for him to toss Kara around. Hatred fueled my adrenaline, and I felt like I could take on an army of Draugr single handed.

Odin stepped forward and placed the tip of the blade under Kara's chin, forcing her to look up at him. The sword hummed with Magik, and she recoiled.

"You have been a blight on the Nine Realms for far too long." Odin slashed the blade against her face, cutting a gash along her cheek. Her face paled, but she held the Alfather's gaze with a determination that sent a thrill through me.

She would not be broken today, no matter what happened.

Thor tangled his fingers in Kara's hair and pulled her up onto her knees. Still, she didn't make a sound, nor did she fight him. How she kept her composure when she looked down right murderous, was anyone's guess.

"Sigurd," Odin motioned me to his side, and he kept his eye trained on Kara.

I stepped forward, and he flipped the sword so the hilt was facing me. I swallowed the lump in my throat as a pulse of Magik sparked between my fingers and Gramr.

My heart slammed against my ribs, making me lightheaded as I reached for the pommel. It must truly be useless in his hands if he didn't bat a lash at giving it up. Though the way Fenrir growled made it clear, he'd swallow me whole if I made one move toward his master.

My fingers curled around the hilt, and warmth spread through my veins like wildfire. I sucked in a breath as raw, unfiltered Magik burned up my arm. My senses sharpened and I could hear the heavy, deep thud of Fenrir's heart. Embers crackled somewhere in the hall and the smell of decay and rot intensified.

Just beyond Odin's shoulder, Freya smiled like a mischievous cat. A soft caress of her Magik swirled around my hand, and I gripped the sword tighter.

"You must offer your blood to ignite the Magik in the steel." Odin's icy gaze zeroed in on me. "It's time to take your place among the legends," Odin held his arms out and took a step back.

I pulled the blade through my fist, and blood coated the steel. I barely felt the bite of pain as the sword flashed with the brilliance of a thousand stars. The hilt warmed in my hand. And Magik poured into my soul like the sun after a long winter. The rush of every battle I've run into galloped through my veins. My muscles tensed and stretched with a strength that was more than any mortal should possess.

I looked down at Kara, and fear crossed her features for the first time. Thor's hands on her shoulders held her in place, but she looked like she was trying to inch away from me. Or was it the Magik of the sword that made her soul cower?

I glanced up at Odin, who wore a smug smile. And then at Freya, who stared at Kara with an intensity that stilled my heart.

"Now is not the time for second thoughts." Odin snarled, and Fenrir snapped his teeth.

I looked down at Kara, and her chest heaved with every breath. Her pulse thrummed wildly at her neck, matching my own. Everything I felt for her over the last hundred years filled my heart—love, loss, anger and betrayal. My visitor's voice echoed in my head.

You will choose Kara, but she won't choose you.

He was right. I would choose Kara.

Peace settled over me, even as the sword pulsed with need in my hand. Kara flinched and my eyes caught on Thor's fingers digging into her shoulders. A cold fury made me grit my teeth. I met the god's eyes, full of confidence now that I wielded a weapon that could kill the unkillable. And I swore I'd make him pay for laying a single finger on her.

I raised Gramr, and let a century of anger and loss flood my veins. My grip tightened around the hilt, my knuckles going white.

I met Kara's eyes, then dipped my gaze to the floor. I hoped with everything in me that she understood what I was asking her to do.

"You're right, Alfather."

Kara loosed a breath, and I swung as she dropped like a stone to the marble. The blade skated past her head, and cut through flesh with such ease, I thought I missed.

"Destinies can be changed."

Thor's arms hit the ground with a thud. Several gasps and a strangled cry filled the air. Thor stumbled back a step and Kara's vibrant, trusting green eyes looked up at me as Fenrir let out an ear-splitting roar that shook The Hall of the Gods.

CHAPTER THIRTY-TWO

KARA

FOR HALF A HEARTBEAT, I'd doubted Sigurd as he raised the sword over my head. The glare in his eye was murderous, and I thought maybe I misread everything. Maybe he wanted me dead after all.

Thank the stars I was wrong.

I stared up at Sigurd, astonished he had the gall to attack a god. His chest heaved with every breath as he held my gaze. Bloody, unfiltered rage was etched into every line of his face and something ancient sparked behind his eyes.

A swell of admiration filled my chest as Fenrir's growl reverberated through the hall, rattling my bones. Everyone shouted, and the sound of swords being drawn filled the air. A million thoughts and emotions ran through me faster than a pack of wolves as Thor's blood spilled across the marble floor.

Odin shouted the order to attack Sigurd, and my heart stopped. We had to get out of here. Now.

I pushed off the cold stone and kicked out my leg, sweeping Thor off his feet. He went down like a solid gold statue, cracking the marble as he hit the floor.

"Let's get out of here." Si grabbed my arm and hauled me to my feet. He dragged me down the stairs. Away from Thor. Away from Odin. And right toward a snarling Fenrir.

Gramr pulsed with another wave of raw power that clawed against my skin, and I recoiled as we dodged to the left. The cloying presence of the sword's Magik set my teeth on edge, and made the ember in my core burrow into the shadows of my soul.

Midnight wings erupted between Fenrir's hind legs, and Talon unceremoniously wrapped an arm around Ezra and shot into the air. Asheria was already airborne with a horror struck Daiman as Fenrir slammed a heavy paw down, sending a tremor through the hall. Relief at their safety flooded through me as the ground buckled under my boots.

"Run," Sigurd ordered and gripped the sword with both hands. His blade connected with another and he shoved one of Odin's fallen backward.

"I'm not leaving you." A blade swung toward me and I ducked. I rushed my assailant, arms still bound behind my back, and shoved my head into his gut, knocking him on his ass.

A familiar icy blast of air crawled over me, and the chains around my wrists froze. The metal burned my skin, then fell away with a clank. Si's shackles hit the marble next to me, and I let out a sigh of relief.

My eyes met Freya, and she tipped her head in acknowledgement as she stepped into the shadows and vanished.

The guard I knocked over rose and I kicked him square in the chest. The kernel of Disir Magik warmed my core, but I still couldn't access it with the brand on my neck. I needed a weapon.

Desperation and anger flushed through me as I grabbed the guard at my feet and swung. My fist connected with his face and his head snapped back against the stone. Stepping on his wrist, I ground his bones into the marble until his grip relented on his sword, and it clattered to the floor next to him.

"Kara," Si yelled, and I felt his concern burn through me like it was my own.

I looked over my shoulder as Odin dropped Fenrir's chains. The order to annihilate us screamed from his lips. My heart shuttered as I looked up at the wolf staring down at me. A deep primal fear shuttered through me as he peeled his lips back, exposing a row of bones shattering teeth.

"This way." Si grabbed my hand, and we ran as Fenrir's jaw snapped toward us. Hot breath licked up my neck as lightning crackled along the ceiling. The hairs on the back of my neck rose and my Magik snarled at the beast pursuing me.

I skidded to a halt and Sigurd whirled on me, eyes wide as lightning struck right in front of us.

"I expected more from you, Sigurd." Odin stood before us, sword in hand, and fire ripped through my veins.

"You were meant for greatness and yet you stand by her side." He sneered when his eyes landed on me.

"He has nothing to do with this." I stepped in front of Sigurd and squared my shoulders. Magik or not, it was time for Odin to pay for stealing my wings and banishing me to Midgard.

Embrace it. Feed it. A fragment of my dream resurfaced and my Magik stirred.

A slow smile crept across his face, and he cocked his head to the side.

"He has everything to do with it." The ground shook with an even cadence as a shadow stretched over us. Fenrir.

"The Norns should've told you the truth about Sigurd." Odin continued and I wanted to punch the smug look off his face.

There was nothing he could say that I'd believe.

Odin's gaze shifted to Si over my shoulder. "The truth of his blood isn't the only bit of knowledge Mimir shared with me."

"Get out of here," I said over my shoulder. All I had was the sword in my hand and one tiny ember of Magik. But it would be enough to save Si. "Find Talon."

"No." His voice carried an edge of finality to it as he took his place next to me. "We leave together, dead or alive."

"Dead it is, then." Sparks of Magik ignited on Odin's fingertips and a deep growl that would haunt my dreams rattled my teeth.

One blue eye bore into me and the fear I'd been living with for over a century turned to acid in my stomach.

I wanted blood. His blood.

I swung my weapon, pushing him back. He wanted to kill me before I even lived. I circled around him and out of the corner of my eye, I saw Sigurd strike out at Fenrir. How he summoned the courage to face that beast was more than impressive.

Odin grabbed the hilt of his sword with both hands and the Magik crackled up the blade, turning the steel blue.

Your blood is stronger than his Magik. A voice snarled in the back of my mind as I reached for the ember inside me.

"Your Magik is child's play compared to what lives in me," I spat. I curled my will around my Magik and pulled it out of the shadows, letting it feed on my fury.

"You know nothing of the power I possess." He lunged forward, and I dodged out of the way as Magik exploded off of his sword, and hot blue embers burned my skin.

I flinched and jumped backward. Looking down at the black and red burn marks on my skin. My Magik dug in, burying its roots in my pain and fueling the hungry storm galloping through my veins.

Fenrir let out a snarl that made the hair on my arms stand up, but I kept my focus on Odin.

A deep laugh rumbled in his chest as he stared at me. "You are a far cry from your ancestors."

"Then why are you so threatened by me?" I stalked toward him as the embers of my Disir Magik grew stronger and more alert to the well of power inside Odin.

"Tell me." His eye flashed with morbid curiosity. "Can you feel his soul?" He looked at Sigurd over my shoulder. "The power he would give you?"

I could. Even with the majority of Magik locked up, I could still feel the strength of him. The power that radiated under his skin and called to me.

"As I thought," he smirked when I didn't say anything. "And what of my soul? Does it call to you?"

I stopped in my tracks as a wave of his power hit me like a brick wall. He'd been holding back, baiting me into this trap. Now that I could feel the full weight of his power, my heart raced as the blast of a battle horn and drums hit me like a physical blow. My hands shook, and the hunger in me roared as I tried to remain neutral.

"No, it doesn't," I lied through my teeth. "Guess you aren't as desirable as you like to believe. Loki, on the other hand." I let a smile twist across my face. "Now he was irresistible."

"You insufferable cow." He rushed forward, sword raised, when the Hall of the Gods exploded.

The blast threw me backward. Stone and branches pelted me like a thousand arrows. Something solid and large hit me hard in the ribs and the air was knocked from my lungs as I tumbled end over end.

A cold spike of fear stabbed me in the chest. I did a quick body scan, and I was fine, nothing but superficial scrapes and bruises.

"Kara," Sigurd yelled over the roar of falling debris. And the fear in my chest consumed me. I turned toward his voice. The windows that overlooked Asgard had shattered. There was nothing between Sigurd and the thousand foot plummet to the forest below, except for his grip on the pillar.

My heart stopped, and the noise of death and battle fell away.

There was only Si, a singular point in my universe. I leapt to my feet and ran toward him as another wave of Magik blasted through the hall.

The momentum threw me forward onto my hands and

knees. His eyes met mine for a fraction of a second as his fingers slipped from the pillar. He flew over the edge as if in slow motion. His arms flayed and his dark hair blew around his face. Gramr reflected the last rays of the sun as Si fell out of sight.

My soul screamed, the sound echoing off the hall, and I shoved to my feet. It couldn't end like this. There was too much left unfinished for him. I wasn't finished with him.

I reached the edge in two strides.

"This isn't over, Disir," Odin snarled and a shock wave of Magik hit the center of my back. The heat of it was almost unbearable, and I shook with the effort to stay standing. He was strong, much stronger than I remembered.

I looked over my shoulder at Odin.

"No, it isn't." My Magik simmered and flickered with need, but my revenge would have to wait.

Without a second thought, I jumped after Sigurd.

He tumbled head over feet, and I tucked my arms and pressed my legs together in a desperate attempt to catch him.

The wind whipped past me, the cold biting into my face and making my eyes water. But I refused to blink or take my eyes off of him for even a second. The sounds of the battle above vanished, leaving only the sound of my shirt rustling in the wind and the frantic beat of my heart.

Panic crawled up my throat, and hot tears burned my eyes. My muscles strained to keep my limbs close to my body as the force of the air tried to throw me off balance.

"Sigurd," I yelled his name as I closed the distance, hoping he could hear me.

He looked over his shoulder, and his body turned with the movement so he was facing me. His eyes met mine, and relief settled over his features. A wave of guilt crashed on the shore of my heart as he stared up at me. I wasn't sure I deserved the trust I saw in his eyes.

How many more times would his life be at risk because of me?

He reached a hand out as I drew closer. His fingers splayed as he strained to reach me.

How many more times would he suffer because of me?

I reached out a hand as I approached. My fingers brushed his, and I grabbed hold. His other hand gripped my shoulder, and we pulled ourselves toward each other. I wrapped my arms around his torso. The solid weight of him against me was a relief. His arms clamped around my waist and his cheek brushed mine.

"For someone who doesn't like flying, you find yourself in the sky more often than a novice Valkyrie." A nervous chuckle blossomed in my chest.

"It's not by choice." His words resonated through me. "Just don't drop me this time." Even with the lilt of humor in his voice, a rush of guilt poured over me at the reminder of what I did to him under Loki's control.

Summoning my wings, I waited for the telltale tingle of Magik across my back.

Nothing.

"I know you like a little danger when you fly, but—" Sigurd breathed against my ear.

"The brand." Realization hit me like a ton of bricks. I'd thrown myself after Si without access to the one thing that would save us. I was so accustomed to being able to fly, I didn't think twice when I jumped.

"Streð mik," I cursed. "I can't access my wings." I was closed off from my Valkyrie Magik. From the Magik that would save us. All I had was the small fire of Disir Magik.

Gods. We were going to die.

Use your Magik. A calm, soft voice whispered in the wind.

I could make out the tops of trees over Si's shoulder and a twinge of panic settled under my breastbone.

"Kara—"

"Just give me a second." I was terrified of what I might become if I started down that path. I'd already struggled to regain myself after the Mara. If I let the Disir Magik grow into the inferno it craved, I might never gain control again.

"We don't have a second."

He was right. The forest below was growing with every beat of my heart. I didn't have time to debate if this was a good idea or not. If we wanted to live, it was our only option.

"If I lose control, use the sword and kill me."

"Your Disir Magik?" He asked, and I was grateful he'd already followed my line of thinking.

"Promise me."

"You can do this. I won't need Gramr."

"Just give me your word."

"Save us, and we'll worry about the rest if we're still alive."

I took a deep breath and reached inside myself for the ember of eager Disir Magik.

"Not to rush—"

"Shut up and let me focus," I snapped at him and closed my eyes. I had seconds at best to get my wings to materialize or all of this fighting will have been for nothing.

Concentrating, I stoked the fire inside me and the Magik flickered brighter. The foreign nature of this Magik slithered through me, slow and unyielding. It was so unlike the power I was accustomed to.

Si cupped my face. "Don't fight it," he breathed as my eyes flew open. His dark brown eyes met mine, but there was no fear in his gaze. He held my stare, strands of his dark hair flying around his face. "Let it take you."

He couldn't know what he was asking of me. But the confidence in his gaze made me pause, and I reached for the Magik again.

"Let go," he pressed his forehead against mine.

I couldn't see anything beyond him, but I didn't need to see the ground to know we were close. Too close.

I exhaled and, one by one, I let my walls fall. The fear of hurting him. The guilt over all the people I killed. The heartache that I recognized all too well in Bryn's eyes. I let all of it fall away until there was nothing but the warm sensation of power buzzing through my marrow.

The Disir Magik—my Magik unfurled inside me like a dragon waking from a deep slumber. What I thought was an ember of Magik rose from my soul and grew until it eclipsed every part of me. I pulled on my Magik again, dragging it out of its cave and forcing my wings from my back.

Power burned between my shoulders, and the song of Sigurd's soul filled my ears, my heart, my every breath. The deep hum of his essence dripped through me like honey, and my arms tightened around him instinctively. His heart beat against my chest and his song was an ancient melody in my bones, calling me home from the highest mountain top.

The trees below were no longer a blotch of green. I could make out individual branches and pockets of empty space.

It took all my careful concentration to ignore the pull of his soul with his body so close to mine. But I was able to quiet my mind enough to feel the wind through each feather.

The snap of my wings opening to their full length sent a shudder through me, but I was too late. My wings crashed against branches, snapping the limbs off the trees as we fell through them.

We were going to hit the ground—hard. But maybe I could slow us down enough to keep us alive.

"Hold on," I grunted.

I leaned forward, and Sigurd followed my lead. He tightened his grip around my waist as my wings beat in an upward motion as fast as I could manage.

His breath warmed my neck. And my Magik took notice of

him once more. The deep melodic hum of his soul sliced through my concentration like an ore through water and I let out a ragged breath.

Not now. I seethed at the monster inside me as we hit a branch and were knocked sideways. I kept beating my wings, kept fighting to slow us down, but we were spinning out of control and my Magik faltered.

I reached into the deepest parts of myself, and with a desperate hand, grabbed hold of the Magik. My wings solidified in time for me to thrust us to the left, narrowly missing a trunk three times the width of us.

"Brace yourself," I warned, as I wrapped my wings around him and turned so I'd hit the forest floor first. The impact ripped the air from my lungs as his body crashed into mine.

We tumbled end over end. Rocks and roots digging into my body, leaving no part of me unpunished. Sigurd groaned as I rolled over him, my wings only able to keep his body close to mine as the unyielding earth assaulted us both.

My head smacked against something solid and sharp, and my vision blurred. I lost hold of my Magik and felt it retreat into the shadows, where I couldn't reach it. My wings vanished, and I was free of Sigurd's weight, as my back slammed into solid, rough bark.

CHAPTER THIRTY-THREE

KARA

I LOOKED through the canopy of branches to the indigo sky above. The rich color reminded me of the flowers that grew at the base of the blue mountains in Folkvang. A single star twinkled in my field of vision, a mirror of the tiny spark of Magik that resided in my chest.

"Kara," Sigurd choked out somewhere to my left. "Are you alright?" His husky voice pulled on the desperate part of me that could still feel the call of his soul. I let out a breath, and I rolled onto my side. The leaves crunched under me as I battled for control of my emotions.

I pushed to a sitting position and my ribs felt like they'd been snapped like twigs. A sharp bolt of lightning shot from my lower back, down my leg, and I hissed.

Was I alright? Undecided.

After everything I felt as we fell to our death—my Magik, Sigurd's soul, our bond—the only thing I was sure of was the throbbing pain in every part of my mind, body and soul.

I could still feel the Disir Magik under the surface, dormant but alive. I was grateful it saved us, but I hated the way it made me crave power. I didn't want to give into the temptation, but abstaining left me feeling empty and unsatisfied in a way that was hard to ignore.

"Kara?" He groaned again and this time there was an edge of worry in his voice.

"Yeah," I exhaled. "I'm here." I called out, getting on my hands and knees as a wave of nausea rolled through me. I took a slow measured breath, filling my lungs as much as they'd allow and exhaled.

Inhale. Exhale. The ground came back into focus, and the fuzzy warmth of sick, gave way to a chill.

I pushed to my feet, my legs weak and aching from the impact. I scanned the area for him, and he was kneeling a few feet away, covered in a layer of dirt and leaves. Blood dripped down the side of his face and his hair was wet with blood and matted at the temple.

He got to his feet, holding his side. His face contorted into a mask of pain, and he sucked in a breath as he rose to his full height. He ran a hand through his dark hair, brushing the strands off his face, and winced when he touched the wound on his head.

"Are you alright?" I asked as I closed the distance between us, scanning him from head to toe. His clothes were back to being disheveled and a little bloody, but there were no obvious wounds that needed immediate tending. And then I noticed his hands were empty and the prickly Magik of the sword was gone. "Where's Gramr?"

"I'm fine, thank Yggdrasil." He limped toward me, one of his legs stiff. "And the sword's around here somewhere." His eyes scanned the immediate area as he closed the distance between us. "I dropped it when we hit the ground." His eyes bore into mine and the memory of his soul song prickled my sensitive skin, sending a thrill through my core that both excited and terrified me.

I shoved the heady melody into the back of my mind and rooted myself in the panic simmering in my chest.

"What the Hel were you thinking?" I shoved him hard enough to knock him off balance.

He stumbled backward, a flash of surprise flickering across his face.

"Ow," he drew out the word like a question. His brow furrowed, and he stared at me like I'd lost my mind.

"That's for saying I deserved to die." I stalked toward him, and before I could shove him again, his fingers wrapped around my arms and pulled me against his chest.

My breath caught, and a different kind of heat simmered under my skin. My anger subsided, and I realized fear was driving my emotions. Fear that I'd lost Si for good this time. Fear that I'd be the one to send him to the stars. Fear that I didn't know how to keep him safe.

"I didn't mean a single word, and you know it." He looked down at me, pinning me to the spot with dark brown eyes that melted the tension in me.

He cocked an eyebrow, and the corner of his lips twitched. "Besides, I can't afford anymore broken bones if we're going to get out of here in one piece." His grip lessened on my arms.

"You're truly okay?" I searched his gaze. So much had happened since the last time we were alone and yet, every time I looked into his eyes, it felt like no time had passed at all.

He nodded, and his gaze fell to my lips. A dull roar filled my ears and I couldn't think. There was only him and the stars that blinked into existence just to witness my self control crumble.

I pulled my arms free of his grasp and took a step back. The loss of contact left my arms cold, and I bristled.

"You alright?" He did a quick scan of my body. "You took the brunt of the impact."

"I'm well enough, all things considered," I panted, not from the pain, but from the effort to keep even an inch of distance between us.

"And your Magik, how are you feeling?" He asked tentatively and brushed the back of his fingers down my arm. As if he too couldn't help the draw between us. Goosebumps rose on my skin and I let out a shaky breath.

"Fine," I breathed, but I wouldn't meet his eyes. I was ashamed of what I felt when we were plummeting to the ground. What I was still feeling as his fingers moved back up my arm.

"Look at me." He pinched my chin between his thumb and forefinger and tilted my head up.

I blinked a few times and swallowed hard as our eyes met. Everything I felt for him bubbled to the surface. Desire, fear, lust, anger, love. I was a jumble of emotions, each demanding my attention.

But the warmth of his gaze hit me with the force of a battle-axe. Slamming through everything else, until there was only him. My heart threatened to beat out of my chest as everything —the forest, the gods, the Nine Realms—faded to the background.

He ran a finger along my jaw and I leaned into the warmth of his touch. "Two truths?" He exhaled and a spark of desire burned in his eyes.

I nodded, and he dropped his hand and squeezed it into a fist by his side. It was comforting to know he was just as affected by me as I was by him.

"Tell me what you're feeling."

My eyes dipped to his mouth. I wanted to close the gap between us. I wanted to get lost in the feel and taste of him. I wanted to remind myself that we were alive.

Instead, I took a steadying breath and searched for the Magik inside me. It was there, ever present, but just a whisper under my skin. Even the siren call of his soul was fading to a soft lullaby.

"The Magik is quiet." I placed a hand on his chest, and the even tempo of his heart was a balm to my frayed nerves. "But I can still feel the memory of you." I admitted as I closed my eyes.

The echo of his soul song burned through my core and made my head spin. "It was almost impossible to ignore."

I took a breath and pulled my hand back like I'd been burned.

"I couldn't think, couldn't breathe."

Si watched me, his gaze roaming over my face like he was searching for a sign of the Magik in me that would be his undoing. Or maybe he was waiting to see how much I'd share with him. I met his eyes, and I knew I didn't want to keep this from him. He needed to know who I really was if we were ever going to be able to move forward.

"I felt it once before," I exhaled. "When you became my charge." The memory flooded me like it was yesterday. "I was drawn to you the way a bird knows true north. It was undeniable and stronger than anything I've ever felt." His gaze met mine, and a fire simmered in his eyes that turned my blood molten. "I crossed realms, oceans, and mountains to find you. But that first summons of your soul was a drop in a shallow well compared to what I felt today."

"What did you feel today?" He grabbed my hand and laced his fingers through mine. The gesture made my heart swell. He was here, in this moment, with me, and he wasn't afraid.

"It was all-consuming, endless." My gaze lingered on his mouth. "You weren't just under my skin, you were in my marrow, coaxing me into an endless ocean that I never wanted to resurface from." My eyes met his and a dizzy heat swirled through me.

"Good to know I'm irresistible even in a life or death situation." His voice came out husky and my core throbbed as the sound reverberated through me.

"This isn't a joke." I shook my head. How he could look at me, and act as if I wasn't talking about turning him into a Draugr, was beyond me.

"I know." He cupped my face. "But we're alive, and you didn't try to kill me while we were a thousand feet in the air. I call that progress." His lips quirked into a smile that I wanted to taste. Gods, he was beautiful.

A small laugh escaped my throat. "One of these days, you're going to tire of risking your life around me."

"Doubtful." The heat in his gaze made the corner of my lips curl. "I've lived more since your return than I have in the last hundred years. If being around you means risking the stars, I'd rather spend every day thinking it might be my last, then a single risk-free day without you."

My eyes bounced between his, and the thread of control I was holding onto cast off into the wind. I grabbed him by his shirt and pulled him toward me. His lips were a breath from mine and I inhaled the heat of him. The familiar scent of spice and wood filled my nose, and a thousand memories tangled in his arms flooded me.

"Does that mean you'll go with me to the end?" I breathed, and the ache in my body gave way to the desire heating my skin.

His lips brushed against mine, and heat flushed my chest. "To the end and into the next life." His hand wrapped around the back of my neck and tangled in my hair.

We shared a breath as the last hundred years melted away and I pressed my lips to his. The shadows of our past weaved together with our present and exploded in a shower of stars as his lips moved against mine. Magik pulsed low in my core, acknowledging the undeniable thread that tied his soul to mine.

His hand gripped my hip and pulled me against him, and a breathy moan escaped my lips. The desperate ache I'd gotten good at ignoring shot through my core like a flaming arrow, igniting the embers of desire that only he touched. All the heartache and loss, the politics of gods and destinies, fell away at his touch.

His mouth moved against my lips with unspoken words. His desire matching my own, and throwing kindling on the fire blazing between us. His hand tightened on my hip, pulling the lower half of my body flush against him. He groaned into my mouth and it reverberated through my blood. Deep, unabiding longing drowned me in a torrent of memories.

Our first chaste kiss, his body moving in harmony with mine. The long nights of heartache and separation. And finally, the moment our eyes locked after a hundred years.

The last shred of my control snapped, as my Magik met my desire and I let go. A flood of warmth spread through my core and between my legs. Every brush of his lips laid claim to my heart as his desire poured into me.

His tongue slid against mine. And the stars rearranged themselves as I melted into him. His fingers tangled in my hair, holding onto me like I was the very breath he needed to survive.

This was nothing like the moonlight kiss we shared before Loki ruined everything. This was all heat and desperation driving us and I couldn't stop even if I wanted to. I needed him to soothe the ache in my soul. I needed him to make me feel alive and whole.

A new merciless hunger sparked in the shadows of my heart and swirled with my own desire. The intensity devoured me, plunging me deeper and deeper into a century of yearning.

My Magik unfurled, and a frenzy burned under my skin as Sigurd's soul called to every part of me. He was everywhere, all over me, in my blood, and I moaned at the sensation of being fully wrapped in the essence of him.

I sucked in a shared breath as his hand made its way from my hip, up my side, leaving a trail of heat as he explored the curve of my body. He stepped into me and I stepped back, both of us moving until my back hit a tree. A thrum of pain spider webbed across my back, but I was far too gone in the feeling of him to give it much notice.

He released his grip on my hair, his hand falling to my neck. He tilted my head up ever so slightly, giving him better access to deepen the kiss, sending a bolt of pure lust through my center. My heart thrummed against the pad of his thumb and he squeezed ever so slightly.

A heady warmth filled my head, and I bit his bottom lip and sucked it into my mouth. He groaned and pressed the full length of his body against mine. The sound of his desire was more intoxicating than any soul song. Blood rushed between my legs and a primal hunger I hadn't felt since the last time we were together burned through me like wildfire.

Every brush of his tongue, every caress, every breathy sigh felt like an unbreakable vow that was being sewn into the stars.

If she wanted my soul right now, there wasn't an ounce of me I wouldn't give to her. Si's husky voice pierced through me and the Magik in me sparked.

"I want all of you." My fingers found their way into his hair, and he gripped my neck tighter and pulled back. His gaze was molten, and I tried to kiss him again, but he kept my head in place. He stared down at me like I was his salvation and damnation.

A soft smile pulled at the corner of my lips and his gaze dipped to my mouth like he was starved, and a throb of need pulsed through my body. He ran his thumb over my swollen lip and the Nine Realms tilted at the teasing sensation.

"Don't stop." I leaned toward him, but he dropped his hand from my neck and took a step back.

"Is it the Magik making you feel this way?" He held my gaze and I could see the war waging inside him as he kept his distance.

"That's not…" I sighed and slumped against the tree. "It's hard to tell where the Magik ends and my own desires begin." The admission was a hot knife in my chest.

What I felt for him all these years was real. I refused to believe it was because of the Disir Magik in my blood. My heritage had already taken too much of a toll on my soul. I wouldn't let it take the beauty of what I felt for him, too.

He closed the gap between us and cupped my cheek. "I want to know that you want me for me, not because my soul calls to the Magik in you." He held my eyes, his thumb stroking my face.

I wanted to reassure him. But the call of his soul, when we were about to hit the earth, was so breathtakingly beautiful it shattered my walls and wormed its way into my very being. I wanted him. I've always wanted him, but this was different. The Magik in my blood was hungry, demanding in a way that was impossible to ignore. And it terrified me.

I've already caused him so much pain. The thought that I might lose control and turn him into one of those soulless monsters turned my insides. If I wanted to keep him safe, to save him from any more heartache, I needed to get a handle on my Magik. Even if it killed me to do it. Even if every sweep of his gaze, every touch, pulled on the invisible thread between us, begging me not to let go. I could do it. I could keep my distance for now, if it meant his soul stayed intact.

My chest constricted, and I let my walls fall into place. I would protect him, keep him safe and alive if it cost my last breath.

Finally, I nodded. "Okay," I stepped into him. "You're right. We should take a beat until I can say with absolute certainty that my Magik has no bearing on what I feel for you."

His gaze sparked with desire.

"Friends?" The corner of his mouth quirked, and he raised an eyebrow like he too wondered if it was even possible to be platonic when we clearly wanted to jump each other's bones.

I nodded and let out a breath. "I could think of worse things." My eyes got caught on his swollen lips. "If only we lived a normal life."

A branch snapped and leaves rustled to our left. Every ounce of my desire vanished as I placed myself in front of Si.

"And here I thought I was going to get a free show," a deep velvet voice stepped out of the shadows.

"Freyr?" A warning went off in the back of my mind.

"You know him?" Si asked.

"We've met." Freyr's gaze perused me, making my skin crawl.

"What do you want?" Caution prickled my skin. Just because he'd warned Freya didn't mean he was here to help us.

"Thought you might want this." He pulled Gramr out from behind his back.

The blood drained from my face. And the Magik within the sword pulsed. It was duller in Freyr's hands than when Si held it. But the stifling darkness still clawed at my skin and turned my insides.

"You didn't use it as it was intended." Freyr stepped forward and Si placed his arm in front of me. "To kill the unkillable."

Freyr's eyes met mine and something sinister flashed under his carefree mask.

"Give me the sword." Si stepped forward like he was approaching a wild animal and held out his hand.

Freyr's lips twisted into a grin that made the hairs on the back of my neck rise.

"Of course," He flipped the blade, so the hilt faced Si. "It's keyed to your blood after all." His gaze flicked to Si, and he nodded as something unsaid passed between them.

Si took Gramr, and the force of the Magik made me take a step back. Every instinct in me screamed to put as much distance as possible between me and Gramr.

"Shall we get moving or did you want to be Fenrir's dinner tonight?" He held out his empty hands. It was a reassuring gesture, but something about the way he carried himself set my teeth on edge.

"We?" I studied him.

"Freya's collecting the others, and I was tasked with collecting the two of you."

"I thought Freya didn't want to get involved?" I narrowed my eyes.

"Things changed." He pinned me with a look that made the Magik in me stir once more.

"What changed?" I demanded as the constant blanket of Magik prickled my skin.

"I like you, red. I do. But if you don't stop asking questions and start moving, I will leave you to fend for yourselves."

As if on queue, Fenrir's howl pierced the night.

"I think we should listen to him." Si grabbed my hand.

"Smart man." Freyr walked past us and motioned for us to follow him.

If I had any other option, I'd take it. But my wings were basically out of commission with the brand on my neck, unless I wanted to dip into my Magik again. I channeled into my center, searching for the telltale spark. It was there, but faint once more. I tried to grab hold, but it quickly slipped through my fingers like fine sand. Either the brand was working its way deeper into my stores of Magik, or saving our lives took more out of me than I realized.

"I guess we're doing this," I sighed.

"Together." Si squeezed my hand and a small smile touched the corner of his mouth.

"Together." I squeezed his hand back, and we followed Freyr into the woods.

CHAPTER THIRTY-FOUR

SIGURD

My LEG ACHED, and my ribs throbbed with every breath as I followed Freyr through the forest for what seemed like hours now. Stars filled the sky, and beams of moonlight filtered through the trees, giving off enough light to see a few feet ahead.

I knew little about the god, other than he was Freya's brother. But there was a slipperiness to him that kept me on edge. And I sure as Hel didn't like the way he was looking at Kara when he held Gramr. There was an explicit threat in his gaze that turned my stomach to knots.

Kara's boots crunched in the underbrush behind me as we made our way deeper into the forest. I'd been more than grateful when she took up the rear of our party. I needed the reprieve from her roaming gaze. I needed a breath that didn't taste like longing, and her. But stars, did she make me feel like the Nine Realms were at my fingertips with just a brush of her lips.

How we were going to manage being *friends* was anyone's guess. But maybe this is what she needs. What we needed. Maybe keeping things simple between us would make it easier to understand the nature of her Magik.

She sighed behind me and my body went taut as I recalled the heat of her exhale on my neck.

I was so screwed.

And so turned on I felt like my skin might burn my clothes off my body. A flash of her mouth on mine, my hand around her neck. The rapid beat of her heart under my thumb made my blood sing with unfulfilled desire.

Deep down, I knew I shouldn't have given into temptation. But facing down death will make any man reckless, and streð mik did I want to be reckless with her.

But I don't think my heart could handle learning it was all a lie. I spent the last hundred years thinking she never really loved me, but if it turns out to be true, and her Magik is the cause of her desire, I might throw myself at the stars and beg for their mercy.

My visitor's warning that I would always choose her, but she wouldn't choose me in return, cleared the lust filled haze consuming me. He was right about my actions. What if he was right about Kara?

The way she looked at me as she described the call of my soul was heady and eager. Even I couldn't resist the hunger in her eyes that made my heart race and ears roar with need. I almost wouldn't blame her if she gave into the darkness within her.

And maybe it wouldn't be the worst thing if she did give in to her Magik. She'd used it—controlled it—to save us, despite the brand on her neck. Her power could be the tipping point in the war brewing around us.

The back of my neck prickled as Freyr veered to the right around a group of saplings. I took a deep breath and my aching ribs screamed at the pressure as I brushed a low hanging branch to the side.

Freyr adjusted course and turned to the left, his deep emerald green cloak billowing behind him. Was he lost? A pang of wariness pricked down my spine. I quickened my pace, even though each step caused a sharp pain to shoot up my leg.

"You're limping." Kara sidled up next to me. Her shoulders tensed and she leaned away from me ever so slightly. "You're hurt worse than you let on."

The sword warmed against my hip, and I twisted my belt so Gramr was on my other side. She let out a little sigh that made my heart clench. I hated that the Magik of the sword made her uncomfortable. It served as a harsh reminder of what it was made to do.

"I'll be fine." My knee was swollen, and now that the adrenaline was wearing off, it was getting difficult to walk. But I'd been hurt far worse in training. I could manage until we got to the others.

"I didn't say you wouldn't." There was a worried edge to her words, and I could feel her studying my profile.

"I assure you, it's nothing. I'm in more danger of a reprimand from Asheria than succumbing to my wounds." I chanced a glance at her out of the corner of my eye.

Her lips twitched into a smile, and my gaze lingered on her as she brushed a low hanging branch out of her way.

Just friends. I forced my eyes back on the path ahead. Freyr had stopped a few paces ahead and was looking around like he was searching for something. He knelt and placed a hand flat against the ground and closed his eyes.

"So you know, Freyr," I said under my breath. "What's his deal?"

"I know of him and I've met him once." A note of distaste colored her words. "And I honestly don't know why he's helping us." She pulled a leaf from a shrub. "Even Freya seemed annoyed by his presence the last time I saw him." She tore a sliver off the leaf and tossed it into the dirt.

"You'll camp here for the night." Freyr rose and dusted off his hands as we drew closer.

My aching body relished in the idea of resting for the night.

But with Odin, Fenrir, and who knows how many others looking for us, it didn't seem wise to stop.

"Camp? No." Kara stepped ahead of me, placing her body between me and the god. "We need to keep moving, Fenrir-"

"There are far worse things in this forest than that beast." He cocked an eyebrow as if challenging her, and I scanned the shadows for anything nefarious.

"And you think making camp here?" She threw out her arms, motioning to the small clearing. "Is going to save us from being dinner?"

"Oh, I don't know. I think it'll do nicely." Freyr's mouth twisted into a grin that had me reaching for Gramr. He raised his hands, and a gust of Magik whipped through the trees, and the ground trembled.

A blend of anxious confusion stirred in my gut and I pulled Gramr from its sheath. Kara took a step back and held her arm out in front of me. Goosebumps rose on her skin, but she didn't shy away from the Magik pulsing off the sword.

"Are you trying to alert every manner of creature to our location?" Kara yelled over the sound of the earth being ripped apart.

Roots rose from the ground. Dirt and rocks falling from the limbs and my mouth fell open. I was no stranger to Magik, but this was unlike anything I'd ever seen. Gnarled serpentine tendrils of wood twisted toward each other and multiplied. Branches grew off at every angle, twisting and turning as they created a domelike structure.

"You worry too much," Freyr called over the rumbled of trees reshaping themselves. "It'll be the death of you."

Freyr waved his hands side to side, up and down, as if he was guiding the roots into position. I had no idea what he was the god of, but I never would have guessed he had power over the natural world.

Long, sinuous roots like vines weaved in between the larger structure, binding them all together to create a small shelter. And leaves sprouted along the tangled roots, making it blend into the forest.

"And you thought being the god of Fertility was useless," he winked at Kara and she stiffened.

"Why are you helping us?" The bite in her words made it clear she didn't trust him.

"Because I want to see Odin fail." Freyr stalked forward and the glint of amusement in his eyes vanished. "I want him to suffer, as so many others have suffered under his rule."

Surprise flickered through me. I didn't expect him to be so forthright with his answer. I glanced at Kara and noticed her hands balled into fists like she was fighting a war with herself.

I stepped forward, hand still gripping Gramr tightly. "What makes you think we have anything to do with whether Odin succeeds or fails in getting what he wants?"

Freyr's eyes met mine, and the mischievous glimmer in his stare made me dread whatever he was about to say.

"For when a heart of flame." He inclined his head toward me. "And soul of steel come together." His eyes darted to Kara. "The final battle for the Nine Realms shall commence."

"The Norns said something similar." Kara's voice held a desperate edge as she stepped forward. "What does it mean?"

I glanced at Freyr, and another stone in the path ahead fell into place and solidified. The Norns had said it, Freya had said it. Odin had alluded to it. As did my visitor. My heart fell into the pit of my stomach and I released my grip on the sword, letting it fall back to my side.

"It means we're the reason Magik is failing. Doesn't it?" I met Freyr's unnerving gaze, and he nodded. "We're the reason Ragnarok has begun." The words fell from my mouth as my body went numb.

"But why now? Why us?" Kara looked at me and there was heartbreak in her eyes. My heart faltered as I stepped closer to her and placed a hand on the small of her back.

"There are forces," Freyr started. "Greater than all of us that want Odin's reign to end."

He turned his back on us and waved his hand once more. The domed cage lifted a foot off the ground as more roots twisted together to create supports.

"Why you were chosen," he shrugged. "That's above my pay grade."

His words rang true, but after everything we've been through, I wasn't ready to believe his word alone.

"But, it just so happens that I too would like to see someone else on the throne."

"Let me guess, you?" Kara scoffed.

Freyr actually looked offended. "Absolutely not. My talents lie elsewhere." He cocked an eyebrow at her and a grin twisted his lips.

"Not this again."

Fenrir's howl split the night. Icy fear burned through my veins and I scanned every shadow, looking for a pair of glowing eyes that would be our end.

"Kara's right, we need to keep moving." I started forward and my leg screamed in agony.

"And how far do you think you'll get on that leg?" Freyr snapped. "Get in." He motioned toward the small, dark opening of the shelter he created. "I'll take care of the rest."

Kara grabbed my hand and looked into my eyes. "If you want to make a run for it, just say the word." The tenderness in her gaze disarmed me. "But if you need to rest, I'll stay by your side without question."

"Don't be fools," Freyr scoffed.

"I don't want to hold you back." I cupped her cheek.

"You said you were in. And so am I." She squeezed my hand. "Together. No matter what."

I glanced at Freyr and the shelter he created. His eyes met mine, and a shiver ran down my spine. We could run. But where would we go? We had no idea where the others were. And Kara couldn't access her Magik easily, if at all after the fall.

I turned back to Kara, and an overwhelming sense of responsibility filled my chest. She was trusting me once again. As much as I wanted to get the Hel out of Asgard, I knew in my bones the right thing to do was to stay put and regroup.

"I think some rest will do both of us some good."

A smile touched the corner of her mouth, and she laced her fingers through mine.

We walked toward the shelter, and my eyes skated over Freyr once more. I didn't trust his help. But if I sensed any foul play, I'd abscond with Kara before he had a chance to wonder where we went.

"Do try to enjoy your *rest*." An impish grin spread across his face as he eyed the two of us.

Kara gently nudged me forward, and I ducked as I stepped into the shelter. The roots formed a solid, mostly flat surface to support my weight, and the dome was tall enough for me to stand up straight.

"One toe out of line and I won't think twice about doing to you what I did to Loki." Kara's soft menacing threat made my heart clench.

It was just a threat, I told myself.

Kara stepped into the shelter, and without warning, the whole structure shifted back and forth. The groan of roots tangling, twisting, and ripping from the ground shuttered around us. Fresh air filled my nose and a beam of moonlight wiggled its way through the roots and kissed the side of Kara's face.

Her pissed off face.

"A little warning would have been nice," she grumbled and turned away from the opening.

"Enjoy the view," Freyr shouted.

The opening now looked out over the top of the forest. For the love of Yggdrasil, would my feet never stay planted on the ground?

CHAPTER THIRTY-FIVE

IF WE WEREN'T DANGLING from what was basically a glorified animal trap, I might have enjoyed the view. The stars glimmered against the velvet black sky. And even the Seven Hens were visible, despite the hazy glow of lights from Asgard in the distance. A cool breeze ruffled the loose strands of my hair as tiny pinpricks of light danced through the trees below. It was serene, if not for the simple fact that Fenrir was stalking the forest, hunting us.

"I hope the others are okay," Kara said, more to herself. "I hate not knowing what happened to them." The roots groaned and creaked as she took a seat and leaned against the makeshift wall.

"Speaking of the others." I moved away from the opening, slowly and carefully, so as not to jostle the roots too much.

"What the Hel happened to Daiman?" I had wondered what happened to him and Ezra since the beach.

I lowered myself next to her, careful to keep the weight off my injured leg. "Because I know you weren't the cause of his injuries."

"Is that what Bryn told you?" She scoffed and rested her head against the twist of leaves and branches.

My gaze traveled over her. The cuts across her hands, the purple bruise blooming along her temple. The scrape against her cheek that Odin had given her. The tiny bits of leaves and twigs still tangled in her hair. The dark circles under her eyes.

She'd taken the brunt of our fall and didn't complain once about her injuries. The brand on her neck peeked through her hair and my stomach tightened.

"They wanted me to believe the worst in you."

"Thank you for choosing not to believe them." She placed a hand on my thigh and rubbed her thumb back and forth affectionately. "I know it would've been easy to after everything I've done."

The small gesture made the cracks in my heart shutter. She was so used to everyone thinking the worst of her. The roots creaked all around us as a gust of chilly air passed through the shelter.

"It was easier not to believe them." I grabbed her hand and laced my fingers through hers. She let out a sigh and leaned her head against my shoulder.

Really, I was starting to believe the worst in everyone else. Time and time again, she had put her life at risk to save others. And as payment for her sacrifice, she was branded and hunted simply because of who she was.

A lingering rage simmered through me. She didn't deserve any of this.

"So, how'd Daiman end up half dead?"

Kara stiffened, and she sat up.

"We were attacked on our journey to Asgard by creatures called the Mara."

There was a frosty edge to her voice and my senses screamed to life at the mention of the Mara.

"The dream feeders?"

"You know of them?" She let go of my hand and twisted toward me. The shelter rocked side to side. My heart sank as I thought about the drop to the ground, and I gripped the roots next to me as if it would save us.

"My mother used to tell me stories." I glanced out at the shadowy forest. "I thought just to scare me into staying in bed. But they're real?" I looked at her and hoped, just this once, she was lying.

"They're real." From the haunted look in her eyes, I knew unequivocally that I never wanted to cross paths with one of them. "And terrible."

The image of a shadowy figure stealing the souls of children flashed through my mind. And the terror I felt as a young boy resurfaced. Freyr wasn't kidding when he said the wolf wasn't the only monster out there.

"Why didn't you just fly to Asgard?" I scanned the shadows a little more diligently. "You could've avoided the Mara altogether."

"Believe me, I wanted to." Kara shook her head with a short, humorless laugh. "But it would've alerted Odin to our arrival, and our plan hinged on him not knowing we'd arrived in Asgard. Clearly, Ragnar had other plans." She played with the ends of her hair, twisting it round her fingers absentmindedly.

"I'm sorry about his involvement in all this." A spasm of guilt tugged at my core. Ragnar was my friend, and I felt responsible in a way for his betrayal.

"Don't be," she glanced at me and a soft smile brushed her lips. "He was trying to save you."

"Most wouldn't be so forgiving." I cocked an eyebrow at her and wondered how she could find it in herself to always justify other's actions.

"I didn't say I forgive him. But I understand why he did it. He loves you, can't say I blame him." She bumped her shoulder against mine and my heart squeezed.

Just friends. I reminded myself.

"So if you didn't fly, how'd you cross the realms so quickly?"

"Ragnar actually." Kara rubbed the back of her neck. "Did you know he's been leaving Folkvang for the last ten years?"

The sharp sting of surprise wound itself around the dull ache in my chest. I didn't know Ragnar as well as I thought.

"No, I didn't. And I'm guessing Freya didn't either. She questioned me and Daiman about our ability to cross the rift."

"She didn't know you could leave?" Shock and curiosity furrowed her brow.

"Nope. And she was less than pleased by the notion." The memory of her Magik searing my skin made me adjust to a more comfortable position.

"I could only imagine what she'd think about Ragnar's adventures over the last decade." She chuckled softly, and it did unbearable things to my insides. Just the curve of her lips teasing a smile made me want to toss my ego aside. Who cares if her Magik is the reason she's drawn to me, if she's mine?

I care. My heart seemed to say as it ached.

I forced myself to look away from her and focus on the conversation.

"So his tunnels aren't just for smuggling ale." I shook my head. "I should have known." Disappointment burned in my chest.

"If it makes you feel any better, no one knew."

It didn't, but I appreciated her trying to ease my irritation.

"So the tunnels led to Asgard? That was lucky."

"Not exactly." She leaned back and her body visibly relaxed as she settled next to me. "They led us to the Nowhere. It's the place between realms," she amended when she noticed the confused look on my face.

"It connects all the realms together." She looked up at me and the naked wonder in her eyes softened the tension in my soul. She's lived longer than me, seen more than me, and still there was something out there that made her glow with adoration.

"I'd never heard of anyone traversing the Nowhere on foot,"

she continued. "We pass through it as Valkyrie, but it's never been a tangible place, until now."

"So anyone can access the Nowhere?"

"If you know how to find it. The rift in Folkvang, the one the Draugr came through, it wasn't the only one. Ragnar found one of them in his tunnels, and the rest is history." She shrugged.

"I knew the man had secrets, but this is—"

"Insane. Ridiculous. Impossible. I know." She sighed. "But it's how you're still alive right now. The Magik that binds you to your realm isn't strong enough to hold you any longer. It allowed all of them to come here to save you."

"When did everything get so complicated?" I said under my breath.

"I think it's always been complicated. We were just living in ignorance. Blissful ignorance." A saccharine smile kissed her lips.

"Do you wish you could remain ignorant?" I glanced at her profile. "Live a mundane life?"

A dry, humorless laugh escaped her throat. "After the last few days, it sounds like a dream."

"If you could give it all up. Never taste battle again, never feel the breeze under your wings. Would you?" I studied her profile.

A soft, sad smile touched her lips, and she let out a heavy breath.

"I asked Bryn something similar when I first arrived in Folkvang."

My heart throbbed with guilt at the mention of Bryn's name. I could only imagine the swirl of complicated emotions Kara was feeling.

"She wondered what it was like for me, in Midgard."

"And?"

"It was fine for a time. It was a relief to not hear the call of the fallen. To be free." She closed her eyes. "But it didn't last."

This was the most she'd ever shared with me about her time in Midgard. And I wanted to know more, to know everything. I wanted to know her, like I once did.

"To answer your question though," she looked up at me. "No, I couldn't live a normal life. At least, not anymore," she said the last part under her breath.

"Anymore?" I raised an eyebrow, wanting—needing her to share more. "But you did, once?"

"Once. for a brief moment." Her eyes met mine and a faint blush touched her cheeks. "A long time ago."

For a heartbeat, we were just two people under the stars. No gods chasing us, no Disir, no Fenrir, or threats of Ragnarok. Just us, the way we once were, before it all got so complicated.

"What about you?" She glanced away. "Do you wish you would have settled down, fallen for a nice girl in your village and had a gaggle of kids?"

"You already know the answer to that." A small smile touched my lips.

"From the moment I could hold up a wood sword, I knew I'd never be satisfied with a quiet life." I said without hesitation. "Being a warrior, fighting for my people, it's all I ever wanted."

Until I met you. I thought as my eyes caught hers.

"What we want and what we need rarely coincide." Her voice turned soft and her hand found its way to my thigh once more, making me feel like I was about to take up arms and rush into battle.

"Maybe, but if you're lucky, they can be one and the same." My gaze trailed down to her lips, the hollow of her throat, the swell of her breast, before meeting her eyes again.

Heat flashed in her hungry green eyes as they skated over me like a promise and a claim.

"And do you count yourself lucky?" Her voice was much too sultry for the fragile walls I'd place between us.

"Most days," I exhaled.

The vulnerability in her gaze undid the armor around my heart. It would be so easy to lower myself and brush my lips against hers. Just like I'd done a thousand times before.

"You asked for two truths earlier," she leaned toward me. "It's your turn to answer one of my questions."

I nodded. I was too wrapped up in the way she was looking at me to form any words.

"You said if I wanted your soul, you'd give it to me."

Heat flushed my face, down my neck, and over my chest. "I didn't mean to say that out loud."

"Did you mean it?" Her eyes searched mine, and a roar filled my ears as a thousand memories of her flashed through my mind. The first time we laid together, the way she smiles over her shoulder when she wants to get her way, the brush of her lips, the feel of her skin.

I gave her my soul many moons ago. "Yes," I breathed as my heart thrummed wildly.

She placed her hand on my chest and pressed her forehead to mine. "Promise me something?"

"Anything." I folded my hand over hers.

"Never let me touch your soul." She pulled her head back and her eyes met mine. "If I ever try, if I lose myself, use that sword and stop me." Pain and heartbreak flashed across her face.

"Kara." I cupped the back of her neck and brushed my thumb along her jaw.

"Just promise me. Please."

My heart trembled as she pleaded with me. "Alright." I agreed, even though I knew I would never use Gramr on her. "But I won't have to." I pulled her toward me and kissed her forehead. "You may carry Disir Magik in your blood, but you are not like them."

A flicker of doubt crossed her face as she settled next to me. "You don't know that."

A howl broke through the quiet of the forest and every muscle in my body went taut. Both of our attention shifted to the opening, wreathed in vines and leaves.

"You should get some sleep." She cleared her throat and put a little distance between us. "I'll take first watch."

Off in the distance, the tops of trees rustled as if something massive was moving through them. Fenrir.

CHAPTER THIRTY-SIX

KARA

SWEAT DRIPPED down my back and temples as we trudged through the forest. It wasn't even midday yet, and the stagnant, humid air was stifling.

Freyr had returned at first light, and unceremoniously lowered us back to the ground. He looked more like a disheveled man who enjoyed half the women of Asgard rather than someone who had spent the night leading Fenrir astray. But I couldn't complain.

The night's rest did wonders for my aches and pains. Even with very little access to any Magik, my body healed quickly, making it easier to face the day. And Sigurd was no longer nursing his leg.

Neither of us had spoken much since we started our trek and a twinge of nervous energy sparked in my chest. We were both dancing around our feelings last night. I could feel it in the way he looked at me. Like there was an endless well of emotion within him I could happily drown in. I knew we had more important matters at hand, but I couldn't help but feel like we were both teetering on the edge of our self control.

"We're almost there." Freyr called over his shoulder as the forest started to thin.

The steady sound of rushing water reached my ears and relief flooded through me. The thought of splashing cool water on my face made me quicken my pace.

The ground shook ever so slightly under my boots and a howl sounded much too close for comfort. The tiny sliver of relief I felt shattered, and every muscle in my body went taut.

The three of us bolted, running for the river winding through the forest. I jumped over a fallen tree and a low hanging branch hit me in the face. My legs burned and I couldn't get a full breath with the heat, but still I pushed harder.

"Just on the other side, about fifty paces, you see that rock?" Freyr panted as Si and I reached the shore.

He pointed to a large boulder protruding from the hillside, covered in ivy. "There's a cave system beyond that boulder that'll take us to your friends. I don't suppose you want to fly us across the water?" Freyr raised an eyebrow.

"If I could use my wings, don't you think I would've by now?" I huffed out of breath.

He leaned in, his deep green eyes searching mine. "Maybe you just need a little encouragement?" He said under his breath as another howl raised the hairs all over my body.

The small flame of Disir Magik prickled faintly along my limbs, like it recognized power nearby.

Interesting. I stored that thought for later, when I wasn't being hunted by one of the Nine Realms fiercest beasts.

"Like I said, I can't." Or at least I didn't want to court the shadows of my Magik just to cross a river.

"Very well." Freyr took a step forward, but instead of stepping into the soft mud lining the riverbank, he vanished.

"What in the name of—" Si stared at the river bank.

"We don't have all day," Freyr called from the other side of the river.

"Ass," I grumbled under my breath.

"Did you know he could do that?" Si glanced at me with a bewildered expression.

"No, I didn't," I said through gritted teeth and took a step.

My boot sunk into the soft earth as I stared at the dark, opaque water.

Si stepped into the river without hesitation.

The sound of branches snapping sounded behind me and I looked over my shoulder. I couldn't see more than a few feet into the trees, but I could feel more than one set of eyes on me. My Magik stirred as a flood of adrenaline seared through me. I wasn't sure if I was strong enough to call it forward again, and hopefully, I wouldn't have to try.

I turned back to the river as Sigurd pushed off the shore. He was favoring his right side. His injuries must still be hindering him more than I realized. A pang of worry echoed through my empty stomach. He'd always been good at hiding his pain, that I'd forgotten to check him—really check him.

I lowered myself into the river and sucked in a breath as the frigid water drenched my boots and plastered my shirt to my body. I took another sharp breath and pushed off the shore. The water felt incredible against my sticky, sweaty skin, and I welcomed the chill.

The current pulled at my body, pushing me in the opposite direction of where Freyr waited for us. I panted with every stroke as I pushed against the current.

Stars, I hated any activity that made my heart pump like it was fighting for every beat.

I caught sight of Sigurd ahead of me, and he was struggling far more than he should be. Worry bled through me quickly, followed by a warm tingling of awareness in my core that made me pause. I looked over my shoulder as a dark mountain of fur and fangs stepped out of the forest and paused on the edge of the river.

Fenrir.

"Streð mik." I tucked into the water, and my Magik flickered brighter, taking notice of the terror rising within me.

We needed to get out of here.

Now.

Magik pulsed through me and I knew Fenrir had stepped into the water.

I caught up to Sigurd within a few strokes. His eye caught mine and whatever he saw on my face was enough that he pushed harder and kept up with me.

Another ripple of power pulsed through the water, and my Magik purred like a hungry cat.

I clamped down on the feeling building inside me. I didn't have the time or energy to dissect what was happening to me.

I reached the shore mere seconds before Sigurd and pulled myself up onto dry land. Half the river dripped off of me like a drown rat, as I reached for Si.

He winced as I yanked him out of the water and pushed him forward. He glanced over his shoulder and I followed his gaze.

Fenrir was halfway across the dark icy water. My gut hollowed and my heart threatened to beat out of my chest. The odds of us out running the beast were slim.

"That's something you don't see every day," Sigurd huffed.

"Come on, almost there," Freyr ordered and ran without waiting to see if we'd follow.

"Go." I pushed Si ahead of me and ran behind him.

He gripped his side like his life depended on it, and he wasn't putting his full weight on his bad leg.

I was one step behind him the whole way, ready to grab him and haul him to safety if his body gave out. I might not be able to fly us out of here, but I wouldn't go down without a fight. I'd do everything in my power to make sure Si didn't fall to the Sun Eater.

Everything in your power? A voice purred through my mind like velvet and my Magik sparked brighter.

The sound of water sloshing off of something large reached my ears.

Yes. Everything.

If I had to reach into the darkest part of my soul and allow their Magik to burn through me to save him, I would.

Panting and admittedly more terrified than I'd been in a long time, we reached the outcropping of stones.

Thank Yggdrasil, thank Ymir, thank the Norns, we might actually make it.

Freyr pushed aside the ivy. His fingers traced the groove of the largest rock and his brow furrowed.

"What is it?" I demanded.

"Someones been here." Freyr continued to run his fingers along the edge of the stone. "They sealed the entrance."

"Then unseal it," I commanded, and my Magik snapped to life, heightening my senses. The crisp mineral scent of the river filled my nose. Sigurd and Freyr's rapid, heavy breaths filled my ears. And the tremor of heavy footsteps vibrated through me.

"While I'm loath to admit it, my gifts have their limitations."

I looked over my shoulder and Fenrir stalked toward us, his gold eyes pinning me to the spot. The water made his gold chains glisten, and his lips peeled back, showing off his canines.

"Then we use brute force," Si stepped to Freyr's side. "Together." They both pushed on the massive boulder, blocking our path to freedom.

I glanced over my shoulder. We had a handful of seconds before Fenrir tore us limb from limb.

"A little more," Freyr encouraged. The boulder scraped against the other stones as it slid a few inches, revealing an opening. But it was still nowhere near wide enough for any of us to pass through.

My heart fell into my stomach, and I knew we weren't going to make it. Or at least I wasn't going to make it. But Si would. Freyr could guide him to the others, and he could escape.

I reached for the simmering flame of Magik as I shoved everything I felt last night into the darkest shadows of my soul. I couldn't worry about what Si would think. I couldn't worry about what it meant if he left here without me.

Odin wanted a Disir, and he was about to get one.

"Keep trying." I grabbed Gramr from the sheath at Si's side. The metal burned my hand, and a cloud of stifling Magik sucked the air from my lungs.

But I was a Valkyrie. I was a Disir.

And a little pain was nothing if it meant Si would make it out of this alive. I gripped the hilt tighter, letting it sear my flesh, and turned to face Fenrir.

"Kara, don't," Si pleaded, but I ignored him as I walked toward the monster in front of me.

A deep growl sounded in Fenrir's chest and he snapped his jaw at me, showing off every ivory tooth in his mouth.

Squaring my shoulder, I planted my feet in the soft earth. I gripped Gramr tighter, letting the pain fuel me as I forced my Magik to the surface. Goosebumps rose over my entire body as a wave of power brushed over me like a breeze. A small smile curled my lips and the fear I felt a moment ago vanished.

Fenrir seemed to recognize the change in my demeanor and his next step was hesitant.

I ignored the tremble in my hand and pushed aside the oppressive blanket of Magik trying to snuff out the fire in me. I dug deeper, wanting—no, needing more. I curled my fingers around the flickering flames, taking root inside me, and refused to let go. I would bend it to my will. I would save Si.

The heavy whoosh of wings sounded somewhere above me. Deep black wings the color of nightmares spread wide and blotted out the sun. Fenrir's eyes tracked the sky, and he took a step back with a snarl.

Taking my eyes off the beast, I watched Freya and her Hrafn dive toward us.

"Go," she yelled from the back of the monstrous crow. She raised her arms and clouds gathered overhead.

Fenrir snarled and leapt forward. He was outnumbered now, and if he was going to kill me, he had one chance.

Fenrir lunged forward, and I raised Gramr to strike. Freya's pet dove between us, its massive talons clawed at the wolfs snout, forcing Fenrir to take a step back.

"Get that rock out of the way," I yelled over my shoulder as I ran back to them. "Now." Freya wouldn't be able to hold him off for long. Now was our chance to get into those caves and leave Asgard behind us.

Si threw his shoulder into the rock, and he winced as it budged another inch.

Fenrir snarled and snapped his teeth so loud it rattled the loose rocks and dirt around us.

Freyr had his back pressed to the stone, with one foot propped up on the cave wall as Si threw his body against the stone again.

And again.

"For the love of Yggdrasil," Si growled and panted as he shoved against the unmovable stone.

Lightning zig-zagged across the sky and a snap of Magik exploded between us and Fenrir.

We all turned to look at the battle of beasts. Freya stood atop the Hrafn, arms raised, eyes glowing. Fenrir lunged into the air, jaws wide open and aiming for Freya as she unleashed another icy blast of Magik.

Sigurd shoved against the stone again, and it was just enough room to squeeze through.

"Kara, let's go," he yelled.

I looked back at him, hunched over in the dark tunnel and back at Fenrir and Freya. Against every instinct, I turned away from the fight for the first time in my existence, and I ran.

I reached the crevice and bent to follow Si when Freyr grabbed my arm and his eyes met mine. There was no humor in his gaze, and it sent a spike of fear through me.

"There's a fork in the path."

"You're not coming with us?" I studied his stoic features.

He shook his head. "And leave all the fun to my sister?" He glanced over his shoulder at Freya.

"You both have a choice to make," he said, turning back to me. "To the right, you'll find your friends and a way out of Asgard. To the left, there's a boat. It'll guide you to the answers you seek."

The Hrafn screeched so loud I flinched and covered my ears.

"Go," he shoved me forward.

"Thank you for helping us." I ducked and forced my shoulder into the tight crevice.

"Choose well Kara. We're all depending on you." He winked and turned his back on me.

Before I had the chance to say anything else, he pulled his sword and ran to help his sister so we could escape.

CHAPTER THIRTY-SEVEN

I GLANCED over my aching shoulder at the small opening. A sliver of golden light spilled into the tunnel. A screech that turned my blood molten with fear echoed through the hollow space as Kara ran toward me.

"Where's Freyr?"

"He's staying behind." She closed the distance between us and handed me Gramr with a trembling hand.

"How are we—" I took the sword and sheathed it.

"He said to follow the path," she motioned me forward. "It'll lead us to the others."

I nodded and started deeper into the tunnel, still dripping half the river.

A flicker of resentment crossed my heart. If Freya hadn't intervened, Kara would be nothing but star dust. It was one thing to give us a fighting chance, but going toe to toe with Fenrir was a death sentence. And she knew that.

I hurried through the dark, uneven tunnel. They reminded me of Ragnar's operation back in Folkvang, except this tunnel seemed forgotten. No torches lined the path. Making it difficult to see, even with the shaft of sunlight pouring in behind us.

Fenrir's roar and snap of teeth echoed through the cavern, and the mountain shuddered around us. Soil and loose rocks tumbled around us like rain. I inhaled the musty, dirt filled air and coughed. Fire ripped through my lungs as my ribs threatened to shatter completely.

My ankle rolled on a loose rock, and I stumbled forward. A jolt of pain shot across my chest and down my arm. Throwing myself against the boulder not only further damaged my ribs, but it also dislocated my shoulder.

I paused to catch my breath and force the pain into a tiny compartment in my mind.

"Si?" Kara huffed, and the warmth of her hand pressed firmly between my shoulder blades. Her touch was soothing, even as I sucked in another painful breath.

"Just give me a moment." I leaned against the crudely carved wall, and the cold earth seeped through my shirt and sent a shiver down my spine. The heat had been oppressive as we walked through the forest, but the freezing swim had chilled me to the bone.

"What is it?" Her fingers coasted over my shoulder, and I winced. "What's wrong?" I could hear the worry in her voice.

I huffed and tried to reposition my arm into a more comfortable position.

"For sorðinn sake, Si. This isn't the time for heroics." Frustration laced her voice as her hands move down my chest, and I sucked in a breath.

If I could just get my shoulder back into place, it would take away some of the pain radiating through me in hot waves.

"Put your hand on my shoulder and press down," I said through gritted teeth.

Her hand moved up my arm to my shoulder and clavicle with a featherlight touch.

I guided the lower half of my arm out to my side, so it was parallel with the ground, and then slowly started to raise my hand above my head. The tension was almost unbearable, and I groaned as the joint slipped back into place with a crunch. I let out a sigh of relief and rested my head against the dirt carved wall.

"Thank you." I cradled my arm to my chest. "Let's keep moving." I wiped the mix of sweat and water from my face and pushed off the wall.

I felt her step to my side, and she kept a hand on my bicep. The gesture was enough to tell me she was concerned, but I was grateful she wasn't making me out to be weak and human as we continued deeper into the tunnel.

The further we walked, less and less light reached us, until I could only see a few steps ahead. The fight had gone quiet, which was almost worse than hearing Fenrir and the Hrafn snarling and screeching. It was unlikely Freya bested the beast, which meant the Sun Eater was still out there.

It was only a matter of time before our paths would cross again. It was a fool's notion to even consider being free of Fenrir and Odin.

The tunnel opened up into a cave, and I halted. A small pool of shallow water sat undisturbed, straight ahead, and reflected a swath of stars from above. My gaze travelled up to the ceiling, and my mouth fell open. Between the dozens of stalactites hanging from the ceiling, thousands of pinpricks of blue light sparkled like the night sky, and a gasp escaped my throat. It looked like an entire realm was shining down on us.

"They're beautiful, aren't they?" Kara's voice was soft next to me.

"I've never seen anything like it." A sense of wonder and melancholy settled low in my core.

The Nine Realms had more to offer than I could ever imagine, and yet I'd been satisfied with Folkvang for the last century. Shame soured the otherworldly glow as I realized how much of my adventurous spirit I'd lost in my second life.

At least I was making up for it now.

The distant sound of voices echoed through the cave from a

tunnel to our right. And I could have sworn I heard Daiman's laugh. I started toward them, and Kara grabbed my arm.

I turned toward her, concern spiking through me. "What is it?"

Her brow furrowed as she took a step backwards and shook her head.

"Freyr said our friends would be down that path," she motioned to the tunnel where their voices could still be heard.

She glanced over her shoulder at another tunnel hidden in the shadows that I hadn't noticed before.

"And where does that lead?" I watched her face carefully. And I already knew she wasn't going back to our friends.

"Answers." Her gaze met mine and the vulnerability in her eyes hit me square in the chest.

I took half a step toward her, and she raised her hand to stop me.

"There isn't a place in the Nine Realms we can hide from Odin."

Her guard was already up and I grit my teeth. She was going to leave without me. After everything we've been through. After everything we said in the forest. She was still going to try to walk away.

"No, there isn't." I closed the distance between us. There wasn't a chance I was letting her leave this cave without me.

I'd made my decision.

I chose her.

"You should go to them," she stepped back and my resolve slammed into place as I closed the distance between us.

"Knowing me has already cost you so much."

I wrapped my good arm around her waist and pulled her into my space. She could be stubborn, and she often got her way. But I was just as hardheaded as she was.

"You've cost me nothing." My words were sharp with frustration. "It's living that takes from us. From the day we're born, until the day we return to the stars, life takes if you're doing it right."

"Si," she let out a heavy breath, like whatever she was about to say would cost her.

"What do you need to hear right now? That I choose you? That no matter what does or doesn't lie between us, I will always want to be by your side?"

Her tentative gaze held mine like a lifeline. Like I might deny her the very words she needed, and she'd shatter in my arms.

I brushed her hair back and let my hand rest on her shoulder. My thumb traced the column of her neck. Her pulse fluttered under my touch, but she held still as stone.

"If I've learned anything over the last century, it's that no matter how hard I tried to unstitch you from the fabric of my soul, I couldn't without destroying the most beautiful parts of me."

Her face softened, and something akin to heartbreak flared in her emerald eyes.

"But this is your chance to start over. To live and explore the Nine Realms. To get back what I took from you." She shook her head and her eyes welled with tears.

"But I can't go with you. There's only one path forward for me." She broke our gaze. "I know we said we'd go to the end together, but you have the chance to go home. You have the chance to live." Her gaze flicked to the tunnel to the right.

I cupped her cheek and forced her to meet my eye. "I know I've given you more than enough reason to doubt me since your return. But I want to make one thing perfectly clear. When my mortal life ended, I wasn't upset that my story had come to an end prematurely. I was heartbroken because I lost my home. When you returned to Folkvang, I was angry, but not because you killed me." I brushed my thumb across her cheek and her breath hitched. "I was angry because you reminded me of everything that was missing in my second life. And when you asked me to be sure I wanted to walk this path with you, I knew my answer the moment the question left your lips. You have always been and always will be, my home. I go, where you go."

She leaned in and brushed a feather light kiss to my lips that made the world tilt on its axis. "I was so used to being on my own." She breathed against my lips. "Floating through the universe untethered and free. I thought I had everything I needed. Until I found you." She looked up into my eyes, the blue star like ceiling reflected in her gaze. Like the entire cosmos lived inside her. "You change my orbit, the way I move through the realms. From the moment our paths crossed, there was no longer a me without you."

My lips pulled into a smile I felt in my whole body, and I pressed my forehead to hers. "Then let's go get you some answers."

She grabbed my hand and pulled me down the tunnel to the left. Neither of us looked back. There was only the path in front of us now.

The path we'd walk together until the end.

OUR BOOTSTEPS, the drip of water and our heavy breaths, were the only sounds that echoed around us as we followed the narrow path. I could barely make out the walls on either side of me. And a sting of worry turned my stomach the further we walked. What if this was a trap, and we played right into Freyr's hand?

His last words echoed through my mind.

Choose well Kara. We're all depending on you.

There was a vulnerable truth to them that felt sincere. Like he and Freya wanted me to choose this path and fight against the storm that was coming. But what if I was wrong?

A cool, damp breeze that smelled like the ocean brushed over my wet clothes and made me shiver.

I stopped without warning, and Si's arm wrapped around my waist, and his hand splayed against my abdomen as his chest hit my back. The solid feel of him calmed the swirling doubt, and I took a breath.

"A little warning." He mumbled against my ear, and a shiver went down my spine for an entirely different reason.

"Do you hear that?" I exhaled and ignored the lingering desire his closeness elicited from me.

Si took a breath behind me, his chest rising against my back as he went still. I breathed with him, letting the warmth of his body sink into me as we stood in the dark and listened.

Just friends. I rolled my eyes. There hadn't been a single moment of knowing him that I wanted anything platonic.

His chest rose again, and I forced myself to focus and listen.

Movement, slow, deep and endless, filled the tunnel. A hiss that split the air, followed by a boom that resonated through my boots.

"The sea," Si breathed and my toes curled in my boots.

"We must be close." I twisted out of his hold, desperately needing some space between us before I put us in a compromising position.

The sound of waves grew louder with each step and an air of freedom surrounded me. I had no idea where this path would lead, but I knew I couldn't continue fighting my Magik. I needed answers, and I needed to gain some semblance of control again.

The tunnel widened and within a few dozen breaths I was spit out onto a bed of sand. Waves flowed freely into the open air cave and an ocean stretch as far as the eye could see. Stars glistened like diamonds and reflected in the black water. Moonlight bathed the white sand beach and at the edge of the water, sat a small boat.

A salty mist clung to the air as my boots sunk into the sand with every step. Small waves lapped at the front of the hull, beckoning the boat into deeper waters. A prominent dragonhead was carved into the prow, its eyes trained on the horizon. A swell of anticipation filled my chest, and my Magik soared to meet the emotion.

"Did Freyr mention where we're supposed to go in a vessel barely fit for the open sea?" Si called from behind me as I reached the boat.

She was a small vessel, but I'd captained many ships just like her, across the realms.

"He did not." I pulled myself up into the boat, and three leather packs sat on the floorboards.

I grabbed the first one and rummaged through it. A canteen of what I assumed was water. The aroma of freshly cooked bread filled my nose as I pushed aside a large lump of fabric wrapped food.

I was grateful Freyr had thought to pack us something to eat, but it wasn't what I was looking for. I pushed the sack aside and grabbed one of the others when Si reached the boat.

"He said it would take us to where I needed." I pulled out a deep blue cloak and several articles of clothing for men and women. He must have known Si would join me.

"Is it spelled then?" He ran a hand along the smooth, dark wood.

I sensed nothing about the ship, but that didn't mean Magik wasn't present. Looking down the length of the boat, I searched for anything that didn't belong on a Dragon ship. But she was as simple as any ship I've ever come across.

"It's possible." I pulled another cloak from the bottom of the bag. "I was hoping there was a star map or some kind of coordinates. But there's nothing." I wrapped one of the cloaks around my shoulders and was immediately grateful for the warmth.

The boat rocked as the tide crept further into the cave and I opened the third bag. It was filled with bandages and small bottles that tinkled as they clanked together.

Si grunted as he lifted himself into the boat. His face contorted into a mask of pain as he let out a measured breath.

"Si." I set the pack aside and stood to check his injuries.

"I'm fine." He leaned against the mast, gripping his side.

"Am I'm the sea goddess, Ran." I grabbed the blue cloak and handed it to him. If he wanted to be obstinate, I wasn't going to push him.

I picked up the pack with the bandages, and started pulling things out one by one. Si wrapped the cloak around his shoulders and pulled it tight around him.

"What did Freyr say exactly?" Si asked as a wave rocked the boat gently.

"He said, 'To the left, there's a boat. It'll guide you to the answers you seek.'"

I pulled out a bronze bottle with handwriting I recognized scrawled across the label.

Asheria.

Warmth spread through my chest. Maybe I didn't give Freyr enough credit if he thought to gather food, water, dry clothes, tinctures, and wound dressings. He was still an ass. But a thoughtful ass.

"Drink this." I crossed the space between us, and the boat creaked as I handed him the tincture.

"What is it?" He held the vial between his thumb and pointed finger and eyed it suspiciously.

"A tonic. It should ease your discomfort."

He uncorked the bottle and sniffed. His face wrinkled in disgust and then he drank it with one pull.

"Why would Freyr send you down this path with no way to move forward?" He wiped his mouth and tossed the bottle into the open pack.

I sat and placed my head in my hands. "I must be missing something."

I closed my eyes and listened to the cadence of the water crashing on the shore and receding. I slowed my breathing and thought back over every interaction with Freyr.

When he burst into Si's and warned Freya—something about an island. The way he just appeared after our fall, as if he'd been waiting for us. His words about flames and steel that echoed the prophecy the Norns shared with me.

A flash of sand falling from the sky wiped Freyr from my memories, as if I was focusing on the wrong thing. My Magik sparked in recognition, and star like butterflies shot out across the ocean. I tried to grab hold of the memory—or was it a dream?

"My dream." I shot to my feet and crossed the boat. I stared out at the water, and there, just above the horizon, was the Seven Hens.

"Kara," Si's voice was a million miles away.

My dream crashed through me and I remembered the woman with wings like wildfire. I remembered the stars, the beach that looked so much like this one I was kicking myself for not recalling it sooner. I remember the forest and a current of Magik that zipped through my veins.

The Nine Realms cannot survive if you don't embrace your Magik.

"Kara?" Si's hand gripped my shoulder as the memory of Jotunheim seared through me. All this time, everything was connected.

Lightning flashed in my memory and the words the Disir carved into the tree made my heart race.

There must be balance. When you're ready, you'll know how to find us, Kara.

A wave hit the boat and we slid further into the water.

"I don't need a star map." I turned toward him and his hand moved down my arm. "They already gave me the coordinates."

"They?" Fear dripped from that one word.

I met his stare. "The Disir."

His brow furrowed, his shoulders tensed. Gramr pulsed at his side and prickled my skin. A wave crashed on the shore with a boom, and a spray of water splashed into the boat.

"Si?" Unease crept through me like a ghost.

"When did you speak with the Disir?" There was no warmth in his voice, and I felt my defenses go up immediately.

"Until the end, huh?" Disappointment pierced my heart and anger leaked into my chest as I turned away from him. It took all of five minutes for him to turn on me.

Another wave washed up the shore, and we rocked side to side as the water pulled on the hull.

"I meant what I said." He grabbed my arm and turned me toward him. "But that doesn't mean I'm not going to question you along the way." His eyes met mine and a mix of relief and apprehension flooded my core. "I'm done playing the loyal lap dog who takes orders blindly. If that's what you want, then maybe—"

"No." I stopped him from saying words I didn't want to hear. "It's never what I've wanted." I had no reason not to trust him. We both just went through Hel and back to save one another. I needed to trust in that, and not let my fear control me.

"Then tell me, when did you meet with the Disir?" His voice was softer this time, but still held an edge of apprehension as he let go of my arm.

"I didn't meet with them." I moved down the ship. "They left me a message when I was in Jotunheim." The boat jostled, and I had to widen my stance to steady myself.

I proceeded to tell him everything that happened in Jotunheim. The attack, the people who were turned to Draugr. The message from the Disir. And about the dream with the Seven Hens and how it all connected back to my Magik and the Disir.

"Why the Seven Hens?"

"I don't know. Maybe it has something to do with balance. The Seven Hens represent the injustice that was done to the sisters of creation. Legend says, once balance is restored, they'll disappear from the night sky."

"Odin wished to seek balance as well." He touched the sword at his waist. "With this."

"All of this has to be about the Magik failing. But why would the Disir care about balance when they're the ones disrupting it?"

"Maybe they're not." He shrugged.

"What do you mean?"

"Over the last few days, I've wondered if the Disir are the real enemy. Maybe the gods and the Norns wrote them as the villain. But we've yet to see them behave as such."

"Then how do you explain Jotunheim? The Draugr?"

"I can't." He shook his head. "And I could be entirely wrong. I just hoped..."

"You hope they aren't as bad as we fear, because you don't want me to become like them," I finished for him.

The boat creaked as the hull was fully submerged, and we left dry land behind.

"There is something else you should know." I glanced out at the water.

I opened my mouth and closed it. I didn't know how to say this next part out loud.

He pushed off the mast and closed the gap between us as the boat was pulled out to sea. His thumb brushed my chin and his fingers curled against my skin.

A gentle smile touched his lips that undid me. "Whatever it is, you don't have to face it alone."

I closed my eyes and took a deep breath.

"I've been hearing voices since the temple."

"I recall." His voice was even, as if there was nothing I could say that would shake him.

I looked up into his dark, endless eyes and forced myself to say the rest. "I don't think they're hallucinations. And I think they belong to the Disir."

His face remained neutral, but he stiffened, and his eyes narrowed. "What do they say to you?"

He was too calm. Like he was gearing up for battle and assessing his opponent.

I swallowed the lump in my throat. He deserved to know the whole truth while he still had the chance to change his mind and find the others.

"They're angry with the gods. They want revenge. They encourage me to embrace my Magik."

"So far, they aren't saying anything I disagree with." The gentleness in his voice undid me. How could he be so calm, so understanding?

"Can you hear them all the time?" His head tilted to the side like he was studying me, and noticing the color of my eyes for the first time.

I shook my head. "Only when my emotions are heightened. Or in my dreams."

His gaze fell over my shoulder, and it was almost like he was searching for them in the dark.

"Si." The word was barely a whisper on my lips. "Tell me what you're thinking?"

His gaze fell back to me. "I'm thinking it must be horrible to have your mind invaded over and over by outside forces."

"You're not afraid of me? Of what this might mean?"

He tucked my hair behind my ear. "Afraid of you, no." The corner of his lips pulled into a soft smile. "Does it make me nervous that you have any connection with them? Yes. But only because I worry about you. About what they want from you."

My heart swelled, and I leaned into him, placing my head on his chest. He wrapped one arm around my waist and his other cradled my head to him. There were many things I cursed the Norns for, but he was not one of them.

"Out of curiosity, can you hear any others? Or just the Disir?" His voice resonated through my chest.

"Just them. Why?" I pulled back to look at him.

His brow furrowed, and his hold on me lessened. "I've noticed since the temple that sometimes it's like you're reacting to my thoughts." His gaze slipped to my lips. "Like when we kissed. I know I didn't speak my desires out loud. But you answered me as if I did."

His eyes met mine again, and my Magik stirred. There had

been moments where I felt like he was speaking directly to me without words. But I chalked it up to the depth of our connection. I'd always been able to read his little expressions, or interpret his emotions from one look.

"I don't know if that's possible," I stepped out of his arms. "But I know someone who might have some answers." I moved to the back of the boat and took up the steering oar. "What do you say we go find the Disir?"

CHAPTER THIRTY-NINE

KARA TOOK the first stint steering the ship. Her hair had dried in the breeze and was blowing around her face and shoulders. Moonlight splashed over the left side of her, lighting up her black cloak and making it shimmer. She stared off into the distance, her arm resting on the steering oar, and keeping the prow pointed toward the Seven Hens constellation.

I offered to take the helm, but I learned long ago not to argue with her when she got that far off look in her eyes. And if I was being honest, I was more than happy to oblige. My ribs and shoulder ached nine ways to the moon, my stomach screamed for sustenance, and I needed a minute to process everything she'd shared with me.

Learning that she could hear the Disir, while mildly terrifying, could be used to our advantage. A pang of guilt spread through my chest at the idea of using Kara like that. But if it could help us find the Disir and stop Ragnarok, then it was a necessary evil.

Still, my heart ached for Kara. To have your mind invaded by hostile forces. To have your dreams tainted by shadows. It wasn't fair. Not for the first time, I wondered where her source of quiet strength came from.

My eyes searched her out of their own accord for the hundredth time since we set sail. I couldn't help it, even if I wanted to. She was a beacon in the dark, endless expanse surrounding us. It'd always been like that with her. No matter the time or place, she'd always radiated a golden warmth that called to the deepest parts of me.

Her gaze slid to me for a fraction of a second. And I wondered if she could hear my thoughts now. Or if she couldn't help the undeniable draw between us either.

Her eyes softened as she gazed out at the water. It was rare to see her so unguarded. Even in my mortal life, she only shared glimpses of herself fully undone in the dead of night. When only the stars dared to glisten.

On some of my darkest nights over the last hundred years, I'd recall the quiet moments where she let me see beyond the armor. And for a few minutes, the memory would banish the ache in my heart.

I reminded myself that I was the only one to blame for the distance between us. I had my reasons, but with each passing moment, it was getting harder to hold the line I'd drawn in the sand.

I forced my eyes back to the small portion of bread, cheese and handful of dry berries in my lap, and sat back. Stretching out my legs, I popped the last bite of cheese into my mouth and savored the sharp, salty flavor.

The swelling in my knee was mostly gone, and the constant ache in my chest and shoulder had eased significantly. Whatever was in that tonic was working faster than anything Asheria had given me in Folkvang.

Thank the stars. I had no idea what was ahead of us, but I knew that I'd be better off at full strength.

I let my head fall back and stared at the vast blanket of stars as they cast their brilliant, ancient light upon us, and opened up my senses.

There was something calming about the rhythmic cadence of the water sloshing around us. The creaking of the wood planks as our boat fought the current. And the gentle rustle and snap of our sail. I'd always felt at peace on the water, and it did wonders to calm the hum of anxious energy inside me.

"You look like you're feeling more yourself?" Kara's voice carried on the breeze.

"It's the best I've felt in days." I rolled my head toward her and a chilly breeze tossed my hair to one side.

"The tonic must be working well then." Her gaze trailed down the length of me before meeting my eyes again. The air crackled between us and heated my skin.

"Or it's the company." I sat up and finished the tart dried berries. "And fresh air."

My gaze flicked to her, and her lips pulled into a shy smile that made my pulse quicken. The tonic was working well, but it was her presence that was healing the ache in my soul.

"Or it's because you're hogging all the food."

I popped the last bite of my bread into my mouth. Grabbing the sack of food, I pushed to my feet.

"If you wanted some, all you had to do was ask." I cocked an eyebrow as I towered over her.

Her lips parted as she looked up at me and her eyes reflected the moonlight, like she was lit from within.

"This is me asking." Her voice was soft and sultry. And a hint of a smile tugged at the corner of her lips.

A flash of heat speared through me. For the love of Yggdrasil, I didn't stand a chance.

I took a seat next to her and pulled the other loaf out of the sack.

I handed her the bread, and our eyes met. "Anything else you want?" Fire sparked in her eyes, echoing my own desire. The faintest scent of lavender mixed with the salty air, and I did my best to ignore the ardent memories it stirred in me.

She slid the bread from my hand. "There are a great many things I want."

"I'm all ears." I kicked my feet up, aiming for nonchalance, when I felt anything but.

"I'd love a hot bath that I could lounge in to my heart's content." She took a bite of the bread and closed her eyes.

"Mmm. What about a plush bed, wrapped in the most luxurious blankets?" It felt like ages since I slept on anything resembling a bed.

"A hot meal. Juicy, spiced meat. Potatoes. And a crisp cup of mead," she groaned and took an angry bite of bread.

"A quiet night under the stars," my voiced turned soft and thoughtful as I looked up at the night sky. "In the prison where Odin kept me. There were no windows. I had no way of knowing if it was day or night. No way to track the passing of time."

She scooted closer to me and placed her hand on my arm. The small comfort warmed my chest.

"I would lie on the cold, unforgiving stone, and pretend I was looking up at the sky." I turned to look at her as her fingers lightly stroked up and down my arm. Goosebumps rose on my flesh and warmth spread through my core. "I wished to lie under their beauty once more, before I joined them."

Her eyes softened as her fingers trailed down my arm and over my hand. My mouth went dry and my heart beat with a fever in my ears.

"I don't know when we'll have a soft place to lie our heads again." I turned my hand over and she drew delicate little patterns across my palm. "Or have a hot meal. But I promise you'll never have to spend another night without the stars."

I looked up at the sky and felt the weight of the Nine Realms stare down at us.

"There was one other thing I thought of often while laying in that prison." I closed my hand around her fingers as my heart thundered in my chest.

"What's that?" Her voice was barely a whisper.

"I hoped that you were safe." I turned my attention back to her. "And that Odin never lays a hand on you again." Heat flashed in her eyes, but it was different from the fire that burned between us.

"You don't have to worry about me." She took a bite of bread and adjusted the steering oar.

"You act as if it's something I can turn off." I studied her profile. "When Odin showed up at the rites demanding Freya hand you over," I shook my head. "I was ready to fight him to the death. Then he threw me in that dungeon, and I had no idea if you were safe or even alive. I can't tell you how relieved I was when I saw you on that beach."

A dry laugh escaped her throat. "I was sure you were anything but relieved."

"I had to make them think they'd turned my mind and heart against you," I sighed and laced my fingers through hers. "Odin was very clear about what he wanted from me. And I wanted that sword." I nodded toward Gramr, nestled with the other satchels.

Kara stiffened as she stared at the weapon.

"Better we have it than him." I gave her hand a reassuring squeeze.

"Do you really think it can kill a Disir?" I heard the unspoken question in her voice. *Do you think it can kill me?*

I turned toward her and tucked her hair behind her ear. "I have no idea if it can do what Odin claims. The Magik feels…"

"Dreadful."

"Extraordinary," we said at the same time. "Which leads me to believe what he learned from Mimir is the truth."

"Mimir?" Her attention snapped toward me as a cool gust made the sail waft vigorously. "What does he have to do with you and that sword?" She adjusted our course and a fine mist brushed over my face.

"He's the one who told Odin that it was my destiny to wield Gramr and end the threat of Ragnarok once and for all."

"So let me get this straight. You and I are the reason Ragnarok is on our doorstep, but we're also the ones meant to stop it according to not just the Norns, but now Mimir as well?" She shook her head.

"I get the distinct impression we're missing something vital." I agreed with her. "From the moment you returned to Folkvang, I've had this sense that you and I are circling something bigger."

"What could possibly be bigger than Ragnarok?"

"I don't know," I sighed. "But something doesn't feel right about all this. Take Gramr for example." My gaze skated over the blade. "I barely gave Odin any indication that I was on his side, and he just handed over the sword. Why?"

"I think he was hoping you'd cut my head off." She raised her brow and finished the last bite of her bread.

I shook my head. "I think he knew I wouldn't. I think he hopes I still will."

"You think he let us get away in the hopes I'd turn on you and you'd use the sword against me?"

My heart leapt into my throat. "I don't think he *hopes* you'll turn on me."

Her eyes scanned the horizon as my words settled over her.

"Mimir," she exhaled and her face went pale. "You think he told Odin I would betray you?" Her eyes met mine, and she shifted away from me.

I nodded and my visitor's words haunted me as I watched a storm brewing in her meadow green eyes. I grabbed her arm to keep her from retreating entirely. She deserved to know everything that had happened in that dungeon. Whether it was the truth or not.

"Someone visited me while I was imprisoned." I wasn't going to tell her it was me from a future realm, because I still didn't believe that myself. "They warned me that you'd succumb to the darkness of your Magik."

"Then why the Hel would you choose to come with me?" She got to her feet, and I matched her movement.

"Streð mik," I cursed. "Because I don't care what Odin says, what the Norns say, what Mimir or some stranger have to say about you—about us." I reached for her, cupping the back of her neck, and forcing her to look up at me. "You and I make our own destiny."

She opened her mouth to say something, but was cut off by a blast of light followed by the telltale rumble of thunder.

We both turned and looked out at the horizon. Dark gray clouds blotted out the stars in front of us and lightning exploded inside the storm.

A wave hit the side of the boat, throwing a spray of water into the air.

"That storm isn't born of nature." She studied the clouds, the water, and jumped up on the railing, letting the wind flow through her hair. "I think it's meant to keep whatever we're searching for hidden."

I couldn't help but wonder if she was being told to go through the storm, or if it was just instinct guiding her.

I walked to the front of the boat and studied the clouds, the movement of the water, and the feel of the wind as it whipped a few drops of rain into my face. Looking to the right, the ocean was deadly calm, inviting even. I leaned over the left railing and the water was choppy and churning with the promise to tear our vessel apart.

"I think you're right." I turned back to her. "But this ship won't make it through a storm like that."

"I don't think we have a choice." I noticed she was no longer manning the steering oar, but our course didn't deviate an inch.

A low rumble of distant thunder punctuated the air. As a fine mist brushed over my skin.

"Skitr," I cursed under my breath.

A gust of wind snapped the sail taut and pulled us forward, right toward the thickest part of the storm.

Kara sprang into action, making her way to the mast. She loosened the rope to the sail, and the fabric collapsed in on itself as we crested a sizable wave.

The moon disappeared behind the clouds, plunging us into total darkness as the mist turned to rain, then transformed into an icy downpour within seconds.

Normally I'd grab an oar, try to fight, try to survive. But there was no fighting the will of this storm, or the Magik that pulled us deeper into its grasp.

My hand clasped the wood railing as I made my way to Kara. The hull creaked and groaned as it was pushed and shoved in every direction. The dragonhead pitched forward as we slid down the back side of another wave.

"Grab the packs!" Kara shouted over the roar of wind and rain as they slid toward me.

I stopped their forward momentum with my boot and reached down to pick up Gramr first. I sheathed the blade at my waist, then grabbed a rope and threaded it through the hilt and around my body. It'd be a waste if it ended up at the bottom of the sea now.

A flash of lightning crawled across the sky, and we headed into the clouds, our visibility going to zero.

I grabbed one of the packs and opened it. Bandages and small bottles jostled back and forth. I wiped a sheet of rain off my face and reached for the other pack. Several pairs of trousers, shirts, vest and furs filled the bag.

"Take this one." I held out the satchel to her as the boat rocked violently up and down. I stumbled forward and caught myself on the railing as she grabbed the pack. "An extra set of clothes might come in handy."

Lightning lit up the clouds in long, jagged branches, and

Kara's eyes went wide. I glanced over my shoulder and my heart plummeted into my stomach. Water crashed against sharp, jagged rocks up ahead.

My blood ran cold. We were heading right for them by some unnatural force.

I pushed past Kara as she fastened her pack to her body. Stumbling back and forth, trying to keep my balance, I reached the back of the ship. My hands slipped over the smooth wood of the steering oar as I tried to grab it.

"It's too late," Kara pulled a dagger from her boot. Her hair was soaked and plastered to her face. Water dripped off of her in sheets as she wound her arm around a rope and cut through it.

Another flash of lightning, and the shadowy outline of mountains filled the horizon as I grabbed the oar and pushed against the current, driving us forward.

"There's an island!" I shouted as a wave crashed over the prow and icy salt water filled the boat. The oar snapped from the pressure and I fell backward.

Wiping the water from my face, I got back to my feet just in time to see the wall of water in front of us.

Kara reached for my hand, rain and ocean water pelting her face. Her eyes were wild with determination as I took her hand.

"Your Magik?"

She shook her head. "Even if I could access it. It wouldn't help us. I can't fly in this," she said as we both stared at the wave that would break this ship apart.

"Get to the island." The urgency in my voice made her look up at me.

Her eyes sparked and Gramr warmed at my side as she squeezed my hand tighter.

A tidal wave of water crashed down on us. The distinct sound of wood shattering into a thousand tiny pieces was the last sound I heard as we were thrown into the icy, churning waters.

The cold hit me like a wall of knives, stealing my breath. My body twisted in every direction as the roar of the ocean barreled down on us.

Still, I held onto kara's hand with everything I had as we were pushed and pulled apart.

My lungs burned for fresh air, but I had no notion of up or down. I opened my eyes, searching the black water for any sign of salvation when lighting flashed above me.

I kicked, pulling Kara with me. My leg still ached and my shoulder throbbed, but it was easy to ignore the pain as I pushed toward the surface.

My head broke free first, and I gulped down a breath of air. Kara's head popped up next to me and relief burned through my marrow until I noticed the look of terror on her face.

I followed her gaze and sucked in a breath, filling my lungs as full as they'd allow as another wave crashed over us

The water hit us with the force of an angry god, and we were plunged into the depths of the sea.

Kara's hand tore out of mine as I was pulled down, down, down.

CHAPTER FORTY

SIGURD

I COUGHED up a mouthful of water as I dragged myself onto a black sand beach. The sound of waves crashing on the shore behind me resonated through my bones as the water struck solid ground.

I rolled onto my back and stared at the sky that was just as dark as the sand beneath me. My lungs burned with every greedy breath, and my shoulder ached. All things considered, I was in one piece and I was alive. I could deal with a little pain.

Sitting up, I pushed to my feet, and felt for the sword at my side, and by the grace of the Norns, it was still attached to me. The satchel slid off my shoulder, sloshing a heap of cold water down my side as I hoisted it back into place.

A streak of moonlight spilled across the beach, but it did nothing to soften the stark landscape around me. I glanced down the shore, looking for Kara, but I was alone. A cold stab of fear dug into my heart as I looked in every direction.

Please be okay.

I turned away from the shore and rocks sprung up out of the ground like pillars forming a steep cliff face ahead of me. Still, there was no sign of her. My heart started to race and my chest constricted as I thought about the frigid water. The unruly current. The storm.

What if she was wrong? What if the Disir lured her here to be rid of a liability?

Shuffling through the sand, I ran down the beach, looking for her in the water or along the shore. But there was nothing but the dark clouds and rain swirling over the sea, a few pieces of debris from our boat, and the waves crashing against the rocks and shore.

I started back the way I'd come and noticed a small cave nestled at the base of the cliff. It was the only shelter from the wind and ocean mist whipping around me.

Maybe she reached the shore before I did.

I ran up the beach, huffing with every breath.

Maybe she'd sought out shelter, thinking I'd perished in the water.

I reached the edge of the shallow cave. It was empty. My heart sunk into my stomach and I dropped the heavy pack into the sand.

"Come on, Kara." I turned toward the water once more, hoping to get a glimpse of her. Nothing.

I brushed my hair off my face. I had no idea what to do or how to move forward. We were here because Kara needed answers, but if she was...

No. I wouldn't think the worst. Not yet.

I unfastened my soaking cloak and let it drop to the sand with my pack in a heap. I looked up the length of the cliff. Maybe she was topside. It would give her a better view if she were looking for me.

I looked around, searching for a footpath when out of the corner of my eye I noticed several runes carved into the geometric stone pillars that made up the cliff face.

Curiosity sparked in my core, and I reached out and touched the smooth carvings etched into the stone. The markings were warm despite the crisp ocean air, and I could feel the Magik crackle under my fingers. Gramr pulsed at my side and a brush of the power I felt in The Hall of the Gods made my heart race.

I traced one of the runes, and Magik burst from the stones, making me take a step back.

Everything to my left came to life as the night sky gave way to daylight. I squinted at the sudden change as I looked over my shoulder. The sun was just beginning to rise as the ocean turned from a dark endless expanse to rough white capped water crashing before me.

To my right was an entirely different story.

The night sky still hung heavy above me and the ocean was a dark blanket stretching as far as the eye could see.

It's like someone drew a line down the middle of the beach, splitting the world into day and night right before my eyes.

I let out a breath as I scanned the shoreline on the day side.

Kara.

Relief so acute, I thought my knees might buckle, surged through me.

The white foam of the waves gathered around her ankles as she marched out of the water. She looked to her right and then her left, taking in this strange land of night and day.

"Kara," I yelled as I jogged toward her, but she didn't look my way.

I yelled her name once more. But the sound of the waves pummeling the beach was too loud for my voice to reach her.

She moved out of the water and toward the rocks jutting out of the sand.

"Kara," I yelled again when I was within a few feet of her, and she finally turned to look at me. "Thank the stars. Are you okay? I thought—"

"I'm alright." Her shoulders sagged and relief washed across her face as she started toward me. "You?" Her gaze traveled over me and I closed the distance between us.

"All in one piece." I reached for her, and my hand hit something clear and solid. Like the barriers in Folkvang.

"I don't understand." I placed my hands against the invisible barrier separating us.

"I don't either." Her eyes moved passed me to the moon rising over the horizon and then turned to look at the sun on her side just peaking over the horizon as well.

"There are some runes on the stones," I nodded toward the cliffs. "When I touched them, the world split in two."

"Show me." She dropped her pack and shrugged off her heavy water logged cloak.

I moved toward the cliff once more and came to a stop in front of the stone pillars with the runes.

"It looks like they're on my side, too," she yelled over the roar of the sea as she ran her hands along the stones on her side. "This is a Mirror World," Kara said. "I've heard of them before, but I've never seen one." She traced one of the runes the same way I did and light exploded all around me, while Kara was plunged into darkness.

"It's a puzzle," she mused as she studied the runes. "One in the light, one in the dark."

"Both in the shadows, miles apart," I finished the line from one of the poems we used to tell around a fire on long winter nights.

"It's the shadows." She inspected the pillars of stone like they might speak to her. "I think I found something," she called out. "Switch me back to the light."

"What is it?" I asked.

Her eyes met mine, and she smiled. "A way into the gray."

I reached out and traced the rune again. Her side of the beach brightened, and night settled over me once more.

"Myrkrún," she smirked as she ran her hand down the seam. "I have the rune for darkness, or night," she said, without taking her eyes off the rune. "Look for Sólrún, or Ljósrún. If our two sides are mirrored, yours should represent the sun or light."

Moving away from her, I searched the rocks carefully, looking for what she described.

About ten feet from the barrier, I noticed the edge of a carving settled in the shadows. "I see it." My heart leapt with excitement. It couldn't be this easy, could it?

My fingers moved over the symbol, tracing the runes.

Kara let out a blood curdling scream. My hand fell from the symbol and I reached for Gramr.

Kara fell to her knees as her wings erupted with a snap from her back.

I rushed to help her and realized that the light from her side was bleeding through to mine. As I reached the barrier, only tiny pinpricks of light seeped into the darkness and quickly vanished.

"Kara." I slammed my fist against the barrier, my heart pounding.

"I'm okay." She picked herself up, her wings hanging behind her as she looked at me.

"Did you see the light? Before you let go of the rune?"

I nodded. "It must be the key to removing the barrier." I sheathed Gramr as my gaze traveled over her.

"And it's the source of my pain."

She looked fine, but that scream. She hadn't made a sound during her wing ceremony. I can only imagine the pain she must have felt just now, if it elicited such a response.

"Which means the rune on your side will take its price from me." My heart felt heavy with the knowledge of what we had to do. "There's always a price."

Her eyes met mine, and she nodded.

"There has to be another way," I argued.

"A Mirror World tests your resolve and forces your hand. If we don't make a sacrifice, we won't find what's on the other side."

"You're sure about this?" A wave crashed on the shore as the cracks in my heart opened up.

"I am. But I'll understand if you're not." Her eyes met mine and though I knew what I had to do, my stomach turned at the thought of causing her physical pain.

"And let you have all the fun?" My lips pulled into a grin as I walked backward toward my rune.

"Whatever happens, don't let go until the barrier is down." Her eyes held mine and her brow furrowed.

The distance between us was only twenty feet, but it felt like the Nine Realms had stretched between us. The wind picked up around me, but the damp air no longer felt cold. Every nerve in my body was solely focused on the rune in front of me and the task at hand.

"On three?"

I nodded as she raised her hand.

"One."

I exhaled.

"Two." Her voice was sure and steady as we both raised our hands.

"Three," we said in unison.

Kara closed her eyes as my fingers touched the rune, and the air was ripped from my lungs. White hot pain shot across my chest and I couldn't breathe. With my free hand, I reached for the wound that had been my end. Only it was no longer a scar. The scar across my chest was opening up once more.

Kara screamed, and I looked her way. Her head was thrown back and her wings crackled as they burned, just like Bryn's.

Sunlight spilled through the barrier as I fought to keep my hand against the runes.

My head spun, and I forced myself to take a deep, painful breath. I could taste the blood in my lungs as if I was still on that battlefield losing the fight for my life.

The sunlight edged across the beach, moving past the barrier and touching the side of Kara's face. The sound of her scream was drowned out by a wave crashing on the shore and I fell to my knees, gripping my chest.

Blood slid between my fingers as my legs went numb.

My vision blurred as the stars gave way to sunrise. The dark sand glistened in the sunlight as far as the eye could see, and I let my hand fall from the rune.

Kara collapsed onto the sand as I pushed to my feet. Taking a ragged breath, I shuffled toward her. Kicking up sand and wheezing with each step as the pain from my wound pulsed.

"Kara," I groaned, but she didn't move. Her exposed wings, or what was left of them, spread out under her. A handful of forest green feathers disappearing into the midnight sand.

Kneeling next to her, I tentatively reached out to touch her. Pushing the wet hair out of her face, I turned her head toward me.

Her eyes met mine, glassy with tears.

"Are you okay?" She sat up and gripped my face between both hands. Her eyes bounced between mine, frantic and scared.

I felt for the wound that had opened in my chest, but there was nothing. I was perfectly fine, though my shirt was stained with blood.

"I'm alright."

Her hand moved to my chest, like she needed confirmation that my heart was still beating.

"Your wings." My gaze traveled over the charred and pitiful feathers hanging at her back.

"They'll heal," she breathed.

"Are you—"

Her lips crashed into mine. She tasted like the sea, and sorrow and home.

I wrapped my hand around the back of her neck and deepened the kiss. Her lips parted for me with ease and my brain clicked off. There was only the solid feel of her in my arms. Her soft, breathy moan as my fingers wound into her hair.

I pulled her against me, desperate to feel the solid warmth of her. I spent too long today thinking I'd lost her forever.

We survived the storm. Fenrir. Odin. And a hundred other things that should've sent us to the stars by now. And for the life of me, I didn't care if her Magik played a role in how she felt about me.

Because I knew that every speck of life inside me loved her.

There was no amount of Magik, or destiny, or gods that could ever change that. Her hand found its way into my hair and she held onto me like I was the very air she needed to breathe.

"Si," she moaned my name against my lips, and it took every ounce of strength I had, not to strip her bare right here on the beach.

"Whatever it is, it can wait." My lips found her neck, and I nipped at the sensitive skin.

"As much as I don't want this to end," she grabbed my face in her hands and brushed a soft kiss against my lips. "We need to find shelter." Her breath was warm on my face.

"I don't care about shelter right now." I traced her lips with mine, our breath mingling and making the argument for me. She melted into me as thunder rolled overhead.

The storm that brought us here was about to make landfall, and she was right. We needed shelter.

I groaned in frustration and rested my forehead against her. "If I ever meet the Norns, I'm going to have a few choice words about their timing."

She laughed. Truly laughed and her eyes sparkled. My heart shattered at how beautiful joy was on her. And I knew I would fight until the end of my days to see her smile like this again.

CHAPTER FORTY-ONE

KARA

Si pulled me up the beach toward a cave. It was shallow and wouldn't provide much shelter from the elements, but at least we'd be out of the howling wind and rain that was about to crash down on us.

He grabbed his cloak and pack, and I stepped into the cave. The air shimmered and the sound of the waves all but disappeared, along with the damp, frigid wind. Magik crawled over my skin, as the shallow opening expanded into a larger cave, and a fire sparked to life to the right.

"Looks like we're in the right place." Si's voice echoed off the rocky walls.

I let out a sigh of relief as Magik brushed against mine in a comforting caress. Awareness prickled down my spine, like I'd been here before and I was being welcomed back.

Si laid out his cloak in front of the fire to dry, and I crossed the space to do the same. He unsheathed Gramr and laid it in the sand. A fresh spike of Magik turned my stomach and my step faltered. I despised the oppressive weight that clung to me every time I got close to that sword.

"Hand me your pack," Si held out his hand, while keeping his body between me and the sword, like he knew how much it bothered me.

"Everything in there is soaked through," I handed over the satchel without getting too close and he rifled through it.

"

Pulling one of the larger shirts out of the bag, he bent and wrapped it around the sword. Immediately, the blanket of Magik suffocating me vanished and I could take a full breath again.

"Better?" His brow rose as he stood and place the weapon a few feet away.

"How'd you know it bothered me?" I breathed a sigh of relief as the small ember of my Magik settled into the shadows.

"I noticed you shy away from it whenever it's close." He walked toward me as I slid my boots off and placed them in front of the fire as I took a seat on the cloak.

It was wet, but so was I, and it was better than sitting in the sand.

"The only exception being when you took it to face Fenrir," he said, towering above me as the heat from the fire warmed my skin.

"That was about as pleasant as feeling my wings burn from my back once more."

My gaze traveled the length of him. His long lean legs, up his torso and over his broad chest. My eyes traced his full lips, and the wet strands of hair falling across his face. And finally, I met his dark eyes that reflected the firelight. The spark of desire I felt outside rekindled low in my core, and my pulse quickened.

His soul song was almost non-existent with the brand on my neck, and I thanked the stars. Being this close, feeling the way I did, would be a recipe for disaster if his song was also calling to my blood.

I grabbed one of the discarded articles of clothing to distract myself and laid it out in front of the fire.

I wasn't sure how he felt about the kiss. I was just so relieved we were alive that I acted on feelings I knew had nothing to do with my Magik. But he was clear in the forest about my feelings and my Magik, and I needed to respect that. Even if every fiber of my being wanted to prove that what I felt for him had nothing to do with the power in my veins.

He kicked off his boots and sat on the cloak next to me as the fire snapped and crackled.

"You told me what Odin did to you, but seeing it. Hearing you scream…" His eyes met mine and the concern in his gaze was almost my undoing. "I'm sorry you had to relive that." He laid his hand on top of mine as I fidgeted with a pair of soggy trousers.

"You have nothing to be sorry for." I slipped my hand out from under his. "If anything, I should apologize to you. Your wound…" I couldn't meet his eyes as I spread out a vest to dry.

"Let's not travel down that path again." His voice was soft and comforting as he leaned back on his side and propped himself up with one arm. "The Magik extracted a cost neither of us wished on the other."

"I fear that's not the only price we'll pay on this island." I glanced at him and it was like taking an arrow to the chest. His eyes were soft and open as he watched me.

"When the time comes, we'll face that too, together." His hand reached for me, but he pulled back and balled his hand into a fist.

"We have no idea what might come next." I brushed a strand of hair off his face. "Today we paid with pain, but there are things far worse the mirror world can extract from us. Are you sure you want to keep moving forward?"

"Do you?" His brow furrowed as his eyes traced my face.

"I don't think I have a choice," I admitted. Even if I wanted to turn back, I didn't think the Disir would let me. They'd brought me this far for a reason. They weren't going to let me walk away now.

"Then neither do I." His lips curled into a smile that made my skin heat.

A beat of silence stretched between us. I'd always admired

his ability to meet the unknown head on with a confidence that rivaled even the Aesir. It was one of the first non-Valkyrie reasons I was drawn to him. That, and it didn't hurt that he was built like a god.

My gaze lingered on him. His full perfect lips, arms that felt like home, and hands I wanted to feel against my skin. The fire flickered, castings shadows and light across his face. A flood of memories, wrapped in the amber glow of the hearth, turned my blood molten.

"You need to stop looking at me like that." Si sat up, placing his back to the fire and resting his arms on his knees.

"Like what?" My cheeks flushed as the fire popped, and the muffled sound of a wave crashed on the shore.

His gaze slid over his shoulder and the warmth in his eyes put the flames burning beside us to shame. "Like you want me to be your undoing."

I leaned closer to him, and he turned toward me. I could see the question in his eyes. I could feel his hesitation in the way he kept the distance between us.

"What if I do?" I placed my hand on his chest. His heart beat wildly and his eyes flared with a dangerous edge I wanted to explore.

His hand cupped my cheek, and I looked up into his deep chestnut eyes.

"We should have met the stars a dozen times already," his voice was full of raw emotion that made my heart swell. His thumb brushed the edge of my jaw, making me lightheaded. "I don't want to waste another moment pretending I'm not utterly consumed by you."

He leaned toward me, forcing me onto my back until he was hovering over me.

"And my Magik?" I exhaled as he brushed my hair off my face.

"Magik or not, I know what I feel for you is real." His thumb traced my bottom lip and heat course through me, making it hard to breathe or think.

"But if you're unsure." His husky voice purred through me. "If you want to wait until you have answers, you're going to have to be the one to walk away. Because I can't."

"I can't either," I cupped his face. "And I don't want to."

I looped my arms around his neck, my fingers tangling in his hair. His lips pressed to mine, soft and sure, and his beard brushed against my sensitive skin. He tasted like salt water and promises whispered in the dark.

He slowly deepened the kiss, like he was savoring the moment, taking his time for all the years we spent a part. The heat of his breath warmed my skin, making me ache to feel his lips on the rest of my body as he started undoing the buttons on my vest.

I kissed him for all the nights I wished I could. I kissed him for all the words I once whispered against his skin. I kissed him for every tear that carried the pain in our hearts. I kissed him because I knew in the deepest part of my soul that Magik had nothing to do with how I ached for him.

With the last button free, I sat up and he moved with me as I shrugged out of my vest. He lifted my top over my head and tossed it behind him. The cool air brushed over my skin, but the goosebumps prickling my bare chest had everything to do with the look of pure lust in his eyes.

My hands found their way to his belt, and I kissed him for every night I spent wishing I could just see his face again. I lifted the soaking shirt over his head and threw it with my discarded clothes. I ran my hands down his chest and kissed the scar that I'd given him.

A deep, guttural noise came out of him as one hand found its way into my hair. I kissed my way up his chest, savoring the solid feel of him. I pressed my lips to the hollow of his throat, and then tipped my head back to look at him.

"There isn't a Magik in the Nine Realms that feels like you," I breathed.

He cupped my face, running his thumb along my cheek. "Promise me, no matter what happens, we never part again."

I smiled up at him, letting the warmth and happiness rise in me like the sun.

"I promise."

His lips crashed into mine as sure as the waves against the shore. The heat of his breath mingled with my own as his lips brushed mine, making me feel alive and whole despite what's ahead of us.

The greedy caress of his hands reached me in places I thought long dead. I wanted him in a way that was more than physical, more than just bodies and a release. I needed him in the way a soul needs to gaze upon the moon to truly feel seen.

I leaned back, pulling him with me. His body hovered over mine and he stared into my eyes in a way that stripped me to my core.

"There isn't anything in the Nine Realms that rivals your beauty." He leaned in and kissed my neck with so much tenderness, my heart shattered into a thousand tiny pieces. His lips brushed mine, and the heat of his passion pieced me back together.

It had always been like this with him. As if we were destined to trade pieces of ourselves until we were no longer two distinct entities. But instead something infinitely more beautiful.

He undid the laces of my trousers and his mouth traveled down my torso, kissing and tasting my skin and making me ache for him in a way that turned my blood to molten lava.

I lifted my hips, and he tugged my trousers off with a few good pulls. His eyes trailed up my naked body like a claim, and I flushed with the need mirrored in his gaze.

He positioned himself over me again, his bare chest brushed against mine. He ran the back of his fingers down my neck, over the swell of my breast, and circled my nipple before trailing down my stomach.

His fingers trailed down my hip, my thigh and I spread my legs in invitation. His hand moved between my legs, and I gasped as his fingers slipped up my center. Heat pooled in my core and my back arched off the ground.

His hand moved back up my hip, my ribs, and cupped my breast as his lips moved down my neck, my collar bone, my chest. His thumb coasted over my nipple, sending a shock of pure lust through me. The warmth of his breath on my chest heated my skin as his tongue swirled around my nipple.

My body rocked to meet his mouth and a low groan of approval escaped his throat that made me squeeze my thighs together. I felt like my heart was going to beat out of my chest as his tongue flicked over my nipple and he sucked it into his mouth. My head fell back and my hips rolled.

I needed more of him—all of him

As if he heard my silent plea, his hand splayed against my thigh and he pushed my leg to the side. He released my nipple with a gentle flick, and his mouth brushed the hollow of my throat and up the side of my neck. His teeth scraped against my throat as his finger slipped inside me.

My very existence narrowed to his touch as he found a slow, sultry pace that was maddening. I rocked my hips against his hand, and his thumb brushed over the most sensitive part of me in response. My fingers dug into his shoulder, and I stopped breathing. His tempo quickened, and his thumb brushed delicate circles over the nerves that begged for his attention.

"Please," I begged with a breathy moan as a dull roar filled my ears as I rocked my hips again as he worked me to the edge of oblivion.

"I spent too many years without you," he breathed against my lips and moved with a rhythm that was meant to destroy my last shred of control. "I want to take in every moan." His lips traced my jaw. "Every breath." He licked up the column of my neck. "Every kiss." He slipped another finger inside me and a rush of pleasure burned through me until I was nothing but pulsing pleasure.

Every stroke of his fingers, every word uttered from his lips, fused the cracks in my heart, and brought me closer to climax. The last century melted away like a bad dream and for the first time in a long time, I felt like I was on the right path.

"Look at me," his voice was commanding.

I opened my eyes, desperate to give him anything he asked for, and I was rewarded with a smirk on his perfect lips as his thumb pressed on the most sensitive part of my arousal.

A wave of pleasure pulsed through me as I stared into his dark brown eyes, that felt like home, My body coiled tighter as a breathy moan escaped my throat and my fingers tug into his arm.

Gods I missed him more than I ever dared to realize. I missed his strength, his beauty, and the way he touched me like I was the most precious thing in the Nine Realms.

His fingers plunged deeper, and my eyes closed of their own accord as I clenched around him. My heart pounded in my chest like a battering ram, and my hips rocked against his hand as every nerve in my body pulled tight.

"You're breathtaking." The husky rasp of his voice lit the fuse that shattered my last shred of control.

Release tore through me stronger than any Magik and ignited the spark I thought I'd lost forever. A swell of raw, unbridled emotion filled my body as his fingers stroked me through the waves of pleasure.

Nothing existed outside us, outside this moment. There was only him. And the feel of my soul coming back to life. Small waves of pleasure lapped through me as I open my eyes to look up at him.

My heart beat with a fever as his heavy lust filled gaze met mine, and my soul burned a little brighter. I've been so afraid of hurting him, of losing myself to the Magik within me. But with him, the darkness felt lighter because of the stars that burned bright in his eyes, and sparked on his fingertips when he touched me.

I sat up on my elbows to kiss him, to feel his light burn against my shadows. His lips were soft and tender as I reached for the laces on his trousers and made quick work of them.

Pulling away from me, he rose to his full height and pushed his trousers down, freeing himself. He may be a man in blood, but Si was a god in every way that mattered. Every muscle across his body was hard steel, and my body pulsed with need as my gaze traveled the length of him.

Our eyes caught once more and the heat in his gaze left my heart thundering in my ears as he knelt down and wrapped his hand around the back of my neck and kissed me with a tenderness that was designed to ruin me.

My head fell to the side in pure bliss, and his lips kissed the side of my cheek, my pulse along my throat, my collarbone, the swell of my breast as he parted my legs and settled over me.

"Si," I murmured, and his fingers dug into my thigh.

"I love the sound of my name on your lips." His deep voice resonated through me, and I pulsed like wildfire as he slid up my center.

A small, desperate moan escaped my throat, and I reached between us, my fingers wrapping around the thick, solid feel of him, as I guided him to my entrance.

He groaned at my touch, and his lips brushed against mine.

"I've waited a hundred years to feel you again," I breathed. "I don't want to wait any longer."

His tongue slid against mine as he pressed into me. I moaned into his mouth as my body shook at the fullness of him. My hips rolled of their own accord, seeking to feel all of him.

My entire body was an exposed nerve as a tidal wave of

unrelenting pleasure coursed through me. Every thought emptied out of my head as he slowly pulled out of me. The loss of him felt like some sort of cruel torture.

Before I can utter even the smallest whimper of need, his fingers found the swollen bundle of nerves between my legs, and he gently swirled his finger as he slid into me slow and purposeful. My body arched off the ground, and he slid out of me once more.

"Si," I whimpered, and a deep rumble of satisfaction and amusement reverberated through his chest.

"I've lived too long with just the memory of you." His fingers continue to work me, making it hard to focus on anything other than the pleasure coiling between my legs. "Let me savor the way you come undone for me." He slid into me again and a throb of pain mingled with the pleasure growing inside me.

"More," I breathed and wrapped my leg around his waist, trying to spurn him into a rhythm that will shatter me. And I'm rewarded with a smirk on his full lips as he slid out of me again, this time a little faster, sending a thrill down my core and between my legs.

Si hovered over me, his hair falling into his eyes, and I pulled him closer, forcing his body to press against mine. His warm, dark eyes sparked in the firelight as he drove into me harder, stealing my breath.

Time may be a chasm between us, but our love, our connection, was bridging the gap and binding us together once more. Each thrust branding us both, solidifying the unbreakable bond between us.

His mouth found my nipple, and he sucked and nipped at the sensitive peak. My whole body went fuzzy with heat, and I lost myself in the sultry pleasure of his touch as the Nine Realms disappeared, leaving only Si. The center of my universe.

"Don't stop," I whimpered as my body went taut. My head spun, my fingers gripped his hair, and I tighten around him. I teetered on the edge of my climax with every swirl of his fingers, every thrust.

Again. In and out. And my body went tight as a bowstring as he thrust again. The fullness of him stretched me to my limit, and I unraveled under his brute strength. Sparks of lightning coursed through my blood, rewriting the fabric of my soul as pleasure barreled down my spine.

"Kiss me," he demanded as waves of pleasure lapped through me.

My lips brush his and his tongue slid into my mouth, teasing and tasting as his hips move to a rhythm that he could no longer control.

I deepened the kiss, losing myself to his passion, his need. I pressed my hand to his chest, and his heartbeat matched my own wild tempo. He groaned into my mouth, the vibration sending a bolt of molten pleasure through me, and I gasped.

"You're going to be the end of me," he breathed as he slammed into me again and his body went rigid, every muscle straining as he completely lost control and shattered on top of me.

"My memory didn't do you justice," he panted and pressed his forehead to mine as we both tried to catch our breath.

"Nor did mine." I cupped his face, his beard tickling my palm as I brushed my thumb over his swollen lip.

He swept my hair back, and his eyes met mine with an intensity that felt more intimate than the pleasure we just shared, and my heart melted the way the sun melts into the sea.

He traced my lips with his, and every corner of my soul warmed. I didn't care what lay ahead of us, I just wanted to stay in this moment, right here until the last stars blinked out of existence.

CHAPTER FORTY-TWO

I woke up with a renewed sense of ease in my heart I hadn't felt in ages. Desire throbbed down my body as the memory of Kara's smooth skin and soft moans flashed through me. I rolled onto my side and reached for her, but my hand gripped a cold, empty cloak.

"Kara?" I sat up and glanced around the cave as I slipped my shirt over my head.

She was gone.

A pang of unease unfurled in my stomach, wiping away the sheen of bliss I woke up in. She wouldn't have left without waking me. Every instinct screamed at me that something was wrong. Kara may be reckless at times, but disappearing altogether after last night was unlikely.

It wouldn't be the first time she bailed when things got heavy.

The memory of her leaving Asheria's the moment she was alone soured my good mood.

I shoved into my trousers and boots and moved toward the cave opening as the fire crackled and burned just as bright as the night before. Maybe she needed some fresh air. Or...maybe she regrets last night. My insecurity about her true feelings reared its ugly head.

As I reached the edge of the cave, relief drowned the unease in my heart.

Kara stood on the shore, staring out at the calm water. Her

hair whipped in the wind, like wild flames, and I took a moment to appreciate her beauty. She was a beacon of color and warmth in a world of muted colors. My heart swelled as I studied her and my lips pulled into a smile I felt in every part of my body.

I finally felt like we were finding our footing again, even amidst the chaos, and it settled the part of my soul I thought would never find peace.

Water slid up the black sand toward her, but she didn't move as the frigid water covered her bare feet. She let her head tip back and the desire to go to her felt like a physical tug on my core.

I stepped out of the cave, and the beach transformed in front of me.

Chunks of ice were scattered across the beach, and the sea was a white sheet of ice. I sucked in a breath as a freezing wind slammed against me, and the heavy smell of salt, rain and ice filled my nose. I shivered against the cold and regretted not dressing warmer.

I turned to grab our cloaks, but was met with a solid wall that resembled the rest of the cliff face. Confusion washed through me, and my shoulders tensed.

The sword. I banged my hands against the stone, to no avail.

The opening was gone. The shelter was gone.

My heart ached as the evidence of our night together was erased. This must be the Mirror World testing us again. The Magik that connected me to Kara tugged once more, and I turned toward her.

The only way through this test was to keep moving forward.

I started across the beach, and the colors of the sky swirled like a storm was brewing. The gray shifted to a deep charcoal blue with streaks of dusty pink. It was beautiful, but something about it felt wrong. Like the environment was trying to conjure up a memory that was too fuzzy to see clearly.

"Kara," I called to her as I drew closer. "Everything okay?" I shivered against the cold.

Her shoulders stiffened, but she didn't turn toward me. Something was wrong.

"I think this is another test." I tried to reassure her as I passed a boulder of ice.

The cold seeped into my bones and rose the hairs on my arm. A prickle of awareness kissed the back of my neck and shadows seemed to skitter along the shore.

I scanned the beach to my right. Reflected on every piece of ice was the image of me and Kara the moment she ended my mortal life.

I froze, and my hand went to my chest instinctively as I watched her shove a dagger into my heart. A century old pain flashed through my chest as Kara's eyes stared out at me from the ice.

"Kara," her name escaped my throat on an exhale. "Are you seeing this?" My chest ached as my gaze bounded from image to image. I turned in a circle as a sheet of ice rose out of the sand behind me. We flew through the sky, fighting and arguing as I tried to save her from Loki's influence.

"You'll never forgive me, and I don't want you to." The Kara in the ice screamed, then dropped me from a thousand feet in the air.

My stomach bottomed out as I recalled the feel of falling and her cold, hard eyes.

No.

I wouldn't let this cursed place turn my heart against her. I made my choice to trust her. I turned away from the scene as it played once more.

"None of this is real," I started toward Kara as I ignored our past. "The Mirror World is trying to manipulate us."

"Si," she turned toward me, tears streaking down her face. "Please, don't come any closer."

I froze mid-step, and a cold spike of fear burned through me. "None of this is real." I held my hand out to her as my heart constricted at the pain etched across her face.

"That's the problem," her voice wavered. "It's all real. I've hurt you, over and over again."

"Kara," I stepped toward her and she stepped back.

"I want to hurt you right now." Her gaze met mine and the invisible thread between us pulled tight.

"You won't." There wasn't a doubt in my mind that she could send me to the stars if she wanted to. But in the marrow of my bones, I knew she wouldn't.

She might. My insecurities voiced their opinion once more, and I ground my teeth.

"The brand," her voice was strained as she shook her head. "It's gone." Her brow furrowed and she let out a heavy breath, like she was fighting an invisible war.

"My Magik." She stepped toward me as a flash of lust that had nothing to do with carnal pleasure crossed her features. The rest of the world went hazy as my vision narrowed on the woman in front of me.

"I can't breathe, I can't think." Her words echoed what she said to me in the forest.

She wrapped her arms around her middle, and I took a step toward her.

"Don't!" she practically growled. "Your soul," she let out a heady breath. "It's too much." She took a step back and one of the glacial boulders melted.

I took a step toward her, partly because her power demanded it. But also, because I refused to give her Magik any measure of control over us.

"I trust you."

Her eyes flicked to mine, and the pain in her gaze vanished. "You shouldn't."

Her wings snapped open and my heart raced as adrenaline

flooded through me. The woman I cared for transformed before my eyes. All her soft edges sharpened. All her warmth vanished, and she stared at me with cold steel in her gaze.

The woman I spent the night with, my Kara, was gone. Standing before was the Disir that lived within her blood.

A heavy weight settled against my palm, and Magik pricked along my skin. Surprise flickered through me as power barreled up my arm, making every muscle in my body flex with the desire to spill blood.

Against my will, my arm lifted Gramr, and pointed it at her chest.

Her smile split her lips, and her eyes flared at the challenge.

CHAPTER FORTY-THREE

KARA

I woke up feeling warm and fully satiated in a way I haven't felt in many, many moons. Heat coursed down my center as the memory of Si's hands, lips, and tongue flashed through me. I rolled onto my back and reached for him, but the place beside me was cold and empty.

"Si?" I sat up and glanced around the—forest.

I rubbed the sleep from my eyes and looked around again.

The cave was gone.

The fire was gone.

Si was gone.

This had to be another test of the Mirror World.

Mist covered the ground, swirling around me with the slightest movement. Giant trees towered over me. And vines curled around the edge of the cloak.

But this place felt unfinished. Like it was mimicking a forest, but it didn't carry the scent of dirt and dew. Nor did it feel steady and ancient, like the forest of Folkvang or Jotunheim.

"Sigurd?" I called for him, even though I knew deep down he wasn't here. The only answer was the branches creaking overhead as they swayed in the wind. My chest ached with the loss of him as I grabbed the shirt lying next to me and threw it on.

One night together and already we were being pulled apart. Again.

I shoved into my trousers and slipped into my now dry boots. The fog swirled at my feet, and a familiar cadence of Magik brushed over my skin as I took in my surroundings. I could only see a few feet in any direction through the thick haze.

The leaves were a muddy green, and the trees were a dark muted brown that almost looked black. Even the sky was an endless gray that hung low and clung to the tops of the trees. A raven cawed somewhere overhead and Magik skittered along my spine.

"Okay Mirror World, let's see what you've got."

I stepped off the cloak, and onto a dirt path that led into the fog. The Magik in my core hummed softly beneath the surface. I wasn't sure if it was the Mirror World itself pulling on my Magik or if there was something out there calling to me.

I took another step, cautiously curious what this test would be. Twigs snapped under my boots, and whispers flittered through the trees. I glanced behind me and the cloak I'd woken up on was gone. Not a single trace of the night we spent together remained.

The bone cold chill of being alone settled under my skin.

The path veered to the right, and out of the corner of my eye, a shadowy figure shot through the trees. Their cloak rippled in the dense air, making the fog swirl unnaturally.

Karaaa. A voice skated along my ear.

"Who's there?" I started forward. Whatever this test was, I wanted to get it over with and get back to Si as soon as possible.

Picking up my pace, I followed the path into the unknown. As I rounded an abnormally large tree with twisted bark, I caught the glimpse of a cloak. Whoever I was chasing turned and looked at me before stepping off the path and disappearing into the overgrown forest.

My heart raced, and instinct told me to follow them. But I

hesitated and took one small step backward. My back hit something solid. I turned, and a wall made of the same rocky pillars we encountered on the beach rose to the sky and stretched out on either side of me.

The way back was lost to me.

A low chuckled rumbled through my chest. Of course it was. In the Mirror World, there's only one way forward.

I stepped off the path and into the forest after the cloaked figure. The brand on my neck flared and my Magik swirled and prickled my skin. Whether that meant I was on the right path or not, only time would tell.

I trudged through the thick underbrush, my shirt catching on brambles and tearing at the fabric.

She's not worth fighting for. A voice whispered above me. A voice that sounded a lot like Ragnar. I glanced at the branches, but no one was there.

She wanted to kill me. Daiman's words slithered through the leaves. *I could see it in her eyes.*

The memory of fighting my Magik in the Nowhere made me sick with shame. I wanted to end his suffering and take his soul for myself.

Slowly, I moved deeper into the forest. Lights danced with the leaves, reminding me of the stars that fluttered like moths in my dream. They jumped forward and twisted above me. I held out my hand and one of them settled against my palm, soft as a petal.

My Magik brightened and my neck ached, as if it was trying to suppress my growing Magik. The little orb of light bounced off my palm once, twice, and then shot up into the sky.

The forest plunged into a night so dark, even I searched the shadows for monsters.

A raven cawed overhead and my Magik crackled. The low growl of a beast sounded to my right, and the feel of several pairs of eyes settled over me, making my heart race.

The heavy thud of boots on soft earth made me take a step back until I was up against a tree. I held my breath, and waited for whatever was out there to pass.

It's not real. None of this is real. I reminded myself.

The sound of steel against wood caught my attention, and I let out a shaky breath as I pushed off the tree.

Keep moving forward.

I shoved my fear aside and took another step. Then another. I moved slowly, each step careful, and soft so as not to alert whatever was waiting for me.

She's a monster! Bryn's words screamed through the forest.

I swallowed hard as I recalled the look of devastation on her face in The Hall of the Gods.

An abomination. Odin's voice sent a spike of anger searing through me and my Magik roiled.

A twig snapped behind me, and I turned on my heel. I scanned the forest and strained to listen for the telltale signs that someone was there. But it was silent. Not the skittering of animals, the cry of a bird, or even the breeze through the trees.

What I wouldn't give to have a weapon right now. Even if none of this was real, it would still make me feel better to have a blade to my name.

I turned back around, and the orange flicker of a fire danced between the trees. A chill ran down my spine as if the mist had found a way into my clothes and I shivered.

The only way is forward.

My Magik mimicked the flames, twisting and swirling in my core, and pain zipped down my neck like lightning. I rubbed the brand as it throbbed and pushed the pain to the back of my mind as I reached a small clearing.

In the center, a fire crackled, and the memory of last night seared through me. A flash of Sigurd's mouth on mine blurred my vision.

The soft creak of a bowstring being pulled back reached my ears as a cloaked figure stepped out of the trees across from me.

My heart stilled as Bryn leveled her arrow at me.

"I've been waiting for you." The bowstring snapped as she released the arrow right toward my heart.

"PUT THE SWORD DOWN." She sauntered forward and let the tip of Gramr press into her chest. A flicker of pain made her eyes crinkle. "We both know you won't hurt me."

"I can't," I said through gritted teeth. I wanted to lower the sword, but the smirk on her face reminded me of the Kara I faced when Loki had control over her.

"You mean you won't." Fire sparked in her eyes, and the sword sent a bolt of lightning up my arm.

Love, hatred, fear, and desperation warred within me. No part of me wanted to hurt her, but for the life of me, I couldn't lower the blade. It wouldn't let me. Like somehow it saw her for the threat she was and refused to back down.

"This isn't you. It's the Mirror World." My voice sounded rough, strained even as I fought the Magik coursing through me, begging me to run her through.

"It is me," she snapped and stepped forward. Gramr dug deeper into her skin and she flinched back a step. "You can't ignore the parts of me you don't like."

"That's not what this is." I stepped toward her and she took another step back. The sky slowly lost its color as if someone was leeching the very life from this place.

My fingers gripped the hilt tighter with a rage that felt bigger than me. My heart beat wildly, my vision blurred until the only thing I could see was her pulse just below her jawline.

"You know I've learned something since the temple about my Magik," she purred as wind whipped around us, but I could no longer feel the cold. My skin was feverish, and sweat beaded on my forehead.

"What's that?" My heart slammed against my rib cage as I watched her every move.

The flicker of her wings. The twitch of her fingers. The subtle inhale as she took a step toward me.

"The closer a person is to death, the harder it is to ignore the siren call of their soul." She swallowed and her hands balled into fists.

"Then it's a good thing I'm far from death," I said with confidence.

With Gramr in my hand, I knew she couldn't hurt me. She was stronger, faster, and she could fly. But I'd fought by her side for years. I knew every single one of her moves, and so long as I kept her on the other side of my blade. My life wasn't in any danger.

"I wish that were true." She closed her eyes and let out a shaky breath. She backed up a few steps and her chest rose and fell like she was fighting for her life. "You have to run," she groaned as fog swirled around us.

"I'm not leaving you." I couldn't move if I wanted to. The Magik wouldn't let me walk away from her. Not until she was dead.

"Please," she groaned.

"No." My resolve slammed into me as I fought the power of the sword. I made a promise to her, and I intended to keep it. "I said I would stand by you until the end. If this is that end, so be it." A calm settled over me.

This is what the Mirror World wanted. To tear us apart. To prove that our alliance—our love—was weak and conditional. To prove that I could only care for her as Kara the Valkyrie, but not Kara the Disir.

It was wrong. I cared for her no matter the Magik she carried inside her. Not walking away from her darkness was the only way to move forward.

Her breathing returned to normal, and she stood up straight. Her vibrant green eyes met mine and the icy fingers of fear clawed down my back.

"I was hoping you'd say that." The struggle in her voice, her eyes, her body was gone. The battle for which Kara I'd face was over.

"You can threaten me, fight me, push me away with everything you have. But I'm not going anywhere. I can shoulder your darkness for as long as you need me to."

"Either you kill me, or I'll finish what I started a hundred years ago." She kicked the blade, and it clanked against the—ice.

My shoulders sagged, and my hand shook as the Magik fled from my body and left me feeling hollow.

Confusion flickered through me as I glanced at our surroundings. The beach was far in the distance, over Kara's shoulder. And somehow, without realizing it we'd ended up in the middle of the frozen sea.

The Mirror World defied logic, and it was a stark reminder that this was just another test of our wills.

"I'm not going to fight you." I squared my shoulders and left the sword on the ice. I would never use it against her.

"This should be easy, then." She launched herself at me like a woman possessed.

I dodged her swing and moved outside of her striking range. Murderous rage filled her eyes, and she shot forward again.

She swung, and I blocked her punch. Kicking, she forced me backward, further away from the shore. Another punch, another kick. She kept up the assault without skipping a beat.

As she moved into my space, her fury got the better of her and she made a mistake with her footing. I grabbed her, pinned her arms to her side, and pulled her back against me.

"You have to fight the darkness, Kara."

Holding her like this, when I held her in my arms so tenderly just a few hours ago, twisted the knot in my stomach.

She tried to squirm free, and I squeezed her tighter to me.

"You have no idea how hard I've fought to keep the Magik at bay." She snarled like a wild animal and kicked her legs, trying to find purchase only to slip on the ice.

"Then keep fighting."

"I don't want to." She bent forward, taking me with her, and flipped me over her head. My back hit the ice, knocking the air from my lungs.

The ice cracked, and freezing water penetrated my clothes. Before I could suck in a full breath, she settled herself on top of me and pressed her forearm across my chest.

She leaned forward, her pupils blown wide, leaving only a sliver of green. I held onto hope that I was right. That choosing her and not giving into fear was my way through this test.

She pulled a dagger from somewhere on her person and pressed it to my neck.

"We both know you can fight better than that." Her words were clipped, but her tone was seductive and the cord between us pulled tight. My body relaxed as I stared into her eyes. Heat flooded my chest and spread to my core.

"I don't want to fight you." I exhaled as my heart swelled and my head slipped into a fuzzy warmth that felt like dreaming. "I want to lay the Nine Realms at your feet." She leaned forward and pressed a feather light kiss to my lips.

The memory of her mouth on mine last night tore through the haze. My senses cleared for a brief moment, allowing my instinct to live kick back in.

She ran her nose along my jaw and pressed the dagger into my skin. A sting of pain zipped across my neck as warmth pooled in the hollow of my throat.

"I've wanted to taste you since the day I shoved that dagger into your chest," she breathed, and I lost myself in the warm cocoon of her Magik.

"What are you waiting for?" I heard the words leave my mouth, but in the back of my mind, I screamed at myself to snap out of it. To stop her. To live.

She won't choose you. A voice seemed to scream from the other side of Yggdrasil.

She pressed her forehead to mine, and my heart ricocheted off my ribcage like a battering ram. She dragged the dagger down my neck and pressed the tip of the blade against my chest.

"For what it's worth," the warmth of her breath on my lips sent a thrill of anticipation barreling down my spine.

The dagger pressed into my chest, and she shivered on top of me. "I will miss you." Her lips pressed to mine and lightning coursed through my blood.

The world shifted around me, the sky turned to night, and Kara was no longer straddling me. Instead, she was sitting next to me, her hand on my chest, and the forest of Asgard was spread out in front of us.

I was back in the memory of Freyr's shelter, but I could still feel the icy grip of the Mirror World seeping into my bones.

Never let me touch your soul. If I ever try, if I lose myself, use that sword and stop me.

Pain fired across my chest, and our sanctuary among the stars vanished with a blink. She slowly pushed the dagger into me. It was like she was enjoying my slow death, savoring it even. Her lips left mine, and she sat up as the dagger sunk a little deeper and blood pooled on my chest.

An awareness settled deep in my soul as I looked up at the wild woman on top of me.

I was wrong.

The Mirror World didn't want me to choose her. It wanted to see if I could do what was necessary should the time come. It wanted me to kill her and save myself.

"Kara." I shuddered as more and more blood left my body. "I know who you really are in your heart." Metal brushed against my hand, and I knew what I had to do.

My fingers wrapped around Gramr and I opened myself up to the raw, unbridled Magik that lay within the steel. Lightning coursed through my veins, and every muscle in my body stretched and snapped as the Magik claimed my soul and reshaped me.

Surprise flickered across her face, and a pulse of Magik blasted off me. Her hand slipped from the dagger as she recoiled from the Magik, surging through my veins.

"Si, what are you—"

The runes of Gramr lit up brighter than a thousand stars, banishing every shadow to the depths of Hel. Another thrust of Magik hit Kara so hard it knocked her backward and she slid across the ice.

I rose to my feet and fury burned through me. I was sick of the games. Sick of the tests. I was done playing by anyone's rules besides my own. I'd rather tear this world apart than give it what it wants.

I ripped the dagger from my chest and threw it to the ice. My blood splattered across the sheet of white and my eyes met Kara's horrified expression.

"I. Won't. Kill. Her." I screamed, and the ice shook under my feet.

Kara scrambled away from me. Away from the Magik that tasted like destruction. Magik that felt like more than Gramr, as it hummed in my blood. I wanted to rip this realm from the fabric of the universe for daring to force my hand.

And I knew in that moment that I could do just that. I could rip this place apart with the hungry, bone melting power churning inside me.

With a strength that was far beyond my own, I stabbed the

sword through the ice. The Magik smoldering through me collided with the Magik of this torturous world.

Cracks splintered in every direction, Magik tearing through the ice like it was parchment. Thunder roared overhead, and I struggled to hold Gramr as power beyond anything I'd ever felt ripped through me. Wind whipped through my hair, and the taste of blood filled my mouth as the sheet of ice exploded with a force that sent me flying backwards.

Time seemed to slow as I flew through the air. Kara turned to ice and broke apart into a thousand tiny pieces that were carried on the wind.

And I realized that the woman I faced was a creation of this realm. Relief flooded through me. Kara hadn't given into her Magik.

Chunks of the sky fell like snow. A cloud burst above me like a dandelion. Tiny specks of ice peppered my face as piece after piece of the Mirror World disintegrated around me.

But if Kara wasn't here with me, then where was she?

I hit the ground, and the air was knocked from my lungs as I tumbled through the black sand and came to a skidding halt.

A shadow leaned over me as I sucked in a desperate breath. "That was impressive." The shadow's face came into view and a man with a scar across his face smiled down at me.

"You?" I stared up at the man who visited me in Odin's prison.

"No one's ever broken out of a Mirror World by force before. Though I should expect nothing less. Sigurd, son of Tyr."

CHAPTER FORTY-FIVE

KARA

I DODGED TO THE LEFT, her arrow whizzing past me and sticking in the bark just ahead of me.

My pulse roared in my ears, and my Magik sparked along my skin. The ground shook, the trees flickered all around me like they were struggling to hold on to corporeal form. The sky flashed between starlight and dawn, and then everything went still all at once.

I held my breath as I looked around the silent forest.

What the Hel was that?

The fire popped behind me in the clearing, and the subtle snap of a bowstring reached my ears.

I dropped to the ground, unsure where the arrow was coming from and the brand on my neck flared, sending a deep ached down my shoulder and up my jaw.

"You can't hide forever, Kara." Her boot steps were light, and near impossible to hear even in this silent world.

"It doesn't have to be like this." I got to my feet but remained crouched behind the tree. I leaned forward and quickly looked at the clearing, but she was nowhere in sight.

"Yes, it does." The venom in her voice made my Magik rise to the surface.

Release your Magik. Stand up for yourself. The voice in my head sounded from every direction.

"Freya wouldn't do what was necessary. Odin failed to deliver your head. So I have to take matters into my own hands."

The branch above me creaked, and I looked up just in time to see Bryn as she fired another arrow.

I bolted from my hiding spot and ran deeper into the forest.

"How long do you think you'll be able to ignore the Magik in your blood before you kill again?" Bryn's voice sounded in front of me, behind me, above me.

"How long until you kill another one of us?" Ragnar jumped from a branch and landed in front of me. Hate filled his eyes, and the dagger in his hand caught the firelight.

Heat flushed my chest and neck, and I grit my teeth so hard I was sure they'd shatter. He betrayed me. Betrayed all of us. My Magik snapped its teeth.

Embrace your Magik. Claim what's yours.

I let out a ragged breath as the flame inside me roared. Bryn's hatred was warranted, even if her actions were questionable. But Ragnar. Ragnar was the real monster. My Magik purred as if it enjoyed the hatred stirring inside me.

"You're one to talk." Anger filled my words. "You led us all to the execution block."

I was through playing nice with Ragnar because he was Si's friend. And though I knew none of this was real. I also knew I wouldn't hesitate to put him in his place outside the Mirror World.

Bryn appeared out of thin air and shoved a dagger into my chest, just below my clavicle. Fire and fury ripped through my veins and my neck burned like I was being branded once more.

I was done apologizing for not being strong enough.

I kicked her feet out from under her, and she dropped to the ground with a heavy thud. I ripped the dagger from my chest, and a warm trickle of blood skated down my skin as I stood over Bryn.

I was done giving my blood, flesh, and tears to their grief.

Show them how powerful you really are. The Disir's voice whispered against my cheek.

"You hate me for something I had no control over." Bryn stared up at me and Ragnar took a step back.

"And yet here you are, fully in control of your actions." Ragnar took another step backward, and I threw the dagger at his head. The blade caught the collar of his shirt and pinned him to the nearest tree.

"You would tear me to shreds." I grabbed Bryn by the front of her shirt, and the anger in my heart spread like shadows across my soul.

"You would rip every feather from my wings and watch me burn," I snarled and my Magik burned down my arms, making my veins glow.

"And you call me a monster?" I let out a shaky breath as I held the power at bay.

"Finally, you show your claws." The deep timbre of Odin's voice slid down the back of my neck.

Bryn burst into a million tiny stars, followed by Ragnar, and they both rose through the trees and disappeared.

And then I remembered that none of this was real.

I turned to face Odin. Now was my chance to say everything that was in my heart. To let all my anger, frustration, and pain go. Maybe that's what this test was. A chance to release a hundred years of weight on my shoulders.

One steel blue eye pinned me in place. "I look forward to the day Sigurd spills your blood and ends your reign of terror once and for all."

Kill him. The voices snarled. *Take your revenge.*

Rage, older than time, ignited in my blood.

"Si will never hurt me, despite your wishes." I stepped toward him without an ounce of fear in my body. "The only way you'll be rid of me is when you meet the stars yourself."

Odin laughed, and a raven's sharp staccato screech pierced the air. "You don't have what it takes to follow through on that threat."

My Magik bucked against the brand, aching for release. I wanted to feel his blood between my fingers. I wanted to look into his eye as I took everything from him.

His blood will run. Run through the streets of Asgard. The Disir's voices roared in my ears.

"You're wrong." My hand shot out and wrapped around Odin's throat. And I dug my fingers into his meaty flesh.

Odin laughed, his vocal cords vibrating against my hand.

He deserved to die. I squeezed tighter, and every one of my senses snapped into focus.

Woodsy smoke filled my lungs. Doubt flickered in Odin's eye. And my heart beat wildly as power surged through me like a thousand lightning strikes.

"You took everything from me," I snarled at him. "You destroyed my happiness out of fear." My nails dug into his flesh and hot, sticky blood dripped down his throat.

His soul song was an ancient battle horn screaming across the night. It was drums and the clattering of bones. I could feel it in my blood. I could taste the raw ancient power that resided inside him, and it made me dizzy with bone deep need.

His soul was pure power. And it was mine.

"Embrace your Magik. Kill him." A woman appeared behind Odin, her dark eyes staring into mine with a fervor that made my blood sing.

The strength of her Magik skated over me, testing and tasting the strength of the beast stirring in my core.

My Magik blazed, making my skin heat and my heart slam against my ribs.

"It's you. You're the one in my head."

Odin turned into a swirl of shadows and vanished before my eyes, taking the heavy beat of his soul song with him.

My heart ached and my Magik snarled as reality settled back in. He was never here. My words were meaningless. And his soul wasn't mine for the taking.

"My name's Astrid." She pushed the hood of her cloak back. She was the Disir that handed Loki to me. I sucked in a breath as a rush of power, stronger than anything I've felt since the brand touched my skin, burned through my blood.

The brand. I touched my neck, and the skin was perfectly smooth. It was gone.

"What do you want from me?"

Someone else stepped out from behind a tree. Her dark skin and piercing honey eyes were striking. A tattoo of a feather graced her right cheek, and she smiled like we were old friends.

Another woman stepped out of the swirling mist. Her sharp, angular features would be breathtaking if they didn't scream death.

Two more of them stepped forward and they could have been two sides of a coin. Their bright blue eyes were the same and their long hair was twisted in the same style of braids. But where one had pale skin and light brown hair, the other Disir's complexion was golden and her jet black hair fell around her like shadows.

"I think you already know what we want." Vines crawled up her cloak as she moved through the forest toward the clearing.

She was right. I did know. I've known for a while that accepting my Magik was the only way to move forward.

But I was scared.

Scared to lose myself. Scared to lose anyone else. Scared to lose Sigurd.

"You want me to accept that I'm a Disir," I said without a doubt in my heart as I followed her.

She turned toward me, and her lips twisted into a smile that the Magik in me seemed to return.

"You have to let go of the woman you were." She motioned someone forward and firelight flickered across her face.

One of the Disir dragged a hooded figured out of the mist and threw him at Astrid's feet.

Dread curdled in my stomach as he got to his knees. She ripped his hood off, and the sharp claws of fury tore at my heart.

Sigurd.

I stepped toward them, and my Magik roared with a vengeance. If she took one step toward him, I'd be the first person to kill a Disir.

Her gaze flicked to mine as if she could sense my thoughts. "So much power," she cooed. "And yet you hinder yourself."

"You even think of touching him." I stepped toward her and squared my shoulders. "And I'll unleash the fury of the Nine Realms on every one of you." Adrenaline turned my blood molten and the last shred of fear left my body.

I didn't care that the Si in front of me was likely a creation of the Mirror World. I would destroy anyone who touched him in any form, in any realm.

"You would choose him," the blonde Disir sneered at Si. "The man destined to spill your blood." She cocked her head to the side and something wicked passed over her features.

"I don't believe in destinies." Si's voice was hard as steel. And it made my heart race.

This isn't real. I reminded myself. He's not real.

"Then why do you carry Gramr?" The Dark haired Disir on the right challenged. The sword fell from the sky and into the dirt with a pulse of Magik that choked me.

"Would you rather it remain in Odin's possession?" I asked, defending Si.

"He's a danger to us all. You shouldn't have brought him here." The Disir with the feather tattoo motioned toward Si.

The blonde with the scar smirked. "Kill him."

An invisible hand wrapped around my heart and squeezed. All the anger, pain and guilt I've been trying to keep at bay exploded in my chest and tears sprang to my eyes.

History was repeating itself. Si's eyes met mine as the tall, blonde Disir with the scar across her face pulled his head back and pressed a dagger to his throat.

The memory of Magnus burned through me and my Magik flared, its wings unfurling into the beast I'd been fighting since the temple.

My breath caught in my throat as my heart revolted against being torn apart again. It didn't stand a chance though. Not when all of me was being held together with promises that would never see the light of day.

Violent tremors of rage ripped through me like ice carving its way through the mountains, reshaping the landscape of my soul.

"The choice is yours. Embrace who you are. Come with us and we'll teach you how to harness the power simmering in your bones. Or he'll be the first to die by our hands in this war." Astrid walked toward me and held out her hand. Her features were warm and inviting, as if she wasn't threatening the other half of my soul.

"He goes free." I met her stare. "If I go with you?"

I wasn't taking any chances with his life. For all I knew, he was real. And even if he wasn't, I couldn't watch him die again. That was a heartache I wouldn't survive the second time around.

"Of course," she smiled. "We don't want to spill his blood."

"At least not yet," one of the Disir snickered in the shadows.

"All of this, just so I'll accept that I'm one of you?"

"All of this, because we need you if we're going to restore balance to the Nine Realms." Astrid's face hardened, like she could sense that I was on the verge of joining them.

Her words rang through me. The Norns wanted balance. Si said Odin wanted balance. And now the Disir.

If I went with them, not only would I be sparing Sigurd, but maybe I could try to stop them from destroying our universe.

I turned to Si, and my heart shattered. I didn't want to say goodbye. I didn't want to choose them. But if I didn't, his death would be on my hands again.

His eyes held mine, and I remembered the words I promised to myself when I thought Fenrir was going to kill us.

I'd do anything in my power to save him.

I stepped forward and dove headfirst into the endless well of Magik that stirred inside me. They wanted me to embrace my Magik, but they had no idea the Hel I planned to unleash on them for daring to lay a hand on the man I loved.

"Let him go." Magik crackled along my skin, and runes glowed along my arms through the fabric of my sleeves.

A wicked grin that made my blood turn to liquid vengeance pulled across Astrid's face.

They were no better than the gods. Playing with people's lives like it was nothing.

The Disir holding Si dropped her knife, and I watched as he faded before my eyes. The piece of me that belonged to him crumbled to ash.

He was never really here.

And that's when I realized what this test was.

To embrace my Magik.

My boots carried me toward Astrid of their own doing and I came to a stop in front of her. Her golden brown eyes danced with the same Magik that burned within me.

I'd been the victim at the hands of the Gods and the Disir for too long. We all had. And now was my chance to make things right. To stop living in fear and create my own destiny.

But playing by the rules wouldn't change a single thing. I couldn't save Magnus, but I could save countless others.

All I had to do was embrace my Magik and become a Disir.

I placed my hand in Astrid's and the Mirror World seemed to exhale as it slowly faded into the mist.

Si had trusted me to use my Magik to save us once. And it was time to trust myself. I could be the victim forever, or the villain in the story that unfolds from here on out. But if being the victim requires me to lose everyone I love, then I choose villain.

THANK YOU!

I hope you enjoyed *Realm of Stars & Shadows*.

In the meantime you can read my other series, Soothsayer. It's filled with Arthurian Magik, Destiny, Love, and lots of Adventure! You can check it out on Kindle Unlimited or buy a physical copy!

I would love to hear from you and what you think about Kara & Si! Please feel free to email me any questions or just drop me a line and say hello on my website.

Until next time, Embrace Your Magik!